AF492207

THE SHAPE OF A BROKEN BOY

STEVEN ALLEN

CONTENTS

CHAPTER 1

THE LOST PUPPY

The alarm blared, shattering the pre-dawn quiet. Danny slapped the cheap plastic box until it wheezed into silence, then lay staring at the faded glow-in-the-dark stars on his ceiling — relics from a childhood that felt like a lifetime ago. Rolling onto his side, his gaze fell on a stuffed elephant, its blue and green worn pale with years of silent comfort. His dad had given it to him, back when laughter still filled the house. Now, "Peanut" was his only solace, a confidante he hid deep in his closet for fear of what his mother might do if she found it.

First day of high school. Starting a new school in the middle of spring semester in March was an uncommon occurrence. The words echoed in his mind, heavy with a promise he wasn't sure he could keep. *Try his damnedest to make an effort to be a normal teenager.* The mantra felt flimsy, a whispered lie against the roaring truth of his life.

Normal. What did that even mean anymore? Not with a father six feet under and a mother who chased ghosts with a needle. The more he'd replayed the last few years, the more the jagged edges of their decline had become sharp, undeniable truths. The picturesque, broken all-American family. A bitter laugh caught in his throat.

He swung his legs over the side of the bed, the thin mattress groaning in protest. The air in his small bedroom was cool, carrying the faint, stale scent of the house – a mix of old dust, a lingering sweetness that was *not* sugar, and the quiet decay of dreams. He pulled on his dad's old NYU hoodie, the faded navy fabric soft against his skin, a small comfort. It was almost a uniform, an armor against the day. His favorite jeans, patched at the knee from an old bike accident, followed. The sneakers, once bright white and black, were two years past their prime, the left one threatening to split open with every step. He ran a hand through his short, shaggy brown hair – it was a mess, as usual, defying any attempt at order. His fingers brushed the faint, faded scar above his upper lip, a ghost of a deeper hurt. He pushed the memory down, swallowing the metallic tang it left in his mouth. He was only seventeen, just a greasy teenager with barely a care in the world. That's what he *wanted* to be.

He skipped breakfast. There was never really any breakfast to skip anymore. The kitchen was quiet, the silence almost louder than any noise. He grabbed his worn Spiderman comic from the counter, its pages soft from countless readings, and slipped out the back door. The early spring air was fresh, clean, and surprisingly easy to breathe in.

As he approached the school, its light-colored brick façade and abundance of large, clear windows seemed almost welcoming, a beacon of normalcy. Maybe this wouldn't be so bad. Maybe. Then he saw them. Clumps of students, already gathered, their voices a low hum that swelled into sharper, more distinct tones as he drew closer. He could practically feel the burning gaze of their judgmental eyes as they sat in their carefully constructed cliques, talking trash about whatever, or whoever, they saw fit. It was a silent gauntlet, and he was walking right into it.

"Could someone please just kill me now?" he thought, the plea a desperate whisper in his mind. *"I really want to try making new friends, it just isn't as easy as most people think."*

His gaze, fixed on the Spiderman comic in his hands, darted up just in time to catch a pair of girls eyeing him from near the front gates. Their whispers were low, but their expressions were clear – a mix of curiosity and thinly veiled disdain. He imagined their thoughts: *"Why is this lost-looking puppy at our school?"* He wanted to go over, to prove he wasn't some disease-ridden fleabag, to show them he was just... Danny. But the words caught in his throat, replaced by the bitter taste of fear. He could almost hear the scowls, the ill-minded retorts, before they even formed. That's just how the teenage world went. Then, their voices sharpened, latching onto a new target.

"I heard that her parents were getting a divorce because her dad cheated on her mom with another man. Disgusting!" exclaimed one of them, her voice shrill with manufactured outrage.

Danny flinched, his stomach clenching. It was almost too much to listen to, the casual cruelty, the effortless demolition of someone's life. Without even thinking, a low groan almost escaped him. He clamped his jaw shut, grateful for the instinctive self-preservation. He didn't need a bullseye painted on his forehead on day one. He just needed to disappear.

Suddenly, a laugh, boisterous and familiar, cut through the low din of the crowd. The sound itself was a punch to the gut. As he slowly walked over to get a closer look, his eyes landed on someone he least expected. Tony was sitting there on the grass with his arm slung around the shoulder of some bubbly looking brunette girl he was talking to, Jessica. Tony looked much better than the last time Danny had seen him: his black hair was long and tied in a loose ponytail, skinny jeans with a chain looped from his belt, silver nose ring, black leather jacket and white T-shirt. Danny thought Tony kind of reminded him of James Dean.

Jessica attempted to stop him from laughing, poking him hard in the chest, which finally got his attention. As Danny stood maybe twenty feet away, he quickly gathered himself, but it was too late. Tony's eyes found him, a flicker of surprise, then something unreadable, crossing his face. Danny, caught in the sudden spotlight, just stood there, staring in amazement at his oldest friend. He wanted to walk over, to say something, anything. But the chasm between them felt too wide, too deep. He felt like he wasn't part of Tony's world anymore, that he would just brush Danny off like dust. A cold wave of despair washed over him, and Danny turned back, continuing his walk toward the front door of the school.

"Danny, wait!" Tony called out unexpectedly, his voice carrying easily across the diminishing distance. "Come back here for a moment." Danny almost instantly doubled back, a desperate, foolish hope blossoming in his chest, trying to hold back the biggest smile ever.

"Maybe… maybe I was wrong," Danny hopelessly thought. Tony remained sitting on the grass, observing him with an unreadable expression. It was seriously just too early for this; class hadn't even started yet. Danny opened his mouth to say something, anything, but the words kept choking in his throat, making him feel like he was about to start stuttering out of nowhere.

"Tony, do you know this lost puppy?" Jessica asked, her head tilted, trying to piece things together.

"Nah baby, just some kid I used to know before his mom went off the deep end," Tony responded in the coldest way possible.

"Baby? Tony had a girlfriend?" Danny internalized, the word twisting in his gut. He almost wanted to turn back and run, to vanish into the swarm of students now beginning to press toward the school entrance. But something stopped him. A stubborn ache, a yearning for the past, a need to understand the chasm that had opened between them. He wanted so much to just curse Tony out, to scream at him for being such a dick, especially when Danny needed a friend more than ever. *"What did I expect though, I mean honestly?"*

The basketball court shimmered under the hazy summer sun. Tony, all lean muscle and effortless grace even then, dribbled the ball, his long black hair, usually tied back, flopping wildly as he faked left, then right. Danny, sitting on the sun-baked asphalt against the chain-link fence, watched him, a quiet smile playing on his lips. He didn't play basketball. Never had. But watching

Tony, seeing the pure, unburdened joy on his friend's face as he moved, as he effortlessly sunk a shot from downtown – that was enough. Danny's role was spectator, supporter, and constant presence. They'd been inseparable since elementary school, two mismatched halves of a whole. Tony, the effortlessly cool one, the James Dean in the making, already turning heads. Danny, the quiet observer, content to bask in his friend's reflected light, finding comfort just being in his orbit.

Later, sprawled on the fresh cut grass next to the court, catching their breath, Tony had turned to him, his expression suddenly serious.

"You know, Danny," he'd said, picking at a loose thread on his jeans, "you're the only one I can really talk to. About… anything." Danny's chest had swelled with a warmth that had nothing to do with the sun. It was a secret, shared language, a bond that felt unbreakable. And it was that feeling, that deep trust, that had finally given Danny the courage to speak the truth that had trembled on his tongue for months.

"Tony," he'd started, his voice barely a whisper, "I… I think I like guys. I'm gay." The immediate silence had been heavier than any noise. Tony had frozen, his hand still on his jeans, his gaze suddenly hard, distant.

"What?" he'd asked, his voice flat. Danny had stammered, tried to explain, tried to convey the terror and the relief of finally saying it aloud to his best friend. But Tony had just shaken his head, slowly at first, then more vigorously. "No. No, Danny, that's… that's wrong. You can't be." His face had contorted into something Danny had never seen before – a mixture of disgust and fear. "That's… that's not right. I can't… I can't be friends with someone who… who's like that."

The words had ripped through Danny, colder than any ice, sharper than any blade. He'd stumbled away, unseen, the warmth of their friendship freezing over, shattering into a million irreparable pieces. He hadn't seen Tony, hadn't spoken to him, hadn't dared to, until this moment.

Even up to the present moment at school, the raw pain of that memory still stung. He made it very clear he didn't want to be friends with a faggot. The casual cruelty of Tony's words just now, throwing Dina under the bus instead of him, felt like a twisted mercy.

"That woman wasn't my mom anymore, and she hasn't been for a very long time." To Danny, Dina was just a shell, an empty shell that only cared about when she was going to get either her next screw, or her next fix. The abuse Danny endured from her had carved out a hollow space inside him, leaving him in a constant, dull ache of depression. The last thing Danny wanted was for everyone to know that he was gay.

He turned to walk back through the crowd of people heading into the school, all the while praying this was the worst he had to endure all day. As he continued walking forward, all of the students outside began swarming toward the front entrance to get inside. It was then Danny felt this overwhelming feeling of anxiety wash over him as he entered the school, watching everyone scramble to find their lockers. The brightly lit entry and fresh paint were almost blinding. Blue and Gold banners for 'Class of 2023' strewn on every wall. Everyone was getting into everyone else's personal space; the idea made it feel like the walls were closing in on him from all angles. The sound of lockers opening and slamming shut made Danny wonder if he'd find a locker with someone discretely hiding in one after trying to escape their own torture. The bell to get the day started rang at exactly 8:50 AM.

"Come on! Honestly?" Danny thought to himself. He decided he'd look for his locker later, and instead he ran to his first class, AP English. The school's hallways felt like a maze, one long corridor after another. Danny spotted someone in the hallway who he could only assume was either a teacher or the principal. He knew that if he wanted to have any chance of getting to class relatively on time, he would have to ask for directions. Danny quickly cleared his throat preemptively in the hopes he wouldn't sound nervous and he reluctantly walked up to his potential savior. As Danny made his approach, his tongue felt like it was tying itself in a knot. "Please God, don't let me make an idiot of myself."

"Excuse me, I'm looking for AP English with Mr. Bodowski. Would you happen to know where that might be?" Danny asked the man standing in front of him. The man put on a gentle smile as he answered Danny. This man seemed very young to be a teacher, possibly in his late 20's, short black hair and short stubble for facial hair. He wore glasses and a tweed jacket. Danny wondered if the man wore the jacket ironically.

"Sure, I don't have anything important going on," the man answered in a coy manner. "I'll escort you myself. You're new here, right? I haven't seen you here before." Danny shook his head slowly. The kind man turned to walk down the hallway to his left, prompting Danny to follow him closely so he didn't get lost. Around the next corner they reached a large blue door. The man walked inside first and commanded everyone's attention quickly by writing his name on the black board at the front of the classroom. The name Danny saw him write, Mr. Bodowski.

"Great, I don't know what's worse," Danny thought. "Asking a teacher for directions to his own class, or showing up with a teacher in front of everyone." Danny then looked around the room for an open desk. "Fuck me, one open seat, and it's right next to…. him….." Mr. Bodowski motioned for Danny to stand in front of the class as he was introduced to everyone. As Danny reluctantly sauntered forward, he couldn't help but notice that Tony glared with daggers in his eyes. Mr. Bodowski reached over to Danny as he inched closer.

"Everyone, this young man joining us is Daniel Sanders," stated Mr. Bodowski. "This is his first day here, so let's all make him feel welcome as best we can." Danny wiggled free of Mr. Bodowski's grip and timidly walked over to his new desk next to Tony. He glanced over at Tony, who was facing the opposite direction, as though he were ignoring Danny's very existence. It broke Danny's heart to feel so rejected by someone who used to make the world disappear.

Danny slid into the empty chair, the plastic seat cold against his worn jeans. He kept his gaze fixed straight ahead, hyper-aware of Tony's presence just inches to his left. He could feel the tension radiating off him, a tangible wall. Tony, still facing away, leaned slightly, his elbow propped on the desk, effectively putting a subtle barrier between them. Danny risked a quick, peripheral glance. Tony's dark hair, neatly combed back, gleamed under the fluorescent lights, his silver nose ring a tiny glint of rebellion. He was tapping a pen rhythmically against his textbook, the sound of a low, irritating thrum that seemed to vibrate directly inside Danny's skull. It was a microaggression, subtle but unmistakable, a dismissive tone set without a single word. Mr. Bodowski, oblivious to the silent drama unfolding in the back row, clapped his hands together.

"Alright class, let's begin. Our first unit will be an exploration of narrative voice. Who can tell me why an author's voice is so crucial to a story?" asked Mr. Bodowski toward his semi-attentive listeners. A few hands tentatively rose. Tony, without turning, sighed loud enough for Danny to hear, a drawn-out, theatrical sound of boredom. It wasn't directed *at* Danny, not overtly, but it felt like it. It felt like every little action, every shift in Tony's posture, was designed to emphasize the distance between them, to remind Danny of his unwanted presence. Danny shrank further into his seat, trying to make himself invisible. He knew the answer to Bodowski's question, or at least he had a good idea, but the thought of speaking, of drawing any attention to himself, especially with Tony sitting there, was paralyzing.

The class settled into a slow rhythm of discussion, Mr. Bodowski's calm voice a steady counterpoint to the nervous flutter in Danny's stomach. Tony occasionally shifted, his knee bumping the side of Danny's desk with what felt like deliberate carelessness, each small jostle a fresh prick. Mr. Bodowski assigned the first reading, a short story by Flannery O'Connor.

"Ugh, this old shit again?" Tony mumbled low enough for only Danny to hear, his voice laced with disdain. It was a comment meant to annoy, to dismiss, to belittle the very subject Danny usually found solace in.

Danny just clutched his Spiderman comic, still tucked under his arm, wishing he could disappear into its colorful pages.

The class crawled by, each minute feeling like an hour. Danny managed to avoid eye contact with Tony, focusing instead on Mr. Bodowski's tweed jacket and the swirling dust motes in the sunlight filtering through the high windows. When the bell finally shrieked, signaling the end of the first period, it was a sound of immense relief and immediate dread. Relief from the suffocating proximity to Tony, dread for what the rest of the day held. Students surged from their desks, a loud, chaotic wave. Tony was one of the first out, not even glancing back, his brunette girlfriend already waiting for him by the door, her arm possessively linked through his. Danny watched him go, a fresh wave of despair washing over him. The world had indeed moved on without him.

The hallways were even more impossibly crowded now, a churning river of teenagers. Danny clutched his comic tighter, navigating the human currents, desperate to find a moment of peace before his next class. He didn't have a map, and his locker was still a mystery. The thought of asking for directions again, or risking another public introduction, made his stomach churn. He could feel the curious glances, the whispers he couldn't quite decipher but knew were about him. *The new kid. The weird kid. The lost puppy.*

He ducked into an alcove, then behind a pillar, trying to get his bearings. The noise was overwhelming – laughter, shouts, the clatter of textbooks, the incessant opening and slamming of lockers. Lunch. That's what everyone was heading for. Lunch. His stomach rumbled in protest, but the thought of the crowded cafeteria, a thousand more judging eyes, was unbearable.

He needed somewhere quiet. Somewhere truly, completely alone. His mind raced, desperate. The library would be too public, the gym too loud. Then an idea, grim but pragmatic, formed. He remembered spotting the bathrooms near the main entrance earlier, before the chaos truly began. They were probably quieter, less monitored.

With a grim determination, Danny pushed through the throng, following the faint signs for the restrooms. He slipped inside the boys' bathroom, pulling the heavy door shut behind him. The sudden silence was a shock, a quiet sanctuary after the roaring ocean of the hallway. The stale air, thick with the scent of disinfectant and something vaguely metallic, was still infinitely preferable to the suffocating social pressure outside.

He walked past the row of gleaming sinks, ignoring the stray paper towels on the floor. At the very end, he found it: a single, unoccupied stall. He pushed the door open, stepped inside, and pulled the latch. Locked. Safe. He sank onto the closed toilet seat, pulling his knees up to his chest. He reached into his backpack, retrieving the brown paper bag he'd packed this morning – a half-smashed peanut butter and jelly sandwich, a bruised apple, and a small juice box.

The soft crinkle of the paper bag was the loudest sound in the small enclosure. He unwrapped the sandwich, taking a small, slow bite. The sweetness of the jelly, the creaminess of the peanut butter, tasted bland and tasteless against the knot in his throat. He chewed slowly, staring at the graffiti scrawled on the stall wall: declarations of love, crude drawings, meaningless dates. It wasn't exactly comforting, but it was private. No one was looking at him here. No one was judging. No one was calling him names. He could almost pretend, just for these few minutes, that he was utterly invisible.

He took another bite, listening to the muffled sounds of the school outside, the distant shouts, the ringing of a bell, all softened by the thick walls. He was alone, utterly and completely, eating his lunch in a bathroom stall on his first day of high school. A profound wave of loneliness washed over him, colder even than Tony's rejection. This was the reality of trying to be normal, he supposed. It was a lot harder than he'd thought.

Just as Danny was about to peel his bruised apple, the heavy swing door of the boys' bathroom creaked open again. Danny froze, apple halfway to his mouth. He held his breath, willing whoever it was to walk past his stall, to choose one of the others. He heard heavy footsteps, confident and unhurried, cross the tiled floor. The distinct squeak of sneakers on linoleum. A low sigh. Danny's blood ran cold. He knew that sigh. He knew those footsteps.

Tony.

He pressed himself back against the cool, grimy porcelain of the toilet tank, making himself as small as possible. His heart hammered against his ribs, a frantic bird trapped in a cage. He could hear Tony moving, the rustle of his leather jacket, the clink of the chain on his jeans. Tony stopped at a sink, just a few feet from Danny's hiding place.

A heavy, frustrated breath escaped Tony, followed by the sharp hiss of a faucet turning on. Danny heard the splash of water, loud in the confined space, then a choked sound, almost a grunt. It wasn't anger, not exactly. It was raw, unadulterated frustration.

Tony began to splash water on his face, the rhythmic sloshing against the basin filling the silence. Danny could picture him: the dark hair plastered to his forehead, the water dripping down his chin, trying to wash away whatever was clearly eating at him. Tony's breathing was heavy, ragged, filling the small bathroom.

"Damn it," Tony muttered under his breath, the words tight, barely audible, as if speaking them aloud would give them too much power. He scrubbed a hand over his wet face, then braced his palms on the edge of the sink, his knuckles white. Danny could almost feel the vibration of his frustration through the stall wall. "This is such... a mess," Tony continued, his voice low and strained. "Why *now*? Why here?" He took another shuddering breath, a sound loaded with unspoken conflict. "I can't... I hate him so fucking much!"

Danny felt a fresh wave of nausea. He knew, with a sickening certainty, who Tony was talking about. Himself. Tony was thinking about him, about their past, about his presence here, and it was clearly disturbing him. He was trying to push Danny away, trying to maintain the carefully constructed facade of his new life, his new image, by distancing himself from anything that might remind him of who he was, or *who he used to be*, with Danny.

He heard the faucet click off. The sudden silence was deafening, amplifying the frantic thump of Danny's own heart. He squeezed his eyes shut, willing Tony to leave, to just go. He didn't want to hear any more. He didn't want to be the source of Tony's obvious distress. It was too much, all of it. The betrayal, the rejection, and now this raw, unwitting confession of discomfort.

Finally, after what felt like an eternity, he heard the heavy swish of the door opening again, then the retreating footsteps. The door clicked shut, leaving Danny alone once more in the disinfectant-scented quiet. He stayed curled on the toilet seat for a long moment, trembling, the forgotten apple lying bruised beside him. He could finally breathe, but the air felt heavy, tainted by the silent echoes of Tony's pain and his own profound heartache.

CHAPTER 2

DECAYED MEMORIES

When Danny left for school at 7:30 that morning, the house was silent except for the low hum of the refrigerator. Dina lay collapsed on the couch, tangled in a thin, stained blanket — the posture of someone who had long given up.

Lately, Danny no longer cared if she woke. The thought of her slurred demands and vacant eyes often felt worse than her stillness. She was exactly as he'd left her, curled on her side amid empty vodka bottles glinting faintly against the wall. The coffee table, once polished wood, now held a bowl of crinkled dime bags, a couple of makeshift pipes, and a single, clean syringe beside a crumpled spoon.

Danny hadn't said goodbye. There was nothing to say.

The morning light, thin and watery, tried to filter through the grime on the windows. The silence stretched, broken only by the occasional distant rumble of traffic.

It was close to eleven in the morning when the fragile peace was shattered by a loud, insistent knock on the front door. The sound, sharp and unexpected, acted like a physical blow. Dina, deep in the murky depths of a restless, drug-addled sleep, convulsed, her eyes snapping open in a spasm of disorientation. She landed with a muffled thud on the sticky, debris-strewn carpet, a sharp pain shooting through her hip.

"Gah!" she grunted, her voice raspy, a strangled sound that barely resembled a human utterance. Her mind was thick, clouded, struggling to piece together where she was, what day it was. The knock came again, firmer this time, more impatient.

Slowly, painfully, she picked herself up, her limbs heavy and unresponsive. Her muscles ached, her head throbbed with a dull, persistent hammer, and her mouth felt like cotton. The world spun for a moment as she pushed herself upright, a wave of nausea washing over her. She stumbled, shuffling across the cluttered living room floor, carefully trying to avoid the broken glass. Each step was an effort, her old, threadbare robe dragging around her ankles.

She reached the front door, her hand fumbling for the peephole. Squinting through the warped lens, she saw him: Leroy, standing on the front step, patient as ever, yet his posture radiating an unspoken expectation.

"Fucking hell," Dina hissed under her breath, the words tasting foul on her tongue. Her voice was scratchy, unused. "What does he want now?" Leroy was the last person she wanted to see, a living, breathing reminder of everything she'd lost, everything she'd become.

She lifted a trembling hand, slapping her own cheeks a couple of times. *Slap. Slap.* She needed to look less like the corpse she felt. She took a deep, shuddering breath that caught in her chest. Slowly, the heavy bolts on the front door began to slide back. Just as the first click echoed, another loud, jarring knock reverberated through the thin wood, making her flinch.

"Dammit Leroy, I'm opening it already!" she yelled, her voice cracking. With a surge of adrenaline, fueled by annoyance and a desperate need to get rid of him, she unlatched the deadbolt and flung the door open, exposing the unkempt chaos behind her. She stood there in the doorway, framed by the wreckage, looking at Leroy not with fear, but with a potent mix of complete disgust and simmering rage.

"About time, Guzman," Leroy began to speak, his voice carefully level despite the immediate stab of pain at her use of his last name. Not Leroy.

Guzman. It was a wall, built of contempt, between them. He motioned to open the screen door separating them, its mesh torn in one corner.

"I was worried I might have to break the door down." Leroy's words were an attempt at lightheartedness, but they died on his tongue the moment he stepped across the threshold. The air inside hit him first – a cloying, sickly sweet smell of stale cigarettes, something vaguely chemical, and the undeniable tang of neglect. It wasn't the scent of a home. It was the smell of a tomb.

He stepped into the living room, his police instincts immediately cataloging the chaos, even as his personal history screamed in protest. Dina slowly shuffled backward, her eyes darting to the floor, trying to avoid the broken glass that crunched under his heavy work boots.

"Jesus Christ, Dina," he managed, the words involuntarily escaping him, his voice rough with shock and a deeper, more profound sadness. "What the hell happened here?" His gaze swept across the room, taking in the devastation. Broken liquor bottles lay scattered like fallen soldiers, glinting in the faint light. There were the crude, homemade pipes he'd seen far too often on calls, discarded like children's toys. Holes, dark and ragged, marred the walls, as if someone had punched through plaster in a fit of pure, unbridled rage. And there, on the floor, torn to shreds, was the framed family portrait. He recognized it instantly: a smiling Rick, his arm around a vibrant, laughing Dina, a much younger Danny beaming between them. A cruel parody of what they once were.

This wasn't just a messy house. This was a war zone, a testament to a life spiraling out of control. And somewhere in this wreckage, a child lived. Danny. *Rick's son.* The thought twisted in his gut. Leroy knew, with a certainty that chilled him to the bone, that this was no place for a young man to be growing up.

"Guzman," Dina began again, her voice thick with her prized South Carolina accent, laced now with venom. "Nice of you to drop by. You here to screw me again? You here to rub it in my face that being a coke whore is all I'm good at? Does Maria know you raped me after you killed my husband?" she spat, her eyes wild, her hands already nervously rearranging the garbage on the coffee table. The accusations, as old as the addiction itself, were flung like poisoned darts. Leroy just stood there, rooted to the spot, not even knowing how to react to the train wreck happening right in front of him. "You don't even have a reason to step foot in this house. I want you gone, now!" Dina's voice rose, shrill and demanding. She reached for her purse, a tattered, overflowing bag, and started sifting through each compartment, emptying the chaotic contents – old receipts, crumpled tissues, loose pills – one by one onto the coffee table, a frantic ritual.

"Dina, I'm only here to help you get out of this hole," Leroy pleaded, trying to inject calm into his voice, to bridge the chasm between them. He took a tentative step closer, but Dina's hand shot out, a thin, bony barrier. "Look," he continued, keeping his distance, his voice softening slightly as he tried a different tack. "You haven't worked since Rick died. You fell into a hole, Dina, and you just kept digging. Maria and I miss you and Danny so much. This is no place for the young man to live. Hell, your neighbour, Mrs. Flores, has started calling me every day for the past month to get me to talk to you. The woman is tired of hearing you yelling at your son. Your son, for Christ sake!" He knew Danny was suffering. He saw the signs, the withdrawn glances, the quietness. Mrs. Flores's calls only confirmed his worst fears.

Leroy surveyed the entire living room again, his eyes desperately searching for a clean place to sit, somewhere to ground himself in this nightmare. The sheer squalor of the house, the physical manifestation of Dina's decline, was almost too depressing to bear. He lifted his head, his gaze drifting into the kitchen. He saw the dining table, laden with more clutter, but in his mind, it transformed. He remembered how he, Rick, Maria, and Dina had shared so many joyful meals around that very table. Laughter, debates, plans for the future. He saw the discolored rectangular outlines on the walls where countless photos had once hung. Those memories felt like a cruel joke now.

"Maybe if the kid wasn't so goddamn useless and got a job, any job at all, then maybe we'd have a better life," Dina said, her voice cutting through his memories like a razor. She picked up a lighter with trembling fingers and began to light a cigarette, the faint click followed by the acrid smell of burning tobacco. "He wants all this stuff, he wants to leave and be his own person, especially when he knows I need the money." She coughed, a wet, rattling sound, as she exhaled a plume of smoke into the already heavy air. Leroy just stood there, silently studying her features, her motions. Her hair, once a vibrant blonde, was now a chopped, uneven mess, streaked with random greys, dull and lifeless. Her eyes were sunken, framed by dark circles, her skin pasty and sickly looking, stretched tight over sharp cheekbones. The track marks running up and down both arms, a map of her addiction, were stark against her pale skin. This wasn't the woman he knew anymore, the spirited friend who had laughed so easily with Maria and Rick. This was just some transient he had the misfortune of having to deal with, a shell of the person he once loved.

Leroy was more than prepared to wash his hands of this whole thing, to walk away and never look back. He was a police sergeant. He saw this kind of destruction every day. But the only reason he stuck around, the only reason he kept coming back to this hellhole, was the gnawing guilt. The ghost of Rick, his best friend, hovered in this decaying house, a constant reminder. He would feel unforgivably guilty should anything happen to Danny. Leroy felt like he had been backed into a corner by the memories of Rick, and all the fun times they had together, the unbreakable bond they once shared. Leroy had done his hardest to give Dina the benefit of the doubt for years, thinking that, with enough patience, enough chances, it would help her kick the drug habit. But it only got worse.

"Dina, you leave me with no choice," Leroy advised Dina, his voice firm, no longer pleading, but edged with a steely resolve he rarely showed. She slowly looked up from her purse, her tear-streaked face a mask of indifference. "I want you to get your act cleaned up, get your life back together. Go back to work. Go back to being a good mother for Danny.

It's not too late. Please, I'm begging you. If I return and this situation hasn't changed, you *will* be taken into custody. And your son *will* be placed. No more chances, Dina.And that's a promise I will keep."

Leroy's words, heavy with the full weight of the law and his personal despair, seemed to ring hollow with Dina. She didn't care what happened to Danny, or at least, that's how it appeared. The addiction had consumed everything, leaving no room for maternal instinct or self-preservation. Leroy waited for a response, a flicker of understanding, anything. There was nothing. He left the house, the heavy silence of his resignation louder than any argument, and softly closed the door behind him. On the other side of the door, he could hear Dina let out an ungodly, frustrated yell, a primal scream of despair.

As Leroy walked down the cracked concrete steps, he finally allowed himself to truly study the exterior of the house, a mirror image of the decay within. The handrails of the porch were rusted, crumbling to the touch. The last step was halfway eroded, a dangerous trap. The grass in the small front yard had overgrown into a wild, uncared-for thicket. A couple of windows at the front of the house had been broken and crudely boarded up with plywood, dark, empty eyesores. Three faded citation notices from the city were tacked to the front door, official demands for Dina to clean up the property. Leroy just couldn't understand why Dina would let this happen, why she would let everything they had built crumble into dust.

He was halfway down the weed-choked driveway when he heard a voice, sharp but not unkind, cut through the quiet afternoon.

"Sergeant Guzman! Just the man I wanted to see," Mrs. Flores called out.

Leroy looked up to see Mrs. Flores, Dina's next-door neighbor, standing by her meticulously manicured rose bushes, a gardening trowel clutched in her gloved hand. Her face, usually etched with a gentle warmth, was now a mask of concern and weary exasperation. She was a woman who missed nothing, her small, watchful eyes taking in every transgression from behind her pristine lace curtains. He forced a weary smile, though it felt like a grimace.

"Mrs. Flores. Everything alright over here?" Leroy asked, already knowing the answer.

She sighed, a heavy sound that seemed to carry the weight of months of worry. She pulled off her gloves, tossing them into a small bucket by her feet. "Alright? Sergeant, how can anything be 'alright' with that poor woman in there, and that boy? Honestly, it's a tragedy." She gestured subtly with her chin toward Dina's house, her gaze lingering on the boarded-up windows.

"Another one of her 'episodes,' was it?" Mrs. Flores barely questioned. Leroy ran a hand over his face, feeling the stubble.

"Something like that, Mrs. Flores. She's… she's not doing well."

"Not doing well?" Mrs. Flores's voice rose slightly, indignation warring with pity. "She's destroying herself, Sergeant. And what about Danny? That boy is wasting away. I hear her screaming at him, late at night sometimes. And that boy, he just takes it. He's so quiet now. He used to be such a bright, lively little thing, playing with your Tony." Her eyes, sharp and knowing, met his. "You remember, don't you? Before… before Rick."

The mention of Rick, and the unspoken 'before' of Dina's decline, hung heavy in the air. Leroy shifted his weight. "I do, Mrs. Flores. I remember. It's why I keep trying."

"Trying isn't enough anymore, Sergeant," she said, her voice dropping to a low, urgent whisper, glancing around to make sure no one else was within earshot. "She had a man over again last night. Different one this time. And the shouting… the noises… it went on for hours. It's not safe. Not for her, and certainly not for Danny." She wrung her gloved hands. "I see him leave every morning, that poor child, looking like he hasn't slept a wink. He's so thin. And he comes home to *that*." She made a sweeping gesture toward the dilapidated house. "What are you going to do, Sergeant? Because something needs to be done. For Danny's sake."

Leroy looked back at the house, the sun glinting off the broken glass in the yard. Mrs. Flores's words weren't news, but hearing them from a concerned neighbor, a direct witness, made them heavier, more concrete. He was a cop. He knew protocol. He knew the steps. But Dina was family, or had been. Rick's wife. Tony's childhood playmate. It was an impossible tightrope.

"I gave her no choice today, Mrs. Flores," Leroy said, his voice flat, devoid of emotion. "I told her if she doesn't get herself clean, get help, and get her life together for Danny, I'm going to take formal action. Arrest her. And Danny would go into foster care. No questions asked." He watched Mrs. Flores's face for a reaction. Her eyes widened, a flicker of surprise and then a slow, reluctant nod.

"It's drastic, Sergeant," she said, her voice softer now, tinged with sadness. "But maybe… maybe it's the only way. For that boy." She paused, then added, "You're a good man, Sergeant Guzman. For sticking with them this long."

Leroy didn't feel like a good man. He felt like a failure. A failure to his best friend, to Dina, and most of all, to Danny. He nodded curtly.

"Thank you, Mrs. Flores. I'll be in touch." Leroy said as he turned and walked to his patrol car, parked a little way down the street, the image of Dina's vacant eyes and Mrs. Flores's worried face burned into his mind.

Leroy unlocked his patrol car, the interior still smelling faintly of stale coffee and police-issue cleaning supplies. He slid into the driver's seat, the worn fabric molding to his tired frame. He pulled his phone from his pocket again, its screen glowing like a small, accusing rectangle in the dim light of the afternoon. His thumb hovered over the contact for Child Protective Services, a number he knew by heart, a number he had used countless times for strangers, but never, *never* for someone like Dina.

For all his might, all his years of training, all the hardened resolve he cultivated as a police sergeant, he couldn't make the call. His hand trembled almost imperceptibly. He couldn't do it. Not yet. The weight of Rick's memory, of the vibrant, laughing woman Dina once was, pressed down on him, suffocating him. He pictured Danny's quiet, haunted eyes, the way the boy used to light up when Rick was around. He had almost set a chain of events in motion, threatening to shatter what little semblance of family Danny had left, even if it was a toxic one.

With a frustrated groan, Leroy shoved the phone back into his pocket. The digital glow vanished, replaced by the grim reality of the moment. He reached into his breast pocket, pulling out a crumpled pack of cigarettes and his Zippo. The familiar click-flick of the lighter was a small, defiant sound in the quiet street. He inhaled deeply, the harsh smoke burning his lungs, a welcome sting that momentarily eclipsed the ache in his chest.

He just sat there, defeated, watching the wisps of smoke curl into the air. He thought about the ultimatum he'd just given Dina. Arrest her. Foster care for Danny. He had laid it all out, a stark, brutal choice. He knew the answer. He knew the statistics. And he knew Dina.

He had put in motion the final act of this tragedy, severing the last fragile thread holding Dina and Danny to any kind of stable life, however broken. He wasn't just a cop anymore; he was a judge, a jury… and a reluctant executioner.

The taste of ash clung to his tongue, bitter as guilt.

CHAPTER 3

FREDDY'S LEGACY

The late afternoon sun, already dipping towards the horizon, cast long, golden shadows through the large front windows of *Freddy's Place*. Inside, the usual after-school bustle was conspicuously absent. It was unusually quiet, the clatter of plates and the murmur of conversation replaced by the soft hum of the refrigeration unit and the faint, tinny music from the kitchen radio. Maria was working a double shift, the afternoon girl having called in sick, leaving her with a skeleton crew of new staff. She moved with an easy, practiced grace behind the counter, wiping down the gleaming stainless steel, her movements efficient and almost automatic after decades in the business.

She sometimes noticed the new waiters, young kids mostly, looking through the framed, sepia-toned photos that still hung at the front of the restaurant. They were relics from a different era, captured smiles from a time when this place truly lived up to its name, a place of joy and camaraderie. Today, one of the newer hires, a quiet boy named Miguel, had gravitated to a specific photograph. Maria watched him from across the room, observing his slight, curious tilt of the head. It was *that* one. The one of her, Freddy, and Dina, caught mid-laugh, heads thrown back, eyes crinkled with genuine mirth. A pang, sweet and sharp, went through Maria's chest. She walked up to him, a gentle smile touching her lips, and placed her hand lightly on his shoulder.

"You guys looked like you used to have so much fun here," Miguel said in amazement, his voice soft, almost reverent, as if peering into a sacred past. "Who are all these people?"

Maria's gaze moved from one vibrant, faded image to the next, a silent film reel of her younger years. "These people, Miguel," she replied, her voice tinged with a nostalgic warmth, "these people were all family. This one in particular was Freddy, the old owner." Her finger traced the image of a beaming man with a wide smile and a mischievous glint in his eyes. "My oldest best friend, Dina," she continued, her voice softening, a complex mix of affection and an unspoken sorrow for the woman Dina had become. "And finally, myself." She pointed to a younger, more carefree version of herself, her arm linked with Dina's.

"The day this photo was taken, we wanted to do something vintage," Maria recounted, a genuine chuckle escaping her. "So, Dina and I went and had our hair and makeup done that morning, all pin curls and red lipstick, before coming in for work that afternoon. And Freddy," her voice held pure affection, "Freddy came in looking like Louis Armstrong, wearing this ridiculously oversized suit and a fedora. He even tried singing *'What a Wonderful World'*. It was so bad, Miguel, so wonderfully, terribly bad, we couldn't keep it together, so my husband, Leroy, shot the picture." Maria snickered again at the memory, a sound that held both joy and profound loss, as she went on through each photo, naming each person, telling this young waiter how much fun *Freddy's Place* used to be when she first started. The air in the restaurant seemed to shimmer with the ghosts of laughter and good times.

"So why did you guys stop taking photos?" Miguel asked, turning to face her, his youthful face earnest. Maria tried to hold it together, the question a gentle probe into a wound that never quite healed.

"Well, after Freddy died about ten years back, and I lost my best friend to… to herself, this place just didn't feel like home anymore," Maria explained, her voice quiet, the words tasting like ash. "No matter how hard we tried, we just couldn't bring back that feeling. Freddy left me this place to manage, said it was the only thing that could keep his memory going, keep a piece of his heart alive." She managed a small, sad smile.

The sterile scent of disinfectant and stale coffee clung to the air in the small hospital room. The afternoon light, muted by blinds, cast long, grey shadows. Freddy, usually so boisterous and full of life, seemed impossibly small against the white sheets of the bed. Tubes snaked from his nose, connecting him to the rhythmic beeping of monitors that punctuated the heavy silence. An oxygen mask obscured most of his face, but his eyes, though tired, still held that familiar sparkle of mischief and warmth as they flitted between Maria and Dina.

Dina, looking pale but resolute, sat on one side of the bed, clutching Freddy's hand. Maria sat on the other, her own hand resting gently on his arm. They were both exhausted, their faces etched with worry, but they were there, together, just as they always were. Just as they had been since Freddy's wife, Linda, had passed away too soon, not long before. Freddy had rallied then, for them, for the restaurant, for his own enduring spirit. And they, in turn, had rallied for him, managing the place, trying to keep his spirits up, pretending not to notice the subtle fading in his eyes.

Freddy cleared his throat, a weak, rasping sound.

"Girls," he whispered, his voice hoarse through the oxygen. "You two… you've been amazing." He squeezed Dina's hand, then Maria's arm. "I'm so proud of you both. Especially… especially how you managed to keep it all together since Linda passed." A faint, fond smile touched his lips, and he blinked back tears. "You both were her girls, too, you know."

He paused, taking a slow, shallow breath.

"That place," he continued, his gaze sweeping around, as if he could see the bustling restaurant beyond the hospital walls. "Freddy's Place. Everything we built. All the laughter. All the good food. It's… it's mine and Linda's legacy. It's family." He looked directly at Maria, then at Dina, his eyes brimming with a profound earnestness. "I want you two to share it. Like the sisters you practically are. You always have been. Look after it. Look after each other. Keep the spirit alive." His eyes closed for a moment, then fluttered open, searching for their faces. "Promise me."

Maria swallowed hard, her throat tight. She gripped his hand, feeling the fragile bones beneath her fingers.

"We promise, Freddy," she whispered, her voice thick with unshed tears. Dina nodded fiercely, her own eyes glistening. A faint, peaceful smile settled on Freddy's face, a sigh escaping him. It was a promise given, a legacy bequeathed, a bond solidified in the shadow of impending loss.

Maria and the young waiter began to walk to the back, through the swinging doors into the organized chaos of the kitchen. On the way through, Maria's steps faltered just for a moment as she walked past her office door. The interior was dimly lit, a small, enclosed space packed with ledgers, receipts, and a worn leather chair. She just stared into it, seeing not the mundane reality, but the echo of Freddy's booming laugh, his reassuring presence.

"I know that if Freddy were still here," she murmured, almost to herself, her voice thick with longing, "He'd say, *'Buck up, baby doll. You helped run this place for a while after Linda passed. You were a rock from the start and will continue to be one long after I'm gone. You got this.'*" She closed her eyes for a fleeting second, just imagining the warmth of his hand on her shoulder, the gruff tenderness of his voice. "How I wish I could hear him actually say that, and believe him." A sharp, resounding slam from the front door reverberated through the entire restaurant, echoing even in the back office. Maria jumped, startled, her melancholic reverie instantly shattered. "What was that?" she exclaimed, her voice sharper than intended.

She and Miguel exchanged a look and quickly made their way back to the front of the restaurant, Miguel navigating the tables with a practiced ease. They found Tony already there, hunched over, his shoulders tense, a furious energy thrumming off him. He was huffing to himself, muttering under his breath, his long black hair, usually so meticulously styled, now slightly disheveled. Maria knew that expression. Knew the rigid set of his jaw, the tightness around his eyes. She figured something must've happened at school to put him in such a foul mood, something far worse than a bad test grade.

Tony went behind the counter, moving with an aggressive swiftness, to drop off his school backpack. He ripped off his black leather jacket, tossed it onto a stack of clean napkins, and snatched an apron, tying it with unnecessary force around his waist. He still had his headphones on, music blaring loud enough for Maria to feel the faint bass vibrations. Without a word, he began clearing the few tables that still held remnants of the afternoon rush, clattering dishes. Maria just watched, her heart clenching, as Tony was consumed by his own frustrated, silent world.

"Fucking fuck, stupid Danny! Why did you have to go to my school??" Tony kept thinking to himself, the words a relentless drumbeat in his skull, the music in his ears doing little to drown them out. "I can't stop thinking about you now…." Each plate he grabbed, each fork he tossed into the bus bin, felt like a miniature act of violence. As Tony picked up the last of the dishes from a table, Maria could see past the superficial anger. She saw that Tony was more than just frustrated. She saw that he almost looked scared, hurt even, a raw vulnerability usually hidden beneath layers of cool indifference. He was scared to bring it up to Maria, to confess the reason for his turmoil. So, he just worked away silently, furiously, trapped in his own turbulent world.

Miguel saw the agitated energy. He approached Tony cautiously, trying to be ever so careful not to startle him with the stack of dishes in his hands. He reached out, his fingers lightly tapping Tony on the shoulder. The unexpected touch forced Tony to fall from his furious train of thought. He flinched, pulling out his headset with a jerk, the music instantly ceasing, and spun around to see Miguel standing behind him. Tony just stood there, momentarily disoriented, then his features hardened into a mask of irritation, mixed with a flash of something that looked like relief, or perhaps just a desperate need for a distraction. Miguel just stood there, a nervous, sympathetic smile on his face. Without a word, he subtly motioned toward the table, as if to offer a helping hand with the remaining dishes.

"Don't come any closer, faggot!" Tony snarled, the word erupting from him, harsh and venomous, a raw projection of his own internal pain and fear. It was so sudden and out of nowhere, so utterly unlike the calm, reserved Tony, that neither Tony, nor Miguel, nor even Maria, who had been watching from the counter, knew how to respond. A stunned silence descended upon the restaurant, broken only by the faint hum of the refrigerators. Before either of them could say anything else, the angriest voice could be heard from across the dining area, vibrating with fury and disbelief.

"Antonio Armando Salazar Guzman!" Maria yelled, her voice a whip-crack that echoed through the quiet space. Her face was flushed, her eyes blazing with an unmeasured fury Tony had rarely seen directed at him. "You get your ass over here right now! I won't tolerate you disrespecting anyone like that, do you hear me? I taught you better than that!" She pointed to the space in front of the counter, commanding him to approach. He dropped the dishes he was holding back onto the table with a clatter, his hands suddenly empty, his movements clumsy. He just stood there, eyes welling with tears of anger and, perhaps, shame. Tony couldn't move; he was frozen, caught between his mother's rage and his own boiling emotions. He quickly tore off his apron, the ties tangling, and without another word, bolted. He ran out the door, the bell above it jingling frantically in his wake. It was at that moment that Maria knew, with a certainty that chilled her to the bone, that something truly serious must've happened for her son to behave like that, to lose control so completely.

"I'm terribly sorry, Miguel," Maria said, crossing the floor to the young waiter, her voice laced with genuine sincerity and profound shame. "I really don't know what's gotten into Tony. You don't deserve that. Are you alright?"

Miguel just shook his head, his face pale, and walked past her, heading into the kitchen without saying anything. Maria tried to stop him, to reach out, to truly see if he was alright, but he deftly evaded her outstretched hand and continued his determined path, walking out the back door behind the restaurant. Maria followed him to the doorway, watching as Miguel leaned against the brick wall, pulled out a cigarette, and lit it. He took a long, slow, refreshing drag, the smoke curling around his head like a protective shroud. Maria just stood in the door, a silent, helpless observer.

"He's not the first person, nor will he be the last," Miguel said, his voice surprisingly calm, almost weary, between drags. He quietly wiped away a single tear that had escaped his eye, the experience still fresh in his mind, despite the years. "No matter how many times you hear it, no matter where it comes from, it never gets any easier." He took another long drag, exhaling slowly. Maria, almost instinctively, reached into her own apron pocket, pulling out a pack of cigarettes and a lighter. She clicked it open, the small flame momentarily illuminating the worry in her eyes, and lit one for herself. Miguel looked at her in astonishment, a flicker of surprise crossing his face; he hadn't realized she smoked. She offered him a silent, shared acknowledgement, then took her own deep drag.

"My parents kicked me out after they found out I was gay. I was only sixteen, and scared as all hell. My boyfriend's family took me in, thankfully." Miguel, now 23, looked at Maria, his expression stoic but with an underlying current of resilience. "I suspect I know why your son acted like that, but that's not for me to say." Miguel continued, wearing an optimistic, almost accepting look on his face, despite the painful memories he had just shared. Such words made Maria pause, truly pause, to think about what Tony might be going through, to consider the deeper reasons behind his sudden, violent outburst. However, she didn't know where to start, or even how to ask him what may be going on, how to penetrate the walls her son had so clearly built around himself.

"Miguel," Maria said, her voice soft, the smoke from her cigarette mingling with him in the cool air. She took another drag, the familiar burning a small comfort against the turmoil in her heart. "What do you think I should do? How do I even approach him when he's like this?

He's so angry. I just… I just want him to be honest, Miguel. About whatever it is that's eating at him." She shook her head, a sigh escaping her. "But teenagers, they don't know how to be honest about themselves, do they? They just bottle it up until it explodes." Miguel took a long drag from his own cigarette, his eyes distant, fixed on some unseen point beyond the restaurant's back alley.

"Honesty is tough, especially when you're that age, and especially when you're scared," he replied, his voice still even, but with a deeper resonance now. "When I was sixteen, the last thing I wanted to be was honest. Because honesty, for me, meant losing everything. It meant being kicked out, being alone." He turned his gaze back to Maria, a quiet intensity in his blue eyes. "Tony's got a lot of anger, yeah. But you're right, Maria. There's something else under it. Something that's scaring him. It might not be what you think, or it might be exactly what you're thinking. But either way, yelling at him isn't going to get him to open up. It'll just make him dig in deeper." Miguel flicked his ash, a thoughtful pause.

"When someone's that angry, that hurt, sometimes they're just pushing you away because they're afraid of what will happen if you get too close. Afraid you'll see something they don't want you to see, or that you'll reject them too." He looked down at his cigarette, then back up at Maria. "My boyfriend's mom, she didn't yell at me. She just… she just listened. And she let me know it was okay. That I was still family. Even when I was a total mess, terrified of everything." He took another drag, then tossed his cigarette butt into a small, overflowing ashcan nearby. "You can't force him to be honest, Maria. But you can show him that no matter what it is, you'll still be there. That he won't lose you. That's usually the biggest fear." Miguel offered a small, sad smile. "Sometimes, it just takes time. And a lot of patience." He pushed himself off the wall. "I should probably get back inside."

"Miguel, wait," Maria said, her voice firm, stopping him before he could re-enter the kitchen. She took one last drag from her cigarette, then stubbed it out with force against the brick wall, tossing the butt into the same ashcan. "Come into my office for a minute. Just… I want to understand what happened to you." Miguel hesitated for a moment, his gaze searching hers. He seemed to weigh his own privacy against the genuine concern in her eyes. He nodded slowly.

"Okay," Miguel hesitantly agreed. Maria led the way, through the quiet kitchen, past the gleaming counters and the stacked dirty dishes Tony had left behind. She pushed open the door to her small office, flicking on the overhead light. The room was cramped, filled with the scent of old paper and aroma of coffee. She gestured to the worn leather chair opposite her desk, where a stack of invoices lay waiting. Miguel sat down, looking a little less stoic now, a hint of vulnerability in his posture. Maria sat behind her desk, leaning forward, her hands clasped.

"You mentioned your parents kicked you out," Maria began, her voice gentle, completely different from the shout she'd aimed at Tony moments earlier. "What… what happened after that? Did you ever talk to them again? Did they ever reach out?" Her concern was palpable, not just for Miguel, but for the echo of Tony's own potential future in his story. She couldn't imagine turning her back on her child, no matter what. Miguel looked down at his hands, folded in his lap, his jaw working for a moment before he spoke.

"No," he said, the word quiet but definitive. "Not really. Not directly. They sent a Christmas card once, maybe two years after. Just a generic one, no message from them, just their names signed. It felt… hollow. Like they were just checking a box." He looked up, his eyes meeting hers, a faint, almost imperceptible tremor in his voice. "I tried calling once, after I'd been with Leo's family for a while. I just wanted to tell them I was okay. My mom answered. She just… she just hung up. My dad never picked up." Maria felt a fresh stab of pain, a physical ache in her chest.

"Oh, Miguel. I'm so incredibly sorry. No parent should ever do that." The words were heartfelt, a stark contrast to Dina's casual cruelty towards Danny. "So, they never apologized? Never tried to make amends?"

"No," he repeated, shaking his head. "They made their choice. They decided being gay was wrong, and I was wrong for it. It hurt. It still hurts sometimes, to be honest. But Leo's family... they became my real family. They didn't care who I loved, only that I was safe and happy. They showed me what unconditional love felt like." His voice gained strength, a quiet pride blooming in his eyes. "They were there for me when my own blood wasn't."

Maria leaned back, processing this. It amplified her fear for Tony. Was he afraid of such a definitive break, not just from her, but from his own carefully constructed image? Was he battling an internal struggle that could lead to such a painful fracture?

"You're a strong young man, Miguel," Maria said, admiration clear in her tone. "To go through all that, at sixteen, and still... still come out on the other side with so much grace." She picked up a pen from her desk, idly turning it in her fingers. "It gives me... a lot to think about with Tony. Your words. They're helping me see this differently."

CHAPTER 4

PEANUT

The turn of the key in the lock was the sound of hope dying. Walking through the door, the scent of stale cigarettes and something vaguely sweet and acrid hit Danny the moment he pushed open the front door. It was a smell he knew intimately, the signature perfume of his 'home'. It clung to the curtains, permeated the worn fibers of the couch, and seemed to lodge itself in the back of his throat, coating his tongue with a film of despair. This wasn't just a smell; it was a constant, suffocating reminder of everything he was desperate to escape, a chemical embrace that choked his lungs and his spirit.

He stepped inside, letting the door click shut softly behind him. His backpack, already feeling impossibly heavy, slid from his shoulders with a quiet thud against the worn linoleum. The sound went unnoticed. Dina was exactly where he'd left her that morning, or perhaps, exactly where she'd collapsed after Leroy's departure: sprawled on the living room floor, not quite reaching the stained area rug, her body twisted awkwardly, one arm flung out as if she'd reached for something and fallen. An empty vodka bottle was still clutched loosely in her hand, resting on the threadbare carpet beside her.

Her mouth was slightly ajar, a soft, ragged snore escaping her lips, punctuated by the occasional wet gurgle. The ashtray on the coffee table overflowed, grey ash and crushed butts, a faint, sickly plume of smoke still curling lazily from a forgotten stub, polluting the already thick air. The crinkled dime bags and an array of makeshift pipes were still scattered around the half-eaten bowl of stale cereal he'd left on the table this morning, a grim still life. Nothing had moved. It was as if time itself held its breath, paralyzed by Dina's inertia, her endless cycle of unconsciousness and craving. The only thing that ever truly changed was the level of liquid in the bottles and the growing pile of ash in the tray.

A wave of crushing familiarity washed over Danny, pulling him under. The anxious knot in his stomach from school, barely loosened by the isolation of the bathroom stall, tightened into a hard, aching ball. The brief, fragile hope he'd felt walking into school that morning, had already extinguished, leaving only the cold, pervasive dread. This was his reality. He didn't even bother to check if she was breathing. He knew she was. She always was. Sometimes he wished she wasn't. He pushed it down, deep, into the darkest corners of his mind, ashamed of its fleeting, traitorous presence.

He stepped carefully over the broken glass, glinting like scattered jewels in the dust-choked light filtering through the grimy windows, navigating the invisible minefield of his living room. The silence, punctuated only by Dina's labored, congested breathing, felt heavy and suffocating, pressing down on him, making it hard to draw a full breath. He just wanted to escape it, even if just for a few hours. Escape was a fragile dream he clung to, a future where the air didn't taste like ash and desperation, where he didn't have to walk on eggshells in his own home.

Climbing the stairs, each creak of the old wood seemed to echo a mournful lament for what was lost. He reached his bedroom, a small, cluttered sanctuary, and pushed the door shut with a gentle click that sounded deafening in the silence. It wasn't much – a twin bed shoved against one wall, a battered desk piled high with textbooks and a few forgotten action figures, faded band posters tacked precariously to the walls – but it was his. It was the only place in the entire house where he felt he could truly breathe, where the air didn't feel quite so tainted.

The small cut on his lip, still a faint pink line against his pale skin, throbbed with a phantom ache, a constant reminder of the physical violence that underscored the emotional. He slid into his desk chair and pulled out his AP English textbook. He tried to focus on the intricate poetry of Shakespeare he'd studied earlier, the words on the page blurring slightly as he tried to force his mind away from the ugliness downstairs. He just needed to lose himself in something, anything, that wasn't here, that didn't smell like *her*. But the scent of stale smoke still seemed to seep through the closed door, wrapping around him like a suffocating shroud, refusing to let him go.

It was the sudden scraping sound from downstairs that jolted Danny out of his half-hearted attempt at studying. The sound of furniture being dragged across the floor. He heard Dina cough, a deep, phlegmy, guttural sound that seemed to tear at her throat, followed by the flick and hiss of a lighter.

A fresh wave of that acrid chemical smell began to waft up the stairs. She was awake. Like a predator rousing from a long, unsettling sleep, she was stirring, and he knew, with a terrible certainty, that he was always her first target. He tensed, gripping his pencil tighter until his knuckles were white. He knew what was coming. It always came. He heard her shuffling footsteps, unsteady and slow, making their way not to the kitchen, but to the stairs. His door, he knew, wouldn't deter her. It was merely a flimsy barrier against the inevitable. The knock was soft at first, then grew more insistent, rapping sharply against the wood.

"Danny?" Dina's voice was hoarse, edged with the false, cloying sweetness she adopted when she wanted something. "Danny, you in there, honey?" He took a deep, shaky breath, trying to calm the frantic, panicked beat of his heart. It never worked.

"Yeah, Mom. What do you need?" Danny asked nervously, his voice thin, barely audible. The door creaked open, revealing Dina framed in the dim, stale light of the hallway. Her hair was a matted, tangled mess, her blue eyes bloodshot and rheumy, but there was a flicker of cunning in them now, a predatory gleam. She leaned against the doorframe, a freshly lit cigarette dangling precariously from her lips, the smoke curling around her face like a malevolent halo.

"Look, honey, I just… I need a little cash," she slurred, exhaling a plume of smoke directly into his air. "Just enough to, you know, get some groceries. And maybe a pack of smokes. I'm all out." Danny's stomach dropped. He knew "groceries" meant another fix, another day lost to the drug-induced haze. It was a worn-out script, each repetition chipping away at a piece of his soul, dulling his spirit.

"Mom, I told you. I don't have any money. I don't even have enough for lunch tomorrow," Danny pleaded, his voice rising slightly in desperation, then quickly flattening. It was the absolute truth. His bank account, a pitiful remnant of his father's final, desperate attempt to leave him something, was practically empty, drained by her insatiable demands. Dina's eyes narrowed, the false sweetness draining from her face, replaced by a familiar, ugly hardening. She took a long, slow drag from her cigarette, the glowing tip flaring like a tiny, malevolent eye in the dim light.

"Don't you lie to me, you little fucker," Dina continued, her words more slurred now, but infused with a raw, dangerous edge. "You always got something stashed away. You know I just need a little to get by." She pushed herself off the doorframe, stepping further into the room, invading his small sanctuary, her bloodshot gaze fixed on him, scrutinizing his face. Then her eyes flickered to his mouth, resting, lingering, on the barely healed scar. "Remember last time, Danny, when you said no?" Her voice dropped, a low, menacing purr that sent a fresh, icy shiver down his spine, prickling his skin with goosebumps. "You got a real pretty mouth, don't you? Wouldn't want anything to happen to it again, would we?" His eyes glistened, filling with abundant, hot tears of fear he desperately tried to blink back. The air thickened, pressing down on Danny, making it hard to breathe, suffocating him with the weight of her threat. The memory of her fist, clenched and surprisingly hard, the sharp crack of impact against his cheek, the metallic taste of his own blood blooming in his mouth – it flashed before his eyes, vivid and horrifying, a replay of the last time he defied her.

The unspoken threat hung heavy, a chilling reminder of the brutal, unpredictable violence she was capable of. Danny swallowed hard, his throat suddenly dry, his gaze falling to his textbook, the words now completely meaningless. He had nothing left to give. And even if he did, giving it to her felt like a complete, utter betrayal of himself, of the last shreds of his dignity. But saying no… saying no came with a price he was desperate to avoid, a physical and emotional cost that left him raw and trembling. He was trapped, caught between a mother who was a monster and the grim, inevitable consequences of defiance. The only question was, how much more could he endure before something finally broke inside him?

"Mom, please," Danny began, his voice barely a raw whisper. He lifted his head, his eyes, swimming with unshed tears, meeting her bloodshot gaze. He tried to project a sincerity he truly felt, a desperation that was as real as the air in his lungs. "I don't have anything. Seriously. I don't have any money. Not a single cent. You know I don't have a job, and what little Dad left… it's gone." His voice cracked on the last word. He spread his hands in a gesture of utter helplessness.

He watched her face, searching for any flicker of understanding, any hint of the mother he vaguely remembered. But her features remained hard, etched with the familiar mask of addiction. Her eyes, narrowed and cold, were still fixed on his mouth.

"Don't give me that bullshit, Danny," she slurred, taking another long drag from her cigarette, the smoke clouding her face like a veil. Her voice was growing sharper, losing the false sweetness, replaced by a cutting edge that always signaled the shift from persuasion to threat. "You think I'm stupid? You think I don't know you hide things?"

"I'm not hiding anything, Mom!" Danny insisted, a fresh wave of panic rising. He pushed himself back against his desk, feeling the solid wood against his spine. "I just… I just want to study. I have AP English homework. And I'm exhausted. I just want to go to bed." The words tumbled out, desperate. He longed for the simple peace of being left alone, to retreat into the fragile sanctuary of his room.

Dina took a step closer, her silhouette looming in the doorway, casting a long, distorted shadow across his small space. The smell of stale smoke and something cloying, sickeningly sweet, intensified, wrapping around him, stealing his breath. Her eyes, still glinting with that chilling cunning, raked over his desk, his books, searching for any sign of hidden currency. Her gaze landed on his worn NYU hoodie, crumpled on the bed. He tensed, anticipating her next move.

"You think you're better than me, don't you?" Dina accused, her voice dropping to a low, dangerous growl that sent a fresh shiver down his spine. "Reading your fancy books. Thinking you're too good for this house, for *me*." She gestured around his room with the cigarette, a careless flick of ash scattering onto his textbooks. "You think you can just escape all this, huh? Just walk away when you feel like it?"

Danny clenched his fists, his nails digging into his palms. The accusation was familiar, a twisted resentment that always surfaced when she felt threatened or denied. He wanted to scream that he wasn't trying to be better, he was just trying to survive. But he knew it was futile. There was no reasoning with her when she was like this. He kept his gaze down, focused on the swirling ash on his book, on anything but her menacing eyes.

"No, Mom. I just… I'm tired. Please. Just let me study." His voice was barely audible, laced with a plea he knew she wouldn't hear. He felt the familiar weight of inevitable defeat settle over him. He was losing this battle, just as he always did. The only question now was how much more she would take before she finally left him alone.

Dina scoffed, a dry, bitter sound that held no humor. She took one last, long drag from her cigarette, the tip glowing fiercely before she slowly, deliberately extinguished it in the overflowing ashtray on his desk, grinding it down with a vicious twist. The acrid smell of burnt tobacco flared, mingling with the ever-present chemical stench. Her eyes, still cold and hard, locked onto his, unblinking.

"Fine," she slurred, her voice a low, dangerous growl. "Be useless. See how far that gets you." She leaned closer, her breath hot and foul on his face. "But if I find out you got so much as a penny tucked away in here, or if you even *think* about telling anyone about me," her voice dropped to a chilling whisper, "you'll regret it. Got it, honey? Really regret it." She emphasized the last words, a promise of pain that settled deep into Danny's bones.

Without another word, she straightened up, a shadow retreating from his doorway. Her shuffling footsteps receded down the hall, then down the stairs, the creaks of the old wood sounding like a mournful echo of her departure. A final, distant thump from downstairs signaled her return to the living room, to her chemical slumber.

Danny didn't move for a long moment, frozen in place, listening until the last sound of her settled into silence. Only then did the rigid tension in his body begin to unravel, his muscles trembling uncontrollably. His breath hitched, a dry, ragged gasp tearing from his throat, followed by another, and then another. The dam broke. Tears, hot and stinging, welled in his eyes, blurring the textbooks on his desk into an indistinguishable mess. He covered his face with his hands, muffling the choked sobs that wracked his slender frame. He couldn't take it anymore. The fear, the humiliation, the sheer, crushing loneliness of it all – it was too much. He wept silently, desperately, the sound of his own pain the only solace in the suffocating quiet of his room.

After what felt like an eternity, when the tears finally began to subside, leaving his face wet and his throat raw, he reached instinctively. Danny rushed to his closet, frantically tearing it apart, his hand fumbled under a pile of discarded clothes, searching, until his fingers brushed against the soft, familiar fabric. He pulled out Peanut, his stuffed blue and green elephant, the only thing in his life that brought any remote comfort. He clutched it to his chest, burying his face in its worn, faded fur, drawing in the faint, lingering scent of dust and memory. The small, familiar weight of it in his arms was a tender anchor against the storm raging inside him.

The touch of Peanut immediately pulled him back, a sudden, vivid warmth flooding his memory.

The air in his dad's barbershop smelled of pomade, antiseptic, and something distinctly masculine and comforting. Danny, a small, fidgety five-year-old, sat perched on a booster seat atop the old leather barber chair, his feet dangling. Rick, his dad, a man whose laughter seemed to fill every corner of a room, stood behind him, clippers buzzing gently around Danny's ears.

"Almost done, sport," Rick murmured, his warm hands steady and gentle. "Just a few more snips, and you'll be the sharpest looking kid in town."

Danny squirmed.

"Is it almost over? My ears are tickling." Danny said as he tried hiding his childish laugh. Rick chuckled, a deep, rumbling sound that always made Danny feel safe.

"Almost. And you've been such a good boy, sitting so still for me. You know what that means, right?" Danny's eyes, wide and curious, met his dad's in the large mirror.

"What?" Danny asked with his eyes full of wonder.

"It means a reward for being the best helper a dad could ask for," Rick said, a mischievous glint in his eye. He finished the last trim with a flourish, then took off Danny's barber cape. "Close your eyes." Danny giggled, squeezing his eyes shut tightly. He heard a rustle, a soft crinkle, then something soft and plump was pressed into his arms. He opened his eyes. There it was: a brand new, vibrant blue and green stuffed elephant, its trunk curled up in a cheerful salute.

"His name is Peanut," Rick said, beaming, crouching down to Danny's level. "Because he's little, but he's tough. Just like my boy. And he's going to be your guardian. To remind you that you're always brave, always loved." He ruffled Danny's newly cut hair. "Think he'll help you study all those big books?"

Danny hugged the elephant tightly, burying his face in its soft fur. It was the best gift ever. Better than any toy car or video game. It felt like a piece of his dad, warm and constant.

"Thank you, Daddy," he'd whispered, his voice thick with unbridled joy. He'd kept Peanut on his pillow every night since, a silent guardian against the dark, a constant reminder of his dad's love and his own quiet bravery.

Danny still clutched Peanut, the old toy a lifeline in the overwhelming current of his despair. He held onto that small, faded elephant like it was the only real thing left in his world, the only proof that love and safety had ever existed, even if only for a little while. The tears had stopped, replaced by a hollow ache, but the memory, bittersweet as it was, provided a fragile shield against the encroaching darkness of his reality. He just held Peanut, listening to the silence, praying it wouldn't be broken again.

CHAPTER 5

WEARING A MASK

"He's not the first person, nor will he be the last... I suspect I know why your son acted like that, but that's not for me to say," Miguel's quiet words echoed in her mind, a haunting refrain. Tony's behavior wasn't just typical teenage angst; it was a desperate cry, a raw wound festering beneath a veneer of manufactured indifference. Maria felt a cold dread begin to seep into her bones. Something serious had happened.

"Miguel," Maria said, her voice softer now, almost a plea, as she stepped back into the cool evening air. He turned, his face softened by the dim twilight. The streetlights were just beginning to flicker on, casting a faint, orange glow. "Can you… just close up when you're done? I need to go." Her gaze locked with his, a silent understanding passing between them, a shared weight of knowing. Miguel simply nodded with quiet empathy.

"Go get him, Maria," Miguel said, his voice low, his eyes soft but steady. She didn't need to be told twice. The words fueled her, hardening her resolve. Maria pulled her keys from her apron pocket, her fingers fumbling slightly, her mind already racing with the day's fragments. The short walk home felt endless, each step heavy with apprehension, the question pounding in her head: What happened? What had gotten into her son? Tony was usually so guarded, so internalized with his struggles. For him to explode like that, with such a vicious slur, especially at someone like Miguel, it had to be something truly devastating.

The front door of their small house was unlocked, a familiar carelessness that usually irritated Maria but now brought a pang of icy fear. It was just *too* easy to walk right in. She pushed it open slowly, the hinges groaning softly in the evening quiet.

"Tony? Are you home?" Maria called out, her voice nervous, thinner than usual. She heard nothing but the beat of her own heart.

Silence. The house felt hushed, unnatural. She walked through the small entryway, past the familiar clutter of the living room – the worn armchair, the dark, unlit television screen, the stack of magazines Leroy had left. Her gaze swept the familiar space, searching, listening. Then she heard it: the faint, insistent thrum of bass, muffled but unmistakable, coming from upstairs. His room. He was here. A small wave of relief washed over her but it ebbed quickly into dread.

Maria climbed the stairs, each creak of the old wood amplifying her growing anxiety, echoing the frantic rhythm of her pulse. She paused outside his closed door, listening to the heavy, insistent thrum of the bass that seemed to bleed through the walls themselves. Taking a deep breath, she knocked, her knuckles rapping softly against the painted wood, more plea than demand.

"Tony? *Mijo*, it's Mom. Can I come in?" Maria asked, her voice calm, carefully modulated. She peered tentatively into the narrow crack of the door. The music abruptly cut off. The sudden silence in the house was deafening, thick and heavy, stretching into an eternity before she heard a low mumble.

"Yeah, whatever," Tony managed to mumble out, his voice choked, devoid of its usual defiance. Maria pushed the door open to find Tony sprawled on his bed, still in his work clothes, his back to her, rigid and unyielding. His headset lay discarded beside him on the rumpled sheets. The air in the room felt charged with a palpable tension. She stepped fully into the room, closing the door softly behind her, cutting off the rest of the house.

"We need to talk about this afternoon, Antonio," Maria said, her voice calm but firm, holding his gaze, refusing to be intimidated by his usual defiance, refusing to let him hide behind the wall he built. "About what you said to Miguel."

"Oh, that? He's a faggot. I just said what everyone thinks," he scoffed, a short, sharp burst of air, turning his face into the pillow. His voice was flat, devoid of real conviction, just a bitter recitation of learned cruelty.

"No, Antonio," Maria said, her voice unwavering, cutting through his pretense. She walked further into the room, her eyes never leaving him, and perched carefully on the edge of his small desk chair. "You said something that hurt him. And you said it with an anger I don't understand, especially from you." She waited, leaving space for the words to land. "What happened today that made you lash out with that kind of cruelty? That's not how I raised you."

"Nothing happened. Just leave me alone." His voice was tight, edged with irritation masking fear, his body still rigid.

"I can't leave you alone, *mijo*," Maria countered, her gaze unwavering, her voice softening, pulling on the thread of their connection. "You ran out of work, you yelled at someone who did nothing to you. That's not like you. Something's wrong." Tony finally rolled over, slowly, reluctantly, his face blotchy and red, his eyes still shimmering with unshed tears, betraying the tough facade he tried to maintain. He pulled his knees to his chest, wrapping his arms around them, making himself small.

"You don't know anything," he muttered, his voice muffled against his knees, half-defensive, half-broken.

"I don't know what happened. But what I do know is that you're hurting for some reason," Maria countered, her gaze unwavering, her heart aching for him. She reached for the familiar wisdom she'd clung to since Freddy's passing. "Freddy always used to tell us 'Anger is just hurt wearing a mask'. And you know you don't have to hide it from me. We talk about everything, remember?"

It was a half-truth, and they both knew it. They talked about school, about the restaurant, about bills. But never about the deeper shadows beneath. He scoffed, a hollow laugh that didn't reach his eyes.

"Yeah, right. Like you'd understand," claimed Tony, his voice thick with hurt and exhaustion, covering himself further with the duvet, trying to disappear.

"Try me," she urged, her voice low, resonating with a quiet strength he hadn't heard in a long time. "Please, Antonio. Just tell me." The silence that followed was suffocating, stretched taut with unspoken fears. Tony's chest rose and fell with rapid, uneven breaths, his body trembling slightly. His gaze flickered frantically around the room, settling on nothing, as if he were trying to find an escape route, a door that wasn't there. Maria waited, patiently, resolutely, refusing to look away, refusing to break the fragile connection. She thought of Freddy's booming laugh, his unwavering support. *"Buck up, baby doll."* This was her baby. And she had to be a rock now more than ever, a sturdy anchor in his storm. Finally, he spoke, his voice barely a whisper, ragged with emotion, breaking the silence like fragile glass.

"It's… it's Danny," Tony managed, the name a painful confession, each syllable scraped raw from somewhere deep inside him.

"Danny?" she asked softly, as if afraid to press too hard. "What about Danny?".

"He… he goes to my school now," Tony blurted, his voice cracking as if the fact alone carried unbearable weight. Then, the dam broke completely. "And I… I can't stop thinking about him, all the feelings came rushing back," Tony choked out, his voice cracking on the last word, the raw emotion finally unspooling. "I just… I hate it. I hate that he's there, and I hate that I feel… I don't know what I feel. It's just… wrong." He trailed off, burying his face deeper in his knees, his body shaking with suppressed sobs, the words dissolving into a desperate, guttural cry. "I just… I can't be that way… I can't be like them." Maria's heart dropped; Miguel's warning now made terrible sense..

"I suspect I know why your son acted like that," Miguel's words rang in her mind, their meaning now painfully obvious, pressing against her chest like a weight she could no longer deny. Tony's anger, his fear, his cruel words to Miguel, weren't aimless—they were tied to Danny's sudden presence, sparking feelings too tangled and frightening for him to face. And the fact that it was Dina's son, a ghost from her own painful past, only deepened the wound, reopening old shadows she had tried to bury.

She rose from the chair, moving slowly, careful not to break the fragile silence. She walked slowly to the bed, her heart aching with a mixture of sorrow and a fierce, protective love. She sat beside him, her hand steady on his rigid back. His muscles were rigid beneath her touch, coiled tight with a lifetime of suppressed emotion.

"Oh, *mijo*," she murmured, her voice thick with a tenderness that surprised even herself, all compassion, no judgment. She wrapped her arms around him, pulling him close, her chin resting on his messy, damp hair, inhaling the faint, familiar scent of him. The truth already settling into her bones, and with it a fierce, aching tenderness that burned brighter than shock. He resisted at first, then collapsed against her, sobs breaking free.

The sobs that wracked his body were deep and raw, years of fear pouring out at once. She held him tighter, feeling the weight of his secret, and the immense, terrifying responsibility that came with it. She didn't need every answer yet—only the resolve to protect him.

Tony's sobs ebbed away, breaking into ragged, shuddering breaths against Maria's shoulder. Finally, he stirred, pulling back slightly, his face still blotchy and tear-strestreaked, but his eyes, though red-rimmed, held a desperate need to explain.

"It's... it's not just that he's at school," Tony mumbled, his voice hoarse, barely above a whisper. He swallowed hard, then continued, each word seemingly dragged from the depths of his shame. "Months ago, Mom. Before... before all of this. Danny... he told me. He told me he's gay."

Maria stiffened, a sharp intake of breath. The truth hit hard. Miguel's words echoed: *"My parents kicked me out after they found out I was gay"*. This was it. This was the source of Tony's terror.

"And I…" Tony's voice hitched, a fresh wave of agony washing over his face. "I freaked out, Mom. I didn't… I didn't know what to do. I just… I started icing him out. I avoided him. I stopped talking to him." He pushed away from Maria, rolling onto his back, staring blankly at the ceiling, his hands clenching and unclenching on the duvet. "Because… because it's wrong, right? It's a sin." Maria's heart constricted.

"Tony, where did you get that idea?" she asked softly, already dreading the answer, a sickening feeling forming in her stomach.

"Tia Isabella," he whispered. He turned his head slowly, his eyes meeting hers, full of a deep, ingrained fear. "Years ago. When she visited. You were at work, and Dad was on shift."

A cold, horrifying realization washed over Maria. Isabella. Pious. Rigid. The sister she had trusted once. She had left Tony with Isabella one evening years ago when Leroy was working a late shift, trusting her sister, believing she would just entertain him, maybe cook him dinner.

"She was watching me one night. We were just watching TV, and then she… she just started talking," Tony said as he closed his eyes, his voice becoming desperate, faltering. "About church. About sin. She said… she said that God hates it when men love men. That it's an abomination. That people like that go to hell. She said they were an insult to God, an insult to their families. That it was a sickness. And if you knew someone like that, you had to cut them out, or you'd be corrupted too."

"She looked me right in the eye, Mom, and she said it." He opened his eyes, pleading, fear carved deep. "That it was the worst sin. And she made it sound so real. So terrifying. I carried those horrifying words with me, Mom. Every single day since then. And then… then Danny told me, and it all just… it clicked. And I just couldn't… I couldn't be friends with him anymore. I couldn't be near him. Because if I was, maybe… maybe it would be wrong for me too. Maybe *I* would be like that. And I can't be like them, Mom. I just can't."

He buried his face in his hands again, sobs muffled, grief and confusion spilling through. Maria sat beside him, silent, her heart aching, burning with a fierce, protective rage at her sister. Isabella had poisoned her son, cloaking fear as faith.

She pulled Tony back into her arms, holding him tighter than before, a silent promise forming in her mind. This was about undoing the damage at its root.

Tony's sobs slowly quieted, fading into ragged, shuddering breaths against Maria's shoulder. Still curled into her, his breaths uneven, he clung to her. Finally, he stirred, pulling back slightly, his face still blotchy and tear-streaked, but his eyes, though red-rimmed, held a desperate need to explain.

Maria held him, stroking his hair, waiting for his breathing to even out. Her mind turned over years of Isabella's quiet poison, and the way it had seeped into her son. This wasn't just about Tony; it was about protecting her son from a poison that had seeped into his very soul.

"Antonio, *mijo*," she finally said, her voice soft but firm, a steady anchor in his storm. "Listen to me very carefully. What Tia Isabella told you… that's not true. Not about God. Not about people. Being gay is a natural occurrence, *mijo*. Just like being straight. It's how some people are born. There is nothing, absolutely nothing, wrong with it. It's not a sin. It's not a sickness. And it certainly doesn't make someone an abomination." She pulled back slightly, gently cupping his face in her hands, forcing him to meet her gaze. Her eyes, filled with unconditional love, searched his, burning against years of fear. "Do you understand me? You are my son. And nothing you could ever feel, nothing you could ever be, would make me love you less. You will not go to hell for loving someone, Antonio. You will only go to hell for hurting someone."

Tony blinked, his eyes wide, still clouded with doubt and remnants of terror, but a flicker of dawning hope remained there. He opened his mouth, but no words came out. Maria took a steadying breath. This was the hardest part, the question that needed to be asked, the truth that needed to surface.

"So, what if you're gay, Tony? And so what if Danny is?" She paused, letting the implications hang in the air, watching his reaction closely. His breath hitched again. "Is that what's scaring you, *mijo*? Is it… is it that you have feelings for Danny?"

Tony flinched, his eyes darting away, then back to her, cheeks flushing hot with shame. He swallowed hard, his throat working. He squeezed his eyes shut again, then, in a barely audible whisper, thick with shame and a lifetime of suppressed emotion, he finally confessed.

"I… I started liking Danny," he choked out. "When we were much younger. Before… before Tia Isabella. Before I even knew what it meant. I just… I just knew I liked being around him more than anyone else. I hated it when he paid attention to other kids. I didn't know how to process it. It felt… confusing. And then Tia Isabella… and then Danny told me… and it just made all those feelings feel even worse. Like a secret I couldn't ever tell anyone. Like something I had to crush inside me." He burrowed his face back into Maria's shoulder, all resistance gone. "I don't want to feel this anger anymore, Mom. I don't want to be like this."

Maria held him, tears finally stinging her own eyes, but these were tears of understanding, of relief, of fierce love. Her heart broke for the little boy who had carried such a terrifying, beautiful secret alone for so long. Now she saw: the anger was fear, the cruelty a desperate shield.

Maria rose slowly, pressing a kiss to his temple before slipping from the room. She needed a moment — to breathe, to keep from drowning in the storm of rage at Isabella and sorrow for her son. The floorboards creaked under her feet as she moved downstairs, the muted hum of the refrigerator grounding her in the ordinary, even as her world tilted. She busied her hands with pouring a glass of water, but her ears strained for the quiet above.

Upstairs, Tony sat still for a long while, staring at the closed door, at the silence Maria had left behind. His hands trembled as they fell to the side of his bed, fingers brushing the familiar curve of wood. The guitar had been sitting there for months, collecting dust, but now — almost without thought — he lifted it onto his lap.

He let his thumb graze across the strings. A soft, imperfect chord rang out, the sound fractured, almost shy. He adjusted, pressing down harder this time, until the notes found one another. His breath caught. Music had always been safer than words, less dangerous than feelings. Now, the strings gave voice to everything his throat had choked back: the confusion, the shame, the strange, aching love he didn't know how to name.

The melody was clumsy, halting, but it carried something truer than speech. Each note lingered like confession, trembling into the quiet of the room. His shoulders hunched over the guitar as if he could hide inside it, pouring himself into the hollow body of wood and sound.

Downstairs, Maria froze mid-step on the return. The faint, hesitant strumming floated through the ceiling. It wasn't much — not a song, not even a tune — but it was Tony, raw and reaching for something beyond fear. She closed her eyes, tears slipping free, and in that fragile sound she heard not just pain, but the start of release.

CHAPTER 6

FOSTER CARE

Leroy gripped the steering wheel, knuckles white, the worn leather cold beneath his sweaty palms. He was already driving, the familiar roar of the engine a dull thrum beneath his feet, but his mind was still miles back, trapped in the grim tableau of Dina's living room. Rick. His best friend. They'd been inseparable, dreamed big dreams, planned futures. And then Rick was gone, leaving Dina, broken and spiraling, in his wake. Leroy had tried. God, he'd tried. For years, he'd held onto the hope that Dina would pull herself out, that the woman he and Maria had loved, the vibrant, funny Dina, would reappear. But each attempt to help, each offer of support, had been met with lies, manipulation, or venom. Now, seeing the wreckage of her life and, more importantly, Danny's, he knew it was cowardice. He'd failed Rick. Rick had trusted him to look out for his family, and Leroy had watched as Dina devoured herself and, now, was devouring their son.

The image of Danny's quiet, watchful eyes, the subtle tension in his shoulders Maria had described, flashed in his mind. That boy was living with a monster, with the constant threat of a volatile, drug-addicted mother. Mrs. Flores, the neighbor, calling him every day – what had Danny endured that had driven a sweet old lady to such desperation? He was actively letting Danny be harmed, betraying Rick's memory with his inaction. The guilt was a physical weight, pressing down on him, making it hard to breathe. The taste of ash from his earlier cigarette was bitter on his tongue, mirroring the taste of guilt in his soul.

After arriving home he opened the front door. The warm glow of the overhead light, the comforting scent of garlic and herbs from dinner, wrapped around him like a soft blanket—a blinding contrast to the darkness he'd just left. He found Maria in the kitchen, humming softly to herself as she tidied up, the rhythmic clink of dishes and silverware, a comforting counterpoint to the chaos still ringing in his head. She turned, a soft, welcoming smile on her face that quickly faded as she took in his expression, the grim set of his jaw, the haunted look in his eyes.

"Leroy? What's wrong? You look like you've seen a ghost." She wiped her hands on a dishtowel, her eyes searching his, immediately picking up on his distress. The cheer in her humming evaporated, replaced by a thin edge of unease. He just stood there, words caught in his throat, a lump of despair choking him. He shoved his trembling hands into his pockets, trying to hide his weakness.

"It's Dina," he finally managed, his voice rough, heavy with the visit's toll. "I went to see her." Maria's face tightened instantly, resignation falling over her like a familiar weight.

"Oh, Leroy. Why? You know how she is. I just… I don't understand why you keep putting yourself through that." Her voice was gentle, but laced with a frustration born of years of failed attempts.

"Because of Danny, Maria!" He snapped, the anger he'd suppressed finally bubbling to the surface, sharp and uncontrolled. He immediately regretted he saw her flinch, her shoulders pulling tight. He ran a hand over his face, sighing heavily, forcing himself to breathe. "I'm sorry. It's just… you wouldn't believe it. The place is a war zone. Broken bottles, holes in the walls, everything ripped to shreds. She's completely gone, Maria. More gone than I've ever seen her." He walked to the kitchen table and sank into a chair, rubbing his temples. "She was talking crazy, accusing me… it was just off the rails."

Maria slowly approached the table, composure crumbling into a growing, sickening concern. She pulled out a chair opposite him and sat down, her hands clasping tightly, white-knuckled on the tabletop. She lingered before sitting, hovering like someone standing at the edge of a cliff, torn between lashing out in anger or breaking down in fear. The scrape of the chair legs on the tile was loud, final, like sealing herself inside whatever truth was about to come.

"What do you mean, 'accusing you'?" Maria asked, her voice tired, yet laced with a new, fearful curiosity. Leroy looked up, his eyes meeting hers, full of a raw pain he almost never let her see.

"She said… she said I raped her after Rick died. That I killed him. Can you believe that, Maria? My own goddamn best friend." His voice dropped to a near whisper, shaking with disbelief. "She's not just sick, Maria. She's delusional. And that poor kid… Danny is living in that hellhole. He's suffering. I know it."

Maria gasped, a sharp, choked sound, pressing a trembling hand to her mouth. Her thoughts immediately went to Tony. His outburst just hours ago, his tearful confession about Danny. Her heart lurched; two broken boys, two poisoned homes, snapping together in her mind like jagged glass. The connection, the horrifying realization of the link between the two broken families, hit her so hard she felt her breath catch and her throat tighten. Her mind flickered unbidden to Tony as a little boy—chubby cheeks, hands sticky with candy, laughing as Leroy tossed him in the air. That innocence felt impossibly distant now, corrupted by Isabella's poison, and the memory made her stomach twist with grief.

"Oh, Leroy," she whispered, every word trembling with dread. "Danny… Antonio told me something tonight. Something about Danny. He's going to Tony's school now." She saw his face, still etched with the raw pain of Dina's accusations, shift to confusion.

"What does that have to do with anything? What did Tony say?" Leroy snapped, his patience worn thin, unable to grasp the sudden turn in the conversation. Maria sank lower into her chair, her fingers knotting together as if bracing for impact. She recounted the entire scene with Tony, his distress, his confused words.

"He said… he can't stop thinking about Danny. He hates it. He said it feels 'wrong.' And he yelled something awful at Miguel, Leroy. Called him a… a faggot. He was crying, he was so scared and angry. I think… I think Antonio is struggling with something, something about himself, and it's tied to Danny being there, and what Isabella filled his head with." Maria paused, her jaw tightening. "It was a bad idea, Leroy. A really bad idea to let her visit when she did. She filled his head with hateful things about people being… being 'wrong' if they're like that. It scarred him, Leroy. Our son." Leroy's jaw clenched, a muscle working furiously.

"Goddammit, Maria! I *knew* it. I told you she was too much. I told you it was a mistake to leave him with her when she started going on about her damn church. Look what she did to our son." His own son. Caught in the undertow of Dina's chaos, of Isabella's hatred. The idea of Danny, Rick's son, living in such squalor, enduring such abuse, and now inadvertently triggering such profound, unsettling turmoil in Tony… it was too much. His initial impulse, to just wash his hands of Dina and her problems, evaporated like smoke. The guilt he'd felt about Rick's memory, the long-standing protective instinct for Danny, and now the burgeoning, terrifying worry for Tony, merged into a singular, urgent need for definitive action. The luxury of inaction was gone.

"I told her, Maria," Leroy said, his voice hard with renewed resolve, stripped of all personal emotion, returning to his police sergeant's tone. "I told her if she doesn't clean up, if she doesn't get her life together, I'm going to have her arrested. And Danny would go into foster care." The words hung in the air between them, stark and brutal. He watched Maria's reaction, bracing himself for her judgment, for her disbelief, perhaps even her plea to relent. But Maria just looked at him, her eyes wide with a mixture of shock, sorrow, and then, a slow, dawning understanding that hardened into shared resolve.

"You… you said that to her?" she asked slowly, her voice barely a whisper, not in judgment, but in awe of his courage.

A deafening silence filled the air. Maria looks at Leroy in near disbelief at the words she had heard. The hum of the refrigerator filled the air, coupled with the rhythmic ticking of the clock on the wall. He watched Maria's reaction, bracing himself for her judgment, for her disbelief, perhaps even her plea to relent. But Maria just looked at him, her eyes wide with a mixture of shock, sorrow, and then, a slow, dawning understanding that hardened into shared resolve.

"Yes, *mija*," he affirmed, his gaze steady, unwavering. "And she didn't care. Not about herself, not about Danny. She just… she just laughed." The memory of Dina's deranged laughter made him sick to his stomach all over again. "I can't just stand by, Maria. Not when Danny is living like that. Not when it's hurting Antonio too. Not when he's carrying this hatred because of Isabella's twisted words." Maria reached across the table, her hand covering his, her touch warm, solid, and utterly steadfast.

Maria pressed her palms flat on the table as if steadying herself. "Leroy, I don't… I don't know anymore." Her voice cracked. "The system isn't safe either. We've both seen it. What if Danny ends up worse? What if he gets lost in there, with no one looking out for him? No family. No one."

Leroy's chair screeched back as he shoved to his feet again. "And what's the alternative, Maria? Leave him there? Pretend we didn't see it?" His chest heaved, his face contorted between rage and despair. "Jesus Christ, I swore to Rick I'd look after them. And I've done nothing but fail."

Maria rose too, hands trembling as she jabbed a finger toward him. "Don't you dare put this all on yourself! We *both* failed. We've been failing for years, Leroy! And now you want to fix it by throwing Danny to the wolves? By letting strangers decide if he eats, if he's safe, if anyone even gives a damn about him?"

"Strangers might be the only ones who can keep him alive!" Leroy shot back, his voice cracking. "What do you want me to do, Maria? Bring him here? Pretend we're not already drowning with Tony?"

"Maybe!" she snapped, eyes wet with furious tears. "Maybe we should! At least then he wouldn't be completely alone!"

Leroy's face darkened, his voice breaking through the silence like a whip. "And what then, Maria? Huh? When he looks at me and sees the man who threw his mother in jail? When Tony sees us dragging another broken kid into this house and realizes I can't even protect my own son?"

Maria shook her head violently, chest heaving. "You think you're protecting anyone right now? You're not saving Danny, you're not saving Tony—you're just punishing yourself for Rick's ghost! That's all this is, Leroy. You're still trying to fix something that died years ago!" The kitchen rang with silence after that, sharp and ugly. Leroy stared at her, breath ragged, Maria's words hanging between them like a slap.

Finally, Maria sagged, her voice lowering to a hoarse whisper. "We're getting nowhere. Absolutely nowhere. You're yelling, I'm yelling. This— this isn't solving anything." She wiped at her face with the heel of her palm. "We need to sleep on it. Just… survive tonight. Decide tomorrow."

Her words didn't end the argument so much as smother it under the heavy blanket of exhaustion. Leroy's jaw worked, muscles twitching with everything he wanted to say and couldn't. He sank back into his chair, eyes burning, and for once, he didn't argue.

He moved toward the kitchen doorway, ready to head upstairs. But just as he reached the archway, a figure emerged from the shadows of the hallway.

It was Tony. Halfway down the staircase, frozen on a step, his back to them. His face was no longer blotchy from earlier tears. It was pale, stark white, his eyes wide with a dawning horror. Every word seemed carved into him, leaving him frozen.

"Antonio, *mijo*?" Maria whispered, her voice a fragile thread, seeing the shock on her son's face, realizing how much he must have heard.

Tony didn't respond to Maria. His gaze was fixed on Leroy, wide and accusing, filled with a raw, panicked betrayal. His breath came in shallow, ragged gasps. The phrase clanged in his head: foster care. Foster care. Like a hammer blow that wouldn't stop. He pushed himself off the step, his legs shaking, stumbling backward as if the stairs themselves had turned against him. His eyes, still fixed on Leroy, were filled with disbelief and a deep, cutting pain.

"Foster care?" Tony whispered, the word a choked accusation. "You're… you're going to put Danny in foster care?" His voice cracked, a fresh wave of tears springing to his eyes. "You would do that? To Rick's son? To… to Danny?" The question wasn't just about Danny; it was about the chilling, impersonal power of the system his father represented, and the implication that such a drastic step could be taken, even against family. Leroy froze, his heart sinking. He hadn't accounted for this, for Tony overhearing.

"Antonio, wait. We need to explain," Leroy started, moving towards the stairs, but Tony recoiled.

"No!" he cried, a high-pitched sound of distress. Tony shook his head furiously, his fear momentarily overcoming his earlier shame and confusion. "You can't! You can't do that to him!" He turned, scrambling back up the stairs, two steps at a time, his footsteps heavy and desperate, disappearing into the darkness of the upstairs hallway. A moment later, they heard the distinct slam of his bedroom door.

"Oh, Leroy. I can't believe he heard, "Maria said as she turned to Leroy, her face pale, her lips trembling. Leroy just ran a hand through his hair, defeated.

Leroy and Maria froze as if the world itself had stopped. The silence after Tony's voice was so sharp it hurt. Maria's lips trembled; she whispered, "He thinks we're betraying him too." Leroy stared at the wall past her shoulder, feeling the slam of guilt like a baton blow. His authority, his fatherhood, his very promise to protect—all of it suddenly felt paper-thin in his son's eyes. The silence that followed was thick with the weight of Tony's pain, and the fragile hope they had just begun to cling to.

Upstairs, the slam of the door echoed the violent crashing inside Tony's own head. He stumbled into his room, pushing the door shut with his foot and leaning against it, gasping for breath as if he'd just run a marathon. Panic seized him, a cold, tightening vise around his chest. *Foster care. They're going to put Danny in foster care.* The words repeated in a horrifying loop, each syllable a fresh stab of fear.

He clutched his head, his fingers tangling in his long black hair. It couldn't be happening. Not to Danny. Danny, with his quiet eyes and his old Spiderman comic. Danny, who looked so lost today, just like a puppy. The thought of Danny, alone in some sterile, impersonal 'system', stripped of even the meager, chaotic comfort of his home, was unbearable. He might hate the confusion Danny stirred in him, might still be terrified of the forbidden feelings that erupted whenever Danny was near, but he didn't want *this* for him. He didn't want him *gone*.

A dizzying wave of nausea washed over Tony. The room tilted, shadows stretching across his posters, his desk, the pile of clothes on the floor. Everything looked wrong, stretched, hostile, as if the walls themselves had turned against him. Even his own heartbeat betrayed him, hammering off-beat, too fast, too loud. He dug his nails into his arms, desperate for something sharp, something that hurt, just to remind himself he was still real.

He slid down the door to the floor, pulling his knees up to his chest, burying his face in them. This was all his fault. If he hadn't reacted so badly. If he hadn't iced Danny out. If he hadn't listened to Tia Isabella's poisonous words. If he wasn't so messed up, if he didn't feel this confusing, wrong thing for Danny, maybe none of this would be happening. His parents wouldn't be talking about Social Services. Dina wouldn't be... like that. It all spiraled back to him, to his own tangled emotions, to the truth he was so desperate to bury.

He squeezed his eyes shut, trying to force the images out – Danny's face, the terrified look when he'd called Miguel that word, the way his mother's eyes had softened when he'd finally confessed. He was a monster. A monster who hated himself for feelings he couldn't control, and now, a monster who had inadvertently doomed his oldest friend. He had to fix it. But how? How could he stop a train he barely understood, a train fueled by his own secret, horrifying desires? The panic escalated, morphing into a desperate, cold dread. He was trapped, and so was Danny, all because of him. His chest tightened as the thought of Danny's voice—fragile, unsure—echoed inside his head. If he lost him now, it wouldn't just be Danny who disappeared. A piece of himself would, too.

He yanked his headphones from the nightstand with shaking hands, slamming them over his ears. Music blasted instantly—louder than safe, distorted, the bass rattling his skull. It drowned out the house, drowned out his parents' voices, drowned out everything but the words in his own head. *Foster care. Foster care. Foster care.* The bass thudded in time with the hammering repetition.

He buried his face into his pillow and screamed, raw and muffled, until his throat burned. The pillow caught it, held it in, because he couldn't let them hear him fall apart. Couldn't let them know how close he was to shattering. He screamed again, until there was nothing left but ragged gasps and the endless roar of music.

When he finally tore the headphones off, the silence was worse. His own heartbeat drummed in his ears. He slid down onto the floor, curling up with his knees to his chest, fists pressing against his eyes. Tears leaked hot and fast into the fabric of his shirt. Danny was going to vanish into some faceless system, and it was his fault. His. And the music that still hissed faintly from the headphones on the carpet seemed to mock him, a broken anthem for a boy coming undone.

CHAPTER 7

MIGUEL'S KINDNESS

The early morning air in the restaurant was cool, carrying the faint, comforting scent of yesterday's fried food—mingling with the sharp, invigorating aroma of fresh coffee. Maria sat hunched over Freddy's old, scarred wooden desk in his cramped office. The single, bare bulb cast a harsh light on piles of invoices, newspapers, and old grease-stained menus.

In one hand, a steaming mug of black coffee; and in the other, a lit cigarette, its cherry a vibrant, pulsing ember in the dimness. It was barely six. Normally, the silence at this hour was a comfort; today, it pressed down on her. Today, it felt heavy, thick with unspoken anxieties and fragile hopes. She was replaying Tony's halting confession, the raw vulnerability in his eyes. A stubborn knot of worry still tightened in her stomach, a familiar ache she'd carried for years. But beneath it, surprisingly, a tentative seed of hope had begun to sprout.

Tony had talked. He had really talked. He had cried, openly and without shame, for the first time in what felt like forever. It was fragile, but it was a start. The image of his tear-streaked face, raw with confession, was burned into her mind, not as a source of despair, but as proof of his desperate need for liberation from the burden he carried.

The soft, almost imperceptible chime of the front door opening broke the quiet, a gentle intrusion into her thoughts. Maria glanced instinctively at her worn watch, the glow-in-the-dark numbers showing precisely 6 AM. Miguel. Punctual as always, a quiet constant in the chaotic rhythm of the diner. She heard his soft, almost reverent footsteps as he moved through the empty dining room, followed by the familiar, gentle clink of glass as he began his ritualistic setting up of the drink station, each movement precise and practiced.

Taking a last, deep drag from her cigarette, letting the smoke fill her lungs before exhaling a slow, misty plume, Maria stubbed it out in a forgotten, overflowing ashtray on Freddy's desk. The accumulated ash was a testament to countless other stressful mornings she had endured alone. With a sigh that carried the weight of a sleepless night, she pushed herself up from the creaky chair. She walked through the kitchen, the cold, tiled floor seeping through her worn slippers, and found Miguel already meticulously wiping down the gleaming stainless-steel counter, his silhouette bathed in the soft, pre-dawn light filtering through the kitchen window.

"Morning, Miguel," Maria said, her voice a little raspy and tired, but with a new, almost imperceptible lightness he immediately picked up on. He turned, his movements unhurried, offering a small, understanding smile that crinkled the corners of his eyes.

"G'morning, Maria. You're in early," Miguel said cheerfully as he noticed the faint redness around her eyes, a sign of recent tears, but also the subtle, almost peaceful quality in their depths, a stark contrast to the usual weary concern. "Everything alright?"

"We talked. Tony and I. Last night," Maria confessed with a fragile, almost tremulous smile. "He opened up, Miguel. Truly opened up. He admitted he's been struggling. With himself. With feelings he doesn't understand, feelings he's terrified of. He admitted to liking Danny, Miguel, from when they were kids. And my sister, Isabella… she filled his head with such hatred. It was like she poisoned him." She paused, the memory of Tony's raw confession, his face streaked with tears, vivid in her mind. "He told me he hates it. Hates himself for it. He's so scared, Miguel. Scared of what it means, scared of what people will think, scared of what I would think." Miguel nodded slowly, his expression one of deep, unreserved empathy. He didn't offer platitudes or immediate solutions, just a quiet, accepting presence that allowed Maria to unburden herself.

"That sounds about right," Migeul began. "It's a heavy burden to carry alone, Maria. Especially when you're young and trying desperately to figure out who you are in a world that often doesn't make sense."

"I told him I love him, no matter what," Maria continued, her voice thick with emotion, a desperate plea for validation in her tone. "And I told him that hate, that kind of self-hatred… it can destroy you. I told him he doesn't deserve that kind of pain." She looked at Miguel, a silent, searching question in her eyes, needing reassurance. "Was that the right thing to say?" Miguel gave a firm, reassuring nod, his gaze unwavering.

"It was the only thing to say, Maria," Miguel stated as he picked up his rag again, resuming his cleaning. "You gave him a lifeline. That kind of acceptance, that unconditional love… that's the only thing that can truly begin to chip away at all that fear and shame he's been carrying. It won't be easy, and it certainly won't be fixed overnight. He's got a lot of unlearning to do, a lot of old wounds to heal. But you've given him the most important tool he needs right now: safety."

"He looked so lost, Miguel," Maria murmured, her gaze distant, fixed on some unseen point beyond the kitchen window. "Like a little boy who just realized he's stranded on an island, with no way home." Miguel stopped his work again, a shadow of recognition passing over his face.

"He probably feels exactly like that. And it's a long road from feeling 'lost' to truly finding yourself, to building that bridge back to solid ground. But now he knows he's not alone. He knows he has you." He hesitated, his voice dropping slightly, becoming more tentative, almost intimate. "If he ever… if he ever wants to talk to someone who's been there, someone who's walked that road, even just a little bit… I'm here. No pressure, of course. Just… let him know the offer stands. Sometimes it helps to talk to someone who just gets it, without having to explain everything, without having to re-live all the hard parts for someone who might not understand."

"Thank you, Miguel. Truly. I'll tell him," Maria sighed out with a profound wave of relief, the kind that steadied her as much as it released her. The idea of him having someone else, someone who genuinely understood, was an unexpected gift.

The quiet broke as the coffee machine sputtered to life, the diner slowly waking around them. But for Maria, the day felt profoundly different. Lighter. A fragile, but undeniably real, step had been taken towards healing for her son, and now, a new, unforeseen possibility for guidance had emerged, quiet and strong, in the form of Miguel's empathetic offer.

The rich, earthy aroma of dark roast, at first a gentle comfort, intensified, becoming a robust call to action. Maria, feeling a newfound lightness in her step despite the lingering weariness, moved from the kitchen's relative quiet into the main dining area. She began her own morning ritual, pulling chairs down from tables, the scrape of wood against linoleum a steady, rhythmic prelude to the day's symphony. Each chair placed felt like an anchor, grounding her in the familiar routine, a small defiance against the storm of emotion she'd weathered last night.

The first regulars trickled in by seven: Mr. Henderson with his newspaper, a pair of construction workers already laughing too loud. The clatter of cutlery, the sizzle of bacon hitting the grill from the kitchen, the hiss of the espresso machine now joined the growing chorus. *Freddy's Place*, a still life just an hour ago, was rapidly transforming into a bustling tableau of morning life.

Maria found herself moving with an almost unconscious efficiency, pouring coffee, wiping down counters, taking orders. Yet, today, each interaction, each familiar face, was tinged with the memory of Tony's confession.

She saw a young couple holding hands across a sticky table, their faces alight with an easy affection. A pang of protectiveness shot through her. "Tony deserves that easy happiness," she thought, "Without the shadows." She felt a surge of energy, a quiet resolve hardening her spirit.

This new knowledge, heavy as it was, also felt like a burden lifted, a truth finally out in the open, allowing her to stand more firmly.

Miguel, a steady, unshakeable presence behind the counter, moved with the grace of a seasoned professional. He anticipated orders, refilled coffee cups before they were empty, and exchanged quiet, knowing glances with Maria across the bustling room. Their brief eye contact was a silent affirmation, a shared understanding that transcended the noise and demands of the morning rush. He was her anchor in the storm, his offer to Tony a beacon of hope she hadn't realized she desperately needed. When a particularly boisterous truck driver slammed his fist on the counter demanding more coffee, Miguel simply offered a calm,

"Coming right up, sir," his voice even, unflustered. Maria appreciated his stoicism more than ever.

The scent of frying eggs and melting butter now dominated the air, a greasy, comforting embrace. The murmur of conversations swelled, punctuated by the clinking of ceramic mugs and the occasional burst of laughter. Maria, wiping down the corner booth after a family had departed, caught sight of her reflection in the darkened window. Her eyes were still tired, but there was a flicker there, a quiet determination she hadn't seen in a long time. The fear for Tony was still present, a dull thrum beneath the surface, but it was no longer paralyzing. It was now intertwined with a fierce, unwavering love and a new, fragile optimism. The road ahead for Tony, she knew, would be long and arduous, full of unseen turns and obstacles. But for the first time in what felt like forever, she felt like they weren't walking it alone.

Just then, the front door jingled, announcing a new arrival. Miguel's head snapped up, a soft smile immediately blossoming on his face, a smile Maria hadn't seen in him when old wounds came up. A young man, barely older than Miguel, entered, moving with the slightly disoriented stumble of someone who'd been up all night. He was slender, with a mop of dark, curly hair and kind eyes that looked desperately in need of sleep. He wore an old, faded college sweatshirt – definitely not a uniform – and clutched a stack of well-worn textbooks.

"Coffee. Large. Strong. Please tell me you have coffee, or I might actually die right here," the young man groaned, half-joking, as he made a beeline for the counter, his eyes fixed on Miguel. Miguel chuckled, a warm, genuine sound. His whole posture shifted, looser now, as if just seeing Leo gave him back a missing piece of himself.

"Leo! You're alive! I was wondering if you pulled another all-nighter." Miguel cheered as he was already reaching for a fresh mug, his movements quicker, lighter than before.

"Barely," Leo sighed, leaning over the counter, running a hand through his hair. His eyes finally met Maria's, and he offered a tired, but polite, smile. "Morning, Maria. Sorry, rough night."

Maria felt an immediate warmth spread through her. Leo. Of course. Miguel's boyfriend, the one whose family had taken him in. This was him. She saw the easy familiarity, the unspoken affection in the way Miguel instantly knew Leo's order, the way Leo gravitated directly to Miguel. It was simple, unforced, and profoundly loving.

"It's no problem, honey. Miguel, make him a double espresso too, on the house," Maria said, her smile broadening. She leaned over the counter, feeling a genuine excitement bubble up. "It's so good to finally meet you, Leo. Miguel lights up when he talks about you." She bit her lip, perhaps saying too much, but the words felt right.

Leo's tired smile softened, a faint blush creeping onto his cheeks. He glanced at Miguel, who simply offered a reassuring squeeze to his arm.

"Nice to meet you too, Maria," Leo replied, a genuine warmth in his voice. "He talks about you too. Says you keep him sane."

Miguel slid the steaming coffee across the counter to Leo, their fingers brushing, a simple, tender touch that spoke volumes. For a brief, precious moment, Maria saw it all: the quiet strength of their bond, the comfort they found in each other's presence, the unspoken history that had led them to this peaceful, bustling diner. It was real. It was beautiful. It struck her, seeing two young men so open, so unafraid. A glimpse of the kind of love she wanted for Tony. Seeing them, a college senior and his supportive boyfriend, a living, breathing testament to what love could be, solidified Maria's resolve. Tony didn't have to carry his secret alone. He didn't have to be afraid. He deserved this. He deserved to find his own version of Leo.

The breakfast rush continued its relentless pace, but for Maria, the noise and demands now faded into a background hum. Her mind kept returning to Tony's tear-soaked confession, the terrifying truth Isabella had instilled in him, and the desperate yearning she'd seen in her son's eyes. She needed to tell Leroy. She had to. But how much? How deep into Tony's personal struggle could she go without betraying his fragile trust, without exposing him before he was ready?

Maria found a brief lull after the initial wave of customers. Miguel was wiping down the counter, Leo seated on a stool, nursing his coffee and poring over a textbook. Maria walked over to Miguel, lowering her voice so only he could hear, her gaze sweeping the room instinctively to ensure privacy.

"Miguel," she began, her voice hesitant, the warmth from Leo's presence still fresh in the air. "I need your opinion. Your honest opinion. I have to tell Leroy. About Tony. About… about all of it. But… should I tell him that Tony… that Tony told me he likes Danny? Or just leave it at Isabella putting these horrible ideas in his head, and that he's confused and scared?"

"That's a heavy question, Maria. And it's not an easy answer." Miguel set the rag down, his blue eyes thoughtful, a crease forming between his brows. He glanced briefly at Leo, then back to Maria. "Look, Leroy's Tony's dad. He needs to know Tony's hurting. And he needs to know *why*. You guys talking about Isabella is definitely important. It explains the cruelty, the fear. It explains why Tony's reacting this way, and it puts the blame where it belongs – on the person who poisoned him." Miguel leaned closer, his voice dropping even further, almost a whisper. "But... Tony just opened up to you. He just took the biggest risk of his life, telling you how he feels. That's *his* truth. And sometimes, when you're that scared, that vulnerable, you only tell one person at a time. It's a very private thing, discovering that about yourself. If Leroy finds out from you, not from Tony, about those specific feelings... he might feel betrayed. Tony might feel exposed, like his secret was taken from him again, even by his own mother." He straightened, resuming his slow, steady wiping of the counter. "My parents found out from a letter. Not from me. And that was almost worse than them kicking me out. It felt like I had no control over my own story. Like they stole it from me." He met Maria's gaze, his expression empathetic but firm. "Leroy needs to know enough to help Tony. To understand the root of his anger. But whether Tony is ready to talk about his feelings for Danny with his dad... that's for Tony to decide. When he's ready. If he's ready."

Maria listened, her heart sinking, then slowly, a painful clarity emerged. Miguel was right. Tony's trust was too fragile, too new, to risk shattering. She had to protect him, even from her own well-meaning husband. Leroy needed to understand the threat, the fear, the source of the prejudice. But Tony's personal journey, his raw, burgeoning identity, was his own. She sighed, a deep, weary breath, and looked at Miguel, a fresh wave of gratitude washing over her.

"Thank you, Miguel. You're right. You're completely right." The decision solidified in Maria's mind, heavy but clear. She would tell Leroy everything he needed to know to help Tony understand and fight against the hatred instilled by Isabella. But Tony's feelings for Danny, the nascent, terrifying truth of his sexuality—that would remain Tony's to reveal, when and if he chose to. For now, her priority was to build a fortress of love and acceptance around her son, and to begin dismantling the walls of fear he had built.

"And Maria," Miguel said, his voice quiet, drawing her attention back before she could fully turn away. He offered a small, resolute smile. "Just remember, I meant what I said. If Tony ever needs to talk to someone who's been through it, I'm here. For him. And Leo too, if he's comfortable. We'll help him through this terrifying period, in any way we can." Maria turned away, and for the first time in years, her chest felt lighter. She picked up a stack of menus from the counter, pressing them to her chest for a moment before carrying them to the tables, grounding herself in that small ritual, a physical anchor for the promise she'd made. For the first time in years, she believed her son might not have to walk alone. She would build that fortress of love around him—and wait until he was ready to step through its gates with his truth.

CHAPTER 8

USELESS

The predawn silence of the house was a heavy blanket, suffocating in its stillness, broken only by the mournful creak of old pipes settling and the faint groan of the refrigerator, a lonely, mechanical sigh. Danny's eyes snapped open at 4:37 AM, the harsh red digital glow of his alarm clock a beacon of urgency in the darkness. He hadn't needed the alarm; his fear was a far more effective wake-up call, a frantic drumbeat in his skull. It felt like it might burst. His chest hurt like it might burst. Every fiber of his being screamed at him to leave, to put distance between himself and the liquor-soaked air of this house before Dina stirred. He didn't want to see her, didn't want to hear her voice. He didn't want to breathe the same air. Not again. Not ever again.

His heart hammered like a bird battering itself against the bars of a cage. He lay utterly still, listening. Nothing. Just the house breathing around him, old bones shifting. He slipped out of bed as quietly as a shadow, his bare feet meeting the cold, grimy linoleum floor with barely a whisper. The air hung thick with the stale scent of cheap cigarettes, and the metallic tang of something he didn't want to name. He moved with practiced stealth, each motion economical and precise, a ritual honed by years of living invisibly. He was a ghost in his own life.

He grabbed the worn backpack from the hook behind his door, its familiar weight a small, grounding comfort. Inside, he meticulously packed the few essentials he owned: a spare change of clothes, his school books, a half-eaten granola bar from yesterday, and the dog-eared copy of *To Kill a Mockingbird*, its pages soft from overuse. Every rustle of fabric, every soft click of a zipper, sounded impossibly loud, echoing like gunshots in the stillness. He paused, holding his breath, listening again for movement from the couch. Still nothing. Hope fluttered —fragile, dangerous. A flicker of hope, fragile and fleeting, ignited in his chest. Maybe, just maybe, he could get out without a scene.

He pulled on a faded NYU hoodie – it was old, but soft, and smelled faintly of a life he wished he had, a life with a present father and a present mother – and a pair of torn jeans that were somehow both too big and too tight, clinging to his skinny frame. His sneakers, silent and well-worn, slipped on without bothering to tie the laces, a habit formed from needing to move quickly, silently. He was ready.

Then, his gaze fell on the small, makeshift bed in the corner, a pile of blankets and clothes where a familiar, comforting lump lay nestled. Peanut. Danny's heart ached with a familiar tenderness, a pang of pure, unadulterated love. He couldn't leave Peanut behind, not now, not ever. Gently, so gently he barely disturbed the air, he knelt and scooped up the stuffed blue and green elephant. Peanut, sensing the shift in routine, felt soft and familiar against Danny's chest, a silent, plush companion. Danny whispered reassurances, stroking the plush fabric, a tiny, desperate prayer for protection. This time, instead of the usual hiding spot deep in the closet, Danny carefully lowered Peanut into his backpack, creating a small, cozy space among his clothes and books, a guardian packed away for the perilous journey ahead. Peanut settled in, a warm, reassuring weight against Danny's back, a silent promise of comfort.

He gripped the backpack straps, his knuckles white against the faded canvas, and slowly, painstakingly, opened his bedroom door. It protested with a faint, drawn-out groan like a wounded animal. He froze, listening intently, his body tense, coiled like a spring. The house remained silent, holding its breath. Taking a shaky breath, he began to creep down the narrow, creaking hallway towards the front door, each floorboard each step a gamble. The living room, littered with bottles and trash, the couch a dark lump, loomed on his left. He kept his eyes fixed straight ahead, on the dim outline of the front door, his only escape, his only salvation.

He was almost there. Just a few more steps. The faint glow of the streetlights outside was visible through the grimy panes, a promise of freedom. He reached out a trembling hand, fingers brushing against the cool metal of the deadbolt. Relief, potent and sweet, washed over him, momentarily loosening the knot of fear in his stomach. He was going to make it.

And then, a sudden, guttural cough ripped through the oppressive silence from the living room. It was thick, wet, unsettling, the sound of an old engine sputtering to life.

Danny froze, every muscle locking. His heart, which had just begun to slow, lurched back into a frantic gallop, hammering against his ribs with renewed fury. A shadow detached itself from the gloom of the couch, rising slow from chemically induced sleep.

"Going somewhere, Danny-boy?" Dina groaned, her voice rough, thick with sleep and dangerous. She shuffled into the hallway, illuminated dimly by the streetlights filtering through the grimy windows, her silhouette gaunt and menacing. Her short, choppy hair was a wild tangle around her head, matted and dull, and her eyes, though still heavy-lidded and bloodshot, fixed on him with an unsettling, malevolent intensity. In her right hand, dangling precariously between two fingers, was a freshly lit cigarette, its cherry glowing like a watchful eye in the dark.

"Just... just going to school, Mom," Danny stammered, his voice barely a whisper, thin, betraying terror. He tried desperately to project an air of normalcy, but his trembling hands and the frantic beating of his heart surely gave him away. He instinctively took a step back, pressing himself against the cool, rough wall, trying to disappear into the plaster.

Dina took another slow, dragging puff from her cigarette, her eyes never leaving his, a faint, cruel smile playing on her lips. The smoke curled around her face before she exhaled a long, lazy plume directly into Danny's face. The acrid stench burned his nostrils, stinging his eyes, and he choked back a cough, desperately trying not to draw more attention to himself.

"School," she sneered, her voice laced with venom, stepping closer, her bare feet silent on the cold floor. "Always school with you. Always your stupid books. Funny how school doesn't pay the bills, huh, Daniel? It sure as hell doesn't put food on the table. Doesn't buy Mommy what she needs." She took another step, closing the distance between them, until she was barely an arm's length away. Her breath, hot and foul, reeked of stale alcohol and cheap tobacco, a physical assault on his senses. "You got something for your mom today, then? After all your 'schooling'? Your big plans?" Her hand, adorned with a large, gaudy ring featuring a jagged, sharp-edged stone, slowly extended towards him, palm up, expectant. The ring glinted menacingly in the dim light.

"Mom, I… I told you, I don't have anything. I don't have any money, I swear. My bank account is empty," Danny pleaded, his stomach plummeting, a lead weight dragging him down. He knew this game. He knew exactly what she wanted, and he knew he had nothing to give. His voice cracked on the last word, a tear pricked at his eyer. "Please, I really have to go, I'll be late." Dina's face twisted, her eyes narrowing to slits, the last vestiges of sleep vanishing, replaced by a cold, burning, familiar rage.

"Don't you lie to me, you ungrateful little bastard!" she shrieked, her voice echoing in the confined hallway, shaking the house itself. "Always lying! Always sneaking! You think I don't know? You think I'm stupid?"

Her hand, the one with the jagged ring, shot out with terrifying speed. Not to his face, not yet. It grabbed the strap of his backpack, wrenching it hard, pulling him forward off balance, slamming him against the wall. Peanut, the stuffed elephant, jostled uncomfortably inside the bag, a silent witness.

"Always got money for your stupid friends, don't you? Always got money for your little toy!" Her voice was a low growl now, vibrating with suppressed fury. She leaned in, her face inches from his, her eyes glittering with promised pain. "You know what, boy? I'm sick of it. Sick of your excuses. Sick of looking at your pathetic face."

And then, with a sudden, violent motion, her hand whipped back. A sickening crack echoed in the confined hallway as her hand, the jagged ring glinting wickedly, connected with Danny's left cheek. The force of the blow was immense, sending his head snapping to the side, his vision exploding into blinding white and black. A sharp, searing line instantly bloomed across his skin, a hot, wet sensation as blood welled up and began to trickle down his face, warm and sticky. The agony was immediate, blinding, but the shock was even greater, paralyzing him.

Danny stumbled backward, hitting the wall hard, his backpack thudding against the plaster, Peanut jostling inside. Danny's hand flew to his cheek, his fingers coming away slick with warmth. He looked at the blood, then at Dina, his eyes wide with disbelief, with pain, with a dawning horror that this was truly happening again. Dina, however, wasn't finished. Her face was twisted with rage, her chest heaving.

"Look at you!" she screamed, her voice hoarse, raw, cutting through the ringing in Danny's ears like a rusty blade. "You're useless! A worthless, pathetic waste of space!" She stalked forward, her voice rising to a fever pitch, spitting words like venom. "I wish I'd never had you! I wish you were never born! You've been nothing but a burden since the day you came into this world! Nothing!"

Danny could only stare, his mind reeling, unable to comprehend her hatred. The words, sharper than the physical pain, pierced him to his core. He slid down the wall, his legs giving out, collapsing onto the cold, grimy kitchen floor, still clutching his bleeding cheek, the backpack with Peanut inside shuffling against his back, a silent, comforting weight. He was stunned, broken, her words echoing in the silence. She stood over him, eyes blazing, until slowly, almost imperceptibly, the rage began to recede from her features, replaced by a cold, unsettling emptiness, as if a switch had been flipped. She took another long drag from her cigarette, the smoke a thick cloud around her head, obscuring her face.

Without another word, without another glance at her son crumpled and bleeding on the floor, Dina turned. She stalked away from him, her bare feet padding softly over the trash in the living room, heading directly for the front door. The deadbolt slid back with a loud thunk, and the doorknob rattled as she pulled it open.

As she stepped out onto the porch, the early morning light, still grey and muted, caught the glint of something. A figure.

"G.. good morning, Dina," a sweet, slightly saccharine voice chirped from the direction of the sidewalk. It was Mrs. Flores, enjoying her early morning coffee on her back step, her gaze unwavering, her smile just a fraction too wide, a silent, unblinking witness. Dina stopped, her hand still on the doorframe. She took a slow, deliberate drag from her cigarette, her eyes fixed on Mrs. Flores, a sneer twisting her lips.

"Enjoyed involving Guzman, did we, Mrs. Flores?" Her voice was low, laced with a threat that hung heavy in the damp morning air. She didn't wait for a response. Without a backward glance at Danny inside, Dina let the screen door swing shut with a soft click and walked away, disappearing down the street, leaving Danny alone, shattered and bleeding on the kitchen floor. The house was silent once more, filled only with the echo of her words and the throb in his cheek.

Danny just sat there on the cold, grimy kitchen floor, completely in shock. The dull ache spreading across his cheek was a physical manifestation of the blow, but the real pain, the searing, unimaginable agony, was in his chest, in his very soul. He didn't want to move, yet staying felt impossible, an unbearable weight. He was suspended in limbo, caught between the urge to flee and the paralyzing numbness that held him captive. His backpack, with Peanut still nestled inside, pressed against his back, a silent, comforting presence he was too numb to fully register. His mind reeled, trying to make sense of the senselessness.

"*You're useless! A worthless, pathetic waste of space!*" Her words, still sharp and echoing, burrowed deep, confirming every insecurity he possessed. He must have done something. Why else would she lash out like that? Why else would she hate him so much? He searched his memory, desperate for a reason, a justification, a fault in himself that would explain the inexplicable. Perhaps he hadn't been quiet enough this morning. Perhaps he'd looked at her wrong. The self-blame, a familiar, toxic companion, coiled in his gut, tighter than any fear.

A different image, soft and blurred with time, flickered behind his eyes. He wished. God, how he wished. He wished his mom was the kind woman she was before his dad died. The laughing mom, the mom who tucked him in, the mom who smelled of sunshine and warm laundry, not stale cigarettes and chemicals. The mom who would never, ever hit him.

The air was heavy, humid, pressing down on everything. Danny, ten years old and feeling impossibly small, stood beside Maria, clutching her hand so tightly his knuckles ached. His suit felt too big, too stiff, chafing at his neck. The scent of lilies and damp earth was everywhere, clinging to the black clothes of the mourners, a cloying sweetness that made his stomach clench. He didn't understand why everyone was so sad. He just understood that Daddy wasn't coming home.

The small gathering was hushed, punctuated by sniffles and hushed whispers. Rick's family, a stoic line of aunts and uncles and distant cousins Danny barely knew, stood on one side of the grave, their faces etched with a grim, shared grief. Dina's family, a quieter, less imposing presence, stood opposite. And then there were the others, their family, their chosen few.

Dina, his mom, looked fragile. Her face was streaked with tears, her eyes red-rimmed and swollen, but she still stood upright, leaning heavily on Leroy. Leroy, tall and grim, his arm a steady anchor around Dina, his face a mask of sorrow. Next to him, Maria held Danny's hand so tightly it almost hurt, her gaze kind but distant. And then there was Tony. Tony, also ten years old, his usually bright eyes wide and confused, stood a little apart from his parents, his hair in his face. He was staring at the casket, a bewildered, desolate look on his face that Danny recognized as his own.

The minister's words were a blur, a meaningless drone. Danny just watched the wooden box. He remembered Peanut, hidden under his pillow, a small, vibrant splash of color in his otherwise monochrome world. He missed his dad's booming laugh, the way he'd swing Danny onto his shoulders, the smell of barbershop and clean soap that always clung to him. Now, there was just this silence, this heavy, suffocating quiet. He snuck a glance at Tony. Their eyes met for a fleeting second, a shared moment of bewildered grief, before Tony looked away, his jaw clenched, his eyes watering.

Later, at the small reception in the church hall, no one knew what to say. Dina sat in a corner, surrounded by well-meaning relatives, her sobs now quiet, replaced by a hollow-eyed stare. Maria kept Danny close, offering him small sandwiches he couldn't eat. Leroy, ever the pillar, moved among the guests, accepting condolences, his face still grim. Danny felt a nudge. It was Tony. He held out a crumbled tissue.

"You okay, Danny?" Tony asked, his voice rough. Danny just shook his head, unable to speak. Tony nodded, understanding in his eyes, and put an arm around Danny's shoulder, a clumsy, comforting embrace that made him feel a tiny bit less alone.

Danny lay curled on the kitchen floor, the phantom ache of Tony's clumsy hug a distant, bittersweet memory. That version of his mom, that version of Tony, that world where his dad was alive and laughter was possible – it was gone. Replaced by this. The throb in his cheek, the metallic tang of blood, the crushing knowledge that he was truly, utterly alone in this broken house. The grief for his dad, sharp even after all these years, mingled with the fresh, searing pain of his mother's latest cruelty. He closed his eyes, pulling Peanut from his backpack, clutching it tight. He didn't know what to do. He just knew he couldn't stay here. Not anymore.

He couldn't. The words *"worthless"*, *"burden"*, *"I wish I'd never had you"* echoed in the silence, sharper than the ringing in his ears. Staying meant accepting those words as truth, meant letting the chemical stench and the broken glass consume him entirely. He didn't want to move, didn't want to feel the fresh wave of agony his cheek promised, but he also couldn't bear to remain in this house, this tomb of shattered memories and present-day horrors.

With a ragged, shuddering breath, Danny gathered what little strength and courage he had left. Every muscle screamed in protest, every nerve ending pulsed with the memory of the blow, but he ignored it. Slowly, painfully, he uncurled himself from the fetal position, pushing his trembling hands against the slick, cold linoleum. He pushed himself up, a grunt of pain escaping his lips as dizziness swam before his eyes. He swayed for a moment, clutching the backpack with Peanut inside, a lifeline against the vertigo. His vision blurred with unshed tears, but he forced himself to focus, to find the front door.

His legs felt like lead, each step a monumental effort as he stumbled across the trash-strewn living room. The silence was deafening now, broken only by his own ragged breaths and the frantic hammering of his heart. He didn't look at the couch, didn't look at the overflowing ashtray, didn't look at anything that might pull him back into the nightmare. His sole focus was the front door, the sliver of grey light around its edges promising escape.

He reached it, fumbling with the deadbolt. His fingers, still slick with blood from his cheek, slipped on the cold metal. Panic flared again, terrified she'd reappear before he got out. With a desperate twist, the bolt clicked open. He pulled the door, and the screen door, open with a strength he didn't know he possessed, ignoring the protest of his wounded face.

He stepped out onto the porch, the cool, fresh morning air, slapping his face with dew and exhaust. He didn't look back. He couldn't. He descended the broken steps, his bare feet hitting the rough sidewalk. He didn't know where he was going. He didn't care. He just started walking, turning in any direction that would get him further and further from the hell he had just emerged from. Further from Dina. Further from the echo of her words. One foot in front of the other, a ghost escaping his own private hell, backpack heavy on his shoulders with the only comfort he had left.

CHAPTER 9

WAS IT KINDNESS?

The cool, predawn air of the schoolyard was a sting on Danny's burning cheek. He didn't know how long he'd been walking, just that he'd moved in one direction, then another, until the familiar brick facade of his school materialized out of the gloom. The sky was bruised purple with the faintest hint of sunrise, the school itself was a dark, silent monolith. No students. No buzzing cliques. No judging eyes. Just emptiness.

He gravitated to a nearby bench, not far from the front steps, its cold metal unforgiving against his exhausted body. He slid onto it, his backpack pressing like a weight against his spine. He was here. He'd made it. But escape didn't bring relief. It only brought the silence, vast and suffocating, and the relentless replay of what had just happened.

"You're useless! A worthless, pathetic waste of space! I wish I'd never had you!"

Dina's words, still laced with corrosive disgust, echoed in his ears, sharper than the throbbing pain in his cheek. He could still feel the phantom sting of her hand, the rough slide of her ring, the metallic tang of his own blood. He touched his cheek gently, his fingers brushing against the raw, tender line of the cut. It was real. It wasn't a nightmare.

His throat tightened, a desperate, aching knot forming behind his sternum. He wanted to cry. To break down. To let the overwhelming tide of pain and terror wash over him. To simply stop holding it all in, just for a moment. But he knew he couldn't. He didn't know how to anymore. And especially not here. Not at school.

The thought of someone seeing him, a student, a teacher, anyone, seeing him vulnerable, seeing his tears, was a fresh wave of humiliation. He imagined the whispers, the pointed fingers, the pity that felt worse than scorn. He was the new kid, the quiet one, the lost puppy. One tear, one visible crack in his carefully constructed facade, and he would be branded. A target. His stomach churned with cold dread. He had to be invisible. He had to be strong.

So, he sat there, rigid, hunched on the bench in the growing pre-dawn light, forcing the tears back, forcing the sobs down, burying them deep inside, where they could fester unseen. He focused on his breathing, shallow and rapid, trying to calm the frantic beat of his heart. The fear was a cold stone in his gut, but it was also a shield. It kept him upright. It kept him from shattering.

A distant rumble, the groan of a garbage truck making its early rounds, broke the stillness. The sound was a warning. The world was waking up. Soon, this empty space would be filled, and his sanctuary would become a stage. The first rays of sun crested the gymnasium roof, spilling a thin orange light across the dew-dampened grass. The light crept forward, slow and inevitable, like an interrogator's lamp swinging in his direction.

The lumpy weight in his backpack shifted as he moved. Peanut. For a second, Danny's rigid posture softened. He shrugged the pack off his shoulder and settled it on his lap, unzipping the main compartment. Tucked between a textbook and his worn hoodie was the small, green and blue plush elephant. One of its black button eyes was missing, and the fuzzy fabric was worn smooth in patches from years of being held.

"You're my only friend," Danny whispered, his voice raspy. He pulled the elephant out, his thumb automatically finding the worn spot on its ear. The plush offered no living warmth, no trusting response, but its familiar, comforting weight was an anchor against the dread. Peanut was a silent keeper of secrets, a witness to every nightmare and every quiet hope. He was the one thing that had never judged him, never hurt him. Danny hugged the small toy to his chest before tucking it carefully back into the bag, zipping it shut. He had to protect this small piece of his past. It was the only thing he had left.

But the light was relentless. It now touched the school's front doors, glinting off the brass handles. He could see the washrooms where he hid at lunch, every detail a new source of dread. The clock was ticking. The janitor would be here soon. Then the vice-principal, with her clinking keys and her too-bright smile. Then the first wave of students, loud and confident, claiming the space that he was only borrowing. He had to move. But where? The question hung like a weight in his chest.

The relentless light brought with it the first sounds of the school day. Car doors slamming, shouts across the parking lot, the rhythmic thump of a basketball. Danny pulled the hood of his old NYU sweatshirt lower over his face, trying to shrink. The trickle of students became a steady stream, their voices filling the silence he had clung to. Then, a familiar voice cut through the noise, loud and self-assured. Tony's.

Danny's head snapped up. There he was, ambling toward the main entrance with his usual entourage. Marko and Jamal flanked him, laughing, while Tony's girlfriend, Jessica, was tucked under his arm. Clad in his signature black leather jacket and faded blue jeans, with his long hair tied back and a silver ring in his nose, Tony moved with an easy confidence that made him the center of any space he occupied. Their path would take them right past Danny's bench. Panic, cold and sharp, seized him.

Just as he was about to bolt, Tony's gaze swept across the yard and locked onto him. The laughter died on Tony's lips. He stopped walking, his friends faltering behind him. He saw Danny, huddled and pale on the bench, looking like a ghost in the sharp morning light. The spell broke. Danny scrambled to his feet, his backpack slung hastily over one shoulder, and turned to flee in the opposite direction.

As he turned his head, the sunlight illuminated the side of his face. It was only for a second, but it was enough. Tony saw it clearly: the angry red line slicing across Danny's cheek, the faint swelling beneath it. It wasn't a shadow. It was a fresh cut. Something visceral, hot and sickening, churned in Tony's stomach. He recognized the look in Danny's eyes—not just fear, but terror he knew too well. The easy morning mood shattered, replaced by a sudden, sharp-edged anger, and a heavy, familiar regret bitter in his throat. He took a half-step forward, his hand clenching into a fist, but Danny was already gone, disappearing around the corner of the gym.

"Tony?" Jessica's voice was soft, pulling him back. She squeezed his arm gently, her brow furrowed with concern. She'd seen the shift in him, the sudden, dark cloud that had eclipsed his easy-going demeanor. She chose not to make a spectacle, but her eyes searched for an answer he wouldn't give.

"Nothing. Let's go. We're gonna be late for practice." Tony just shook his head, forcing the tension from his shoulders.

He started walking again, his pace faster now, more purposeful. Marko and Jamal fell into step beside him, casting confused glances at each other. The easy banter was gone, replaced by a tense silence that followed them into the school and down the hallway toward the gym. The squeak of their sneakers on the polished linoleum floor echoed around them.

As they pushed through the double doors into the cavernous gym, the smell of varnish and old sweat hit them. Marko clapped Tony on the shoulder, his voice a low rumble.

"Man, what was that about? Did that new kid really piss you off that much just by sitting there?" Marko asked. "You want us to go have a word with him?" Tony shrugged off his hand, the anger in his gut twisting into something sharper.

"No. Just drop it." Tony retorted as he threw his bag onto the bleachers with more force than necessary, the sound echoing loud in the gym. It wasn't Danny he was angry at. It was Dina. And it was himself.

The piercing shriek of the first bell cut through the air, but on the court, it went ignored. The squeak of sneakers, the rhythmic pounding of the basketballs, and the sharp barks of the coach filled the gym. Tony moved with fury, his game all sharp angles and aggression. He drove to the hoop, his movements less fluid grace and more brute force. The ball slammed against the backboard and spun out. A miss. An easy shot he'd make in his sleep.

"Your head's not in it, Guzman!" the coach yelled. From the bleachers, Jessica hugged her knees to her chest, her gaze fixed on Tony. She didn't see the star player. She saw the storm brewing behind his eyes, the one he always tried to hide.

Meanwhile, the bell was a muffled sound by the time Danny slipped into the art room. The chaos of the hallways faded, replaced by the calming scent of turpentine and damp clay. Keeping his head down, he navigated to his usual stool in the back corner, a small island of anonymity. He could feel the throbbing in his cheek in time with his pulse, a dull, persistent reminder. The art teacher, a kind woman with paint-splotched hands, wrote the day's assignment on the whiteboard: *Draw Your World*. Danny stared at the stark white expanse of the drawing paper. He picked up a charcoal pencil, the cool, dusty stick solid in his hand. His hand hovered, then began to move. He didn't draw a face or a place. He drew thick, dark lines, pressing so hard the charcoal threatened to snap. The lines intersected, overlapped, and closed in on each other, forming a cage. And inside the cage, a small, hunched figure, its features indistinct, almost erased. He stared at the grim image, at the prison he had created on the page. This was his world.

This was the truth. But then a thought, quiet and defiant, surfaced. This was his paper. His charcoal. His world to create. Maybe he could draw what he wanted instead. A memory long passed, a longing for something brighter, an escape into a fantasy. His world was what he made it. He just needed to focus. Then he remembered. Peanut. Peanut is his world. The realization was like light cracking through a door. He grabbed the large eraser, and with firm, deliberate strokes, he smudged the cage into a gray, hazy background. It wasn't gone, but it was no longer the focus. He turned his attention to the figure inside.

With a lighter touch now, he began to give it shape. The hunched form softened, becoming rounder. He drew a long, curved trunk, and big, floppy ears. He gave it a single button eye and the faint curve of a stitched smile. Then, he started to draw the world around him. The hazy gray of the erased cage became a soft, downy blanket. He drew a forest of giant, friendly-looking mushrooms and a river that glittered like starlight. He drew a sky with two moons and gentle streaks of falling light. It was a world built for a small, beloved elephant. A world with no sharp edges, no angry voices. A world that was safe. And slowly, his chest loosened, his heartbeat easing. As he worked, a shadow fell over his paper. He flinched, but it was only his teacher. She looked at the drawing, her eyes soft.

"That's a kind world you're creating, Danny," she said quietly. "There's something so innocent about him." Danny just nodded, unable to speak, but a faint warmth spread through his chest. He clung to the faint spark of peace, as the bell rang, signaling the end of class.

The day wore on in a blur of hallways and classrooms. Danny moved through it all like a sleepwalker, the trauma of the morning a constant, humming background noise. When the lunch bell finally shrieked, his stomach gave a hollow pang, and he realized he hadn't packed food in his scramble to leave.

The cafeteria was a roaring sea of noise and motion. Danny found an empty table in a far corner, a small, undesirable island near the trash cans, and made himself as small as possible. He stared at the tabletop, tracing the patterns in the cheap laminate.

From across the room, Tony watched him. The regret that had been simmering in his gut all morning boiled over. He saw Danny's pale skin, the way he hunched his slim frame, trying to disappear. He saw the empty space on the table in front of him. Something inside Tony clicked. He stood up abruptly, ignoring the questioning looks from Jessica and Jamal.

He walked to the cafeteria line, bought a pre-wrapped sandwich and a carton of milk, and walked directly to Danny's table. He placed the food down without a word. The plastic crinkle of the sandwich wrapper seemed to echo between them. Danny looked up, his blue eyes wide with alarm. He saw Tony, then the sandwich, then back to Tony. His mind raced, trying to compute the gesture. Was it kindness? Or was it a trick? A setup for some new humiliation? He didn't reach for it. Tony didn't wait for a response. He just turned and walked back to his table, the weight on his shoulders shifting, but no lighter. He slid back onto the bench next to Jessica.

"Was that for real?" Marko asked, his mouth full of fries. "You just bought the new kid lunch?"

Tony didn't answer. He unwrapped his own sandwich, but the food tasted like cardboard. He ate in silence, lost in his own head, the noise of the cafeteria fading into a distant roar. The rest of lunch was a tense affair. Marko kept shooting confused, almost amused glances between Tony and Danny's lonely table. Jessica just watched Tony, her expression unreadable, a quiet concern settling deeper than words. Tony was becoming harder to understand.

The final bell of the day sent students flooding into the hallways, but for Tony and Danny, there was one class left: AP English. The room was bright, the walls covered in literary posters. Danny took his usual seat in the back, while Tony slumped into a desk near the front with Jessica. Mr. Bodowski let the class settle before clapping his hands together.

"Alright, everyone. For our final unit of the semester, we're diving into a classic: *To Kill a Mockingbird,*" Mr. Bodowski called out. A few groans rippled through the class, but in the back corner, Danny's ears perked sharply. He'd read the book twice on his own. He knew the characters, the themes of justice and prejudice, the quiet courage of Atticus Finch.

Tony, on the other hand, felt a fresh wave of dread wash over him. He stared at the cover of the book on Mr. Bodowski's desk, seeing only another complication in a day already full of them.

"And," Mr. Bodowski continued with a grin, "to make it interesting, we'll be doing a group project on interpretive analysis. I'll be assigning your partners." A collective sigh swept the room. Tony closed his eyes, praying for a miracle. Anyone but him... He didn't even have to look back to know who *he* was. The universe, he was sure, was just waiting for the chance to be cruel.

"Alright, let's see here...," Mr. Bodowski began as he picked up a clipboard. "Group one will be Marko and Jessica." Jessica gave Tony a quick, apologetic smile. Marko just grinned. "Group two, Jamal and Connor." Jamal gave a thumbs-up to a lanky kid across the room. Mr. Bodowski continued as he assigned group after group. Tony held his breath with each pick. There weren't many people left. "And for our final group..." Mr. Bodowski scanned the room, his eyes landing first on Tony, then shifting to the back corner. "Tony... and Danny."

The name hung in the air. Tony's prayer went unanswered. He didn't move, just stared blankly at the back of the head of the student in front of him. A muscle in his jaw twitched. Beside him, Jessica put a hand on his arm, a silent question.

In the back of the room, Danny's head shot up. His heart hammered against his ribs. He looked at Tony, whose back was ramrod straight, and felt a fresh wave of panic. This was worse than the cafeteria. This was a forced collaboration. An inescapable interaction.

"Okay, people! Find your partners!" Mr. Bodowski called out, oblivious to the drama he had just orchestrated. "You've got the rest of the period to brainstorm. I want a preliminary thesis statement from each group before you leave."

The room erupted in the scraping of chairs and chatter. Jessica gave Tony's arm a final squeeze before getting up to join Marko. As soon as she was gone, Tony stood and strode to the teacher's desk.

"Mr. Bodowski," Tony said, his voice low but tight, "can we redo the assignments?"

"Is there a problem, Tony?" Mr. Bodowski looked up, patient but firm.

"I just think... a different partner would be better," Tony pleaded

"The decision is final, Tony. It's a group project. The point is to learn to work with different people." Mr. Bodowski gestured to the back. "Now please, go join your partner so you two can get started." Defeated, Tony turned. The entire class was now pretending not to watch him. He walked the long aisle to the back corner, the sound of his own footsteps pounding in his ears. He pulled a chair up to Danny's desk but didn't sit, instead leaning against it with his arms crossed. The tension between them was a physical thing, a thick, suffocating blanket.

"So," Tony said, his voice short and curt. "What's our thesis?" Danny flinched at the harsh tone. He opened his mouth to speak, but no sound came out. The words were stuck somewhere in his throat, trapped by fear. He looked down, his hands trembling slightly. Instead of speaking, he pulled a clean sheet of paper from his binder, picked up his pen, and began to write. After a moment, he slid the paper across the desk.

Tony looked down. On the paper, in neat, careful handwriting, were three bullet points:

- *The concept of "mockingbirds" as symbols for innocence (Tom Robinson, Boo Radley).*
- *Atticus Finch as a model of moral courage vs. the town's cowardice.*
- *How prejudice blinds people to the truth.*

Tony read the points, his expression unreadable. They were good. Annoyingly good. A part of him wanted to ask why Danny wasn't just saying any of this, but he crushed the impulse. He kept silent. He took out his own pen, circled the first bullet point, and slid the paper back. Danny looked at it, then gave a tiny, almost imperceptible nod.

The awkward silence returned, hanging in the air as they both stared at the paper, the designated thesis for a project they would have to somehow complete together. When the bell finally rang, signaling the end of the day, Tony grabbed the paper and walked it up to Mr. Bodowski's desk. Danny was already stuffing his books into his backpack, desperate to escape.

"Here," Tony said, dropping the paper on the desk. Mr. Bodowski picked it up, his eyes scanning the page. He let out a low whistle.

"Well, I'll be," Mr. Bodowski said, looking from the paper to Tony. "The concept of the mockingbird as a symbol for innocence... This is better put together than anyone else's in the class. Good work, you two."

The praise took Tony completely by surprise. He glanced back at Danny, who was now hovering by the classroom door, ready to bolt. For a split second, their eyes met across the room. Tony saw the same flicker of shock in Danny's expression before he ducked his head and disappeared into the crowded hallway. For the first time, Tony saw Danny not as a rival or a ghost, but as someone who mattered. And then he was gone.

CHAPTER 10

I THINK....

Danny was a ghost. The moment the bell shrieked, he was gone, melting into the river of students flooding the hallway before Tony had the chance to speak. Tony stood there for a moment, the praised thesis paper feeling foreign in his hand. He'd wanted to say something—not an apology, not a thank you, but... something. To acknowledge the weird, silent truce they'd formed over a shared piece of paper. But Danny was already gone. He walked out of the classroom and scanned the crowded hallway, searching for that faded NYU hoodie, but Danny had already slipped away. Danny had a knack for disappearing. Tony felt a familiar, frustrating mix of anger and helplessness. The hallway still throbbed with the slam of lockers and the acrid bite of floor polish, kids shouting over each other in bursts of laughter. But for Tony, it all sounded muted, as if Danny had carried the air out of the building with him.

He pushed his way through the main doors and out into the bright, late-afternoon sun. That same schoolyard—Danny's sanctuary this morning—buzzed now with shouts and laughter. Tony scanned the departing crowds, half-expecting to see Danny hurrying away, but there was nothing.

"There you are!" Jessica called out. Tony turned to see Jessica, Marko, and Jamal catching up to him, their backpacks slung over their shoulders. Jessica's brow was creased with the same concern she'd worn all day. Marko just looked confused.

"Dude, what is going on with you?" Marko asked. "You were a disaster in practice, you bought the new kid lunch—which, by the way, was weird as hell—and then you actually did the work in English class. Are you sick or something?"

"I heard you two got the best thesis," Jessica added, her voice softer than Marko's but just as probing. "What's going on, Tony?"

Tony felt the walls go up. How could he explain the sickening lurch in his gut at the sight of Danny's cut? Or that it felt like his fault? He couldn't. They wouldn't get it.

"It's nothing," Tony said, his voice flat. "Just drop it. It was a weird day." He started walking toward the student parking lot, but Marko jogged to cut him off.

"No, man, we're not dropping it," Marko persisted. "This isn't just today. You started acting weird the moment you saw that kid yesterday. Today was just... next level. Talk to us."

"There's nothing to talk about!" Tony snapped, his voice sharper than he intended. He saw Jessica flinch, and a fresh wave of guilt washed over him. He scrubbed a hand over his face, feeling exhausted. "Look, I'm sorry. I'm just... tired." The four of them stood in an awkward silence, the noise of students spilling past filling the gap. Marko, ever the peacemaker, finally broke the tension. He slung an arm around Tony's shoulders.

"Alright, alright. I get it. You're in a mood," Marko said, trying to lighten the mood. "I'm driving today, so how about this: we go grab some pizza at Sal's, maybe catch that new horror flick at the cineplex? My treat. We'll just chill. Forget about... whatever this is." Tony hesitated. A dark theater and two hours of pretending sounded tempting. He looked at Jessica, who gave him a small, hopeful nod. He finally let out a long breath, the tension in his shoulders easing just a fraction.

"Yeah," Tony agreed. "Okay. Pizza sounds good." Even as he followed them toward Marko's beat-up sedan, his thoughts kept racing. It was Friday—he should've been ready to laugh and blow off steam. But he couldn't. Instead, all he could see was Danny—haunted eyes in the pre-dawn yard, that red mark on his cheek, the quiet defiance in his neat handwriting. His internal struggle, a beast he usually kept caged, was clawing at the bars, getting worse. He felt a knot of guilt tighten in his stomach. Not knowing what to do was the worst part. He followed his friends, a ghost at their party before it had even begun. Tony's thoughts were a mess. The thought of laughing over greasy pizza felt like a lie. He shook his head, pulling away from Marko's arm.

"You know what, man? I think I'm gonna pass tonight," Tony said, shaking his head. The group stared at him, surprised.

"What? Why?" Jamal asked.

"I'm just not feeling very social," Tony said, his voice quiet but firm. "I think I just need to be alone for a bit. Figure some things out." He gave Jessica an apologetic look. "I'm sorry, Jess. I'll call you later."

Before they could protest further, he turned and walked away, leaving his friends standing there in stunned silence. The walk home was a blur. Autopilot carried him home, his mind storming. Streetlights flickered over cracked sidewalks, casting long shadows across chain-link fences and graffiti-tagged walls he'd passed a thousand times. As the sun slowly set, every mark felt alien, like the whole neighborhood knew something he hadn't admitted to himself yet. He kept hearing the words of his Tía Isabella, whispers from years ago, curling around him like smoke. *It's unnatural, Antonio. A sickness. Something to be ashamed of.* For years, those words had been a shield. But the shield hadn't kept the world out—it had locked him in. It was the justification for the anger he aimed at Danny, because it was easier to hate him than to face the terrifying truth.

The truth was, the moment he saw Danny yesterday, something had sparked. Something he'd been crushing his whole life. And today, seeing him up close—the vulnerability, the quiet intelligence, the sad, beautiful blue of his eyes—it was becoming impossible to ignore. His anger was fear. His disgust, a twisted fascination. He was drawn to Danny, and that terrified him more than anything.

He tightened his fist, his knuckles white. His aunt's poison had been easier to swallow than his truth. He had a girlfriend he cared about, friends he loved. His life was set. But Danny's arrival had thrown a grenade into all of it. He was wrestling with his own reality, and the internal struggle was becoming unbearable.

By the time he walked up his driveway, one thing was clear: he couldn't untangle this mess on his own. He needed help. Maybe his mom, who had always been quieter and more thoughtful than his fiery aunt, could offer some tiny insight, a thread he could pull to start unraveling the knot in his chest.

He walked into the house, the familiar, comforting scent of garlic and sofrito wrapping around him. His mom was home early from the restaurant, standing at the stove, stirring a large pot. She looked up as he came in, her warm smile faltering slightly as she saw the look on his face.

"*Mijo?* Is everything okay?" Maria asked softly, worry threading her voice. Tony dropped his backpack by the door and walked into the kitchen. He leaned against the counter, watching her stir the pot for a moment.

"Mom?" he said, his voice barely above a whisper. "I need to talk to you."

Maria's hand stilled. It had been a long time since her son had come to her like this, since he had wanted to talk about anything more serious than basketball or school. Hope flickered in her chest, but she kept her face calm. She turned the heat down on the stove and gave him her full attention.

"Of course, Tony. Talk to me," Maria quietly said gently.

"It's about Danny." The words came out of Tony in a rush, hesitant at first, then gaining momentum. Maria's expression tightened almost imperceptibly at what Tony said. "I saw him this morning, before school," Tony continued, his eyes fixed on a crack in the linoleum floor. "He was just... sitting there. And he had this cut on his face, Mom. It looked bad." He took a shaky breath. "My head was so clouded, I couldn't focus. I failed miserably at practice. Coach was yelling, my friends were looking at me... I felt like I was going to explode." He finally risked a glance at her. Maria's face was a mask of careful neutrality, but he saw the flicker of old pain in her eyes.

"Then, in English class, we got paired for a project. Me and him." Tony let out a short, humorless laugh. "I was so angry. But then... he just started writing down these ideas for the assignment. And they were good. Really good. He's the reason we got the best thesis in the class." He pushed himself off the counter and started pacing the small kitchen. "I wanted to talk to him after. To say something, I don't know what. But by the time the bell rang, he was already gone. Just… disappeared." He stopped, running a hand through his long hair in frustration. "I'm so confused, Mom. I've been so angry at him for so long, and now... I don't know what I feel. But it's not anger. Not anymore."

Maria watched him pace, her heart aching for him. She knew this was about more than a bad day or a school project. She moved to the counter and pulled out the old coffee maker.

"*Mijo*," she said softly, her voice a gentle invitation. "What is it you really want to say?" The question stilled him. He stopped pacing. The scent of coffee grounds filled the kitchen as she started the machine, a familiar, comforting sound from his childhood. She knew. She had to know. He leaned back against the counter, the fight finally draining out of him.

"I think..." he started, his voice cracking. He swallowed hard, forcing himself to meet her gaze. "I think I'm in love with him." The words, once spoken, seemed to echo in the sudden quiet of the kitchen, broken only by the gurgle of the coffee maker. "I think I have been for years," he confessed, the admission a painful, liberating weight off his chest. "But I was so scared. Scared of what you and *papi* would say... scared of what everyone would say. Of what it meant." He finally said the part that had locked him in his own cage. "I was just so scared."

Maria's face softened completely, the years of her own worry melting away to reveal only love for her son. She moved toward him, but stopped when the coffee maker gave a final hiss. She poured the dark liquid into two mugs, her movements calm and deliberate. She handed one to Tony, her fingers brushing against his.

"*Mijo*, listen to me," she said, her voice full of a warmth that wrapped around him like a blanket. "Your father and I, we love you. Nothing changes that. Do you understand? Nothing." Tony could only nod, his throat tight with unshed tears.

Maria took a sip of her coffee, her gaze steady and serious. She set the mug down. "But I want you to circle back for a minute. The cut on Danny's face." She paused, letting the weight of the topic settle. "That cut wasn't there yesterday, was it? What do you think happened to him, Tony?"

The question landed like a stone in Tony's gut. The warmth from his mother's acceptance was instantly chilled by the cold dread of reality. He didn't have to think. He knew. It was a truth he'd been avoiding for years.

"It was her," he said, his voice dropping to a harsh whisper. "It had to be Dina." He looked at his mother, his own fear and guilt reflected in her worried eyes. "He was at school before sunrise, Mom. Hiding. He looked like a lost puppy, scared and with no home to go back to." The image overwhelmed him. "I'm so worried about him. What if she... what if he's not safe there tonight?" His voice cracked with a plea. "I have to do something," he whispered, but the city was too big. He had no idea where to start.

The city bus was a rattling, fluorescent-lit purgatory. Each hiss of the air brakes, each groan of the engine, marked the time Danny didn't have to make a choice. He sat in the very back, huddled against the vibrating window, the cold of the glass seeping through the thin fabric of his NYU hoodie. Outside, the city lights smeared into long, watercolor streaks of red and gold as the bus rumbled through the deepening night.

He was cold. Not just from the early spring air, but the emptiness in his stomach. He hadn't eaten the sandwich. He couldn't. After Tony had dropped it on the table and walked away, Danny had stared at it, torn between terror and confusion. A gift or a trap? He couldn't decide. So he'd left it there, untouched, fleeing the cafeteria as soon as the bell rang. Now, the hunger was a hollow ache, a constant companion to the sharp, throbbing pain on his cheek.

He hugged his backpack to his chest, his fingers digging into the worn canvas. It was the only solid thing in his world. Inside, tucked away safely, was Peanut. The small, lumpy weight of the plush elephant was his only comfort, a silent friend in a world of noise and pain.

He pressed his forehead to the glass, replaying the day in a merciless loop.

"Why?"

The question echoed in his mind, aimed squarely at Tony Guzman. Why the look this morning? Why the sandwich? For too long, Tony had been a source of a specific kind of torment—the cold shoulder, the muttered slur just loud enough to hear, the embodiment of the hate his Tía Isabella had preached. Tony was a wall of anger and disgust Danny had learned to navigate, to avoid at all costs.

But today, the wall had cracked. He'd bought him lunch. He'd looked at him like… something else. And then he was his partner.

The memory of English class was even more confusing. Tony had started curt, but then just circled Danny's idea—let him own it. Danny had felt a flicker of pride when Mr. Bodowski praised their work, snuffing out the moment he saw Tony watching him. He couldn't decipher the expression on Tony's face before he'd turned and fled.

"He didn't have to use my ideas. He could have just taken over. He could have made fun of me. But he didn't."

Was it a trick? A long game humiliation? The thought twisted in his gut. It had to be. Kindness from Tony felt more dangerous than his hatred. The hatred was predictable. This new, confusing behavior was a mystery he was too tired and scared to solve.

"End of the line. This bus is now out of service." A recorded voice, tinny and distorted, announced the final stop.

The bus groaned to a halt, the doors hissing open, spilling a rectangle of yellow light onto the dark, empty street. The driver glanced in the rearview mirror, his eyes finding Danny's.

"Everybody off, kid. Time to go home," the driver's low raspy voice startled Danny. Home. The word was a punch to the gut. Danny's throat tightened. He had no home to go back to. Not tonight. He slowly, reluctantly, slid his backpack onto his shoulders, the weight of his small, plush world doing little to comfort him now. He stood up on shaky legs and walked toward the open doors, toward the cold, unforgiving night. He stepped off the bus and into a semi busy inner city street. The bus pulled away with a final sigh of its brakes, leaving him utterly alone under the pale orange glow of a single streetlight. Nowhere waited down the long road.

A profound wave of despair washed over him, so heavy it made his knees feel weak. He missed his best friend. Not the angry, hateful boy Tony had become, but the Tony from before. The one who knew which branch on the old oak tree was the best for climbing, the one who could always make him laugh so hard his stomach hurt. Would Tony ever see him again? Or was he just a ghost now, a problem to be ignored?

He felt so unloved. So unwanted. A waste of space, just like Dina had screamed at him this morning. For the first time, he believed her words. What was the point? Why keep going?

He clutched the strap of his backpack, the plush shape of Peanut inside a small, final anchor. Peanut was the only good thing left in his life. The only thing that hadn't hurt him. But a stuffed elephant couldn't keep him warm. It couldn't feed him. It couldn't give him a reason. He had no home. He had no hope. And as he stood shivering under the lonely streetlight, he wondered if there was any point in keeping going at all.

Just as the thought began to solidify, a sound cut through the city hum. It was a low, rhythmic thumping. A bassline. It wasn't coming from the passing cars, but from down a side street, a steady, magnetic pulse. It was music.

He hesitated, the despair warring with a flicker of something else. Something he hadn't felt all day: curiosity. A fragile spark in the dark. He had nowhere to go. Nothing to lose. He turned his head toward the sound and took a tentative step.

He followed the beat down the street, past darkened storefronts and shuttered offices. The thumping grew louder, a physical vibration he could feel in his chest. It led him to an unmarked black door, tucked away in a brick alcove. The only indication of life was a small, weathered rainbow flag sticker peeling at the edges and the muffled, joyous sound of music and laughter spilling from within. A large, bored-looking bouncer stood near the entrance, his attention focused on his phone. It was a gay club. The door was loosely guarded. For a boy with no home and no hope, it looked, for a fleeting moment, like a doorway to another world. Cold air bit at his skin, but the muffled bass carried warmth— bursts of laughter, rainbow light spilling faintly through the cracks of the door. The street was empty behind him. Ahead was noise, color, and the terrifying possibility of belonging.

CHAPTER 11

POTENT AND POISONOUS

The bass from within the club wasn't just a sound; it was a physical force, a vibration that traveled through the soles of Danny's worn-out sneakers and up into his chest. It felt like a heartbeat, steady and insistent, a stark contrast to the erratic panic fluttering in his own ribs. The unmarked black door looked like a void in the brick wall, but the weathered rainbow flag sticker was a tiny, defiant splash of color in the gloom. It was a symbol he'd only ever seen online or in news stories—a symbol of a world he was supposedly part of, yet from which he felt completely disconnected.

The bouncer, a mountain of a man in a black bomber jacket, finally looked up from his phone. His gaze swept the street and slid right over Danny as if he were invisible. It was a familiar feeling, but for the first time, it felt like an advantage. He was just a shadow. No one would notice if he slipped inside.

His hand trembled as he reached for the heavy metal door handle. It was cold, colder than the night air. For a second, Dina's voice, sharp and cruel, echoed in his head.

"You know what they do in places like that? Filth," Dina's cruel voice played over and over in Danny's head. The shame was a conditioned reflex, a jolt of ice in his veins. But then he remembered the sting on his cheek, the hollow emptiness of the bus, the terrifying silence of the street corner. What was worse? The imagined danger behind the door, or the certain despair in front of it?

He pulled. The door was heavy, and for a moment he thought it was locked. Then it gave way with a low groan, opening just enough for him to slip through. He was immediately swallowed by a wave of heat, sweat, and overwhelming sound. The music was a living thing in here, pulsing and loud, interwoven with a tapestry of laughter and shouting voices. Lights—blue, pink, and green—strobed across a sea of moving bodies, catching on glitter, leather, and sweat-slicked skin. It was chaotic and terrifying, but no one was looking at him. For the first time all day, Danny felt the strange relief of being just one more anonymous face in a crowd. He pressed himself against the wall near the entrance, his heart pounding in time with the music, and just breathed.

The coffee mug was warm in Tony's hands, a fragile anchor in the storm that had just ripped through his kitchen. The words "I'm in love with him" still hung in the air, spoken and real. He watched his mother, who was looking at him not with shock or disgust, but with a fierce, focused intensity.

"So what do we do?" Tony's voice was raw, threaded with a rising panic. "I can't just sit here, Mom. He's out there somewhere. He's hurt."

"I know," Maria said, her decision swift. "We'll find him." She looked at him pointedly. "You have to call your friends. You can't do this alone." Tony felt a flash of shame, remembering how he'd walked away. He was about to argue when his phone buzzed violently on the countertop. They both stared at it. The screen read: Jamal.

"Jamal?" Tony's heart leaped into his throat, his voice tight.

"Tony? Hey man... you're not gonna believe this." Jamal's voice was quiet, hesitant, and confused.

"What is it?" Tony asked, his patience frayed by his own anxiety.

"Okay, so I bailed on pizza… I just had a weird feeling. I ended up on the Route 9 bus to clear my head, and Danny was on it. He looked… man, he looked like a ghost." Tony froze, the world narrowing to the sound of Jamal's voice. Maria moved closer, her eyes locked on Tony's face.

"He got off at the end of the line, downtown," Jamal continued, "And this is the weird part. The part I thought you'd want to know, 'cause of how weird today was. He… he went into this club."

"A club? What club?" Tony demanded.

"You know where the old Paramount theatre used to be?" Jamal said. "It's there. In that spot. It's got a rainbow flag sticker on the door. I'm pretty sure it's a gay club, man. He just looked so lost, and then he walked right in. With everything that happened today… I don't know. I just thought you should know." Tony's mind reeled. *A club. A gay club. Where the Paramount used to be.* The place he should be terrified of was the one place Danny had found to hide. He turned to his mother, his eyes wide with a wild mix of fear and an electrifying surge of hope. They had a specific place. They knew where he was.

"Mom, he's at a club downtown. Where the Paramount was. Jamal saw him go in." Maria didn't hesitate for a second. She was already grabbing her keys from the hook by the door, her face set with grim determination.

"Let's go," she said, her voice a firm command that cut through Tony's shock. "We are going right now."

"Jamal, don't move. We're coming to get you. Stay right where you are," Tony said as he put the phone back to his ear, adrenaline sharpening his voice. He hung up without waiting for a reply, his heart hammering against his ribs. The fear for Danny was still there, a cold knot in his stomach, but it was now overlaid with something else: fierce, unwavering purpose. He grabbed his leather jacket and followed his mom out the door.

For a long moment, Danny just stood there, pressed against the rough brick of the interior wall, letting the chaos wash over him. It was a total sensory assault. The music was a physical presence, a deep, rhythmic bassline that vibrated through the floor and hummed in his bones. Strobe lights painted the scene in flashes of electric blue and hot pink, freezing the dancing crowd in fractured, jerky snapshots. Faces, slick with sweat, laughed and shouted, mouths open in unheard conversations or singing along to the pounding music. It was everything he wasn't: loud, vibrant, and alive.

He clutched the strap of his backpack, the familiar lump of Peanut inside his only anchor to reality. He watched the swarm of bodies on the dance floor, a roiling sea of leather, denim, and glitter. It was terrifying, but in a way, it was a relief. Here, his own misery felt small, diluted by the sheer volume of life around him. No one noticed the slim, pale boy trying to merge with the wall. He was anonymous. He was safe.

Then, someone jostled past him, heading toward the bar. The movement sent a new wave of smells crashing over him—spilled beer, sweet, cloying cocktails, and sweat. Underneath it all was a sharp, acrid chemical scent, something cheap and alcoholic that wasn't from a drink.

The smell hit him like a punch to the gut, instantly and viciously transporting him.

Suddenly, he wasn't in the club. He was back in the cramped, stuffy hallway of Dina's house that morning. The stale smell of her cigarettes was thick in the air, but beneath it was that same chemical tang—the cheap vodka on her breath as she leaned in close, her face contorted with rage.

"A waste of space," her voice hissed in his memory, a venomous whisper that cut louder than the club's music. He could feel the phantom sting on his cheek where her hand had struck him, and could see the wild,

unfocused look in her eyes. The world had tilted then, just as it was tilting now, the scent of her anger and despair filling his lungs.

Danny's breath hitched, and he was back in the thumping darkness of the club, the memory clinging to him like a shroud. The very air he was breathing felt poisoned. He had run all night, only to end up in a place that smelled exactly like the monster he was running from. The fragile sense of safety shattered, leaving him more exposed and terrified than he had been on the empty street corner.

The memory of Dina, potent and poisonous, sent a fresh wave of adrenaline through him. He had to get out. Not out of the club, not back onto the cold street, but away from *this*. Away from the open space, the suffocating press of the crowd, the air that smelled of his morning's trauma. His eyes darted around, wide with panic, searching for an escape. He saw a small, flickering neon sign over a doorway past the bar: RESTROOMS.

It was a beacon. A small, enclosed space. A place to lock a door.

He pushed off the wall and plunged into the outer edges of the crowd, keeping his head down. Apologies died in his throat as he bumped into people, their laughter and loud talk a jarring cacophony. He felt like a mouse scurrying through a herd of elephants, desperate to reach the small hole in the wall before being crushed.

He finally reached the doorway and pushed through into a short, graffiti-covered hallway that led to the men's room. The heavy bass of the music was slightly muffled here, but it was replaced by a high-pitched ringing in his ears. He shoved the bathroom door open and stepped inside, desperate for a moment of quiet.

The room was anything but.

The air was thick and humid, smelling sharply of cheap air freshener failing to mask something foul. Under the harsh fluorescent lights, two guys were hunched over the porcelain sinks. One of them straightened up, sniffing hard, and quickly wiped a line of white powder from the countertop with the side of his hand. He caught Danny's eye in the mirror, his gaze sharp, before turning back to his friend.

Danny froze, his heart hammering against his ribs. He was momentarily brought back to a vision of his living room, of Dina passed out, of needles and broken glass littering the floor. Then, a sound from the row of stalls to his left made his blood run cold. It was a low, rhythmic grunt, guttural and animalistic, followed by a sharp hiss of breath. It was unmistakably the sound of two people, violent and urgent. The door of the stall rattled against its lock.

Danny's mind recoiled. This wasn't a sanctuary; it was a cage filled with different kinds of predators. The need to hide, to be completely unseen, was overwhelming. His eyes scanned the row of stalls. The first two were closed. The last one, at the far end, was slightly ajar.

He moved on shaky legs, his gaze fixed on the floor, skirting wide around the men at the sink. He didn't breathe until he reached the last stall and slipped inside, quickly and quietly pushing the flimsy metal door shut. He fumbled with the latch, his trembling fingers struggling to slide the bolt home.

With a final, loud *click*, it locked. Danny sagged against the door, trapped in the tiny, foul-smelling space. He squeezed his eyes shut, but he couldn't block out the sounds: the sniffing and low muttering from the sinks, the sickening grunts from the stall nearby, and the relentless, muffled throb of the music from the world outside. He had found his hiding place, and he had never felt more trapped in his entire life.

The minivan screeched to a halt in a loading zone across the street from the club. The building was an old, brick two-story that had clearly seen better days, wedged between a darkened laundromat and a boarded-up pawn shop. The grand marquee that had once announced films at the Paramount was long gone, leaving only a ghost of its outline on the weathered bricks. The only sign of life was a single, unmarked black door, the peeling rainbow sticker next to it barely visible in the orange glow of the streetlights. Tony was out of the car before it was fully in park, his eyes scanning the empty sidewalk.

"Jamal?" he called out, his voice swallowed by the city noise. "Jamal!"

There was no answer. The street corner where Jamal had been waiting was deserted. "He's gone," Tony said, a fresh wave of frustration washing over him. He ran a hand through his hair. "He left. I can't believe he left."

"Maybe he got scared, *mijo*," Maria said, getting out and joining him on the sidewalk. She looked at the club's entrance. The bouncer they might have expected to see was nowhere in sight; the doorway was unguarded. "Maybe he didn't want to be here when we arrived. He didn't want to be in the middle of it."

Tony knew she was right. Jamal had done his part; he'd made the call. The rest wasn't his fight. Tony's gaze fixed on the black door.

"Okay. I'm going in," Tony said, his resolve unwavering.

"No," Maria said instantly, putting a hand on his arm. "I'll go. You wait here."

Tony turned to face her, his expression incredulous.

"What? No way. Mom, you can't go in there," Tony argued.

"I am a mother, Antonio," she said, her voice firm, leaving no room for argument. "He is a scared boy in a place he shouldn't be. He will listen to me. You... you might just frighten him more." Her words hit him harder than she intended, but he knew she was right. To Danny, he was a monster, a bully, a source of pain. But that reason would be Tony's argument.

"That's why it has to be me," Tony argued, his voice pleading, desperate for her to understand. "Don't you see? I'm part of the reason he's in there. I've been... awful to him. For too long. If he's going to trust anyone, if he's ever going to feel safe, he needs to know that *I'm* the one who came for him. He needs to see that I'm here to help." He looked at his mother, his own fear and shame laid bare in his eyes. "Please, Mom. I have to do this. I have to be the one to walk through that door."

Maria searched her son's face, seeing the raw conviction, the painful sincerity. This wasn't just about rescuing Danny anymore; it was about her son trying to rescue himself. The fierce, protective instinct in her heart warred with the knowledge that he was right. Letting him go in there was a risk, but keeping him out might break something inside him for good. She slowly pulled her hand back from his arm, giving him a single, sharp nod.

"Be careful," she whispered, her voice thick with emotion. "Find him. And bring him out."

Tony gave her a grateful, terrified look. He took a deep breath, turning his back on his mom and the relative safety of the street. He faced the black door, the muffled bass thumping against his chest like a second, frantic heartbeat, and walked forward to bring Danny back from the dark.

Tony pushed the heavy door open and was hit by a wall of sound and heat. The bass was so intense it felt like a physical punch to his chest, and the air, thick with the smell of sweat, alcohol, and cloying artificial fog, was hard to breathe. For a split second, every prejudice his aunt had ever drilled into him screamed in his head. Seeing men with men under pink and blue lights felt alien, his first instinct to recoil.

But then the image of Danny's face—haunted and hurt that morning—flashed in his mind, and it cut through the noise and his own fear. He wasn't here to judge. He was here for Danny.

His heart hammered against his ribs, a frantic rhythm that fought against the club's beat. He took a step inside, letting the door swing shut behind him, and began to scan the room. The dance floor was a writhing mass of bodies, a chaotic sea he had no intention of diving into. Danny would never be in the middle of that. He was a ghost, a creature of the edges.

Tony began to move, hugging the wall just as Danny had. He pushed through clumps of people who were talking and laughing, his eyes constantly moving, searching. He ignored the curious glances he received; his leather jacket, faded jeans, and intense, searching expression probably made him stick out. He didn't care.

He was looking for an escape route. A place someone would go to hide. He scanned the perimeter of the large room, his eyes tracing the walls, looking for any break in the chaos. He saw the long, crowded bar, a dark corner with a few shadowed figures, and then, past the bar, he saw it. A small, flickering neon sign hanging over a dark hallway.

RESTROOMS.

It was the most logical place. The only place in this entire chaotic world that offered a door to lock. A place to retreat. Tony's focus narrowed to that single point. He started moving toward it with renewed purpose, pushing more forcefully through the thick air and the anonymous bodies, his entire being zeroed in on that hallway. That's where Danny had to be.

With a deep breath, Tony shoved the bathroom door open, letting it slam against the wall. The scene that greeted him—the hostile glares from the men at the sink, the sudden silence from the occupied stall—barely registered. His focus was absolute.

"Danny!" he yelled, his voice echoing off the grimy tiles. "Danny, are you in here?" The two guys at the sink exchanged a look, grabbed their stuff, and pushed past him out the door without a word. Tony ignored them. He strode to the first stall and banged his fist on the door. "Danny!"

Nothing.

He moved to the next one, where the unsettling sounds had come from. A moment later, the lock clicked and two flushed, startled-looking men hurried out, fumbling with their clothes and refusing to meet his eyes as they fled.

That left only one. The stall at the far end.

"Danny? Are you in there? It's me. It's Tony." Tony's heart was a frantic drum against his ribs. He approached it slowly, his voice dropping from a yell to a tight, urgent plea. He knocked, gently at first. There was no response, only a faint, shuffling sound from within. He knocked again, harder this time, rattling the flimsy door in its frame. "Danny, please. I know you're in there."

He jiggled the lock, and with a pathetic metallic snap, the cheap latch gave way. The door swung inward with a low groan, revealing the tiny, cramped space.

And there he was. Danny was huddled on the floor, his knees drawn up to his chest, looking smaller and more fragile than Tony had ever seen him. His face was pale, his eyes wide and terrified, shimmering with unshed tears. He looked like a cornered animal, expecting a blow. All the anger and urgency drained out of Tony, replaced by a profound, aching tenderness. He knelt down in the filthy doorway, careful not to crowd him.

"Hey," he said softly, his voice gentle. "It's okay. I'm here." He saw the terror in Danny's eyes and knew he had to say the words, the ones that mattered most. "I'm here to get you out of this. I'm here to rescue you."

Danny just stared, trembling, his expression a mixture of disbelief and raw fear.

Seeing him shiver, Tony acted on pure instinct. He shrugged off his heavy leather jacket, the one that was like a second skin to him, and gently draped it over Danny's thin, shaking shoulders. It was huge on him, swallowing his slim frame in worn, protective leather.

Tony then spotted the worn backpack clutched in Danny's lap. He reached out slowly, his movements calm and deliberate.

"Let me get this for you," Tony suggested as he reached for the bag. Danny didn't resist, allowing Tony to carefully take the backpack from him. Tony stood up and slung the pack over his own shoulder, then offered his hand to Danny. "Come on," he said, his voice still low and steady. "Let's go home." For a long moment, Danny didn't move. Then, hesitantly, he looked at Tony's outstretched hand, at his face, searching for the trick, for the punchline. He found none. There was only a desperate sincerity in Tony's dark eyes. Slowly, shakily, Danny placed his small, cold hand into Tony's.

Tony's fingers closed around his, warm and strong. He gently pulled Danny to his feet and, without letting go, led him out of the stall, out of the foul-smelling bathroom, and back toward the noise and the lights of the club, ready to carve a path through the crowd to get them both to safety.

Tony kept a firm, grounding grip on Danny's hand as they pushed through the club's exit. The cool night air felt shockingly clean after the suffocating atmosphere inside. The muffled bass was replaced by the distant hum of city traffic, and for the first time all night, Danny took a breath that didn't feel contaminated.

Across the street, Maria saw them. She had been standing by the minivan, a statue of pure anxiety, but the moment the door opened and she saw the two boys emerge, she moved. She didn't walk; she rushed, her heart soaring with a relief so powerful it almost buckled her knees. She crossed the street in a few quick strides, her arms instinctively starting to open, ready to pull both her son and the boy he'd saved into a fierce, protective hug. But as she got closer, she stopped.

Under the orange glow of the streetlight, she saw Danny's face clearly. He was practically hiding behind Tony, swimming in the black leather jacket, his eyes wide and vacant with shock. He was trembling, not from the cold, but from a terror that went bone-deep. Maria's overwhelming urge to comfort him was instantly tempered by a wave of profound empathy. A loud, sudden embrace from a woman he didn't know would only be another assault.

Her arms slowly lowered to her sides. Her expression softened from frantic relief to a look of gentle, heartbreaking sorrow. She looked at Tony, a thousand questions and a world of love in her eyes. Tony gave her a small, almost imperceptible nod of understanding. He was in charge here. He knew what Danny needed.

"Come on," Tony said softly to Danny, giving his hand a gentle squeeze and guiding him toward the minivan. He opened the rear passenger door and waited as Danny slid inside, huddling against the far window. Tony placed the worn backpack carefully on the seat beside him before shutting the door with a quiet click.

He got in the front passenger seat, and Maria started the engine. No one spoke. It was the silence of exhaustion, of trauma, of emotions too big and too raw for words. Maria pulled away from the curb, and in the rearview mirror, Tony watched the dark facade of the old Paramount theatre and its lonely, peeling rainbow sticker recede into the night, leaving it behind as they drove the three of them, in silence, toward home.

CHAPTER 12

A MOMENT

The ride home was a silence so thick it felt like a fourth passenger in the minivan. The only sounds were the steady hum of the engine and the rhythmic *swoosh* of the tires on the damp pavement. Streetlights painted long, slow stripes of orange and white across the interior, illuminating fleeting details: his mother's white-knuckled grip on the steering wheel, the worn dashboard, the faint outline of Danny in the rearview mirror.

Maria was a statue of resolve, jaw set, eyes locked on the road. She was their anchor, steering them through the night. Her focus was so absolute it was a tangible presence, a shield around the car.

Behind Tony, Danny had shifted. He had moved from the far window to the seat directly behind Tony. He hadn't said a word, but Tony could feel his presence there, a small, trembling satellite in his orbit. In a quick, nervous glance into the rearview mirror, Tony saw the silent tears tracking down Danny's pale cheeks, catching the light of a passing car. It wasn't the loud, ragged sobbing of a tantrum; it was the quiet, exhausted weeping of someone who had nothing left.

Tony's hands felt huge and useless in his lap. In the club, it had been simple. There was a mission: find Danny. There was an obstacle: the club. There was a solution: get him out. Action had been easy.

But this? This was different. No map, no mission — just silent tears he couldn't fix.

He was Danny's rescuer, the one who had walked through the dark to find him. But sitting there in the heavy silence, listening to the ghost of a sob from the back seat, Tony felt utterly and completely lost, with no idea what to do next.

The minivan's engine cut out, plunging them into an even deeper silence. The headlights clicked off, and the familiar shapes of Tony's house and driveway emerged from the darkness. For a long moment, nobody moved. It was as if the car had become a sanctuary, a bubble protecting them from the world and the difficult reality that lay just beyond the doors.

Finally, Maria unbuckled her seatbelt. She didn't look back at the boys. She simply opened her door, got out, and walked toward the house, her footsteps soft on the concrete. She left the car door slightly ajar, a silent permission for them to stay as long as they needed. She understood that the journey from the driveway to the front door was now the longest, most difficult part of the trip.

Inside, the warm, comforting light of the kitchen spilled into the entryway. Leroy was standing at the counter, his work uniform loosened at the collar, a half-empty glass of water in his hand. He looked up the moment Maria walked in, his brow furrowed with a concern that melted into relief when he saw her.

"There you are," he said, his voice a low, steady rumble. "I got home, the house was empty. I was starting to worry." Maria let out a long, weary breath and leaned against the doorframe.

"I'm sorry, *mi amor*," Maria's tone was exhausted. "We had to go out. There wasn't time to call."

"Go out where? Is everything okay?" Leroy asked while putting his glass down and giving her his full attention, his police officer's instincts sensing the gravity in her tone.

"It's Danny," she said softly. "He was in trouble. He found himself in a... a dangerous situation downtown. We went to go get him." Leroy's expression shifted from concern for his family to surprise, and then to a deep, professional worry for the boy. He knew what "dangerous situations" downtown could entail. But overriding all of that was a simple, profound relief.

"He's okay? He's safe?"

"He's safe," Maria confirmed, nodding. "He's with us."

"Where are they now? Where's Tony?" Leroy scanned the empty entry behind her. Maria glanced back toward the front door, toward the dark driveway beyond.

"They're still in the van," she said, her voice filled with a heavy tenderness. "Both of them. Just... sitting there. Processing."

"Processing? Processing what? What happened out there, Maria?" Leroy's brow furrowed deeper. The cop in him took over, running through a list of possibilities, none of them good. Maria met his gaze, her own eyes weary but firm.

"It's a long story, Leroy. And it's not mine to tell." She shook her head slightly. "It's Tony's. He needs to be the one to explain it."

Out in the driveway, the dome light of the minivan finally flickered on. Tony had turned to face the back seat. He couldn't see Danny's face, which was bowed down, but he could see the slight tremor in the shoulders of his own leather jacket.

"Danny," Tony said, his voice quiet but clear in the small space. "We're home. Let's get you inside."

There was a long pause, then a small, hesitant nod. Tony got out and opened the sliding door. He didn't rush. He just stood there, waiting, a silent, steady presence. After a moment, Danny slid out, his movements stiff and uncertain. He stood on the driveway, looking small and lost under the single porch light. When Tony offered his hand again, Danny took it without hesitation, his cold fingers lacing with Tony's.

Together, hand in hand, they walked toward the front door. Leroy saw them through the kitchen doorway as they stepped into the house—his son, tall and dark, holding hands with the slim, pale boy who was swimming in his leather jacket. The uneasy peace between them, the quiet solidarity, was so contrary to everything he knew about their history that it stopped him cold. He took a step forward, his mouth opening to ask the questions that were burning in his mind.

"Leroy," Maria's voice was soft but carried a steel edge. She put a hand on his arm, stopping him. "Not now." He looked from her to the two boys, who had stopped just inside the entryway, seemingly unsure of where to go next.

"Maria, what is going on?" he whispered, his confusion warring with his concern.

"They need to talk," she insisted, her grip firm. "The two of them. Alone. To clear the air." She looked at her husband, her expression pleading for him to understand. "Then you can talk to Tony. Then we'll get our answers. But first... this moment is for them."

Leroy let out a long sigh, the sound a mixture of frustration and defeat. The cop in him was screaming for a report, for facts, for answers. But the parent in him, the husband who trusted his wife's intuition, knew that she was right. He gave a short, tight nod, stepping back from the doorway and yielding the floor. Tony didn't seem to notice the silent parental negotiation. His focus was entirely on the boy whose hand was still clasped in his.

"Come on," Tony said softly, giving Danny's hand a gentle tug. "My room's upstairs, remember?" He led Danny through the kitchen, past his parents, and up the narrow staircase. Each step felt deliberate and loud in the quiet house. He pushed open the door to his room and led Danny inside.

The room was pure Tony. It was small and messy, with clothes draped over a chair and the floor. Two electric guitars were mounted on one wall, hanging like trophies. The other walls were a collage of band posters—The Clash, The Ramones, Bad Brains—their edges curling slightly. A double bed was pushed against the far wall, its covers in a rumpled heap. In the corner, a desk was cluttered with sheet music and unopened textbooks.

Danny hadn't been in this room since they were kids, back when it was filled with action figures and comic books. It felt like a lifetime ago. He barely recognized the space, now a shrine to a version of Tony he barely knew. He let go of Tony's hand and, as if on autopilot, sat down on the edge of the bed. The oversized leather jacket slid slightly off his shoulders. He sat perfectly still, his blue eyes silently cataloging his surroundings, from the guitars on the wall to the boy who had just saved his life.

Tony watched him for a moment, seeing how small and out of place he looked amidst the chaos of his life. Wanting to give him space, he pulled the cluttered chair away from his desk, pushing a pile of clothes onto the floor to clear it. He sat down opposite Danny, leaving a few feet of open air between them.

The silence in the room was deafening, charged with years of unspoken history and the raw trauma of the night. Tony opened his mouth to say something, anything, to break the tension. *I'm sorry. Are you okay? I was so scared.* The words were all there, a logjam in his throat. But what could he possibly say that would mean anything? He closed his mouth, the uneasy silence stretching on, thick and suffocating.

Tony's hands clenched and unclenched on his knees. The silence was a physical weight, pressing down on him. He had to say something. He had to be the rescuer, the one in control. He cleared his throat.

"Are you... okay?" The words came out sounding stiff and formal, like a line from a bad movie. He immediately cringed. Danny didn't answer. He just continued to stare at a patch on the floor, his shoulders hunched inside the massive jacket. "Did... did she do that to you?" Tony gestured vaguely toward his own cheek, referencing the cut he'd seen that morning.

Tony was shaking. A fine tremor ran through his hands, a physical manifestation of the war raging inside him. He was so terrified. Terrified of the raw, unfiltered emotions churning in his gut—the fear, the guilt, the overwhelming tenderness he felt looking at the broken boy on his bed. These feelings were a language he didn't know how to speak.

For too long, he had hidden behind a carefully cultivated facade of anger and disgust. That facade was his armor, protecting him from his own terrifying truth. It was the version of himself he showed the world, and it was the only version Danny had been subjected to since their falling out. Now, sitting here, he didn't know how to take the armor off. He didn't know how to be the person he desperately wanted to be at this moment.

Every question, every clumsy attempt at conversation, was just him rattling the bars of his own cage. He was a dam, cracks spiderwebbing across its surface, holding back a flood of guilt and confession. And he was about to burst.

The silence stretched, taut and agonizing. Tony stared at Danny, at the empty space between them, and something inside him finally snapped. The frustration, the fear, the guilt—it all came rushing to the surface in a torrent of words he couldn't control.

"It was because of my Tía Isabella," he blurted out, the name tasting like ash in his mouth. "She poisoned my head for years, calling it a sickness, something to be ashamed of. And the worst part is, I knew it was wrong. Deep down, I knew it was all just... poison. It was easier to believe her, to let her words become my shield, than to face how I really felt when I looked at you." The confession hung in the air, heavy and ugly. "So I pushed you away. I was cruel because I was terrified of what you made me feel. I hated you for it, because it was so much easier than hating myself." Tony's voice dropped to a raw, broken whisper. He sank back into his chair, the energy draining out of him, leaving only a hollowed-out shame.

"I know... I know it doesn't change anything. It doesn't make up for any of it. There's nothing I can say that will ever make it alright," Tony heaved the last breath in his declaration

Danny sat on the bed, staring at Tony, words crashing over him without sinking in.

What was real? Was the sneer in the hallway real? The muttered slurs? The cold shoulder that felt like a physical blow? Or was this real? This shattered boy confessing that his cruelty was a shield forged from his aunt's hatred and his own weakness? It was too much to process. His heart locked up, refusing to choose between hate and hope.

He heard the words. He understood them on a logical level. But he didn't know what to do with them. He didn't know what to say, how to feel, or how to process the confession of the boy who had caused him so much pain and had just saved his life the very same night. So he said nothing at all.

Tony watched the emotions flicker across Danny's face—or rather, the complete lack of them. The silence was his penance. He understood it. He deserved it. A selfish part of him wanted to beg for forgiveness, to plead with Danny to scream at him, to hit him, to do *something* to release the years of pent-up poison between them. But what good would that do? It would only be for his own absolution, another selfish act in a long history of them. So he waited, accepting the silence as his due.

Danny felt like he was floating in a deep, dark ocean. The room, the boy in front of him, the words that had been spoken—they all felt distant, muffled, like he was hearing them from underwater. His mind was a haze of despair and nothingness. He had been hurt for so long that he had built walls around his heart, and Tony's confession hadn't torn them down; it had simply vaporized them, leaving him exposed and shivering in the ruins.

After what felt like an eternity, his gaze slowly lifted from the floor and met Tony's. His lips parted, and a sound, fragile and broken, escaped.

"I..." Danny choked on the word, swallowing hard against the lump in his throat. He tried again, his voice a raw, trembling whisper that was barely audible. "I just... wanted you... to see me." The simple sentence, stripped of all anger and accusation, landed with more force than any scream could have. It wasn't about hate, or fear, or Isabella's poison. It was about him. About being invisible. About the one person in the world whose opinion had once mattered most looking right through him, or worse, looking at him and seeing only a monster. "Just... me," he whispered again, a single tear finally breaking free and tracing a path down his pale cheek. He just wanted to be seen for who he was. That was all he had ever wanted.

The simple, heartbreaking confession shattered the last of Tony's defenses. The sound that escaped his throat was a raw, strangled sob. He buried his face in his hands, his shoulders shaking with the force of his own tears.

He had messed up. He hadn't just been a jerk; he had actively erased the person he cared about most. A flood of memories washed over him— two small boys with scraped knees, building forts in the woods, him pushing Danny on a swing higher and higher. He used to be Danny's biggest cheerleader. They were inseparable. And he had taken that, all of it, and violently ripped it apart with fear and loathing. He lifted his head, his face wet with tears, his eyes red and pleading.

"You're right," Tony choked out, the words thick with a guilt so deep it was soul-crushing. "My God, I can't believe what I've done. I stopped seeing you. I did. I forced myself to look at you and see... something else. Something ugly. Because it was easier than admitting the truth." He leaned forward, his hands outstretched as if to bridge the impossible distance between them.

"The guilt... it's been eating me alive, Danny. And then yesterday... when I saw you at school, standing there by the lockers. Seeing you hurt... it all came crashing down. I saw you, really saw you for the first time in forever, and I wanted so badly to break free. To break these chains. But I was still a coward." Tony's voice dropped to a broken whisper. "I am so, so sorry that I made myself blind to you."

Danny watched him, his mind slowly, cautiously, beginning to clear. The haze of nothingness was receding, replaced by a fragile, tentative curiosity. He had been seen. He had been heard. The apology, raw and broken, felt real. But it was all about the past.

"So..." Danny's voice was barely a whisper, still rough with unshed tears. "What does this... mean? Now?"

Tony looked up, meeting Danny's searching gaze. The question hung in the air between them, simple and profound. This was it. This was the moment to burn the old bridge and build a new one.

"It means I'm done running," Tony said, his voice gaining a strength and clarity it hadn't had before. "I'm done being a coward. And I'm done lying—to you, and to myself." He took a breath, the last barrier crumbling away. "It means how I feel about you... it's not something I'm scared of anymore. It's the only thing that feels real." He moved from the chair to sit on the bed, not too close, but closing the formal distance between them. "And it means I'm going to protect you," he vowed, his voice low and fierce with conviction. "From now on. Not just from people like Dina, but from anyone who tries to hurt you. And from me." He looked at Danny, his dark eyes intense and unwavering. "I see you, Danny. And from now on, I'm going to make sure the whole world sees you, too. I promise."

Danny stared at him, his blue eyes wide and searching, trying to process the vow. A promise of protection. A promise of visibility. It was more than he had allowed himself to hope for in years.

Tony saw the fragile hope warring with years of hurt in Danny's expression. He had laid the groundwork, cleared away the debris of his own making. There was only one thing left to say—the final, terrifying, liberating truth.

"There's more," Tony said, his voice barely a whisper. He looked down at his hands, then forced himself to meet Danny's gaze again. "The reason I was so scared… the feeling you made me feel… it wasn't just because you were my best friend." He took a shaky breath, the words catching in his throat. "Even when we were kids… I didn't have the words for it then. I just knew that being with you felt… different. Better than anything else. And when my Tía started saying those things, I finally understood what I was feeling, and I was terrified that she was right. That it was something wrong, something sick."

He leaned in closer, his voice raw with the weight of his long-held secret.

"I'm in love with you, Danny."

The words, spoken aloud for the first time, seemed to hang in the air, both earth-shattering and perfectly simple.

"I think I have been my whole life," Tony confessed, the admission a final, painful, liberating weight off his soul. "That's the truth. That's what I was running from. That's why I hurt you. It was all because I'm completely in love with you."

CHAPTER 13

INSULT TO INJURY

The words settled into the quiet room, not with a crash, but with the soft, heavy finality of a coffin lid closing on the past.

"I'm in love with you."

Danny stared, his mind a static hum. The confession didn't register as joy or relief. It was just another loud noise in a night that had been full of them. It was information he couldn't process, a puzzle piece from a different box entirely. The terror from the club, the smell of the bathroom, the feeling of being trapped—it was all still clinging to him, a cold film on his skin.

"How...?" he started, his voice a dry, cracking whisper. He had to swallow before he could continue. "How can you... be sure? Of that?" He looked at Tony, but his gaze was unfocused, still seeing flashes of strobing lights and hostile faces. "After everything..." He trailed off, shaking his head slowly as if trying to clear it. A memory, fragile and persistent, pushed through the haze. "Even... when you were..." he struggled for the word, "...awful. You always... you looked at me." He seemed to be piecing it together as he spoke, the thought forming slowly out of the fog. "Everyone else... they didn't. They looked away. But you... you always... *looked*." The memory seemed to cause him more pain than comfort. He hugged his arms around himself, the oversized jacket long forgotten. "It never made sense," he whispered, mostly to himself. "Your eyes... they weren't... just mean." He finally focused on Tony, a flicker of pained understanding in his own gaze.

"And now... this." Danny looked down, away from Tony, as if the connection was too much to bear. "It's... too much," he finally managed to say, his voice breaking. "It feels... like it's just... another way to be hurt."

Tony felt Danny's words like a physical blow. *It feels... like it's just... another way to be hurt.* The sentence ripped his heart out of his chest, threw it on the floor, and kicked it across the room. Because Danny was right. He was absolutely, devastatingly right. It *was* cruel. For him to unload this confession now, after inflicting this pain, was the height of selfishness. He should have done this years ago. He should have been brave enough to accept himself, to accept Danny, to protect what they had instead of destroying it. To say it now wasn't just too little, too late; it was an insult to the injury Danny had endured.

And for Danny, the whiplash was profound. This was the first real kindness he had experienced in what felt like a lifetime, and it was coming from the one person he both feared and adored most in the world. The source of his pain was now the source of his comfort, and his mind couldn't reconcile the two. The wires were crossed, short-circuiting his ability to feel anything clearly.

All he could feel was the familiar, crushing weight of his own perceived inadequacy. He had spent so long as the object of Tony's scorn that he had internalized it, believed it. He had to be the problem. He had to be the one who was wrong.

Danny looked at Tony's anguished face, and a single, devastating thought surfaced from the depths of his despair. He finally understood. Tony had been cruel to him for years because he was a disappointment. And now, even in this moment of supposed rescue and confession, he was still failing. He couldn't even accept an apology correctly.

Tony watched him through the blur of his own streaming tears, and his heart didn't just break; it atomized. He saw the shift in Danny's expression, the subtle tightening around his eyes, the way his shoulders curled inward just a fraction more. It was a look of quiet resignation, of self-blame. It was the look of someone who had just decided they were the problem. And Tony knew that look. He knew it because he had seen it a thousand times before their falling out.

Even through the bitter silence, Tony had never lost the ability to read him. It was a language they had developed as children, a silent communication built over thousands of hours of shared existence. No matter how hard Danny tried to build walls, he could never hide his feelings from Tony. It was impossible.

In that moment, a flood of details, things Tony didn't even know he remembered, rushed into his mind: The way Danny chewed on his lower lip when he was concentrating. And the scar—the thin, faded white line on his upper lip. It wasn't from childhood. Tony knew that. It had appeared sometime in the last few months, a new, jarring detail on a face he knew better than his own. He had noticed it, registered it, and then willfully ignored it, never once asking where it came from. He knew Danny's soul. But he had chosen to be blind to the new wounds on his body. Looking at him now, seeing that familiar, soul-crushing look of disappointment aimed squarely at himself, Tony knew exactly what Danny was thinking. And it was the most wrong, most tragic thought in the world.

The weight of Tony's confession settled, and beneath the layers of shock and pain, a deeper, older feeling began to stir in Danny's chest. It was a fragile, desperate yearning. He *wanted* to forgive him. More than anything in the world, he wanted the gaping wound in his life to close. He wanted his best friend back—the one who knew how to make him laugh, the one who made him feel brave. He wanted to feel comforted. He wanted to feel wanted. He wanted, for the first time in years, to just feel *normal*, whatever that even meant anymore.

But how? How could he bridge the chasm of pain that separated them? The desire was there, a tiny, flickering candle in the vast darkness of his hurt, but he didn't know how to take the first step toward it.

Tony saw the war playing out on Danny's face. He saw the flicker of longing, the deep-seated pain, the utter confusion. The silence between them was no longer empty; it was thick with Danny's struggle. Acting on pure, unthinking instinct, Tony started to reach out. His hand lifted, moving slowly across the space between them, his fingers wanting to close around Danny's, to offer a physical anchor in the emotional storm. But then he stopped. His hand froze mid-air, hovering in the space between them. The realization crashed down on him with brutal clarity. He had no right. After everything he had done, his touch wasn't a comfort; it was a transgression. He hadn't earned the privilege of offering solace. To touch Danny now would be another selfish act, taking something he hadn't been given freely.

Slowly, painfully, he pulled his hand back, resting it on his own knee. The best, most respectful thing he could do for Danny right now was to stay on his own side of the divide and wait. Danny saw the movement out of the corner of his eye. He saw Tony's hand lift, saw it move through the space between them, and he braced himself for the touch. He didn't know if it would feel good or bad, only that it was coming. And then... nothing.

He watched, confused, as Tony's hand stopped dead in the air. He saw the conflict on Tony's face, the flicker of pained realization. He watched as Tony, with visible effort, pulled his hand back. The non-action hit Danny with the force of a physical shock. For once, he wasn't bracing for pain. This touch was his choice, not Tony's. For the first time all night, he wasn't being pulled—he was reaching.For so long, Tony's presence had been an invasion—of his space, of his peace of mind. Tony took. Tony pushed. Tony hurt. Even his rescue tonight, as needed as it was, had been an act of force, of pulling him from one place to another.

But this? This was different. This was a conscious choice *not* to take. It was a moment of restraint born out of respect for Danny's pain. Tony had wanted to offer comfort, but he had realized, on his own, that he had no right to. He had put Danny's unspoken need for space above his own desire to connect. It was the first truly selfless thing Tony had done. And in that small, aborted gesture, Danny saw something clearer than he had in the tearful confession. This wasn't just guilt. This wasn't a lie. This was real. The shock of it, the quiet, undeniable proof that Tony genuinely cared about his feelings, pierced through the layers of his pain like a ray of light.

A quiet understanding passed between them in the space where Tony's hand had been. For the first time all night, Danny felt a flicker of agency, a sense that he wasn't just being swept along by the current of Tony's emotional storm. Slowly, his own hand lifted from his lap. It trembled slightly, but it moved with a purpose that was all his own. He reached across the small gap and gently, tentatively, laid his hand on top of Tony's.

Tony flinched at the contact, his breath catching in his throat. Danny's touch was light, almost weightless, but it felt like a brand. He looked down at their hands, at Danny's pale, slim fingers resting on his own, and then back up at Danny's face.

"I believe you," Danny whispered, his voice still fragile, but clear. The words were a gift, and they landed with a quiet, staggering force. He took a shallow breath, choosing his next words carefully. "But... it's going to take time. For me." He looked at their joined hands. "There's... a lot of things I have to unlearn. A lot of things I have to... figure out." He finally met Tony's gaze, his blue eyes filled with a plea for understanding. "You're going to have to be patient with me." Tony's heart swelled with a fragile hope.

"I'll be patient," he promised, his voice thick with emotion. He squeezed Danny's hand gently before letting go. "I'll wait as long as it takes." He glanced at the clock on his desk. The red numbers glowed: 2:17 AM. "You need to sleep," he said softly. "You're exhausted." Danny didn't argue. He nodded, but as Tony stood to pull back the covers, Danny's eyes darted to the corner of the room where his worn backpack sat on the floor.

"Tony?" he asked, his voice barely a whisper. "My... my backpack?"

Tony stopped, confused for a second before understanding flooded him. He didn't ask why. He just walked over, picked up the bag, and brought it to the bed, placing it gently beside Danny.

Danny unzipped the main compartment and reached inside, his fingers closing around a familiar, lumpy shape. He pulled out Peanut, the small, worn plush elephant, and clutched it to his chest. He looked at Tony, a flicker of old shame in his eyes, as if expecting to be made fun of. Tony just gave him a small, soft smile. He pulled back the covers of the bed.

"Get some sleep," he said again.

Danny slipped out of his torn jeans and crawled under the blankets, holding the stuffed elephant tightly. He curled onto his side, facing the wall. Tony watched him for a long moment, his heart aching with a tenderness so fierce it almost hurt. He quietly laid his leather jacket over the back of his desk chair, turned off the main light, and left, closing the door softly behind him.

The walk downstairs felt like a mile. He could hear the low murmur of his parents' voices from the kitchen. He stepped into the warm light to find them sitting at the small table, two half-empty mugs of coffee between them. They both looked up the moment he appeared. Maria's face was soft with concern. Leroy's was a mask of tired, worried neutrality. They were waiting for him to speak.

Tony leaned against the counter, taking a deep breath.

"*Papi*," Tony began, his voice quiet but steady. "I need to tell you what I told *Mami* earlier tonight." Leroy straightened, his gaze intense. Tony didn't look away. "The reason I've been so... angry. The reason I was so awful to Danny for so long." He swallowed hard. "It's because I'm in love with him. I have been for years."

The words hung in the warm kitchen air, heavy and irrevocable. Leroy stared at his son, his face unreadable. The cop in him was trained to absorb shocks, to categorize information, to look for motive. But the father in him was reeling. He picked up his cold coffee mug, stared into it for a long moment as if the answer was at the bottom, and then set it down with a soft click.

"Antonio," he said, his voice low and measured. He needed a minute. He needed to process the confession alongside the image of the terrified, rail-thin boy asleep in his son's bed upstairs. "Are you sure? About what you're saying?" It wasn't a challenge. It was a father's plea for certainty, a need to know that his son wasn't just confused or caught up in the drama of the night. Tony had expected anger, maybe disappointment, even disgust. But the quiet, serious question was somehow harder. It demanded absolute honesty, not just about his feelings for Danny, but about his own identity.

"Yeah, *Papi*," Tony said, his voice clear, all traces of his earlier tears gone. The fear had been burned out of him, leaving only a quiet, solid truth. "I'm sure."

He pushed himself off the counter, standing tall, no longer a boy confessing, but a young man stating a fact. "I'm gay," he said. "And I'm in love with Danny."

Tony walked over to the coffee pot on the counter and poured the last of the lukewarm, sludgy coffee into a mug. The simple, mundane act was a brief respite, a moment to breathe after laying his soul bare. He leaned against the counter, wrapping his hands around the warmth of the mug. Leroy watched him, his mind processing the two stunning revelations of the night. His son was gay. And the boy upstairs, the boy his son was in love with, had been in serious trouble. He shifted from father to cop, his focus narrowing on the immediate threat.

"Okay," Leroy said, his voice low and serious. "So now tell me what happened tonight, Tony. Why was Danny in a place like that? A downtown club... that's no place for a kid, he could've been hurt, or taken, or much worse." Tony took a sip of the bitter coffee.

"He couldn't go home," Tony said, his gaze dropping to the floor. "He had a cut on his face, *Papi*. A fresh one. Angry looking." He looked up, meeting his father's sharp, analytical gaze. "He never said the words. He never said *she* hit him." Tony didn't need to specify who 'she' was. "But... you see him. You see the way he looks. You can't ignore it." The unspoken accusation filled the quiet kitchen. Dina. The name was a poison that had seeped into all of their lives, and tonight, it had finally drawn blood.

A heavy, weary sigh escaped Leroy's lips, the sound seeming to carry the weight of years of unspoken worry. He scrubbed a hand over his face, the exhaustion of his shift compounding with the emotional toll of the night. He looked at Maria, then at Tony, his expression one of profound, regretful resolve.

"Rick," he said, his voice low and gravelly. "His dying wish. He made me promise I'd look out for his boy. Keep him safe." He shook his head slowly, the guilt evident in his tired eyes. "And I let this happen. I knew things weren't right over there, but I kept telling myself it was better than the alternative." He looked at Tony, his voice laced with a self-recrimination that was painful to hear. "I couldn't bear the thought of him getting thrown into the system. Bouncing from house to house. I thought... I thought I was protecting him by staying out of it." He let out a short, bitter laugh. "Some protection." He pushed his chair back and stood up, the decision made. The paralysis was gone.

Leroy and Rick were at Sal's, arguing about baseball over greasy meatball subs. Leroy was off-duty, but the weight of his service weapon was a familiar pressure against his hip. It was always there, just in case. Then the call crackled over the police scanner app on his phone. Armed robbery, two blocks away, at the convenience store on the corner. Shots fired.

"Stay here," Leroy had commanded, his voice already shifting, the friend disappearing and the cop taking over. "This isn't your business, Rick. Stay put." Rick knew it wasn't his wheelhouse. But Leroy was his best friend. He

nodded, but Leroy saw the worry in his eyes. Leroy was out the door and running.

He arrived in chaos. Two patrol cars were already there, officers using their doors for cover. The gunman was still inside. Gunfire erupted—a series of sharp, terrifying cracks that echoed off the brick buildings. Leroy drew his weapon, joining the line, shouting for Rick, who had inevitably followed him, to stay back, to get behind the line.

The firefight was an eternity compressed into thirty seconds. A back-and-forth of muzzle flashes and the scream of ricocheting bullets. Then, a final shot from one of the officers, and a heavy silence fell over the store. It was over. Leroy's training took over. He scanned the scene, his heart still hammering. And then he saw him. He saw Rick lying on the sidewalk, twenty feet behind the police line, a dark, blossoming stain on his chest. A stray bullet. One single, random piece of flying metal had found him. Leroy's world collapsed. He was at Rick's side in an instant, his hands pressing down on the wound, slick with blood. He begged, pleaded with him to hold on, for the paramedics to hurry. But Rick knew. His breathing was shallow, his eyes losing focus. He grabbed Leroy's wrist with a strength that was already fading.

"Leroy," Rick rasped, his voice a wet gurgle. "My boy... Danny..."

"Dammit Rick, don't talk, you're gonna be fine," Leroy lied, tears streaming down his face.

"No," Rick insisted, his grip tightening. "Promise me. Look after him. Promise me you'll keep him safe."

"I promise," Leroy sobbed, pressing down on the wound, on his dying best friend. "I promise, Rick."

The words had followed him ever since, a ghost at his shoulder, whispering every time he looked at Danny.

"But that's over," he said, his voice firm now, the cop taking over. "The situation has changed. He's out of that house. He's here. He's safe, for tonight." He walked over to the sink, placing his empty coffee mug in the basin. "First thing in the morning, I'm making a call to Child Protective Services. We're going to do this the right way." He paused, his back to them, and the next words came out with the cold weight of steel. "And I'm going to have to place Dina under arrest. For child endangerment, at the very least."

Maria gasped softly, her hand flying to her mouth. She had known things were bad, but to hear it framed in the stark, legal language of her husband's profession made it terrifyingly real. To have Dina arrested... it felt like a final, terrible severing. But as she looked at her husband's rigid back, at her son's exhausted but resolute face, she knew it was the only way. It was the only way to truly break the cycle. The only way to guarantee that Danny would never have to go back. She slowly lowered her hand and gave a single, solid nod that only Leroy could see. It had to be done.

CHAPTER 14

FURIOUS

The Saturday morning sun was a merciless intruder. It sliced through the greasy film on the house window and the thin, nicotine-stained curtains, landing squarely on Dina's face. She groaned, a low, guttural sound of protest, and rolled over, burying her face in a pillow that smelled of stale smoke and her own sweat.

Her head pounded, each throb a hammer blow, her mouth dry as sand. She blindly reached for the nightstand, her fingers fumbling around an overflowing ashtray and a half-empty glass of vodka before finding her pack of cigarettes.

With a grunt of effort, she pushed herself into a sitting position on the edge of the lumpy mattress. The room swam for a moment. She lit a cigarette, the first drag a harsh, chemical burn that did little to soothe the tremor in her hands. She sat there for a long moment, smoking in the dusty silence, letting the nicotine do its work.

Finally, the need for coffee overrode the desire to stay inert. She pushed herself to her feet and shuffled out of the bedroom, her bare feet sticking slightly to the grimy linoleum floor.

"Danny!" she yelled, her voice a raw, gravelly rasp. "Get your lazy ass up and make some coffee!" The only response was the hum of the ancient refrigerator. "Did you hear me?" she shouted, her irritation growing. "I'm not your damn maid! Get up!" Silence. A flicker of real anger sparked through the fog of her hangover. The nerve of that kid, ignoring her in her own house. She stomped to the closed door of his bedroom and threw it open without knocking. The room was empty. The small, neat bed was untouched, the thin blanket still pulled taut over the mattress from the day before. There was no backpack, no hoodie slung over the chair. There was no sign of him at all. He hadn't come home. "Lousy, fucking kid," Dina muttered, the words a venomous hiss in the quiet house. "Where the hell could he be?"

A surge of paranoid anger propelled her through the small, cramped space. She tore through the living room, kicking aside piles of old magazines and takeout containers. She ripped open the door to the single bathroom, finding only a damp towel on the floor and a dirty mirror. She checked the coat closet by the front door, a cramped space that smelled of mothballs and mildew. Nothing.

"Ungrateful little shit thinks he can run from me," she muttered, anger quickly eclipsing the flicker of unease. "Fuck it," she finally snarled, abandoning the search. If he wanted to run off, fine. Let him. She'd deal with him when he finally crawled back. Right now, she needed coffee. She stomped back to the kitchen and slammed a pot onto the stove, scooping grounds into the filter with a shaking hand. She waited for it to brew, tapping her foot impatiently on the floor. When it was done, she poured the black, steaming liquid into a chipped mug and turned to the fridge for milk.

She yanked the door open. The small, weak light flickered on to reveal a landscape of near-total emptiness. On the top shelf sat a single, shriveled lemon. The door held an open box of baking soda and a half-empty jar of mustard. There was no milk. No food. Nothing. The sight of her own neglect, reflected back at her in the pathetic emptiness of the refrigerator, only fueled her rage. She slammed the refrigerator door shut with a curse, the force of it rattling the mustard jar inside. The pathetic state of her life, reflected in that empty fridge, was a bitter pill to swallow on a Saturday morning. It was his fault. All of it. If he were here, if he had a job, if he weren't such a useless, sullen lump...

KNOCK. KNOCK. KNOCK.

The sound was so loud and forceful it seemed to shake the flimsy front door in its frame. It wasn't a polite rap; it was an official, demanding summons.

Dina swore under her breath.

"Fucking Guzman," she spat. "Here for his early morning bullshit." It had to be Leroy, no one else would bother talking to her willingly. He had a habit of showing up unannounced, his eyes full of quiet judgment, asking questions she had no interest in answering. She stomped to the door, her mug of black coffee sloshing in her hand. "What do you want?" she yelled through the cheap wood. "It's Saturday! Piss off!" There was a brief pause on the other side, and then a voice she recognized, but with an edge she had never heard before. It was cold, official, and utterly devoid of familiarity.

"Dina Sanders, this is Sergeant Leroy Guzman with the City Police Department. Open the door. Now." The voice was forceful, determined, and it was absolutely not fucking around. A cold, defiant smirk touched Dina's lips.

"Over my dead body, Guzman!" she muttered to herself. She took a deliberate, slow sip of her coffee, the picture of nonchalance. "Go get a fuckin' warrant!" she shrieked back, her voice dripping with contempt. "You can't just come here ordering me around!"

"Dina, I have reason to believe a minor is in danger. I'm warning you, open this door." There was no negotiation in Leroy's reply. His voice was louder now, harder, echoing outside.

"Go to hell!" Dina shrieked.

Silence. Then Leroy's voice, harder, colder.

"Final warning, Dina. Open the door, or I'm coming through." The threat hung in the air, vibrating with a terrifying finality. Dina stood frozen in her dingy living room, her bravado faltering for the first time.

He wasn't bluffing. This wasn't the friendly, worried Leroy she knew how to manipulate. This was a cop about to break her door down.

Before Dina could even process the threat, the world exploded. A deafening *CRACK* like a thunderclap inside the house was followed by the splintering shriek of wood and metal tearing apart. The front door didn't just open; it flew inward off its hinges as if kicked by a giant, slamming against the interior wall with enough force to send a framed picture crashing to the floor. Dina stumbled back, coffee sloshing over her hand, her mind blank with shock. In the gaping, splintered doorway stood a uniformed officer holding a battering ram. Behind him, Leroy Guzman stepped through, his face a mask of cold, grim determination. He wasn't alone. Three other officers followed him in, their movements swift and professional, filling the small, cluttered living room with an overwhelming, authoritative presence.

"What the hell?!" Dina shrieked, a mix of terror and rage. But there was no time for argument. Before she could take another step, two of the officers were on her, one grabbing each arm in a firm, unyielding grip.

"You're under arrest," one of them said, his voice flat and impersonal.

"Get your fucking hands off me!" she screamed, struggling uselessly. As they turned her around and expertly pinned her arms behind her back, she saw the third officer begin a methodical sweep of the house, his eyes scanning for any other people or immediate dangers. Leroy stood before her, his gaze unwavering, his presence dominating the room. The casual neighbor was gone. The worried friend was gone. All that remained was the law.

"Dina Sanders," Leroy said, his voice cold and official, cutting through her panicked screams. "You are under arrest for child endangerment." The click of handcuffs, followed by Dina's stream of furious, incoherent curses, faded as the officers escorted her out to the waiting cruiser. The door slammed shut, cutting off the noise and leaving Leroy in a sudden, profound silence, broken only by the quiet movements of the officer completing his sweep of the house.

Leroy took one hard look around the living room. He walked slowly toward the kitchen… And then, the memory hit him, sharp and vivid. He and Rick had done this renovation themselves… It was the day Tony and Danny had met. They were both only four years old.

He walked slowly toward the kitchen, his shoes crunching on something gritty on the floor. He surveyed the damage from the forced entry, the splintered doorframe, but his gaze was drawn to the chipped countertops and peeling linoleum. And then, the memory hit him, sharp and vivid. He and Rick remodeled the kitchen one hot summer weekend. They'd been covered in sweat and sawdust, arguing over measurements while Dina and Maria sat outside in lawn chairs, watching the boys. It was around the time of both their birthdays, and they had each been given new water guns.

A sun-drenched backyard. A tiny, scrawny Danny, all big blue eyes and boundless energy, was running in frantic circles, his laughter high and breathless. A slightly bigger, more serious Tony was watching him, a look of fascination on his face. Danny, in a final burst of speed, wasn't watching where he was going. He ran headfirst into one of the wooden posts holding up the tree fort. There was a sickening little thud.

Leroy remembered dropping his hammer, ready to rush out, but Rick held up a hand. Danny stumbled back, his hand flying to his mouth. He stood there for a second, stunned. Then he slowly pulled his hand away. In his small, grubby palm sat a single, pearly baby tooth. There were no tears. He didn't cry at all.

Tony, his face creased with concern, ran over to him.

"Are you okay?" Tony asked. Danny looked at the tooth in his hand, then up at Tony, and a wide, gap-toothed grin split his face.

"I'm good. I like to live dangerously," Danny announced proudly, perfectly mimicking a line from the Austin Powers movie Dina had been obsessed with that summer.

The memory faded, leaving Leroy standing in the dim, squalid kitchen. The ghost of that brave, funny little boy, quoting his mother's favorite movie, felt a million miles away from the terrified, silent child who was currently asleep in his son's bed. The contrast was a physical ache in his chest.

"All clear, Sergeant." The officer said after he finished conducting the sweep, giving him a thumbs-up from the hallway. The words snapped Leroy out of his reminiscent trance. He gave the officer a curt nod, turned his back on the squalor and the ghosts, and walked out into the bright, indifferent morning.

He gripped the handle to his patrol car, mindlessly opening the door and slowly sat himself in the seat. For years he told himself keeping Danny out of the system was protection. Now, staring down the aftermath, he wondered if it had just been cowardice.

His mind was a complete haze, a chaotic storm of memory and consequence. It was done. The thought was stark and simple, but it offered no peace. The monster had been put down. But monsters were once people, and he could still see Dina's laughing face at a backyard barbecue, a ghost of a happier time before her own demons had consumed her.

He gripped the steering wheel, his knuckles white. Had he done the right thing? The question was a circular saw in his gut, cutting deeper with every rotation. For several years, he had told himself that keeping Danny out of the foster care system was the priority. He had seen the system chew up and spit out good kids, leaving them with more scars than they started with. He had feared that for Rick's boy.

Was his fear a valid excuse, or just a coward's justification for inaction? The image of Danny's face from last night—pale, terrified, and lost in Tony's bedroom—flashed in his mind. Then, the memory of the brave, gap-toothed four-year-old in the backyard. The two images warred, a testament to the damage that had been done while he stood by, "protecting" him.

There was no saving Dina at this point; he knew that with a cold certainty. She had chosen her path long ago. But Danny... had he saved Danny, or just traded one uncertain hell for another? The road ahead with CPS, with family courts, was long and fraught with its own kind of dangers.

He turned onto the final street leading to the station, the familiar brick building coming into view. He just hoped he had done right by Rick. He hoped his friend, wherever he was, would see this not as a failure, but as a final, desperate, and necessary fulfillment of a sacred promise. He pulled into his designated spot, killed the engine, and sat for a long moment in the sudden silence of the car, the weight of it all pressing down on him like a physical force.

Leroy pushed the car door open, the hinges groaning in protest. He stepped out into the parking lot, the asphalt already radiating the morning heat. His movements were stiff, automatic. He reached into his pocket, his fingers finding the familiar shape of his pack of cigarettes. He shook one out, lit it with a flick of his Zippo, and took a long, deep drag. The smoke burned his lungs, a familiar, grounding pain. Leroy took this precious moment to send Maria a text.

Arrested Dina this morning, we'll talk more tonight, mi amor.

Send. Leroy placed his phone back in his pants pocket. He leaned against the warm hood of his cruiser, the cigarette held loosely between his fingers, and stared at the back entrance of the station. He had just arrested Dina Sanders. He rolled the thought around in his mind. It wasn't just some random perp; this was Dina. A woman he had shared holidays with, whose son was his son's best friend. A woman who was once one of his closest friends. The ghost of her laughter at a backyard barbecue echoed in his ears, a cruel counterpoint to the memory of her venomous shrieks as she was put in the cruiser.

What was he even going to say to her when he went inside? There were procedures, questions he had to ask. But beyond the badge and the uniform, what could he say? *"I'm sorry it came to this?" "Why did you let it get so bad?"* There were no words. There was nothing left but the grim, official process.

He took another drag from his cigarette. Child Protective Services had been called before he'd even left her house. The dispatcher had confirmed it. The worker was already inside, waiting for his report. The reality of the situation was a physical weight, pressing down on his shoulders, making it hard to breathe. This wasn't just about an arrest anymore. This was about the entire trajectory of a boy's life, a life he had promised to protect. He just had to make it through the next couple of hours. He had to talk to this CPS agent. He had to process Dina. He had to write the report. He took one final, long pull from the cigarette, dropped it to the ground, and crushed it under the heel of his boot. Then, with a deep, steadying breath, he turned and walked toward the station door to face what came next.

The fluorescent lights of the interview room hummed, casting a sterile, unflattering glare on everything. The room was small, cinderblock-grey, and smelled of stale coffee and disinfectant. Dina sat handcuffed to a metal ring on the table, her leg bouncing uncontrollably. The morning's hangover had morphed into the frantic, jittery beginnings of withdrawal. She needed a fix, a drink, something to quiet the screaming hornets in her head.

Her mind darted back and forth, weaving a new narrative. This was all Leroy's fault. He was obsessed with her, with Rick's memory. He was trying to frame her, to take Danny away out of some twisted sense of ownership. And Danny... that ungrateful, lying brat. He had probably run to Leroy with some sob story, setting this whole thing in motion. The hate she felt was a hot, coiling thing in her gut.

The door opened, and Leroy stepped inside, closing it behind him. He didn't sit. He stood opposite her, his face an unreadable mask of professionalism.

"Dina," he began, his voice flat.

"Guzman, you bastard!" she shrieked, lunging forward as far as the handcuffs would allow. "You think you can do this? You think you can just break down my door and kidnap my son?" Leroy didn't flinch. He let her tirade wash over him, his expression unchanging.

"You've been made aware of your right to legal counsel," he stated, his voice calm and detached. "I'm asking you now if you wish to waive that right and speak with me."

"I'm not telling you anything, you pig!" she spat. "I want my lawyer! I'm going to sue you, the department, this whole damn city!" Leroy looked at her for a long moment, at the wildness in her eyes, the desperation. There was nothing left of the woman he once knew. There was no point to this. He couldn't get a coherent statement from her, and frankly, he didn't need one. The state of the house and the condition of her son spoke for themselves.

Without another word, he turned and walked out of the room, leaving her screaming threats and obscenities at the empty space where he had been. Through the small, wired window in the door, he saw two uniformed officers enter and uncuff her from the table. It was time for her to be processed.

Leroy walked out of the observation area, the sound of Dina's muffled screaming still echoing in his ears. He ran a hand over his face, feeling the grit of exhaustion, and made his way through the bustling bullpen toward his desk. It was an island of organized chaos in the corner, piled high with paperwork, cold coffee cups, and a single framed photo of Maria and a much younger Tony.

A woman was sitting in the chair beside his desk, waiting patiently. She was in her late forties, with tired but kind eyes and an air of professional calm. She stood as he approached.

"Sergeant Guzman?" she asked, her voice even. "I'm Carol Jenkins. From CPS."

"Ms. Jenkins," Leroy said, nodding as he sank into his own worn-out office chair. "Thanks for coming in so quickly."

"It sounded urgent," she said, her gaze direct. "I've read the preliminary dispatch report. I understand you have the minor, Daniel Sanders, in your care at the moment?"

"He's at my home. With my wife and son," Leroy confirmed. "He's safe."

"Good. That's the most important thing," Ms. Jenkins said, opening a folder on her lap. "Now, I need to get your official statement on the situation at the mother's residence, and we need to discuss the immediate plan for Daniel." Leroy leaned forward, his elbows on his desk.

"The plan is he stays with us," he said, his voice leaving no room for argument. "My wife and I. We want him."Ms. Jenkins looked at him, her expression softening slightly. "Danny doesn't need another stranger," Leroy added firmly. "He needs us."

"I understand, Sergeant," Ms. Jenkins declared. "And given your pre-existing relationship with the family, that's certainly the preferred outcome. We call it kinship care. It's always better than placing a child in a receiving home." She tapped her pen on the folder. "But there's a process. We'll need to declare you and your wife as emergency guardians. There will be a home visit, interviews... paperwork. A lot of it. For now, he can stay with you, pending an emergency hearing first thing next week. But we need to make it official." Leroy nodded, a small measure of relief cutting through the exhaustion. A process. A plan. It was concrete. It was a start.

"Whatever it takes," he said. "We'll do whatever it takes."

CHAPTER 15

BOSS LADY

The first hint of dawn was a pale, grey light filtering through the kitchen window. Maria sat at the table, a fresh mug of coffee steaming in her hands. She hadn't slept. After Leroy had left for the station and Tony had finally gone upstairs, she had stayed, keeping a silent vigil in the quiet heart of her home. The house felt different, holding its breath, charged with the presence of the sleeping, broken boy in her son's room.

She looked at the clock on the stove. It was half-past five. On any other Saturday, she and Tony would already be getting ready to head to the restaurant for the morning prep shift. The thought of chopping onions and simmering sauces felt absurdly normal, a relic from a different lifetime. But maybe normal was exactly what they needed. She pulled out her phone, the screen's light harsh in the dim room. She opened her messages and found Miguel, her ever-reliable head waiter.

Hey Miguel.

Tony and I are going to be late this morning. Something came up. Can you get the sauces started and let the prep cooks know what to do? We'll be there in a couple of hours.

Gracias.

She hit send. It was decided. Tony needed a distraction, something to do with his hands other than wring them with worry. And Danny... Danny needed to sleep. He needed silence and safety and the freedom to not wake up until his body and soul were ready.

A few minutes later, she heard the soft creak of floorboards from upstairs. Tony appeared in the kitchen doorway, looking like he hadn't slept either. His hair was a mess, and there were dark circles under his eyes, but the frantic fear from last night was gone, replaced by a quiet, heavy exhaustion.

"Morning," he mumbled, heading straight for the coffee pot.

"Morning, *mijo*," Maria said softly. She watched him pour a mug. "I texted Miguel. Told him we'd be late."

"We're going in?" Tony looked at her, confused.

"We are," she said, her tone gentle but firm. "You're going to come with me. We'll chop vegetables for a few hours. It'll be good for you to keep busy." She met his eyes, her meaning clear. "And it will give Danny the quiet he needs. Let him sleep."

Tony nodded slowly, understanding. The idea of being anywhere else felt wrong, but the thought of sitting in the house, waiting, listening for any sound from his room, felt like a special kind of torture. His mom was right. He needed to work. He needed a distraction.

"Okay," Tony agreed, his voice rough. "Yeah. Okay." He downed the rest of his coffee in two quick swallows and left the mug in the sink.

He ran upstairs, his body feeling heavy and foreign, as if he were piloting a machine that was low on fuel. The events of the last twelve hours had settled deep in his muscles, a profound physical and emotional exhaustion. He stripped off his clothes from the day before—the white t-shirt, the faded blue jeans—and stepped into the shower, cranking the handle all the way to hot.

The water was almost scalding as it hit his skin, but the shock of it was exactly what he needed. He leaned his hands against the cool tile wall, letting the steaming water cascade over his head and down his back, washing away the grime of the club, the stale scent of fear, the lingering chill of the night. It was the first moment he had been truly alone since this whole thing had started, and his thoughts, held at bay by the frantic pace of the crisis, came rushing in. *"Will they take him away?"* The question was a cold spike of fear in his gut. His dad had said he was calling CPS. Tony knew that was the right thing to do, the only thing to do. What if they decided his family wasn't a good fit? What if they sent Danny to a foster home, to live with people he didn't know? The thought of Danny, after all this, being taken away again was unbearable.

And then there was the other, more immediate fear. *"How am I supposed to act around him?"* Everything was out there now. His confession of love, his cruelty, his promise to protect him. The old, toxic dynamic was shattered, but the new one was a fragile, terrifying unknown. How do you make small talk with someone whose heart you broke and then saved in the same night? Do you pretend things are normal? Do you talk about it? Every possibility felt wrong, awkward, and impossibly complicated.

He stood there until the water started to cool, the steam clearing around him. He felt cleaner, but the weight in his chest hadn't lifted. He had no answers. All he knew was that the boy sleeping in his bed was his responsibility now, in every sense of the word. And he was terrified he was going to mess it up all over again.

The water finally ran cold, forcing him back to reality. Tony turned off the faucet, and the sudden silence of the house rushed in to fill the space. He stood dripping in the quiet, the steam slowly clearing around him. He grabbed a thick towel from the rack and scrubbed it over his hair and body, but as he reached for the doorknob, he stopped, cursing under his breath. His clothes. They were in his room.

He wrapped the towel securely around his waist, tucking the corner in tightly. He opened the bathroom door, wincing at the soft click of the latch, and peered out into the hallway. All quiet. He moved on silent, bare feet across the worn wooden floor to his bedroom door. Every instinct screamed at him not to go in, not to risk waking Danny. But he couldn't exactly go to the restaurant in a towel. He turned the old brass knob with painstaking slowness, preventing the tell-tale squeak, and pushed the door open just enough to slip inside.

The room was dark and still, the curtains drawn against the morning light. His eyes immediately went to the bed. In the dimness, he could see the small, still shape of Danny's form under the covers, rising and falling with the deep, even rhythm of sleep. He was curled on his side, clutching the little stuffed elephant to his chest. He looked impossibly small and young in Tony's bed.

Tony held his breath, his heart thumping a slow, heavy beat. He tiptoed over to his dresser, his movements careful and deliberate. He pulled open a drawer, the sound loud in the quiet room. He grabbed a clean t-shirt and a pair of jeans, holding them against his chest to muffle any sound. He backed away from the dresser, then slowly, carefully, retreated toward the door. He slipped back into the hallway and pulled the door shut until he heard the faintest, softest *click* of the latch catching.

He leaned against the wall in the hall, letting out a long, shaky breath he hadn't realized he was holding. The simple act of getting dressed had felt as tense and high-stakes as disarming a bomb.

He quickly dressed in the hallway, pulling on the familiar comfort of his jeans and t-shirt. He felt more like himself, more grounded. He ran a hand through his damp hair, not bothering to tie it back, and headed downstairs. His mom was still at the kitchen table, but she had stood up and was rinsing out her mug in the sink. She looked up as he entered, a question in her eyes.

"Ready?" she asked.

"Yeah," Tony said. He walked over to the hook by the door and took down her car keys, jingling them in his hand. "I'll drive." Maria raised an eyebrow. "You've been up all night," he explained, his voice quiet. "You look tired, Mom. Let me drive."

A small, warm smile touched Maria's lips. It was a simple gesture, but it was full of a new consideration, a maturity she hadn't seen in him just yesterday. The crisis had shaken something loose in her son, and in the midst of all the pain, she saw a flicker of the good man he was becoming.

"Okay, *mijo*," she said, her voice soft with gratitude. "Thank you." She turned back to the counter. "In that case," she said, reaching for two travel mugs from the cupboard, "let me make us some real coffee for the road. The pot is practically mud by now."

As Maria started a fresh pot, the rich aroma filling the quiet kitchen, Tony stood by the door, keys in hand, waiting. The house was still, the only sounds were the gurgle of the coffee maker and the soft ticking of the clock on the wall. He glanced up the stairs toward his room, toward the sleeping boy who had changed everything. The silence pressed on him like a weight, accusatory.

"Mom?" he asked, his voice so quiet she almost didn't hear him.

She turned from the counter, a travel mug in each hand.

"Yes, *mijo*?" she asked.

"Last night," he started, his gaze dropping to the keys he was turning over and over in his hand. "Telling him everything... confessing. Was that... was that the right thing to do? Did I just make it worse?" Maria put the mugs down and gave him her full attention. She looked at her son, at the genuine anguish and uncertainty on his face.

"Telling the truth is never the wrong thing, Antonio," she said softly but with conviction. "Honesty is never a mistake." She took a step closer, her voice dropping. "But the truth can be heavy. And you gave him a lifetime of it in one night." She paused, letting the weight of that sink in. "He is a very fragile boy, and you handed him a very heavy truth. What matters now is what you do next. You gave him your honesty. Now you must give him your patience. You must give him time and space, and you must prove with your actions, every single day, that your words were real." The coffee maker gave a final gurgle, sputtering to a finish. She gave him a sad, loving smile. "It was a start, *mijo*. A painful, difficult start. But a start." She picked up the travel mugs, filled them with the fresh, hot coffee, and handed one to him. Their fingers brushed. "Now," she said, her tone shifting to one of gentle purpose. "Let's go chop some onions."

The bell above the door of *Freddy's Place* chimed, announcing their arrival. The sound was immediately swallowed by the controlled chaos of the Saturday breakfast rush. The small, cozy restaurant, which Maria had inherited from her old boss and father figure, was packed. The air was thick with the scent of sizzling chorizo, fresh coffee, and the happy din of conversation.

Miguel was a blur of motion, flying between tables with a coffee pot in one hand and a stack of plates balanced on his arm. The moment Leo spotted Maria walking through the door, his face flooded with a relief so profound it was almost comical.

"Oh, thank god, the boss lady is here!" he exclaimed, rushing over to them. "Maria, you have to save me. Miguel gets so *mean* when he's stressed. He told me I have the grace of a startled flamingo." Miguel shot him a look from across the room that seemed to confirm Leo's assessment.

He then noticed who was with Maria, and his sharp expression softened into surprise. Tony. On a Saturday morning, Tony was usually a thundercloud of teenage moodiness, doing his prep work with a sullen silence. But the boy standing behind his mother today was different. He was exhausted, that much was clear. There were dark circles under his eyes. But the usual anger, the coiled tension in his shoulders, was gone. He looked... lighter. As if a massive weight had been lifted from him. Miguel caught Leo's eye, and they shared a silent, curious look.

"Leo, you are a lifesaver. Thank you for helping," Maria said, giving his arm a grateful squeeze. She turned to her son. "Come on, *mijo*. The onions aren't going to chop themselves." Tony gave a small, tired nod to Miguel and Leo and followed his mom through the swinging doors into the familiar, comforting heat of the kitchen.

The next few hours were a blur of focused, repetitive motion. For Tony, the rhythmic *thump-thump-thump* of his knife on the cutting board was a kind of meditation. Onions, peppers, cilantro—he chopped until his hands ached and his mind was blessedly empty, filled only with the task at hand. He worked side-by-side with his mom, their movements synchronized and familiar, a silent dance they had done a thousand times before.

Shortly after eleven, the frantic energy of the restaurant began to ebb. The wave of the breakfast rush had crested and broken, leaving behind the calmer waters of late morning. The frantic clatter of plates softened, the din of conversation lowered to a comfortable hum.

Miguel, looking ten years older than he had three hours ago, ran a hand through his hair and let out a long, theatrical sigh of relief. He untied his stained apron, hung it on a hook, and pushed through the back door into the alley, pulling a cigarette from a pack in his pocket as he went. A moment later, the door creaked open again. It was Maria. She leaned against the brick wall beside him, wiping her hands on her own apron.

"You're a miracle worker, Miguel," she said, her voice full of sincere gratitude. "I walked into a warzone. Thank you for holding the line." Miguel took a long drag from his cigarette, the smoke pluming into the cool morning air.

"Anything for you, boss lady," he said, a genuine smile finally reaching his eyes. "Besides, Leo got a crash course in why he, as a college senior, should probably stick to his studies." They stood in comfortable silence for a moment, the sounds of the kitchen muffled behind them. "So," Miguel said casually, his eyes on the glowing tip of his cigarette. "Not my business, but... Tony looks different today."

"Does he?" Maria asked, pretending not to know who he meant.

"Yeah," Miguel said, glancing at her. "He looks like he's been through hell, but... the anger is gone. He looks... peaceful. It's weird." He took another drag. "Whatever happened the other day, I hope it was a good thing." Maria looked out at the empty alley, a soft, sad smile on her face. She let out a long breath she didn't realize she'd been holding. She trusted Miguel completely. He was more than her head waiter; he was her friend, a part of the restaurant's family.

"It was a hard thing," she said quietly. "But yes, Miguel. I think, in the end, it was a very good thing." She paused, then decided to share the weight. "He told us. Last night. Tony finally told us he's gay." Miguel stopped with the cigarette halfway to his lips. He didn't look shocked, just attentive. He waited for her to continue. "And he's in love," Maria added, her voice thick with a mixture of pride and sorrow. "With a very special boy." She looked at Miguel, her eyes conveying the depth of the situation. "But the circumstances... they are challenging. And they are going to continue to be challenging for a very long time."

Miguel took a slow, thoughtful drag, processing her words. He nodded, a deep understanding in his eyes. He didn't ask for details. He didn't need to. He knew that love and coming out were rarely simple, and he could hear the unspoken weight of a much larger story in her voice.

"Well," Miguel said softly, crushing the cigarette under his shoe. "It's a good thing he's got you, then." He gave her a small, supportive smile. "And it's a good thing he's got a place like this to come to." Maria nodded, her heart aching but also filled with a fierce resolve.

"I'm going to encourage him to talk to you, Miguel. If he's ready." She looked him in the eye, her own expression pained but determined. "And I'm going to tell him that he owes you an apology," Maria declared. Miguel's eyebrows raised slightly. "He called you... well, you know.... a couple of days ago," Maria reminisced, her tone noticeably irate from the memory. Miguel's face softened into a look of deep understanding. He gave a slow nod.

"He was having a bad day, Maria," Miguel said slowly.

"That's not an excuse," she said firmly. "I know he was battling his demons. I know he was scared and lashing out. But it's not an excuse. He hurt you. And he needs to face that. He needs to own it." Miguel looked at this incredible woman, at her strength and her unwavering love for her son, even as she refused to make excuses for him.

"He's lucky to have you," Miguel said again, his voice full of sincerity. "When he's ready to talk, I'll be here." Maria gave him a grateful smile, the weight on her shoulders feeling just a little bit lighter. She glanced back toward the bustling restaurant, wanting to change the subject to something less heavy.

"Speaking of lifesavers," she said, a playful glint in her eye. "If Leo ever wants to make some extra cash... we could always use the help on weekends. He's a good kid." Miguel let out a short, sudden laugh, the sound genuine and amused.

"Maria, I love you, but no," he chuckled. "After this morning, I think he'd rather face a final exam he didn't study for." He shook his head, a grin spreading across his face. "I think his exact words were, 'I never want to see another egg again unless it's safely in a carton.' Let's let the college senior stick to his books. It's safer for everyone, especially our customers." Maria laughed along with him, a real, warm sound. It felt good. For a moment, things almost felt normal.

The back door creaked open again, and Tony stepped out into the alley, blinking in the bright sunlight. He was wiping his hands on a dish towel, his hair still damp and falling into his eyes. He saw his mom and Miguel standing together, and then he heard them laughing—a real, easy sound that felt a world away from the tense silence of the morning. He stopped, his hand frozen mid-wipe.

An immediate, hot flush of self-consciousness crept up his neck. His face felt red. He was sure they'd been talking about him — the heat in his chest said enough. Their laughter died down as they noticed him standing there. Miguel, ever perceptive, saw the look on Tony's face and took pity on him.

"Don't worry, kid," he said, pushing off the wall with a grin. "We weren't talking about you. We were just establishing that my boyfriend has the coordination of a newborn deer and should never be allowed to carry a tray of drinks again."

He clapped Tony on the shoulder as he walked past him toward the door. "Your mom's a saint for not firing him on the spot." Maria smiled as she walked past Tony and Miguel to get back inside, not wanting to admit that Miguel was right. Miguel was about to take another drag of his cigarette when Tony decided this was his chance to show he had changed.

"Hey, man... I need to... I need to apologize."

Miguel stopped with the cigarette halfway to his lips, his expression turning from casual to attentive. He just waited.

"A couple of days ago," Tony continued, the words a difficult, shameful rush, "I was a complete asshole to you. What I called you... it was messed up. There's no excuse for it." He finally looked up, his own eyes full of a deep, painful regret. "I was... battling some stuff. My own stuff. But that's not an excuse. I took it out on you, and it was wrong. I'm really, really sorry, Miguel."

Miguel took a long, slow drag from his cigarette, processing the raw, unvarnished apology. He had seen the storm in this kid for months. He had been on the receiving end of his anger more than once. But he had never seen this. This quiet, vulnerable honesty. He let the smoke out in a slow, thoughtful plume.

"I know," he said, his voice surprisingly gentle. "I know you were." He looked at Tony, his gaze full of a deep, knowing empathy. "It takes a real man to admit when he's wrong, kid. Apology accepted." He took another drag. "Your mom told me... a little bit. About what's going on."

He looked at Tony, his expression all support. "If you ever need to talk, about any of it... I'm here. I get it. More than you know."

Tony felt a profound sense of relief wash over him, so strong it almost made him dizzy. He just nodded, unable to speak.

"Now get back inside," Miguel said, a small, genuine smile on his face. "Before your mom puts us both on dish duty for the rest of the day." Tony laughed, a real, genuine sound.

"Yeah. Okay." He turned and went back into the kitchen, the weight on his shoulders feeling just a little bit lighter.

CHAPTER 16

SIGNED, T.

The sun was high in the sky, casting warm, lazy rectangles of light across the floor of Tony's bedroom. The deep, dreamless sleep that had claimed Danny finally began to release its hold. He surfaced slowly, adrift in that disorienting space between oblivion and consciousness. For a moment, he didn't know where he was. The bed was soft, the blankets were heavy, and the air smelled clean, like laundry soap instead of Dina's smoke. He blinked, his eyes slowly focusing on a poster of a punk rock band he didn't recognize tacked to the opposite wall. Tony's room.

The memories of the previous night didn't come back as a nightmare, but as a slow, overwhelming flood of facts. The club. The bathroom stall. Tony's face in the doorway. The confession. *"I'm in love with you."* The words felt impossible, a jarring contradiction to the fresh, painful memory of the last year's cruelty. He sat up, the blankets pooling around his waist. He was still in his t-shirt. On the floor beside the bed, he saw his torn jeans in a messy heap. He felt a profound sense of dislocation, like a misplaced object in someone else's life. He was safe. He was warm. He had slept without fear for the first time in recent memory. And he had no idea what to do next.

He looked down at his hands and realized he was still clutching Peanut, the small stuffed elephant. The house was completely quiet. For all he knew, it was empty. He had no idea if Tony and his mom were home, if they had left hours ago, or if they were just downstairs, waiting. The uncertainty was a knot in his stomach. Should he stay hidden in the room? Or risk going downstairs? His throat was parched, his mouth dry. A glass of water. That was a simple, achievable goal. It was a reason to move. With a deep, steadying breath, Danny slid out of bed. He pulled on his jeans, his movements slow and deliberate. He picked up Peanut, holding the elephant in one hand, and quietly walked to the bedroom door, turning the knob as if he were a burglar in his own life. He peered out into the empty hallway, then took the first tentative step out of the room.

He stood in the upstairs hallway, a silent ghost in the quiet house. To his left was the closed door of what he assumed was Tony's parents' bedroom. To his right, the bathroom he hadn't dared to use. Straight ahead, a set of stairs carpeted in a worn runner descended to the main floor. There were no sounds of life—no television, no voices, no movement. The only sound at all was the slow, steady *tick-tock* of a tall grandfather clock that stood at the head of the stairs. His eyes found the clock's face. The long hand was pointing past the six, the short hand just past the two. It was already 2:30 PM. He had slept for more than twelve hours, a deep, bottomless sleep unlike any he could remember. The realization was startling. And with that awareness came another, more familiar sensation: a sharp, hollow ache in his stomach. He was hungry. It wasn't just the normal hunger of having missed a meal; it was the gnawing, familiar emptiness that had been a frequent companion for too long. Thirst had gotten him out of bed, but now hunger was pulling him toward the stairs, toward the kitchen. He tightened his grip on Peanut and took another slow, cautious step forward.

Each step down the stairs was a calculated, silent placement of his foot. He was a stranger in someone else's home, and the feeling of being misplaced was a physical weight on his shoulders. He reached the bottom of the stairs and found himself in a small, tidy living room. It looked comfortable and lived-in, with family photos on the mantle and a soft-looking afghan draped over the back of the couch. Everything felt warm and normal, which only amplified his own sense of otherness. He crept into the kitchen. It was sparkling clean, a stark contrast to the grime he was used to. A pot of coffee sat on the counter, and the air smelled faintly of it. The gnawing hunger in his stomach intensified, but he pushed the feeling down. He wouldn't dare. He couldn't just open their fridge and take something. In his experience, taking something that didn't belong to him resulted in screaming, or worse. He was terrified of getting in trouble, of breaking some unwritten rule and shattering the fragile peace he had been granted.

So he stuck to his original, humble mission. Water. That was free. He could have a glass of water. He padded over to the sink and reached for a glass from a drying rack next to it. As he turned on the tap, something on the counter caught his eye. A piece of notebook paper, torn from a spiral binder, folded neatly in half.

Written on the front in bold, familiar handwriting was a single word: *Danny*. His hand froze on the faucet. He stared at the note, his heart beginning to beat a little faster. He picked it up, his fingers trembling slightly. It felt heavy, important. He unfolded it. There were only a few sentences scrawled on the page At the bottom, a simple, stark signature. Signed, T. His heart pounded as he unfolded the paper. The writing was a bit messy, rushed, but clear.

Danny,

Mom and I went to the restaurant. Didn't want to wake you. Make yourself at home. Seriously. There's food in the fridge, help yourself to whatever you want.

If you need anything, the number for the restaurant is on the list by the phone. Just ask for me.

T.

Danny read the note once, then twice. He ran his thumb over the initial, "T." It was such a simple, practical message. But to Danny, it was a revelation. It was permission. It was an acknowledgment of his presence, not as an intruder, but as someone who was being cared for. *Make yourself at home.* The words felt foreign, a concept he couldn't quite grasp. He looked from the note to the refrigerator. The fear and hesitation were still there, a conditioned reflex from years of neglect.

But Tony's words were a quiet counter-spell. He had permission. He was allowed. Slowly, cautiously, he walked to the fridge and pulled the door open.

Danny stood there in the quiet kitchen, the note in one hand, the cold air from the open refrigerator door washing over him. The bed. The clean air. The note. These simple, decent things felt so profoundly alien that he didn't know what to do with them. A part of him, a desperate, hopeful part he thought had died long ago, wanted so badly for this to feel like home. He wanted to relax, to breathe, to believe the words on the paper. But another, louder part, the part conditioned by years of cruelty, was screaming that this was a trap. A cruel, elaborate joke. The kindness felt fragile, temporary, like it could be snatched away at any moment, leaving him looking like a fool for ever believing it was real.

His eyes scanned the contents of the refrigerator. It was a wonderland. Milk. Leftovers. Fresh vegetables. It was full. It was normal. It was everything his own fridge wasn't. The sight of so much food, so readily available, was almost as overwhelming as the confession had been. Tony's note said to help himself, but the ingrained fear of taking something, of overstepping, held him paralyzed.

He decided to start small. A test.

His eyes landed on a bright red apple in the fruit drawer. That seemed safe. It wasn't part of a future meal. It was just an apple. His hand trembled slightly as he reached in and took it. He closed the refrigerator door and leaned against it, holding the cool, smooth apple in his palm. It was the first thing he had taken for himself all day. He took a bite. The crunch was deafening in the silent kitchen, and the sweet, sharp taste that flooded his mouth was so clean and real it almost made him dizzy. He ate the entire thing quickly, methodically, right down to the core, as if he was afraid someone would take it from him mid-bite.

Emboldened by the small act of nourishment, a sliver of curiosity pushed back against his fear. He deposited the apple core in the trash can and let his feet carry him out of the kitchen and into the living room. He drifted through the space like a ghost, his fingers lightly tracing the back of the comfortable-looking couch. His eyes were drawn to the fireplace mantle, which was crowded with framed photographs. It was a timeline of a happy life. There was Tony as a little kid with a gap-toothed grin, holding up a soccer trophy. A picture of Maria and Leroy on their wedding day, looking young and impossibly happy. A photo of a teenage Tony mid-laugh, his arm slung around his dad's shoulders. Then he saw it.

Tucked in the back was a smaller, older photo in a simple frame. Two little boys in a backyard. One, slightly bigger, had his arm slung around the smaller, scrawny one. Both were grinning at the camera. Tony and him. Before. Before everything had changed. Before last year had ripped their shared history to shreds. He stared at the picture, at the ghost of the boy he used to be, and felt a profound, bottomless ache. He was so lost in the memory, in the ghost of that easy friendship, that he didn't hear the car pull into the driveway. He only registered the sound of a key scraping in the lock of the front door.

Panic, cold and absolute, seized him. They were home.

His heart hammered against his ribs. He wasn't ready. He couldn't face them yet, not here, not in the open. His eyes darted around the room, searching for an escape, a place to hide. He scrambled back toward the kitchen, his only thought to retreat, to disappear, just as the front door swung open. Tony was the first one through the door, shrugging his shoulders to loosen the ache from hours spent hunched over a cutting board. He was tired, but it was a good, physical exhaustion, a welcome change from the soul-deep weariness of the night before. The first thing he saw was Danny.

He was standing by the entrance to the kitchen, frozen mid-retreat like a deer caught in headlights. He was up. He was dressed. He was just... there. And Relief buckled Tony's knees — some part of him had been sure the room would be empty. But he was still here. Tony's heart swelled, and every instinct in his body screamed at him to close the distance between them. He wanted to rush forward, to wrap his arms around Danny's slim shoulders and hold on tight, a desperate, physical confirmation that he was real, that he was safe, that he hadn't disappeared.

But he stopped himself. The memory of Danny's quiet, hesitant voice in his bedroom last night echoed in his mind, a clear, sharp warning.

"You're going to have to be patient with me."

Patience. It wasn't his strong suit. But he had made a promise. So he held his ground by the door, clasping his hands together behind his back to keep from reaching out. He swallowed the lump in his throat and offered a small, tentative smile.

"Hey," Tony said, his voice softer than he intended. "You're up." Maria came in right behind Tony, her purse slung over her shoulder. Her face, etched with the morning's fatigue, broke into a warm, genuine smile the moment she saw Danny.

"Danny, *mijo*," she said, her voice full of a gentle warmth that was impossible to resist. "It is so good to see you up." She stepped around Tony, moving into the living room but keeping a respectful distance. "How are you feeling? Did you just wake up? Can I get you anything?" The barrage of kind, maternal questions made Danny shrink back a little. He clutched Peanut a bit tighter, his eyes darting from Maria's kind face to Tony, who was still standing by the door.

"I'm... okay," he mumbled, his voice quiet.

"Did you sleep well?" she asked.

"Yes."

"Are you hungry? I can make you something."

"No, thank you." His answers were short, non-descript, barely above a whisper. But they were answers. He was engaging, however hesitantly. It was a start.

Tony could see the overwhelm on Danny's face. His mom's kindness, as well-intentioned as it was, was a floodlight on a boy who was used to living in the shadows. He decided to offer something more practical, less emotional.

He stepped forward, finally moving from his spot by the door.

"Hey, man," Tony said, his voice low and even. He gestured toward Danny's torn jeans and the t-shirt he'd been wearing for more than twenty-four hours. "Do you... do you want to maybe take a shower? I can get you some clean clothes. Something that isn't ripped." The offer hung in the air. It wasn't a question about his feelings or his trauma. It was simple. Concrete. A clean shirt. A hot shower. It was a small, tangible piece of normalcy, and for the first time since he'd woken up, Danny felt a flicker of something other than fear or confusion.

The offer of a shower, of clean clothes, seemed to break a small dam inside Danny. It was a kindness he could understand. He looked down at the floor, his voice barely a whisper.

"I... I only had an apple," Danny confessed, as if admitting to a crime. "From the fridge. I hope... I hope that was okay." Maria's warm smile faltered, and a look of something fierce and protective took its place. She sounded almost insulted.

"Okay?" she said, her voice full of disbelief and a deep, aching sadness for what he must have gone through to even ask that question. She took a step closer, her voice softening but losing none of its intensity. "Danny, you listen to me. This is your home now. You eat when you are hungry. You can have anything you want in this house, anytime. Do you understand?" Danny could only manage a small, overwhelmed nod.

"Good," Maria said, her tone shifting immediately into one of purpose. Her love was not just words; it was action. She pointed a finger at her son. "Tony. Take him upstairs. Get him in the shower *right now*." She then turned on her heel and marched into the kitchen, already pulling pans from cupboards with a determined clatter. "I am going to make him so much food he won't know what to do with himself."

The unspoken declaration was clear: In this house, he would never have to ask if it was okay to eat an apple again. Tony watched his mom, a small smile touching his lips, before turning back to Danny.

"You heard the lady," he said gently. "Let's go find you some clothes." Tony led Danny back up the stairs and into his room. The afternoon sun was now angled differently, and the space felt warmer, less like a strange hotel room and more like what it was: a teenage boy's bedroom. "Okay," Tony said, trying to sound casual as he went to his dresser. "Let's see." Danny sat on the edge of the bed, watching him, his hands clutching Peanut in his lap. He felt like a visitor from another planet, observing the strange, mundane rituals of a functional household. Tony pulled open a drawer and took out a soft, worn-out t-shirt with a faded band logo on it.

"This should be comfortable." Tony opened another drawer and grabbed a pair of gray sweatpants. "And these." He added a pair of clean socks and new boxer briefs still in their packaging from a multipack. He then disappeared into the bathroom for a moment and came back with a new toothbrush, still in its plastic case. He placed the small pile of items gently on the bed next to Danny. "The bathroom is all yours whenever you're ready," he said, taking a step back to give him space.

Danny looked at the pile of clothes—the soft shirt, the clean socks, the new toothbrush. Each item was a small, concrete piece of kindness. He took a steadying breath, his mind feeling clearer than it had all day.

"Tony," Danny said, his voice quiet but steady. Tony stopped, turning to face him, his expression immediately turning anxious and expectant. "I had a chance to think," Danny said, looking down at the pile of clothes, then finally up at Tony's face. "About what you said last night. About... everything." Tony stood frozen, bracing himself for the verdict. He watched as a storm of emotions clouded Danny's blue eyes—pain, confusion, and a deep, soul-crushing weariness. He was ready for anything. Anger. Rejection. More silence. Danny looked down at the pile of clean clothes on the bed, then back up at Tony. He took a small, shaky breath.

"Last night... and just now... I keep thinking about before," Danny began, his voice barely a whisper. "Before this year. When we were kids." He finally looked Tony square in the eye, and his next words were filled with a profound and simple longing that cut through all the noise of the past twenty-four hours. "I miss my best friend, Tony." The words weren't an accusation. They weren't a declaration of love or a grand gesture of forgiveness. They were just the plain, unvarnished truth. It was a statement of loss, a quiet admission that the person he mourned most was the one standing right in front of him.

For Tony, the simple sentence was both a gut punch and a lifeline. It was an acknowledgment of the good that had existed between them, a shared memory of a time before the poison had set in. Tears welled in his eyes, hot and immediate. This was Danny's answer. It was his way of saying that the friendship was worth more than the pain, that the boy from the past was worth fighting for. He choked back a sob, nodding because he didn't trust his own voice. After a moment, he managed to speak, his words thick with emotion.

"Me too, Danny," he rasped. "More than you know." A fragile understanding settled between them, a single, tentative bridge built across a canyon of hurt. The tension in the room didn't disappear, but it changed, softening from something sharp and painful into a quiet, shared ache. Tony gestured toward the bathroom, his expression gentle. "Go on," he said softly. "Get cleaned up."

Danny closed the bathroom door behind him, the click of the lock feeling like a seal on his own private world. He turned on the shower, the rush of water a welcome noise that drowned out the silence of the house. He stripped off his dirty, torn clothes—the physical remnants of the last day's horror—and kicked them into a corner. He stepped into the spray, the hot water a shock against his cold skin. He let it cascade over him, washing away the grime of the club. And as the steam filled the small room, fogging the mirror and isolating him from the world, the dam inside him finally, silently, broke.

There was no sound, no ragged sob. He simply slid down the tiled wall until he was sitting on the floor of the tub, curling his knees to his chest. The tears came then, hot and silent, mingling with the shower water, their path invisible. The water disguised his crying so completely, even he almost believed it wasn't happening. It was a release of everything. The terror of the club. The gnawing hunger. The sting of his mother's hand. The confusion of Tony's confession. And the fragile, terrifying hope that bloomed after he had spoken his own truth. It was all too much. He huddled there, his shoulders shaking, and let it all pour out of him in the safety of the steam and the running water, completely unseen.

Tony stood outside his bedroom door, listening to the muffled sound of the shower running. He took a deep breath, the air feeling lighter in his lungs than it had in a year. He felt a fragile, trembling hope take root in his chest. *"I miss my best friend."* It wasn't everything, but it was a start. It was the only thing that mattered. He turned and went back downstairs, a new energy in his step. His mom was in the kitchen, wiping down the counters, her movements slow and tired. She looked up as he entered, her face etched with worry.

"Is he okay?" Maria asked softly. Tony couldn't stop the small, watery smile that spread across his face. He walked over to her, his own eyes shining with unshed tears of relief.

"He... he said he missed his best friend," Tony told her, his voice thick with emotion.

Maria's hand flew to her mouth, her own eyes immediately welling up. She understood instantly the immense weight of those simple words. It was forgiveness. It was an opening. It was a chance. Without a word, she closed the distance between them and wrapped her arms around her son, holding him in a tight, fierce hug. Tony buried his face in her shoulder, holding onto her just as tightly. Unaware of the silent breakdown happening upstairs, they stood together in the quiet kitchen, sharing a moment of pure, unadulterated hope. Maria held him for a long moment, then pulled back, her hands resting on his shoulders. She looked into his eyes, her expression searching.

"And how do you feel about that, *mijo?*" she asked softly, her voice full of gentle probing. "You poured your heart out to him. You told him you love him... and he said he wants his friend back." It was a fair question. A confession of love met with a request for friendship could feel like a rejection. A step back. But Tony shook his head, a look of profound, tearful gratitude on his face.

"Mom, it's everything," Tony said, his voice earnest. "It's more than I had any right to expect. It's more than I deserve." He wiped at his eyes with the back of his hand. "After everything I did... the things I said to him... I can't just expect him to fall into my arms. I broke everything between us." He looked toward the stairs, his voice dropping with reverence. "Friendship... that was the foundation of it all. If he's willing to let me try and earn that back, to rebuild that... that's all I can ask for. That's the only place we *can* start." He met his mother's eyes again, his own full of a quiet, steely resolve. "If I can be his best friend again... that's enough. That's everything right now."

"I'm so proud of you, Antonio." Maria's heart swelled with pride. This was the man she had raised. He wasn't the angry, scared boy from yesterday; he was thoughtful, patient, and selfless. She smiled, a true, brilliant smile, and squeezed his shoulders.

CHAPTER 17

FIRST STEPS

The afternoon settled into a long, quiet lull. The sun, now lower in the sky, slanted through the windows, painting the clean kitchen in warm, golden tones. It was nearing five o'clock. Maria, having long since returned from the restaurant, found a familiar comfort in the rhythm of preparing dinner. The steady, therapeutic chop of a knife against a cutting board was a sound that had grounded her for years. She was starting early, wanting to have a warm, welcoming meal ready for whenever Leroy got home, which she figured would be in about an hour. Her phone buzzed on the counter, but she ignored it, assuming it was just a game notification from the chime. She hadn't even looked at the text Leroy had sent her hours ago; the day had been a whirlwind of emotion and activity, and she'd been focused entirely on the two boys under her roof.

Tony drifted into the kitchen, restless. He had tried watching TV, tried reading, but his mind was too agitated to focus. He opened the fridge, stared into it for a moment without seeing anything, and then closed it again.

Maria paused her chopping, her eyes finding her son's. She saw the nervous energy radiating from him, the uncertainty of what to do with himself now that the immediate crisis was over.

"Tony," she said gently, wiping her hands on a dish towel. "I was talking to Miguel today at the restaurant." Tony looked up, his expression wary. "He knows you're going through a lot," she continued, her voice soft and even. "He wanted me to let you know that if you ever want to talk...

about anything... he's there. He understands." She paused, letting the offer settle. "You also owe him an apology."

Tony flinched, looking away in shame. He knew exactly what she was talking about. The memory of his cruel words to Miguel a few days ago was a fresh, hot sting of guilt.

"I know," he mumbled. "I actually spoke to him at work today," he said. Maria stared at Tony with her eye brow raised in surprise. "And I apologized to him. He offered to talk if I ever wanted."

"Oh, *mijo*," Maria said, not unkindly. "You of all people know how important it is to face the things we've done. To own them." She gave him a small, encouraging smile. "Miguel is a good man. He doesn't judge you."

The familiar sound of the front door opening, followed by the soft thud of a heavy bag hitting the floor, broke the quiet rhythm of the kitchen. A moment later, Leroy appeared in the doorway. He looked drained, the long, emotional day settled deep in the lines around his eyes. He saw Maria at the stove and Tony leaning against the counter, and a small, tired smile touched his lips. He walked over to the coat rack by the door and hung up his Sergeant's hat, a silent, daily ritual that separated his work life from his home life.

"Smells good in here," Leroy said, his voice rough with fatigue. He went straight to Maria, leaning in to kiss her cheek. It was a brief but meaningful press of lips that spoke of a long day and the comfort of coming home. He looked from her to Tony, giving his son a weary but steady nod. "Hey," he said, his eyes lingering on Maria. "Did you see my text from this morning?" Maria turned from the stove, wiping her hands on her apron.

"Oh, no, *mi amor*. I'm sorry," she said, her expression apologetic. "It's been... well, it's been a day. I haven't even looked at my phone." She reached for her phone on the counter, a flicker of concern on her face. "Is everything okay?"

"Everything's okay now," Leroy said, reassuring her. "It's just... an update." He ran a hand over his tired face. "I arrested her this morning, Maria. Dina. It's done."

Tony, who had been quietly observing, pushed himself off the counter, his full attention now on his father. "The house..." Leroy shook his head, the memory clearly distasteful. "It's a wreck. Unsanitary. It'll probably be condemned. There's no way he could have stayed there. We did the right thing." He pulled out a chair from the kitchen table and sank into it, the long day finally catching up to him. "I spent most of the morning with the CPS agent, a woman named Jenkins. We had a long conversation." He looked at Maria, then at Tony, making sure they were both listening. "She agrees that for now, this is the best place for him. We'll be his emergency guardians. But it's just the first step. There's going to be a process. Home visits, interviews... a hearing next week to make it official."

He leaned forward, his elbows on the table, his expression serious.

"She's going to need to speak with him, of course. And with both of you. She needs to understand the whole situation. But she was... good. She seemed to get it. She wants what's best for Danny." Leroy looked at his son, his gaze softening. "The hardest part is over," he said, a quiet finality in his voice. "He's safe. Now we just have to do the paperwork." A heavy silence settled over the kitchen. Maria turned back to the pot she was stirring on the stove, the motion slow and automatic. A part of her, the part that remembered backyard barbecues and shared laughter, couldn't let it go.

"And Dina?" she asked, her voice barely a whisper, her back still to the two men. "How... how was she?" Leroy let out a long, weary sigh.

"Not good, Maria. It was ugly." Maria flinched, her shoulders slumping. She regretted asking the moment the words left her mouth. "She was in a bad way," Leroy continued, his voice flat and tired. "Coming down from whatever she'd had last night. She screamed, she cursed. Blamed me, blamed the department... blamed Danny. Said he was a liar, that he made it all up."

Maria didn't turn around. She just stood there, staring down into the simmering pot, the memory of her old friend being violently overwritten by the ugly, tragic reality of the woman she had become. She shouldn't have asked. The air in the kitchen was thick with the weight of Leroy's words. Maria stood frozen at the stove, her back to the room. Tony leaned against the counter, staring at nothing. Leroy sat at the table, the picture of weary authority. None of them heard him.

He was so light on his feet, so accustomed to moving through the world without making a sound, that he was already at the bottom of the stairs and standing in the kitchen doorway before any of them sensed his presence. It was Maria who noticed first. A flicker of movement in her peripheral vision. She turned, a small gasp escaping her lips. Tony and Leroy followed her gaze. There stood Danny. He was wearing Tony's faded band t-shirt, which hung loosely on his slim frame, and the gray sweatpants, which were a little too long. His shaggy brown hair was damp and clean, curling slightly around his ears. His face was scrubbed clean, making the old scar on his lip and the faint, angry bruise on his cheek stand out in stark relief. He was clutching Peanut in one hand, his blue eyes wide and uncertain as he took in the three solemn faces staring back at him. He looked from Maria's pained expression to Tony's worried one, and finally to Leroy's serious, tired face. He knew something had happened.

"What?" he whispered, the single word fragile in the tense silence. Leroy's expression softened instantly. He pushed out the empty chair next to him, a quiet invitation.

"Come sit down, son," he said, his voice gentle. "There's... there's something we need to tell you."

Danny hesitated in the doorway, the invitation to sit feeling more like a summons to his own sentencing. The air was thick with unspoken things. He clutched Peanut tighter and, on shaky legs, walked to the table. He didn't sit in the empty chair next to Leroy, the one that felt too much like an interrogation spot. Instead, he chose the one next to Tony, creating a small, subconscious alliance. He sat on the very edge of the seat, ready to bolt, his eyes fixed on the wood grain of the table.

Leroy looked at Maria, a silent communication passing between them. He would handle this. He turned his chair slightly to face Danny more directly, his movements slow and deliberate.

"Danny," he began, his voice low and steady, the voice he used when talking to victims, not criminals. "A lot has happened today. And it's important you know everything. No more secrets, okay?" Danny gave a tiny, almost imperceptible nod, his gaze still glued to the table. "As part of my job," Leroy continued, choosing his words with care, "I had to go to your house this morning. Based on the events of last night, and... other things, I had a responsibility to make sure it was a safe environment." He paused. "It wasn't, son. It wasn't a safe place for you." He saw Danny's shoulders tense up, anticipating the worst. "So, we had to intervene. Dina... she was arrested this morning." Danny flinched, a sharp, visible tremor running through him. His knuckles went white around the stuffed elephant. Maria immediately reached across the table, her hand covering one of Danny's. Her touch was warm and firm.

"You are safe here, Danny," Maria said, her voice a fierce, protective whisper. "That is the only thing that matters. You are safe." Danny stared at her hand on his, then pulled his own back slowly, not out of rejection, but as if the touch was too much, too intense. He wrapped both his arms around Peanut, creating a small shield. Leroy waited a beat before continuing, letting Maria's words sink in.

"She was arrested for child endangerment, Danny. Because you were not being properly cared for. My job, my *most important* job, is to protect kids. And that's what this is about. Protecting you." He leaned forward slightly. "Because of this, another group is involved now. They're called Child Protective Services. Their only job is to make sure you have a safe, stable home to live in."

At the mention of "Child Protective Services," a new wave of fear washed over Danny's face. He had heard stories. Kids taken away, thrown into foster homes with strangers. His gaze darted toward the door. The words felt almost like a death sentence to Danny. Tony saw the panic in his eyes. He broke his silence, his voice quiet but firm.

"We want you here, Danny," Tony said. "With us. That's the plan."

"I spoke with the woman from CPS, Ms. Jenkins," Leroy continued. "I told her about our families, about my promise to your dad. I told her we want you to stay here, with us, for as long as you need. She agrees that's the best option. It's called 'kinship care.' It means you stay with family, or people who are like family."

He let out a long breath. "There's going to be paperwork. And meetings. And she'll need to talk to you, when you're ready. But the bottom line, the only thing you need to know right now, is that you are not going anywhere. You are staying here. This is your home now." Leroy finished, the weight of the information settling over the table. He had laid all the cards out. Dina was gone. The state was involved. But the Guzmans were his anchor.

Danny sat in silence, processing it all. His home was gone. His mother was gone. His entire life, as miserable and terrifying as it had been, had been completely dismantled in the space of a day. He was free, but it was a terrifying, disorienting kind of freedom. He looked from Leroy's serious face, to Maria's kind, tear-filled eyes, to Tony's steady, watchful gaze. He didn't know what to feel. So he just held on tighter to his elephant.

He looked from Leroy's serious face, to Maria's kind, tear-filled eyes, to Tony's steady, watchful gaze. He didn't know what to feel. So he just held on tighter to his elephant. Leroy's eyes, which had been focused on Danny's face, drifted down to the object clutched in his hands. Peanut. He'd almost forgotten about the little blue and green elephant. A wave of memory, so sharp it almost hurt, washed over him. He remembered the day Rick had bought it, holding it up in the store with a goofy grin on his face.

"Every kid needs a buddy to tell his secrets to," Rick had said. It was for Danny. Leroy felt a profound ache in his chest. He was so glad to see that this one thing, this one tangible piece of Rick's pure, uncomplicated love for his son, had survived the horror of that house. It had made it through.

Tony noticed the elephant, too. He didn't have the memory of its origin, but he had the fresh, painful memory of Danny pulling it from his backpack last night, clutching it like a lifeline. To Tony, the worn plush toy was a stark symbol of how much comfort Danny had been denied, that he had to cling so desperately to this one small friend from a childhood that felt a million miles away. The rest of the weekend unfolded in a strange limbo. Danny stayed mostly in Tony's room, venturing out only for meals Maria insisted he eat at the table. The conversations were careful, halting, but they were conversations — a fragile start.

By Monday morning, the house carried a nervous energy. Tony came downstairs dressed in his usual uniform: a clean white t-shirt, faded jeans, and his black leather jacket. His dad sat at the kitchen table with the paper, his mom packing lunches at the counter. It was a scene of perfect domestic normalcy that felt anything but normal.

A moment later, Danny appeared at the top of the stairs. He was wearing another one of Tony's faded band t-shirts and a pair of Tony's older, less-worn jeans that were still a bit too big on his slim frame. He walked down the stairs slowly, his eyes on his feet, clutching his worn backpack. Tony watched him, his heart doing a familiar, nervous flip. This was it. Their first time going back to school, back to the place where their roles as tormentor and victim had been so clearly defined.

"Hey, can I... can I take the car today? To drive Danny and I to school?" He turned to his parents, his voice clear. Leroy looked up from his paper, over the rim of his reading glasses. Maria stopped packing the lunches. It was a simple request, but they all understood the weight of it. It wasn't just about a ride. It was a public statement. Tony driving Danny to school was an act of protection, an undeniable alliance that would be visible to everyone. Maria smiled, a proud, warm expression on her face.

"Of course, *mijo*," she said, handing him one of the lunch bags. "Your father and I were just talking about it." Leroy folded his newspaper and set it on the table, giving Tony a long, appraising look.

"Just be careful," he said, his voice even. "Eyes on the road. No distractions." It was fatherly advice, but the underlying meaning was clear: *Take care of him.*

"I will," Tony promised.

Danny took the lunch bag Maria offered him, his fingers brushing against hers. He mumbled a quiet "thank you" without making eye contact and quickly put it in his backpack, zipping it up as if to protect the small act of kindness from the outside world. The walk to the car was a silent, nerve-wracking affair. Tony led the way, keys in hand. Danny followed a few steps behind, his head down, watching his own feet. The familiar suburban street, the morning sunlight, the sound of a distant lawnmower—it all felt alien, like a scene from a movie he wasn't supposed to be in. Tony unlocked the doors of his mom's minivan. He got into the driver's seat, the familiar space feeling strange and new. Danny slid into the passenger seat, a place once occupied by Jessica or Marko, and immediately turned to stare out the side window, presenting Tony with nothing but the back of his head. He clutched his backpack on his lap like a shield.

Tony started the engine. The silence in the car was deafening, a completely different entity from the heavy, exhausted silence of Friday night. This was a silence filled with unspoken questions, with the frantic thumping of two hearts bracing for impact. He pulled out of the driveway and started the short drive to school. Every turn was a countdown. Tony gripped the steering wheel, his knuckles white. He wanted to say something, anything, to break the tension.

"It's going to be okay." "Don't worry about what people say." "I've got your back." But the words felt hollow, like promises he hadn't yet earned the right to make. He glanced over at Danny. The boy was ramrod straight, his gaze fixed on the passing houses, his jaw tight. He looked like a soldier heading into battle.

They turned onto the final street before the school. The parking lot, already filling up with students, came into view. Tony could see the familiar cliques gathering — the jocks by the gym doors, the skaters by the bike racks. The normal, chaotic ecosystem of their high school.

He pulled into a parking spot far from the main entrance, hoping to give them a bit of a buffer. He killed the engine, and the silence rushed back in, more intense than ever. This was it. The point of no return. Tony finally turned to Danny.

"Hey," Tony said softly. Danny flinched but didn't look away from the window. "You don't have to do this," Tony said, his voice earnest. "We can just... I don't know. We can go somewhere else. We can turn around." For the first time since they got in the car, Danny turned his head and looked at him. His blue eyes were full of a deep, terrifying fear, but underneath it, there was a flicker of something else. A fragile, stubborn resolve.

"No," he whispered, his voice barely audible. "I'm tired of running."

He took a deep, shaky breath, his gaze shifting to the school building in front of them. "Let's just... get it over with."

CHAPTER 18

NOT THE WHOLE STORY

With Danny's quiet declaration hanging in the air, they both got out of the car. The morning air was cool, but to Tony, it felt charged and heavy. The familiar sounds of the school parking lot—shouted greetings, the aggressive bass from someone's car stereo, the distant rumble of a school bus—seemed amplified, each one a potential threat. He watched Danny pull his worn backpack higher onto his shoulders, a subconscious defensive gesture that made Tony's stomach clench.

As they started the long, exposed walk toward the entrance, a figure detached from a group near the bike racks and jogged toward them. It was Jamal, looking nervous, his hands shoved deep in his pockets as if to keep them from fidgeting.

He stopped in front of them, his eyes darting from Tony's carefully neutral expression to Danny's pale, withdrawn face.

"Hey," Jamal said, his voice low and tight. He focused on Tony. "Man, I'm sorry about Friday night. For not sticking around downtown after I called. I just... I saw him go in there, and then your mom was on the way, and I just... I got scared, man. I didn't want to get mixed up in anything." The old Tony might have felt a flash of anger, a sense of betrayal. But the new Tony just saw a friend who had been put in an impossible situation and had still made the right call. He stepped forward and pulled Jamal into a quick, firm hug, clapping him on the back.

"Don't even worry about it," Tony said, his voice sincere as he pulled back. "You did the right thing. You made the call. That's what mattered.

Thank you. Seriously." Jamal's shoulders sagged with visible relief, a grateful smile spreading across his face. He finally looked at Danny, his expression softening with genuine concern.

"Hey, man. You good?" Tony asked as Danny slung his heavy backpack over his shoulder. Danny, who had been standing silently beside Tony like a shadow, clutching his backpack strap so tightly his knuckles were white, gave a small, almost imperceptible nod.

"Yeah," he whispered, his voice raspy from disuse. The first bell shrieked across the parking lot, a piercing, unwelcome sound that made Danny flinch. He looked at Tony, his eyes pleading for an escape. "I'm... I'm gonna go," he said quietly. "I need to... focus. On school." It was a clear, gentle dismissal. He needed to disappear into the anonymity of the crowded hallways.

Tony understood immediately.

"Okay," he said, his voice soft. "Yeah. I'll see you later." Their eyes met for a brief, charged second—a silent acknowledgment of the morning's journey, the promises made, and the challenges that lay just inside the school doors. Then Danny turned and melted into the stream of students, his slim frame and faded hoodie disappearing into the chaos. Tony watched him go, a mix of pride and a deep, protective anxiety churning in his gut.

"Dude, are you coming or what?" a familiar voice boomed from behind him. "Coach is gonna have our heads if we're late again."

Tony turned to see Marko and Jessica approaching. Marko was already spinning a basketball on his finger, but his usual jovial expression was replaced with one of intense, frustrated confusion. Jessica walked beside him, her books clutched to her chest, her face unusually quiet and watchful. She wasn't asking questions; she was just observing, her intelligent eyes trying to piece together the puzzle of Tony's sudden transformation.

"What was that?" Marko demanded, gesturing with his head in the direction Danny had gone. "First Jamal bails on us Friday night all freaked out, then you drive that Danny kid to school? Are we in the Twilight Zone? Did you get body-snatched over the weekend?"

"We'll talk later," Tony said, his voice firm as he looked at Jamal, who just shrugged helplessly. "We've got practice." He started walking toward the gym entrance, and the others fell into step beside him, a cloud of bewildered silence hanging over them.

The gym was already filled with the rhythmic squeak of sneakers on polished wood and the sharp echo of bouncing basketballs. The boys changed quickly and hit the court. Usually, Tony's practice style was aggressive, almost violent. He played with a barely concealed rage, all sharp elbows, reckless drives to the hoop, and furious shots that seemed aimed at punishing the rim. But today was different.

The anger was gone. His movements were still powerful, but they were controlled, focused. He saw the whole court, passing to an open man when he should have shot, setting a solid pick for Jamal that allowed him an easy layup. He moved with a quiet purpose that wasn't about his own frustration. Marko and Jamal exchanged more than one confused look during the drills. This was a Tony they hadn't seen on the court in a long, long time, if ever. After practice, the locker room was thick with the smell of sweat and steam. Marko, unable to contain his bewilderment any longer, slammed his locker door shut and turned on Tony.

"Alright, dude, I can't do this anymore," he said, throwing his hands up in exasperation. "What the hell is going on? You ditch us Friday, you show up today driving *him* to school, and you play like... like you're not trying to murder the basketball for the first time all season. It's like you're a completely different person. Talk to us, man." Tony sat on the bench, slowly untying his sneakers, gathering his thoughts. He owed them an explanation. Not the whole story, but enough.

"A lot happened this weekend," he began, his voice low and even. "Danny's... his life kind of blew up. And he had nowhere else to go." He looked up, his gaze steady and unwavering. "So he's living with us now. At my house. My parents want him there. It's... a long story." He stood up, pulling on his jeans, a clear signal that the conversation was over. "Look, I know it's weird. And things are uneasy. But that's how it is right now. And you're just going to have to learn to live with it."

The school day passed in a blur of crowded hallways and ringing bells. At lunch, the four of them sat at their usual table, the mood still awkward. Tony unwrapped his sandwich, but his eyes immediately scanned the room. He found him. Danny was sitting by himself at a small, isolated table near the windows, his back to most of the room, making himself as small as possible.

"Okay, I can't do this," Marko said, dropping his fork with a clatter. "Are we seriously not going to talk about this? He's just *living* with you now?"

"Marko, lay off," Jamal cut in, his tone cautious.

"No, man, I'm not laying off," Marko shot back, gesturing with his fork toward Tony, his voice full of frustrated disbelief. "A week ago, *you* were the one leading the charge. You hated the guy. And now you're his bodyguard? It makes no sense. I just... I don't get what's happening."

Jessica, who had been silent all morning, finally spoke, her voice quiet but firm.

"Marko, stop." She looked at Tony, her expression soft and understanding. "Just tell us what you need from us."

"You don't have to do anything," Tony said, finally tearing his gaze away from Danny. "You don't have to be his friend. You don't have to talk to him." He paused, his gaze sweeping over them, landing on Marko. "You just have to leave him alone. The stuff from before... it's over. All of it. It has to be." It was then that he saw it. Kyle, a loud-mouthed jock from the football team, was swaggering toward Danny's table, a cruel smirk on his face.

"Well, well, look what we have here," Kyle's voice boomed across the cafeteria, drawing attention. "New clothes, Sanders? Did you finally get tired of smelling like garbage?" Danny didn't look up; his whole body went rigid. "Or are you just sad your whore mom finally got arrested? I heard the cops had to break the door down."

Before anyone could react, Tony was out of his seat. He moved with a terrifying, silent speed that was more intimidating than any shout. He grabbed the front of Kyle's letterman jacket, twisting the fabric and yanking him backward, half-lifting him from his feet. His face was inches from Kyle's, his eyes burning with a fury so cold and absolute it was paralyzing.

"Remember last football season?" Tony breathed, his voice a quiet, venomous hiss that only Kyle could hear. "After the Northwood game? In the locker room. You told me something. You trusted me." The color drained from Kyle's face. His arrogant smirk vanished, replaced by a look of pure, panicked recognition as the memory surfaced. "If you ever look at him again," Tony continued, his grip tightening until his knuckles were white, "If you even *think* his name, everyone in this school will know exactly what you told me. We clear?" Kyle, pale and trembling, nodded frantically, unable to form words, his eyes wide with terror.

Tony held him there for a second longer, letting the threat sink deep into his bones. Then he shoved him backward. Kyle stumbled, caught his footing, and practically fled from the cafeteria, his tough-guy persona completely shattered.

The area had gone silent, students staring in stunned silence. Tony ignored them all. He looked at Danny, who was watching him with wide, terrified, and utterly disbelieving eyes. Tony gave a small, almost imperceptible shake of his head, a silent apology, before turning and walking back to his table. He sat down and picked up his sandwich.

Marko and Jamal were staring, their faces pale. They had seen Tony get into fights, but this was different. This was surgical. It was scarier than any punch.

"Dude," Marko whispered, full of a new, unfamiliar respect. "What did you say to him?"

"That," Tony said calmly, "was me keeping a promise."

The final bell of the day was a welcome relief. He walked into AP English and slid into his usual seat. A moment later, Danny slipped in and took his seat near the front. Mr. Bodowski stood at the front of the class.

"Alright, settle down," he said. "Today we are diving back into our group projects on *To Kill a Mockingbird.*" A collective groan went through the class. "Now, now," Mr. Bodowski chuckled. "On Friday, you all submitted your thesis statements, and some were excellent." His eyes landed on Danny, then flickered to Tony. "In fact, the strongest, most insightful thesis, as we all remember, came from the partnership of Mr. Sanders and Mr. Guzman." Tony saw Danny's shoulders tense slightly. "So," Mr. Bodowski continued, "for the remainder of the class, I want you to pair up with your partner and begin outlining your report."

As students began shuffling desks, Tony stood up and walked to the front of the room, stopping beside Danny's desk. Danny looked up at him, his expression uncertain. Tony looked at the teacher.

"Mr. Bodowski," Tony said, his voice clear. "Danny and I are going to go to the library to work on the outline." Mr. Bodowski stopped mid-sentence, his eyebrows shooting up. He clutched his head in mock surprise.

"Saints be praised, I think I'm having a stroke," he declared dramatically. "Tony Guzman, suggesting the library? The world must be ending." He shook his head and pointed a playful finger at Danny. "Let me guess.

His idea, right?" Tony glanced down at Danny, then back at the teacher, a small, genuine smile touching his lips.

"Yeah, sir," Tony said. "All his idea."

The boys left the noisy classroom and entered the vast, hushed space of the school library. The air smelled of old paper and silence. They found an empty carrel in a deserted corner. They worked for a while, the only sound was the soft scratch of Danny's pencil on a legal pad. Danny did most of the writing, his focus intense. Tony just watched, following his lead.

After about twenty minutes, Danny put his pencil down. He looked at Tony, his blue eyes full of a quiet, searching question. It was the same look he'd had in the cafeteria, a look that asked *why* without making a sound. Tony knew exactly what he was asking. He leaned back in his chair.

"What I did to Kyle," he began, his voice low, "I'm sorry you had to see that. I didn't want to... be that person. Not in front of you." He took a breath. "But I told you I would protect you. And that meant from everyone. I wasn't going to let him talk to you like that. I couldn't."

Danny was hesitant. He digested what had happened earlier, replaying the scene in his mind. He remembered Tony's vow from Friday night. He was surprised, and a little terrified, that Tony was actually keeping his word. The threat was scary, but the protection... that was new. It was real. Slowly, his own hand lifted from the table. It trembled slightly, a testament to the war going on inside him, but it moved with a purpose that was all his own. He reached across the small space of the carrel and lightly touched the back of Tony's hand, his fingers barely grazing the skin.

The touch was a supernova. Tony's entire nervous system seemed to light up at once, a jolt of pure electricity that shot from his hand straight to his heart. He froze, his breath catching in his throat. He could feel the faint, cool touch of each of Danny's fingertips against his skin, a delicate pressure that was both impossibly light and overwhelmingly heavy. He stared down at Danny's pale, slim fingers resting on his own, his heart hammering against his ribs like a trapped bird trying to escape. A deep, sudden flush of heat crept up his neck and into his face. He didn't move a muscle, didn't breathe, terrified that the slightest motion would break the spell and make Danny pull his hand away forever.

The silence stretched, thick and charged. Danny finally broke it, his voice a raw, hesitant whisper.

"That was... scary," he said, his eyes fixed on their hands as if they were the only two objects in the universe. "What you did to Kyle." He took a shaky breath, mustering his courage. "But... no one's ever... done that for me before." He finally lifted his gaze to meet Tony's, his blue eyes wide and vulnerable. "Stood up for me." Tony looked into those eyes and felt like he was drowning. He was completely at a loss for words, his mind short-circuiting from the touch, from the confession, from the look on Danny's face. All he could manage was a single, choked whisper.

"Danny..." He had to know. The question clawed its way up his throat. "Does this... does this mean you forgive me?" he asked, his voice fragile, terrified of the answer.

Danny didn't answer right away. He just looked at Tony, and in the quiet safety of the library, he finally let himself feel it. The feelings he had for Tony, the ones he had crushed and buried under a year of pain and neglect, hadn't died. They had just slept. And Tony's actions— the rescue, the confession, the protection—were like a slow, warm sunrise, waking them up. The light touch of their hands was the final spark, a current passing between them, reigniting everything. He didn't have to say anything. His eyes told the whole story. The fear was still there, a shadow in their depths, but it was now mingled with a deep, aching affection that was impossible to hide. It was a look of profound, heartbreaking vulnerability.

Tony saw it. For the first time, he wasn't just guessing or hoping; he was reading Danny's feelings as clearly as if they were written on the page between them. This new intuition was a terrifying, exhilarating thing. It was a bridge forming between them, one he was terrified of breaking. He felt a dizzying mix of elation and sheer panic. He took a shaky breath, his heart pounding. He had to ask. He had to give the power back to Danny, to make sure this was real, to make sure he wasn't pushing.

"Can I kiss you?" Tony whispered, his voice thick with an emotion so intense it almost hurt. He saw a flicker of panic in Danny's eyes and immediately added, his words tumbling out in a rush to reassure him. "Not here. Not now. But... someday. Soon. When you're ready. Can I?"

The house was unnervingly quiet after the boys left. The silence they left in their wake was heavier, more charged than the usual weekday morning emptiness. Leroy sat at the kitchen table, a fresh cup of coffee in his hands, staring at the front door as if he could still see their retreating figures. Maria had taken the day off from the restaurant. She knew it would be slow on a Monday and that Miguel could handle it; he would have called if there was a real emergency. Right now, her place was here.

"You think they'll be okay?" Leroy asked, breaking the silence. His voice was low, laced with a worry he couldn't quite hide.

"They have to be," Maria said, joining him at the table. She reached across and placed her hand over his. "Tony will look out for him. He knows what's at stake."

"It's not Tony I'm worried about," Leroy admitted. "It's everyone else. Kids can be cruel." They sat in silence for a moment, both thinking of the challenges the boys were facing in the crowded hallways of their high school. The weight of the weekend, of Dina's arrest, of their new reality, felt immense. Maria sighed, a sad, nostalgic sound. She looked at her husband, at the deep worry etched on his face, and decided they needed a distraction, a memory from a happier time.

"You know," she began, a small, wistful smile touching her lips, "this whole thing... it reminds me of our wedding day."

"Our wedding? How?" Leroy looked at her, confused.

"Just the chaos," she said, her eyes distant. "The feeling that everything was happening all at once." She squeezed his hand. "Do you remember my *Papi* that morning? He was so stressed, he was about to lose his mind. Dina and I were in the kitchen at my parents' house," she said, her voice taking on a storyteller's cadence. "She was helping me with my veil, trying to keep me calm. And suddenly, the kitchen door swings open, and in comes *Papi*, his face all red, looking frantic."

A much younger Maria sat at a kitchen table, a cloud of white tulle around her head. A vibrant, laughing Dina stood behind her, pinning the veil into her elaborate updo. The door flew open, and Maria's father, a stout man with a thick mustache, rushed in, fanning himself with his hand.

"¡Ay, Dios mío!" he exclaimed, his voice a dramatic whisper. "¿Dónde está el brandy?"

"Getting an early start, Papi?" Dina laughed.

"Maria, your madre," he said, ignoring her and pointing a thumb back toward the living room, "is acting crazy! She says the flowers are wrong, the tablecloths are crooked, that the priest looks too young! She is going to give me a heart attack before I can even walk my own daughter down the aisle. I need something strong. For my nerves."

He found the bottle in the cabinet, poured a generous two fingers into a glass, and downed it in one gulp. He shuddered, then let out a long, satisfied sigh. His panic seemed to recede.

"Ah, much better." He turned and finally looked at his daughter, his eyes softening. "Mija, you look so beautiful. Like an angel." He then turned his

attention to Dina, who was watching him with an amused smirk. "And you, Dina! Stunning as ever," he said, pointing at her. "The hair. It's so short now. Different." He squinted at her, a thoughtful, calculating look on his face. "Tell me something, Dina. Are you a…. uh…. lesbian?"

"What?" Dina choked on a laugh, her smirk turning into a look of pure shock.

"A lesbian," Papi repeated, completely serious. "Because Leroy, he has a sister, Jessie. She's a very nice girl, a mechanic. Very strong hands. But she doesn't like boys, I think anyway. I was thinking, maybe you two would get along. I could set it up."

Leroy laughed until tears welled in his eyes, wiping them away with the back of his hand.

"Oh, man," he finally gasped, catching his breath. "I forgot about that. Your ol' man... he was one of a kind."

CHAPTER 19

PROJECT

The final bell shrieked through the library, a harsh, unwelcome intrusion that shattered the fragile bubble around their table. The sound jolted Tony back to reality. He blinked, and Danny immediately pulled his hand back as if burned, tucking it safely into his lap. The connection was broken, but the phantom feeling of Danny's fingertips lingered on Tony's skin, a warm, electric hum. They packed their books in a silence that was no longer awkward or tense, but thick with unspoken possibilities. Tony's mind was a chaotic, buzzing hive.

"He didn't say no. He looked at me... he looked at me like he felt it too." The thought was a wild, hopeful drumbeat in his chest. He was so dizzy with it, he almost forgot to breathe.

The walk to the car was a masterclass in feigned nonchalance. Tony shoved his hands in his pockets to keep from reaching for Danny's again. He was hyper-aware of the way Danny's worn-out sneaker scuffed the linoleum, and the charged space between them. For the first time in what felt like a lifetime, the silence between them wasn't a wall; it was alive, charged with a terrifying, exhilarating energy. Danny, for his part, felt like he was floating. He had touched Tony. He had let him see the truth in his eyes. The fear was still there, a cold knot in his stomach, but it was now tangled with a feeling so warm and so long-forgotten it almost felt new: hope. He risked a sideways glance at Tony. He was just staring straight ahead, his jaw tight, but the tips of his ears were bright red. The sight sent a tiny, fragile flutter through Danny's chest.

They got into the minivan, the familiar space now feeling intensely intimate. Tony started the engine, the radio coming on low with some generic pop song. He immediately turned it off, plunging them back into silence. He pulled out of the parking lot, his movements careful and deliberate, every motion controlled, cautious.

He wanted to say something, anything. *"So... what you said... what I said... what does it mean?"* But the words felt too big, too clumsy. He had promised patience. He had asked for permission for "someday, soon." He couldn't break that promise now, not when the first, tentative "yes" was still hanging in the air. It was Danny who finally broke the silence.

"My dad," he said, his voice quiet and a little rough. "He used to love that song."

Tony glanced at the now-silent radio, then back at Danny.

"The one that was just on?" Danny nodded, his gaze fixed on the passing houses.

"Yeah. He was…. a terrible singer, but he'd always try to hit the high notes. It drove my mom crazy."

It was a small, simple offering. A memory. A piece of his past offered freely. To Tony, it felt like a monumental gift. It was the first step back toward being friends.

"I remember," Tony said softly. "He used to sing in the backyard when he was grilling." A tiny, sad smile touched Danny's lips.

"Yeah. He…… did."

The rest of the drive passed in a new kind of quiet. It was a comfortable silence, filled not with tension, but with shared memory and the soft, humming possibility of a future. When they walked through the front door, the warm, savory scent of Maria's cooking enveloped them. She was standing at the stove, and Leroy was at the table, reading the paper.

They both looked up, their expressions carefully neutral, but their eyes were searching, trying to gauge the temperature of the day.

Maria saw it first. The boys were still separated by a few feet of space, but the frantic, fearful energy from the morning was gone. They were quiet, yes, but it was a different quiet. It was calm. She saw the faint blush that still lingered on Tony's cheeks and the way Danny, for the first time, didn't immediately look at the floor.

"Hey, boys," she said, her voice warm and welcoming. "How was school?"

"It was okay," Tony said, dropping his backpack by the door. As Danny gave a small, shy nod in greeting, Maria's expression shifted slightly.

"School was really okay? No trouble?"

"No trouble," Tony confirmed, deliberately leaving out the cafeteria incident. He didn't want to worry them, and he had handled it. "Practice was good. I was actually focused for once." He glanced at Danny. "And we got a good start on our English project. We went to the library during class."

"The library?" Leroy said from behind his paper, his voice laced with amusement. "Wonders never cease." Maria smiled, pleased. For a moment, it almost sounded like a normal day.

"Well, that's good," she said. "Why don't you two go upstairs and get started on your homework? Dinner will be ready in about an hour."

"Okay, Mom," Tony said.

He looked at Danny, a quiet question in his eyes. Danny met his gaze and, after a beat of hesitation, gave another small nod. Danny turned and headed up the stairs, but as Tony went to follow, Maria put a gentle hand on his arm, stopping him.

"A word, *mijo*," she said quietly, waiting until Danny was out of earshot.

Tony turned to face her, his stomach tightening.

"What's up?"

"I need to ask you about Jessica," she said, her voice low. "Have you spoken to her? Have you told her anything about... well, about any of this?" Tony's gaze immediately dropped to the floor. He felt a hot, familiar flush of shame.

"No," he mumbled. "Not yet. I haven't said a word." He looked up at his mom, his own expression pleading for understanding. "I know I have to, Mom. I know it's the right thing to do. It's just... everything has been happening so fast. I wanted things to calm down first, to figure out what's even going on in my own head before I... before I break her heart." Maria sighed, her heart aching for him, but also for the girl who was being kept in the dark.

"Antonio," she said, her voice firm but full of love. "There is never a 'good time' for a conversation like that. Waiting will not make it easier. It will only make it harder. The longer you wait, the more you will hurt her. She is a good girl, and she deserves the truth, even if it's a painful one."

Tony stood there, the weight of her words settling on him. He knew she was right. It was another promise he had to keep, another hard conversation he had to have. The road to being an honest man was littered with them. He gave a slow, reluctant nod.

"I know," he said quietly. "You're right. I'll... I'll talk to her."

With the conversation over, Tony headed back upstairs, his mind a swirl of guilt about Jessica and a nervous anticipation of seeing Danny again. He pushed the door to his room open quietly. Danny was sitting cross-legged in the middle of the bed, propped up against the pillows. He had already changed back into the comfortable sweatpants and t-shirt Tony had given him. In his lap was their copy of *To Kill a Mockingbird*, open and face down, a pencil marking his place. He was already getting a head start on their project.

A fresh wave of guilt washed over Tony. Of course Danny was already working. He was the smart one, the one who cared about school. Tony, on the other hand, felt like he'd have nothing valuable to add. He wasn't book smart, not like Danny. It was the same old inadequacy, the one that always made him feel smaller beside Danny. It made him feel bad that Danny had taken on all the work, both in class and now.

Trying to be respectful of the quiet, studious atmosphere, Tony grabbed the cluttered chair from his desk. He pushed a pile of clothes onto the floor and dragged the chair over, setting it down a few feet from the bed. He was giving Danny his space, just like he'd been trying to do all day. He sat down, unsure of what to say. Danny looked up from his book, his expression unreadable. He watched Tony settle into the chair, creating a deliberate, respectful distance between them.

"You can come closer, you know," Danny said, his voice quiet, almost shy. He patted the empty space on the mattress beside him. "If you want." Tony's heart gave a hard thump against his ribs. He looked at the empty space on the bed, then at Danny's expectant face.

"I just... I wanted to give you space," he said, his voice a little rough. "If you wanted it."

"I don't," Danny said simply.

Slowly, reluctantly, Tony stood up from the chair and moved to the bed. He sat down on the edge, his back to Danny, still maintaining a careful distance. The invitation was one thing, but actually being that close felt like a new level of terrifying intimacy.

They sat like that for a moment, a silent, awkward tableau. Then Danny shifted, moving closer until their shoulders were almost touching. He picked up the book.

"I found…. a good quote for the part……. about Boo Radley," he said, his voice soft, breaking the tension with the simple, normal task at hand.

The evening melted away like that. They worked on the project, their heads bent together over the book. Tony, to his surprise, found himself engaged, asking questions, offering ideas. For the first time in a long while, it felt like sharing, not competing. The physical space between them slowly shrank, until their arms were brushing against each other as they wrote.

"Dinner!" Maria's voice called from downstairs, startling them both.

At the dinner table, the atmosphere was lighter than it had been all weekend. Danny was still quiet, but he answered Maria's questions with more than one word, and he ate everything she put on his plate. Halfway through the meal, Tony looked at his dad.

"Hey, *Papi*," he started, a nervous energy in his voice. "That old Triumph in the garage... the one under the tarp." Leroy looked up, surprised.

"What about it?"

"I was wondering... if maybe I could try to get it running," Tony said, the words coming out in a rush. "I've been reading about them online. I think I could figure it out." He took a breath. "I've been thinking about getting my motorcycle license. I've been saving up for it."

Leroy looked at his son, really looked at him. For the first time in a long time, he saw a spark of genuine passion in Tony's eyes that wasn't tied to anger or basketball. He was asking for a project, for a purpose. A small, proud smile touched Leroy's lips.

"We'll see," he said, but the warmth in his tone was a clear and definite yes. For a heartbeat, it almost felt like normal again. But as they were finishing their meal, Leroy's expression turned serious again. "Speaking of getting things done," he said, setting his fork down. "I got a call this afternoon. It was Ms. Jenkins, from CPS."

The light, happy mood at the table vanished instantly. Tony's head snapped up, and he immediately looked at Danny. Danny froze, his fork halfway to his mouth. He slowly lowered it back to his plate, his appetite gone. He hunched his shoulders, making himself smaller, and stared down at his half-eaten food.

"She wants to do her initial home visit," Leroy continued, his voice calm and steady, though his eyes were on Danny. "She needs to have a chat with all of us. She's coming over on Wednesday, after school."

The news landed like a stone in the quiet kitchen. Wednesday. It was a deadline. A countdown. Maria's hands clenched in her lap, her mind already starting to race with preparations. Tony just watched Danny, a fierce, protective instinct rising in him. He saw the fragile peace of the day shatter in Danny's eyes, replaced by the old, familiar terror of being scrutinized, of being judged, of having his fate decided by a stranger. Leroy saw the panic on Danny's face and immediately softened his tone.

"Hey," he said, his voice gentle but firm, commanding the boy's attention. "Look at me, son. There is nothing to worry about." Danny slowly lifted his gaze from his plate to meet Leroy's. "This is just a formality," Leroy explained calmly. "It's part of the process. Ms. Jenkins just needs to see that you're in a safe place. She needs to talk to us, and to you, to make sure this is the right home for you. That's it. It's not a test." He leaned forward, his expression full of a steady reassurance "In fact, she was very optimistic on the phone. She said that in situations like this, placing a child with people who already know and care about him is the best possible outcome. She's on our side, Danny. She's here to help, not to hurt."

Leroy's words, as reassuring as they were, did little to dispel the sudden, heavy cloud that had descended over the dinner table. The rest of the meal was eaten in a silence weighted by Wednesday's approach. Danny barely touched the rest of his food, his eyes downcast.

Tony was the most worried of all. He ate without tasting anything, his mind racing. A stranger was coming into their home to evaluate them, to evaluate Danny. The thought of Danny having to recount his story, of having to justify his presence here, was nauseating. The thought of

Danny being taken away curdled into something sickly in his gut. But he remained silent, knowing that showing his own panic would only make things worse for Danny.

When dinner was finally over, Tony and Danny cleared their plates and, without a word, returned to the quiet sanctuary of Tony's room. They didn't pick up the book. They didn't talk. Tony sat in the chair, and Danny sat on the bed, each lost in their own thoughts, the comfortable quiet from before the meal now replaced by a shared, anxious silence as they both processed what Leroy had said.

Danny lay on his side on the bed, curled into a tight ball, facing the wall. Tony, sitting in the chair across the room, could see the fine, uncontrollable tremor running through his slim frame. He was shaking. The news about the CPS visit had burrowed deep, reactivating a terror that was bone-deep.

Tony's heart felt like it was being squeezed in a vise. He wanted so badly to go to him, to sit on the bed, to put a hand on his back, to say something, *anything*, to make the shaking stop. But he was paralyzed. What if he made it worse? What if his touch was unwelcome? He had no idea how to offer comfort, no idea how to navigate this fragile, terrifying new landscape. So he just sat there, a helpless, silent guardian. The silence stretched for what felt like an hour. Finally, a small, muffled voice came from the bed.

"Tony?"

"Yeah? I'm here." Tony leaned forward, his heart leaping into his throat.

There was another long pause. Then, the request, so quiet and so vulnerable it almost broke Tony's heart.

"Can you... can you just lie here with me? On the bed. Not... not touching or anything. Just... here. So I know you're not going to leave."

"Yeah," he breathed, his voice thick with emotion. "Of course."

He stood up and quietly moved to the bed. He lay down on top of the covers, on his back, a careful foot of space between his body and Danny's curled form. He stared up at the ceiling, every nerve ending hyper-aware of the small, trembling boy beside him. He could feel the shuddered breaths Danny was trying to suppress, the tiny movements as his muscles clenched with anxiety. The helplessness gnawed at him, being close but unable to reach. He was right there, but he couldn't do anything.

Danny lay facing the wall, his own internal battle raging. The instinct to curl into a tighter ball, to protect himself, was overwhelming. But a stronger, deeper need was pushing back. The need for comfort. The need to not be alone in his terror. After a long, silent moment, he spoke again, his voice muffled by the pillow.

"Tony?"

"I'm here," Tony answered instantly, his voice a low rumble beside him.

"Is it okay...?" Danny's voice was a fragile whisper, full of a hesitation that tore at Tony's heart. "Am I allowed to... to touch your chest?"

Tony's throat tightened, and he couldn't form words. He just made a soft, affirmative sound, a choked noise of pure, desperate permission.

That was enough. Slowly, reluctantly, Danny fought against the urge to withdraw. He uncurled his body just enough to shift onto his back. Then, with a movement so hesitant it was almost painful to watch, he reached out. He didn't grab or cling. He simply laid his hand on Tony's chest, his fingers splayed out over the steady, solid beat of his heart. He then went a step further, turning onto his side and pressing his face into Tony's arm, seeking the simple, grounding comfort of his presence.

The moment Danny was that close, Tony's senses kicked into high gear. His anxiety, his fear, his overwhelming love—it all sharpened his awareness to a razor's edge. He caught Danny's scent, a faint, clean smell of his own soap mixed with something that was uniquely, achingly

Danny. He could feel the soft tickle of his shaggy brown hair against his bicep, the light weight of his hand rising and falling with every frantic beat of his own heart.

Every instinct, every fiber of his being, screamed at him to wrap his arms around the trembling boy, to pull him close and shield him from the world. It was an almost unbearable urge, a physical ache in his chest. But he resisted. He kept his arms rigidly at his sides, his hands clenched into fists on the mattress. He had promised patience. He had been given permission for a touch, not an embrace. He wouldn't break that trust.

He lay there, a statue of forced stillness, his body thrumming with a protective energy he had no outlet for. Through the thin fabric of his t-shirt, Danny could feel it. He could feel the rapid, heavy thump of Tony's heart under his palm, the rigid tension in his arm, the sheer, vibrating heat of him. He could sense the monumental effort it was taking for Tony not to pull him closer, and in that restraint, he felt safer than he had in his entire life.

CHAPTER 20

DESERVE THE TRUTH

Tony woke up slowly, pulled from a deep, heavy sleep not by an alarm, but by a subtle warmth against his side. He didn't move. He didn't even open his eyes at first, wanting to exist in this peaceful, pre-dawn moment for as long as possible. Sometime during the night, after the fear had finally receded and sleep had claimed them, they had shifted. Danny was no longer just a hand on his chest; he was curled against Tony's side, his head resting on his shoulder, one arm draped loosely across his stomach. Tony's own arm was around him, a protective, instinctual embrace he must have made in his sleep.

He could feel the soft, even puff of Danny's breath against his neck. The house was silent. He knew, without looking at the clock, that it was early. He also knew, with a certainty that settled deep in his bones, that neither of them were going to school today. The thought of the crowded hallways, the noise, the prying eyes, the sheer effort of pretending to be a normal student on a normal day, felt impossible. They were both so emotionally drained from the night before, from the looming threat of the CPS visit, that the idea of facing the outside world was nauseating. They needed a day. A quiet, safe day, just for the two of them, to just... be.

Carefully, so as not to wake Danny, Tony reached for his phone on the nightstand. The screen glowed, showing it was just after six-thirty. He knew his parents would have already left for work—his dad to the station, his mom to open up *Freddy's Place*. He opened his messages and typed out a quick text to his mom.

Hey Mom.

Feeling a little under the weather this morning. Danny too. Think we're gonna stay home from school today. Don't worry, we're fine. Just need a day to rest.

Love you.

He hit send, the message a small, necessary lie to buy them the peace they so desperately needed. He placed the phone back on the nightstand and settled back into the pillows, the weight of Danny a warm, comforting presence beside him. He closed his eyes, not to sleep, but just to exist in the quiet stillness of the morning, with Danny safe in his arms.

A little while later, Danny began to stir. His consciousness returned not with a jolt, but as a slow, peaceful tide. He became aware of the warmth first, a solid, steady heat pressed against his back and side. He could feel the slow, rhythmic rise and fall of a chest that was not his own, could hear the soft, steady beat of a heart that was not his. He slowly opened his eyes, his gaze landing on the faded logo of the t-shirt he was wearing. Tony's t-shirt. He realized Tony's arm was wrapped around him, holding him securely, and his own head was tucked into the space just under Tony's chin. He was completely enveloped.

The old Danny, the one conditioned by a lifetime of flinching, would have recoiled. He would have scrambled away, terrified of the proximity, of the vulnerability. But he didn't. He lay perfectly still, his body relaxed, his mind quiet. He didn't try to get out. He didn't feel trapped. Instead, for the first time in his life, he learned what it meant to be up close and personal with someone and feel completely, utterly safe. It wasn't just the locked room he'd always clung to. Safety was this—the solid weight of an arm, the steady sound of breathing, a peace that seeped into his bones. He closed his eyes again, not to sleep, but to savor the feeling, to commit it to memory.

And in that profound, unprecedented safety, another truth, one he had spent the last year violently suppressing, finally had the space to surface.

Lying there, with Tony's heart beating a steady rhythm against his ear, Danny realized with a startling, quiet clarity that he couldn't deny his own feelings anymore. The love he had for Tony, the love he had tried to kill, to starve, to pretend didn't exist, was still there. It had been there all along, buried under the pain and the fear. But in this moment, held and protected, it was the only thing that felt real. It was no longer a source of shame or a dangerous secret; it was just a simple, undeniable fact, as real and as steady as the rise and fall of Tony's chest beneath his cheek.

Tony drifted in that peaceful state for a while longer, his mind still half-submerged in sleep. But as the light in the room shifted from grey to a soft gold, he became more aware, his senses sharpening. He realized Danny's breathing had changed. It was still quiet, but it was the conscious, deliberate breath of someone who was awake.

Slowly, carefully, Tony opened his eyes. He found himself staring directly into Danny's wide, blue eyes, which were just inches from his own. Danny was awake. And he was watching him. A jolt of pure, unadulterated panic shot through Tony. His face flushed a deep, hot red. He had crossed a line. He had taken advantage of Danny's trust. He immediately tried to pull his arm back, to disentangle himself, the words tumbling out in a rushed, mortified whisper.

"Oh, man. I'm so sorry. I... I don't know how that happened. I must have moved in my sleep. I'm sorry." But as he tried to pull away, Danny's hand, which had been resting on his stomach, moved to his arm, holding him in place. The grip was surprisingly firm.

"Don't," Danny whispered, his voice still thick with sleep. "Don't apologize." He took a shaky breath, his gaze unwavering. "I liked it." Tony froze, his mind struggling to process the words. *He liked it?* The simple, honest admission was so unexpected it short-circuited his panic, leaving only a profound, buzzing confusion.

"You... you did?"

Danny just nodded, but then a familiar look of conflict clouded his features. His lips parted as if he wanted to say more, to explain, but the words wouldn't come. He looked down, a wave of frustration and shame washing over his face. He wanted to say it. He needed to say it. But a lifetime of silence had stolen his voice.

Tony watched him, his own heart aching with a sudden, intuitive understanding. He saw the struggle, the desperate need to communicate warring with the deep-seated fear. He knew, with that same terrifying clarity he'd felt in the library, exactly what Danny was trying to say. The realization was a dizzying, terrifying leap of faith. He took a slow, steadying breath, his voice dropping to a gentle, impossibly soft whisper.

"Is it the same for you?" he asked. Danny looked up, his eyes wide with a silent, pleading question. "What I said to you," Tony clarified, his heart pounding. "On Friday night. The real reason. Is it... is it the same for you?" He saw the answer in Danny's eyes, the raw, unguarded truth of it. He saw the silent, desperate nod Danny couldn't quite make. "Can I...?" Tony whispered, his voice thick with emotion. "Can I say it for you? Just so it's out there?"

Danny looked at him, his eyes shimmering with unshed tears. He gave a single, slow, deliberate nod. An almost imperceptible smile, fragile and hesitant, touched the corner of his lips. It was permission. Tony's heart felt like it was going to beat right out of his chest. He didn't say, *You love me too.* The words felt wrong, presumptuous. Instead, he decided to ask the only question that mattered, the same one he had asked in the library, the one that held the future of everything in its fragile balance.

"Can I kiss you?" he whispered, his voice thick with emotion. "Not someday. Not soon. Right now. Can I?"

Danny didn't answer with words. He didn't need to. His answer was in the way his grip on Tony's arm softened, in the way his eyes fluttered half-closed, in the way he tilted his chin up just a fraction of an inch. It was a silent, complete, and total surrender.Slowly, carefully, as if he were handling the most precious, fragile object in the universe, Tony leaned in. He closed the small distance between them, his own eyes closing as he finally, finally, pressed his lips against Danny's. The first touch was impossibly soft, a tentative question. It wasn't a kiss of passion or pent-up desire, but one of pure, reverent discovery. Danny's lips were even softer than Tony had imagined, and he tasted faintly of sleep and something uniquely, achingly sweet. For a second, that was all it was—a gentle, chaste press.

Then, Danny's hand, which was still resting on Tony's arm, slid up to his shoulder, his fingers curling into the fabric of his t-shirt, a silent plea for more. That small, instinctive movement was all the encouragement Tony needed. He deepened the kiss, and joy nearly bowled him over. He was so in love with this boy he felt like he couldn't contain it, like it was going to burst right out of him. But even in the overwhelming rush of affection, a small, clear voice in the back of his mind screamed at him to be careful. *Patience.* This was fresh. This was new. And it was terrifying for them both. He had to be Danny's safe place, not another storm. With a monumental effort of will, he kept the kiss gentle, pouring all of his love, his regret, and his promises into that one, simple, perfect connection, letting it be a vow of a new beginning.

He pulled back slowly, his forehead resting against Danny's. They were both breathing heavily, their eyes still closed. The silence in the room was no longer empty; it was humming with the energy of what had just passed between them.

Tony finally opened his eyes. Danny's were still closed, his face flushed, his lips slightly swollen. He looked beautiful. He looked peaceful.

"Maybe..." Tony's voice was a rough, unsteady whisper. "Maybe you want to... take a shower? I can get you some clean clothes." Danny's eyes fluttered open. He looked dazed, overwhelmed, but he gave a small, slow nod.

While Danny disappeared into the bathroom, the sound of the shower a welcome, grounding noise, Tony made his way downstairs. His mind was racing, a chaotic, replaying loop of the last ten minutes. *Did that just happen? Did I imagine it?* His lips still tingled from the kiss. He ran a hand through his hair, a dazed, disbelieving laugh escaping him. It was real. He walked into the kitchen, needing to do something, anything, with his hands. Breakfast. He could make them breakfast. He pulled a carton of eggs and a package of bacon from the fridge, his movements automatic. As he set the frying pan on the stove, his phone buzzed on the counter. It was a text from his mom.

Okay, mijo.

I understand. Get some rest, both of you. Let me know if you need anything.

Love you too.

Tony smiled. He typed a quick reply.

We will. Thanks, Mom.

He put the phone down and cracked an egg into the hot pan. The sizzle was a normal, everyday sound in a morning that was anything but. But just as a sense of calm began to settle over him, his mother's voice from the night before echoed in his head, sharp and clear.

"The longer you wait, the more you will hurt her. She is a good girl, and she deserves the truth."

Jessica.

The bliss from upstairs evaporated, replaced by a cold, sickening wave of guilt. He had just kissed Danny, a kiss that felt like the beginning of his real life, but he was still Jessica's boyfriend. He hadn't said a word to her. The thought of telling her, of seeing the hurt in her eyes, was a knot of pure panic in his stomach. She had been so good to him, so patient, and this was how he was repaying her. The future, which had felt like a beautiful, simple promise just a moment ago, was suddenly a tangled, complicated mess.

He stared at his phone on the counter, the sizzling of the eggs fading into the background. His thumb hovered over his contacts, over her name. He knew his mom was right. He knew the only way for anything to get resolved, for him to be the honest man he so desperately wanted to become, was for him to be the one to say something. He couldn't let her find out from someone else. He couldn't let this lie fester.

He took a deep, shaky breath, his stomach churning. He opened a new message, his fingers feeling clumsy and foreign. He stared at the blank screen for what felt like an eternity, his heart pounding. Then he typed.

Hey Jess.

Can we meet up this morning before you go to school? Maybe at the park? There's something important I need to talk to you about. Something you need to hear from me.

He read the message over and over, each word feeling like a small, sharp betrayal. He felt sick. But he knew he had to do it. With a final, grim resolve, he pressed send. Before he could even take a breath, his phone chimed. The reply was almost immediate.

K.

Tony's heart sank. The single, cold letter was worse than any angry paragraph. It was a wall of ice. He hastily finished cooking the eggs and bacon, his hands shaking slightly.

Just as he was sliding the food onto two plates, Danny appeared in the kitchen doorway. He had showered and was wearing a clean pair of Tony's jeans and another faded band t-shirt. The clothes were far too big for him, the sleeves of the shirt hanging down past his elbows, the jeans bunched up at his ankles. He looked small and lost in them, but also clean and safe. For Danny, the sight of eggs and bacon on the table—the first breakfast someone had made *for him* in a long time—was almost as grounding as the shower. Tony forced a smile, his own turmoil momentarily forgotten. He walked over to Danny and, without a second thought, leaned down and gave him a long, soft kiss on the cheek.

"Breakfast is ready," he said quietly.

He stepped back, his expression turning serious. He had to tell him.

"Hey," he started, his voice low. "I... I have to go do something this morning. Something I should have done a while ago." He took a breath. "I'm going to talk to Jessica. To tell her... everything." He looked at Danny, his eyes full of a new, vulnerable question. "Is that... are you okay with that?"

Danny looked at Tony, at the undisguised conflict and guilt on his face. The dizzying, wonderful feeling from upstairs was suddenly grounded by this messy, painful reality. He looked down at the plate of food Tony had made for him—a simple, tangible act of care. He thought about Jessica, about her kind eyes, about the way she always looked at Tony with such open affection. A pang of something—not jealousy, but a sad, empathetic ache—went through him. For him to have this, she had to lose something.

This was what being honest looked like. It wasn't easy. It hurt people. But after a year of lies and cruelty, it was the only thing he wanted. He wanted what was real, no matter how complicated. He looked back up at Tony, his blue eyes clear and steady. He gave a single, slow, deliberate nod.

"Yeah," he said softly. Then, with a quiet strength that surprised them both, he added, "You should." The simple, selfless affirmation hit Tony harder than any accusation could have. He felt a surge of gratitude so strong it almost knocked him off his feet. He just nodded, unable to speak.

"I have to... go change," he finally managed, his voice rough.

He rushed upstairs, his mind a whirlwind. He tore off the t-shirt he'd slept in and pulled on his uniform: a clean white t-shirt and his faded blue jeans. He ran a hand through his long hair, tying it back quickly. He was ready to leave, ready to get this over with, when he saw it. His black leather jacket was still draped over the back of his desk chair, right where he'd left it last night. He had forgotten it.

He grabbed it and headed back downstairs. Danny was sitting at the kitchen table, slowly eating the breakfast Tony had made for him. He looked up as Tony entered, a question in his eyes.

Tony walked over to him, the dread of the coming conversation with Jessica warring with the overwhelming need to connect with the boy in front of him one last time. He leaned down and placed another soft, lingering kiss on Danny's cheek.

"I'll be back as soon as I can," he whispered, his voice a low, earnest promise. "Okay?"

Danny just nodded, his cheek flushing a faint pink.But as Tony straightened and reached for the door, a small, gnawing fear stirred in Danny's chest—the old terror that someone could leave and never come back. He swallowed it down, clinging to Tony's promise like a lifeline.

The walk to the park was the longest ten minutes of Tony's life. The morning sun was bright, the air was cool, but he felt none of it. All he could feel was the frantic, sick thumping of his own heart and the cold dread coiling in his stomach. His mind was racing, a chaotic slideshow of worst-case scenarios. What if Jessica hates him after this? What if she screams at him? What if she just looks at him with that disappointed expression he knows so well, the one that's a thousand times worse than anger?

He was expecting the worst reaction possible, and he knew he deserved it. Jessica had been with him for over a year. A whole year of his moods, his anger, his secrets. She had seen the meanest, ugliest parts of him, and still, she'd never flinched. And he was about to repay all of that loyalty by shattering her heart.

His steps felt like they were encased in cement, each one heavier than the last. The familiar swing set and the old oak tree where they'd had their first real date came into view, and the memories were a fresh wave of guilt. He saw her then, a solitary figure sitting on their bench, her back to him. He took a deep, shaky breath, steeling himself for the conversation. He could do this. He had to do this.

But as he got closer, his stomach dropped. She wasn't alone. Sitting on the grass a few feet away, looking just as grim and expectant, were Marko and Jamal.

Fuck.

This wasn't just a breakup. It was an ambush.

CHAPTER 21

HYPOCRITE

The sight of his friends flanking Jessica like sentinels stopped Tony cold. His first instinct was to turn around, to run back to the safety of his house, back to the quiet understanding in Danny's eyes. But he couldn't. He had sent the text. He had made the promise to his mom, to Danny, and to himself. He was done running.

He squared his shoulders, the worn leather of his jacket a familiar but flimsy shield, and forced his cement-block feet to move forward. Each step scraped against the cracked asphalt, the faint squeak of his sneakers sounding too loud in the heavy morning air. As he approached, the three of them turned to face him. Jessica remained seated on the bench, her hands clasped tightly in her lap, her expression unreadable. Her knuckles were white around each other, like she was holding herself together by force. Marko stood with his arms crossed, a look of grim, protective anger on his face. Jamal just looked sad, leaning against the tree as if he didn't want to be there at all.

"What is this?" Tony asked, his voice rough as he stopped a few feet away from them. "I asked to talk to Jess."

"And we're here to make sure you do," Marko said, his voice low and hard. "After the way you've been acting, we're not letting you corner her by herself."

"Marko," Jessica said, her voice quiet but firm, never taking her eyes off Tony. "It's okay." She looked at her boyfriend, at the boy she loved, and saw a stranger. The anger was gone, yes, but it had been replaced by a haunted, guilty look that was almost worse. "You said you had something to tell me."

Tony's gaze flickered from Marko's hostility to Jamal's quiet disappointment, and finally landed on Jessica. He couldn't do this in front of them. He couldn't shatter her heart with an audience.

"Can we... can we talk alone?" he asked, his voice pleading.

"No," Marko cut in. "Whatever you have to say, you can say it in front of us."

"Marko, please," Tony said, his own frustration starting to build.

"It's okay, Tony," Jessica repeated, a profound sadness in her voice. "They already know, don't they?" It wasn't a question. "They saw you yesterday. The way you looked at him. The way you defended him." She finally looked away, her gaze settling on a crack in the pavement. Her foot tapped once, a nervous stutter against the concrete, before going still. "I'm not stupid. I just... I needed to hear it from you."

Her words disarmed him completely. The fight went out of him, leaving only the cold, heavy weight of the truth. He owed her that. He owed her everything.

He took a deep, shaky breath, the words tasting like poison and freedom all at once.

"I'm sorry, Jess," he began, his voice cracking. "I am so, so sorry. For everything." He finally met her eyes, forcing himself to hold her gaze. "It's not... it's not you. It's never been you. It's me."

"Don't," she whispered, a single tear breaking free and tracing a path down her cheek. "Don't give me that line, Tony. Just... be honest. For once."

The command, as gentle as it was, hit him like a physical blow. He closed his eyes for a second, then opened them, stripped of all his defenses.

"I'm gay, Jessica," he said, the words clear and undeniable in the quiet morning air. "And I'm in love with him. I'm in love with Danny."

The confession hung in the air, stark and brutal. Jessica flinched as if he had slapped her, a small, wounded sound escaping her lips. She quickly pressed her hand to her mouth, stifling a sob. Marko took a step forward, his expression hardening, but Jamal put a hand on his arm, holding him back.

The four of them stood in a tableau of raw, fractured emotion. The silence was deafening, broken only by the distant sound of a lawnmower and the faint metallic rattle of the chain-link fence as a breeze pushed through it, Jessica's breath catching sharp against the stillness. It was Jamal who finally broke the spell.

"Let's... let's not do this here," he said, his voice a low, calming presence. He gestured with his head toward the nearby basketball court, empty on a Tuesday morning. "Come on."

No one argued. They walked in a silent, funereal procession to the court. Marko grabbed a stray basketball, needing something to do with his hands, and started shooting lazy, aimless free throws. Each bounce against the pavement was a gavel strike, each clang of the rim another verdict. Jamal leaned against the chain-link fence. Jessica sat on the bottom bleacher, wrapping her arms around herself. Tony stood in the middle of it all, feeling like he was on trial. He had to explain. He had to make them understand.

"It's... it's not new," he began, his voice rough with unshed tears. He looked at them, at the friends he was about to lose. "It's been my whole life. And for my whole life, I've had my Tía Isabella's voice in my head, telling me it was a sickness, that it was something to be ashamed of. And I was a coward. I believed her." He started pacing the painted key, the words tumbling out in a rush of long-suppressed truth. "So I got angry.

I built this... this wall around myself. Being mean, being a prick... it was easier than facing the truth. And Danny... he was the biggest threat to that wall. So I aimed all of it at him." He stopped, running a hand through his hair. "And then I saw him again last week, really saw him, and something just... broke. I couldn't do it anymore. I couldn't be that person." He looked at them, his expression pleading. "I know it doesn't make it right. I know it was messed up."

He glanced at Jamal, a silent acknowledgment passing between them.

"Friday night... he was in trouble. He ended up at some club downtown, and I had to go get him out of there." He didn't say how he knew. He wouldn't put that on Jamal. "This whole weekend... it just put everything into perspective." He swallowed hard, the sound loud in his own ears. The ball swished through the net. Marko caught it, then turned, his face a mask of conflicted emotion.

"So you're gay," he said, the words coming out flat. "Okay. Hell, I don't care about that, man." He bounced the ball once, hard. "But the way you treated him... for almost a year, you made his life a living hell. Because you were scared? That is the messed up part, Tony. You were a hypocrite."

"I know," Tony said, his voice barely a whisper. He looked at Marko, his own shame laid bare. "You're right. It wasn't right. It was cruel. And I have to live with that." Jessica had been listening silently, wiping away her tears with the sleeve of her sweater. She finally stood up, her movements slow and deliberate. The sound of the bleacher creaking under her weight was the only thing that marked her decision to rise. The boys all turned to look at her.

"The part that hurts, Tony," she said, her voice trembling but clear, "is that I knew. I always told you that the anger, the meanness... that it wasn't the real you. I defended you. I stood by you, waiting for the boy I knew was underneath to come back." She gave a small, heartbreaking laugh. It cracked halfway through, jagged and raw. "I guess I was right. He was in there. He just... he wasn't for me."

She took a step closer, her eyes full of a deep, profound sadness. "You used me, Tony. As a shield. As a cover. And that's what I can't forgive. Not right now."

"Jess, I..." Tony started, but she held up a hand.

"No," she said, her voice gaining strength. "I need you to listen. I'm hurt. And I'm angry. But I'm not going to hate you." She pressed a trembling hand against her chest, grounding herself, looking at Marko, then at Jamal. "And neither are they." She looked back at Tony. "But we can't... I can't be here right now. Good bye, Tony." The words, as much as he had expected them, hit him like a physical blow. He just nodded, unable to speak. "And Marko is right," she continued, her gaze unwavering. "You being gay isn't the issue. But you have a lot of work to do. On yourself. And on making things right with Danny. He's the one you really hurt." She turned and started to walk away, then stopped and looked back at him one last time. Her voice dropped to almost a whisper, but it carried like a verdict. "For what it's worth," she said softly, "I'm glad you're not hiding anymore."

And with that, she walked off the court and out of the park, leaving a stunned silence in her wake. Jamal pushed off the fence.

"She's right, man," he said quietly. "About all of it." He looked at Marko, who was just staring at the ground, bouncing the basketball slowly. "We're your brothers, Tony. But this is... this is a lot. We need some time."

Marko finally stopped bouncing the ball. He looked at Tony, the anger in his eyes replaced by a deep, conflicted hurt.

"Just... fix it, man," he said, his voice rough. "Fix yourself."

He tossed the basketball to Tony, a final, symbolic gesture. Then he and Jamal turned and walked away, leaving Tony standing alone in the middle of the court, the basketball in his hands, the truth finally out in the open, and his entire world completely, irrevocably changed.

Tony didn't try to pursue them. He didn't try to justify his actions or beg them to stay. He just stood there on the cracked asphalt, the rough texture of the basketball a grounding, familiar presence in his hands. He watched them go, the two best friends he'd ever had, and the girl who had loved him more than he deserved. He didn't feel angry. He didn't even feel sad, not yet. He just felt... empty. Stripped bare.

They were right. All of them. Every single word they had said was the truth. He had been a coward, a hypocrite, and he had used Jessica as a shield. Hearing it out loud, seeing the pain it had caused, was a brutal but necessary mirror. He took a good, hard look inward, at the wreckage he had made of his own life and the lives of the people he cared about.

"Fix it, man. Fix yourself." Marko's words echoed in his head. He knew what he had to do. He had to fix things, not for them, but for himself. For Danny.

He dropped the basketball, letting it bounce away with a hollow, lonely sound. He began the walk home. The short distance back to his house felt infinitely longer than the walk to the park. His feet, which had felt like cement blocks on the way there, now felt disconnected from his body, moving on autopilot. His mind was a battlefield. He replayed the entire conversation, every pained look from Jessica, every ounce of disappointment from Marko and Jamal. But underneath the shame, a new, more urgent anxiety was building. How was he going to explain this to Danny? How could he put into words that the first step toward their new beginning had meant the complete destruction of his old life? He had just left Danny in a state of fragile, hopeful peace. Now he had to return, trailing the ghosts of a broken relationship and two fractured friendships behind him. He just prayed Danny would understand.

When he finally reached his front door, he hesitated, his hand hovering over the knob. He took a deep breath, composed himself, and walked inside.

Danny was in the living room, curled up on the couch under the afghan, reading. He looked up the moment Tony walked in, his expression open and questioning. The peaceful, domestic scene was a stark, painful contrast to the emotional warzone Tony had just left. Tony dropped his keys into the bowl by the door.

"Hey," he said, his voice sounding hollow and foreign in his own ears. Danny sat up, sensing the shift in the atmosphere immediately.

"Is... is everything okay?"

Tony walked over and sank onto the opposite end of the couch, a chasm of space between them. He couldn't bring himself to look at Danny. He just stared at his own hands. "We broke up," he said, the words flat and dead.

"Jessica and I. And... Marko and Jamal, they need some space. They're... pissed. And confused."

He finally risked a glance at Danny. And he saw it. The flicker of hope in Danny's eyes from this morning was extinguished, instantly replaced by that familiar, soul-crushing look of guilt. Danny's shoulders hunched. He curled in on himself, making himself smaller, his gaze dropping to the floor. He didn't say a word, but his entire body screamed, *This is my fault. I did this. I ruined your life.*

The sight of that look, of Danny immediately internalizing the blame for a mess that Tony alone had created, snapped something in him. The emptiness he felt from the park was instantly replaced by a fierce, protective clarity.

"Hey," he said, his voice sharp, commanding Danny's attention. Danny flinched but looked up. "No. Don't you dare." Tony moved across the couch, closing the distance between them. He knelt on the floor in front of Danny, forcing him to meet his gaze. "Do not do that," he said, his voice low and intense, but gentle "Do not blame yourself for this. This is not on you. Do you hear me?"

Danny just stared, his eyes wide and uncertain.

"This," Tony said, gesturing vaguely toward the front door, toward the world outside, "is the mess *I* made. I lied to them. I lied to Jessica for over a year. I used her, just like she said. I was a coward. What happened today... it's just the consequences of my own actions. It has absolutely nothing to do with you." He took a breath, his expression softening. "Danny, look at me." He waited until Danny's eyes focused on his. "You are not the reason my life is falling apart. You're the reason it's finally starting to make sense. You're the reason I'm finally being honest. Don't you get it? This... this had to happen. For me to be... for us to be..." He trailed off, the words still too new, too fragile. "This was the price. And I'm willing to pay it."

Leroy's world was a sea of monotonous paperwork. He sat at his cluttered desk in the middle of the bustling station, the phone cradled between his ear and shoulder, trying to finalize a report on a weekend burglary. The emotional chaos of the past few days felt a million miles away, replaced by the mundane, procedural reality of his job.

"...no, the inventory list is still pending," he said into the receiver, his eyes scanning the form in front of him. "I'll follow up with the homeowners this afternoon. Yeah. Okay. Thanks." He hung up the phone with a sigh, rubbing his tired eyes.But the truth was, every word he said on the call felt hollow. His mind was nowhere near the burglary. It was at home, circling the thought of the two boys who'd skipped school. It was on his son—Tony, wound tight and secretive, clearly carrying something heavy—and the quiet, fragile kid under his roof who looked like he might break if the wrong wind blew. Leroy's badge work demanded focus, but his father's mind kept drifting back to them. Just as he was reaching for his cold coffee, the phone on his desk rang again. He snatched it up, his voice the clipped, professional tone of a busy cop. "Guzman."

"Sergeant," the voice of the officer at the front desk came through the line. "You've got a call from county lockup. The detainee, Sanders? She's requesting to see you." Leroy froze, his hand tightening on the receiver. Dina. Of all the things he had to deal with today, this was the last one he wanted. His stomach immediately twisted into a tight, acid-filled knot. He had hoped he wouldn't have to see her again, that he could just let the system handle it from here. But a direct request was different. He couldn't ignore it.

"Did she say why?" Leroy asked, his voice strained.

"No, sir. Just that it's urgent and she'll only talk to you."

Leroy closed his eyes, a wave of pure dread washing over him.

"Alright," he said, his voice heavy with resignation. "Tell them I'm on my way."

He hung up the phone and pushed his chair back, the legs scraping loudly against the floor. He grabbed his keys from the desk, the familiar jingle doing nothing to soothe his frayed nerves. The walk to his patrol vehicle in the station's lot was a long one. Every step was a fresh wave of dread.

He slid into the driver's seat and just sat there for a moment, the engine off, the car silent. The idea of seeing Dina again hollowed him out. He knew he couldn't just walk in like this—unarmored. He needed caffeine, he needed to breathe, and he needed Maria to know where he was headed. He pulled out his phone and sent a quick text.

Dina asked to see me. Heading to the lockup now. I'll call you after.

He started the car, the engine rumbling to life. He pulled out of the parking lot and headed not toward the county jail, but toward a small, 24-hour coffee shop a few blocks away that cops frequented for its strong, black, no-nonsense coffee. He needed it.

On the way, he took a detour, a morbid curiosity pulling him down a familiar street. He passed by Dina's old house. It was a grim sight.

The front door, splintered and broken from the battering ram, was now covered with a large, ugly sheet of plywood. The windows were boarded up. A bright yellow sign from the city was plastered near the door, its official language declaring the property condemned and uninhabitable. More citations were taped nearby, fluttering in the breeze. The place looked less like a house than a crime scene left to rot. To Leroy, it felt like a tombstone marking the death of a family.

The sight settled a cold, heavy stone in his gut. He turned away and continued toward the coffee shop. His mind was already a frantic, replaying loop of what Dina might say, what she might do. Would she scream? Threaten him? Try to manipulate him with old memories? Plead? He could picture it all—her voice too sharp, or too sweet, or too broken, each one another way of pulling him back in. The one good thing, if you could call it that, was that she would be sober. But she would also be detoxing, which could be even worse. The desperation, the anger, the raw, frayed-nerve volatility of a body screaming for a substance it wasn't getting—he'd seen it a hundred times. It was never pretty. He pulled into the coffee shop, his hands tight on the wheel, feeling like he was just delaying his own execution.

CHAPTER 22

SECRET LANGUAGE

"This was the price. And I'm willing to pay it." Tony's words hung in the quiet living room, a raw and desperate vow. Danny stared at him, at the fierce, protective sincerity burning in his eyes. For the first time, the crushing weight of guilt that had settled on his shoulders began to lift. He saw the truth in Tony's expression—the pain, the regret, but also the unwavering resolve. He finally, truly, believed him. This wasn't his fault. This was the consequence of a lie that had festered for far too long, and Tony was the one who had finally lanced the wound.

He didn't have the words to express the complex swirl of emotions inside him—the sorrow for Tony's loss, the gratitude for his sacrifice, the terrifying, fragile hope for their future. So he did the only thing he could. He reached out, his hand trembling slightly, and placed it on Tony's knee. It was a small, simple gesture of acceptance, of solidarity. A quiet acknowledgment that they were in this together now.

Tony's entire body seemed to relax at the touch, the tension draining out of him in a long, shuddering breath. He placed his own hand over Danny's, his fingers lacing through his. They stayed like that for a long moment, kneeling on the floor in the quiet house, the unspoken wreckage of Tony's old life settling around them like dust.

"What do we do now?" Danny whispered, the question not about the next five minutes, but about the rest of their lives. Tony looked at him, a small, tired smile touching his lips.

"Now," he said softly, "we just... be."

The rest of the day unfolded in a slow, quiet rhythm. They ate the breakfast Tony had made, sitting in a comfortable silence at the kitchen table. Danny, noticing the hollowed-out look in Tony's eyes from his confrontation at the park, surprised him by asking,

"Are *you* okay?" The question, a simple act of reciprocated care, was so unexpected it almost made Tony choke up. He just nodded, unable to speak, and a new, more balanced quiet settled between them.

Afterward, they drifted back to the living room and ended up on the couch, watching some old, mindless action movie from the 80's that was playing on TV. At first, they sat on opposite ends, a respectable distance between them. But as the movie roared on with car chases and cheesy one-liners, the space slowly shrank. Tony stretched an arm out along the back of the couch. A little while later, Danny, lulled by the warmth of the house and the mindless noise, leaned his head tentatively against Tony's shoulder. Tony's arm came down to rest around him, a simple, peaceful intimacy that felt both brand new and as old as time itself.

When the movie ended and the credits rolled, the quiet of the house rushed back in, and with it, the anxieties of the real world. Tony could feel a slight tremor start in Danny's shoulder and knew exactly what he was thinking about.

"Hey," Tony said softly, breaking the silence. "About tomorrow. With Ms. Jenkins." Danny tensed, but didn't pull away.

"You don't have to do it alone," Tony continued, his voice a low, steady rumble. "I'll be right there. My mom and dad, too. We're all in this with you. You just have to tell the truth. That's it."

"What if..." Danny's voice was a muffled whisper against Tony's shirt. "What if she doesn't believe us? What if she thinks... I should go somewhere else? To a foster home?" It was his deepest fear, spoken aloud for the first time. The words themselves seemed to terrify him. Tony's arm tightened around him, a firm, protective gesture.

"That is not going to happen," he said, his voice leaving no room for doubt. "I will not let that happen. My dad won't. This is your home now. Period." They sat in silence for another moment, Danny absorbing the certainty in Tony's voice. He seemed to relax, the trembling subsiding. "After this is over," Tony said, his voice softer now, more hesitant. "After the stuff with CPS is settled... we'll have to figure out... us. At school. What that looks like."

He felt Danny stiffen immediately. The idea of a public identity, of being a "we" for everyone to see, was clearly a terrifying one.

"I... I can't think about that right now, Tony," Danny whispered, pulling away slightly to look at him, his eyes wide with a familiar, hunted look. "It's too much. Everyone... staring. Judging." Tony saw the panic on his face and immediately kicked himself. He was pushing too fast. He had promised patience.

"Hey, hey, you're right," he said quickly, his voice gentle. "I'm sorry. It's too soon. Forget I said anything." He met Danny's gaze, his own expression full of earnest reassurance. "One day at a time. Just us. That's all that matters." He paused, an idea forming in his mind, a potential solution. "But... what if we had a signal?" he asked softly. "Something just for us. That no one else would get." Danny looked at him, his expression cautious and confused. Tony lifted his hand and, with his thumb, gently tapped the space over his own heart twice.

Tap. Tap.

"This," he said, his voice a low, intimate whisper. "If you're ever across the room, or in the hallway at school, and you see me do this... it just means I'm thinking of you. It means I wish I could be holding your hand, or... you know, be your shield." He felt his own face flush, but he held Danny's gaze. "It's a way for me to tell you, without saying anything. And you don't have to do anything back. Ever. But... if you ever felt the same, and you wanted to... you could do it back. And I'd know."

For Danny, the idea landed like something sacred. It wasn't just a gesture—it was a hiding place in plain sight, a private tether in a world that always seemed to want to strip him bare. He imagined it, seeing Tony across a crowded hallway and catching that *tap-tap* meant for him alone, and the panic that had gripped his chest loosened.

He let the idea settle in the quiet space between them. It was an offering of a secret language, a private world that could exist in the middle of a crowded room, with all the power to participate, or not, resting entirely with Danny. He stared at Tony, at the open, vulnerable look on his face. He thought about it—the idea of a silent message, a connection that no one else could see or judge. The panic that had seized him just a moment ago began to recede, replaced by a sense of quiet wonder. It was the most thoughtful, considerate thing anyone had ever offered him.

Slowly, a small, grateful smile touched his lips. He gave a single, solid nod and leaned his head back against Tony's shoulder, the last of the tension draining out of him. Tony held him for a moment longer, his heart swelling with relief. Then the new, better idea sparked in his mind.

"Come on," he said, his voice brighter. "I want to show you something."

He led a curious Danny out the back door and into the garage. The air was cool and smelled of gasoline, sawdust, and old memories. In the corner, under a dusty, faded blue tarp, was a large, lumpy shape. "My dad and I were talking about it last night," Tony said as he walked over and grabbed a corner of the tarp. "It's been sitting here for years."

With a single, dramatic pull, he yanked the tarp off. Underneath sat a vintage Triumph motorcycle. It was a beautiful, classic machine, but it was in a state of long neglect. The chrome was dull and pitted, the black leather of the seat was cracked, and a fine layer of dust covered everything.

"It was my dad's, from before I was born," Tony said, a note of reverence in his voice. "He always said he was going to fix it up 'someday'." He ran a hand over the dusty fuel tank. "I told him I wanted to be the one to do it. To get it running again." He turned to look at Danny, a hopeful, nervous energy in his eyes. "I don't really know what I'm doing," he admitted with a small laugh. "I was thinking... maybe... you could help me?"

It was an offering. Not of a complicated future, but of a simple, shared project. Something they could build, together. Danny circled the bike slowly, his eyes wide with a genuine, unforced curiosity. He ran a hand over the cracked leather of the seat, a thoughtful expression on his face.

"My dad loved bikes," Danny said quietly, the memory surfacing easily. "He always..... wanted an old Indian, but he said a Triumph..... was a close second." Danny's voice softened further, almost to himself. "He used to say a bike was freedom on two wheels." He crouched down, peering at the engine block. "He showed me some stuff once. How to clean a carburetor... how to check the spark plugs." He looked up at Tony, a flicker of something—not quite confidence, but a quiet competence—in his eyes. "I remember.... some of it." Tony felt a grin spread across his face, pure and uncomplicated.

"You're kidding me. That's... that's perfect."

"We should clean it first," Danny said, his voice gaining a bit of strength. "See what we're..... really working with..... under all this dust."

And so they did. They found old rags and a bucket of soapy water. They worked in a comfortable, easy silence, side by side. Tony tackled the chrome fenders, scrubbing away years of grime to reveal the bright, shining metal underneath. Danny, with a surprising gentleness, wiped down the engine, his small hands carefully navigating the intricate web of pipes and wires.

Every so often, Maria's laughter from some old memory would drift through Tony's head, and he glanced at Danny—this boy who was already weaving himself into those memories without even knowing it.

They didn't talk about their feelings, or about school, or about the looming dread of Wednesday. They just worked. And as the afternoon sun streamed through the dusty garage window, illuminating the slow transformation of the forgotten machine, it felt like they were doing more than just cleaning a motorcycle. They were polishing away the tarnish of the last year, uncovering the bright, solid thing that had always been there, waiting underneath. They were, piece by piece, starting to build something new.

The sun began to dip lower, painting the garage in long, orange shadows. The air grew cooler. Tony, wiping a smudge of grease from his forehead with the back of his hand, glanced up at the old clock on the garage wall.

"Whoa," he said, his voice full of surprise. "It's almost six. I didn't realize how late it was. Mom's probably going to be home soon."

Danny stopped his careful polishing of a spoke and looked at the clock, his own eyes widening. The entire afternoon had melted away without him even noticing. He looked from the clock back to the motorcycle. It was still a long way from being rideable, but it was no longer a dusty relic. The chrome gleamed, the engine block was a clean, dark gray, and the frame was free of its grimy shroud. It looked like a machine full of potential again. He felt a small, unfamiliar flicker of pride.

"We got a lot done," he said, his voice quiet but pleased.

"Yeah," Tony said, a wide, genuine smile on his face as he looked at their handiwork. He then looked at Danny, who was standing in a beam of golden, late-afternoon light, a smudge of grease on his cheek. In that moment, with the satisfaction of a shared accomplishment between them, Tony's heart felt so full it was almost painful. He didn't think. He just acted. He lifted his hand and, with his thumb, gently tapped the space over his own heart twice.

Tap. Tap.

Danny saw the gesture. His breath hitched. He knew what it meant. It was their signal. *I'm thinking of you. I wish I could be holding your hand.* A soft, shy blush crept up his neck. He looked at Tony, at the open, hopeful, and slightly nervous look on his face. He thought about returning the signal, but it still felt too bold, too public, even in the privacy of the garage. Instead, a real, genuine smile spread across his face, reaching his eyes for the first time all day. It was a small, quiet thing, but it was brilliant. Then, he took a single, deliberate step closer to Tony, closing the distance between them, a silent answer that was clearer than any gesture.

The sound of the minivan pulling into the driveway broke the spell. Maria was home. She walked through the front door with a weary sigh, dropping her purse and a large, flat pizza box onto the kitchen counter. It had been a long, quiet day at the restaurant, a day spent mostly worrying about the two boys she had left at home. She hadn't felt like cooking, so she'd had the guys at the restaurant make up a couple of large pizzas for dinner. Simple. Easy.

She came into the house to find it empty and quiet. The living room showed clear signs of their lazy day—the afghan was still crumpled on the couch where they had been sitting, and two empty glasses sat on the coffee table. She smiled. It was a good sign. She walked into the kitchen and saw the remnants of their breakfast—two plates in the drying rack, the faint smell of bacon still in the air. But there was also a mess of crumbs on the counter and an empty milk carton sitting out.

"Antonio Guzman!" she called out, her voice a familiar, maternal mix of affection and exasperation. "Come clean up your mess!" She opened the back door, expecting to see him in the yard, but there was no one there. "Tony!"

The door to the garage creaked open, and Tony emerged, blinking in the evening light. He had a smudge of grease on his cheek and was wiping his hands on an old rag. He looked happier and more at peace than she had seen him in years. A moment later, Danny appeared behind him, looking equally grimy but with a small, shy smile on his face. Maria's eyebrows shot up in surprise.

"The garage?" she said, a curious smile playing on her own lips. "What have you two been up to in there?"

Tony's face lit up with a boyish, unrestrained excitement she hadn't seen since he was a little kid.

"You gotta see, Mom! Come on!" He started toward her, his hands outstretched as if to cover her eyes for a surprise.

"Ah, ah, ah!" Maria said, playfully slapping his grimy hands away. "Don't you dare touch me with those hands, Antonio. I just got home."

She laughed and followed him into the garage, Danny trailing shyly behind. Her eyes adjusted to the dim light, and then she saw it. Leroy's old Triumph, uncovered and gleaming, the centerpiece of the cluttered space. A wave of pure, potent nostalgia washed over her, so strong it almost took her breath away.

"Oh, my God," she whispered, walking slowly toward the bike. She ran a hand over the newly polished chrome of the fuel tank, her fingers tracing the iconic logo. "I haven't seen this bike out from under that tarp in... fifteen years?" She looked at the two boys, a wistful, faraway look in her eyes. "Before you were born, Tony," she said, her voice soft with memory, "Your father and I, we went everywhere on this thing. We rode it up the coast one summer, all the way to the mountains. We slept in cheap motels and ate at greasy diners. I'd hold on to him so tight, the whole world just a blur of green and blue." A small, sad smile touched her lips.

"We were so young. We thought we had all the time in the world." She turned back to them, a playful, teasing glint in her eye. "Truth be told," she said, lowering her voice to a conspiratorial whisper, "this bike is half the reason I fell in love with your father. A man who can handle a machine like this... it's a very attractive quality." Maria's laughter filled the dusty garage, a warm, welcome sound that broke the nostalgic spell. "Alright, you two," she said, clapping her hands together. "Go wash up. Both of you look like you wrestled a chimney sweep. Pizza's on the counter." She looked pointedly at her son. "And after we eat, that kitchen better be spotless."

As the boys headed back toward the house, their shoulders almost brushing, Maria lingered for a moment. She was about to follow them when her phone chimed in her pocket. She pulled it out, expecting a message from one of her sisters or a notification from the restaurant's supply company. Instead, she saw a text from Leroy, sent hours ago. Her smile faded as she read the words:

Dina asked to see me. Heading to the lockup now. I'll call you after.

Her hands shook as she slid the phone back into her pocket, her heart pounding too fast. The warmth of the garage drained away, replaced by a cold certainty: whatever Dina wanted from Leroy, it would not be simple. And it would not be safe. *What could Dina possibly want?* Was she trying to fight the charges, to manipulate him, to spin some story about Danny and CPS? Or was it a desperate plea for help, a promise to get clean that they had heard and been burned by so many times before? Whatever it was, it couldn't be good.

Just as the cold knot of panic tightened in her stomach, her phone began to ring, vibrating in her hand. The screen lit up with his name: *Leroy.* She answered on the first ring, her voice tight with a mixture of relief and anxiety.

"Leroy? I just got your text. The one from this morning. Is everything okay?" There was a long, weary sigh on the other end of the line, the sound of a man who had been through a war.

"Maria," Leroy's voice was rough, drained of all its usual strength. *"I'm on my way home now. It's... it's been a long day."*

CHAPTER 23

BROKEN

The drive to the county lockup was a familiar route, one Leroy had taken hundreds of times over his career, usually with a suspect cuffed in the back. But this time was different. This time, he was the one who felt like a prisoner, heading toward a sentence he had to endure. The coffee he'd picked up was already cold, sitting untouched in the cup holder, its bitter aroma doing nothing to cut through the sour taste of dread in his mouth.

His mind was a relentless interrogation room, and he was both the questioner and the suspect. *Why does she want to see me?* The question played on a loop, each repetition spawning a new, more venomous possibility. Was this a desperate plea for help, a tearful promise to get clean that he knew, from bitter experience, would be broken before she even made bail? Or was it a threat? Was she going to try to spin some lie, accuse him of having a vendetta, of setting her up, in a last-ditch effort to poison the case with CPS? The thought of her using their shared history, their friendship with Rick, as a weapon made his stomach churn.

He gripped the steering wheel, his knuckles white. His anger, a slow, simmering fire that had been burning for years, was now an undeniable inferno. He thought of what he wanted to say to her, the words he should have said long ago. He wanted to hold up a picture of the boy he had seen on Friday night—terrified, alone, and hiding in the filth of a nightclub bathroom—and scream.

"Look at what you did! Look at what you've done to him!"

How could she have let it get this bad? How did the vibrant, laughing woman from his wedding day, the one who had been like a sister to Maria since high school, transform into this? She wasn't just a neglectful mother anymore. She had become the monster that haunted Danny's every waking moment and his sleepless nights. She was the reason a boy who used to grin with a missing tooth and declare he liked to live dangerously now moved through the world like a ghost, terrified of his own shadow. The anger was so potent, so righteous, it almost choked him. He knew he couldn't go in there like this. A hot-headed, grieving friend couldn't conduct this interview. A cop had to. He had to be cold, detached, and professional. He had to be a wall she couldn't manipulate or break down.

He pulled into the visitor's parking lot of the county jail, the imposing concrete building looming in front of him. He killed the engine and sat for a long moment in the sudden silence, the setting sun glinting off his windshield. He took a deep, steadying breath, pushing the anger down, locking it away behind years of training. He was here to do a job. To close a chapter. To keep a promise. With a final, grim resolve, he got out of the car and walked toward the entrance, ready to face the ghost of his friend.

The inside of the lockup was a sterile, cold hell of fluorescent lights, echoing footsteps, and the clanging of steel doors. Leroy moved through it on autopilot, his badge getting him through checkpoints, his face a grim, unreadable mask. An officer escorted him to a small, windowless interview room. "She's on her way," the officer said, before leaving Leroy alone in the suffocating silence.

A moment later, the door opened again. Two guards brought Dina in. And Leroy's professional mask shattered.

The woman they pushed into the chair opposite him was a horrific caricature of the person he had arrested on Saturday. The angry, defiant Dina was gone, replaced by a broken, brutalized shell. One of her eyes was swollen, completely shut, a grotesque, purple and black mess. Her bottom lip was split and puffy, dried blood crusted in the corner of her mouth. The bruises mottling her skin were fresh, their colours angry and violent. The attack hadn't been days ago; it had been yesterday. This was a "warning," delivered with brutal efficiency.

He sank into the chair opposite her, his mind struggling to process the sight. He had come in here ready for a fight, armed with his anger and his resolve. But the woman in front of him was already defeated, already punished in a way he never could have imagined. This is what happens, a cold, hard voice in the back of his mind whispered. This is what happens when you lay a finger on a child. Dina didn't look up at first. She just sat there, trembling, her cuffed hands shaking on the metal table. When she finally lifted her head, her one good eye was wide with a raw, animal terror. The fight was gone, the defiance extinguished. All that was left was fear.

"Leroy," she rasped, her voice a broken, painful croak through her split lip. "You... you have to help me." Leroy just stared, the carefully constructed wall of professionalism crumbling inside him. "They know," she whispered, a tear leaking from her good eye and tracing a path through the grime on her cheek. "They know why I'm in here. They told me this was just a warning. That next time... next time they'll kill me." The words were a torrent of pure, unadulterated terror. "You're a cop. You have to do something. Get me into solitary. Protective custody. Anything. Please, Leroy. They're going to kill me." She leaned forward, the desperation making her bold. "This is your fault," she hissed, a flicker of the old, manipulative Dina surfacing through the fear. "You put me in here. You did this to me. You owe me." Leroy found his voice, and it was colder than he could have imagined.

"The only thing I owe," he said, his words like chips of ice, "is a promise to a dead man. A promise to keep his son safe. From you." Dina flinched back as if he had struck her. The manipulation had failed. She had one card left to play.

"Then take him," she said, the words a desperate, final bargain. "You want him? Take him. I won't fight you. I'll sign the papers. I'll tell the social worker whatever you want. Just... get me out of gen pop. Get me somewhere safe." She started to sob then, a raw, ugly sound of a soul that had finally hit rock bottom. "He's better off with you anyway. He always was."

Leroy looked at the broken woman in front of him. He felt no pity. He felt no satisfaction. He just felt a profound, bottomless emptiness. This was the end of it all. Not a dramatic courtroom battle, but a pathetic, desperate bargain in a sterile interview room. He stood up, his chair scraping against the concrete floor.

"I'll talk to the warden," he said, his voice the flat, detached tone of a cop closing a case. "I'll see what I can do about getting you moved."

He turned and walked to the door without looking back, leaving Dina weeping at the table. He had his confession. He had her surrender. He had, finally, kept his promise. And it didn't feel like a victory at all. Leroy didn't go straight back to his car. He walked down the long, sterile hallway to the administrative section of the jail and found the warden's office. He knocked on the heavy wooden door.

"Come in," a gruff voice called out.

Warden Miller was a large, imposing man with a bald head and a no-nonsense expression permanently etched on his face. He looked up from a stack of paperwork as Leroy entered.

"Guzman," he said. "What can I do for you?" Leroy closed the door behind him.

"I was just in with the detainee, Dina Sanders," he began, his voice all business now. "She's been beaten, Warden. Badly. She's terrified for her life and is requesting a transfer to protective custody."

Warden Miller let out a short, humorless sigh. He steepled his fingers on his desk.

"Sergeant, you and I both know the unofficial laws that govern a place like this. The other inmates found out about her charge. Child endangerment. They have their own way of dealing with that." He shrugged, a gesture of cold, bureaucratic indifference. "It's an unfortunate but predictable reality."

"She's detoxing, she's terrified... she's not going to make it another night in gen pop," Leroy pressed. "She's also cooperating. She's agreed to surrender her parental rights. It will make everything smoother for the boy." The warden considered this, his gaze shrewd.

"A smooth case is a closed case. I'll see what I can do about finding a spot for her in the infirmary, but I'm not making any guarantees." Just as he finished speaking, a series of sharp, urgent beeps erupted from the warden's desk intercom, followed by the panicked voice of a guard.

"Code Blue, women's block showers! Code Blue, women's block showers! We need medical, now!"

Warden Miller was on his feet in an instant, his bureaucratic indifference vanishing, replaced by the sharp, commanding presence of a man in charge of a crisis. He stabbed a button on his console.

"What's the situation?"

"It's the new detainee, Sanders!" the voice crackled back. *"She was attacked. It's bad, Warden. Real bad."*

Leroy's blood ran cold. He and the warden exchanged a single, grim look. They were too late. They moved quickly, their footsteps echoing down the sterile hallways. They arrived at the women's block to a scene of controlled chaos. Guards were securing the area, and two paramedics were already working over a figure on the wet, tiled floor of the showers. The water swirling around their boots was tinged pink.

It was Dina. Her face, already nearly unrecognizable from the first beating, was now a pale, waxy mask. Her orange jumpsuit was soaked, a darker, spreading stain covering her abdomen. One of the paramedics looked up at the warden, his expression grim and focused.

"She's got multiple stab wounds to the abdomen and chest, looks like they used a shiv. Massive blood loss." He applied more pressure to a makeshift bandage. "She's circling the drain, Warden. We need to get her to the hospital, now."

Leroy stood back, a helpless observer, the smell of blood and industrial soap thick in the air. He watched as they loaded Dina onto a stretcher, a broken, pathetic shell of a human being. He had come here to close a chapter, and instead, he had witnessed its brutal, bloody final sentence being written. He slowly lowered his head as they wheeled her past. Dina was gone. Not dead, but gone. A ghost in a hospital bed, a ward of the state. The threat was neutralized, permanently. The CPS case, the custody battle... it was all over before it had even begun. Danny was theirs now, free and clear.

He should have felt relief. He should have felt a sense of grim victory. But as he stood there in the cold, damp air of the jail, all he felt was the profound, soul-deep exhaustion of a war that had left no winners, only survivors. He turned to the warden, who was already barking orders into his radio.

"Miller," Leroy said, his voice rough. The warden lowered his radio.

"Yeah, Guzman."

"She was a friend once," Leroy said, the words feeling inadequate. "Whatever happens... she deserves a little humanity. Get a guard on her door at the hospital."

The warden looked at him, a flicker of something—not pity, but professional understanding—in his tired eyes.

"I'll take care of it," he said, and it was a real promise this time.

Leroy nodded, turned, and walked away, not looking back. He moved through the sterile hallways, the sounds of the lockdown echoing around him, and finally pushed through the doors into the cool evening air. He walked to his car and leaned against the driver's side door, his legs feeling unsteady. He pulled out his pack of cigarettes and shook it, a single, solitary cigarette falling into his palm. His hands wouldn't stop trembling; the lighter slipped once, twice, before he managed to spark the flame. When he drew in the smoke, it wasn't steady—it hitched, shaky, almost desperate. His badge, pinned to his chest, suddenly felt like it weighed fifty pounds. For the first time in years, Leroy felt like he might break under it.

His mind was a slideshow of horrors. The blood on the tile. The waxy, pale color of Dina's skin. The paramedic's grim face. It was like something from a movie, too brutal to be real. He took a long, deep drag, the smoke a harsh anchor in the swirling chaos of his thoughts. He had seen a lot in his years on the force, but this... this was different.

He finished the cigarette, crushing the butt under his heel with a final, weary gesture. He got into the car and just sat there, the keys in the ignition, his hands on the wheel. The sun had set, and the parking lot was bathed in the pale, orange glow of the security lights. He couldn't go home like this. He couldn't walk through the door with the ghost of what he'd just seen clinging to him. He drove back to the station, not home. He pulled his patrol car into its designated spot and killed the engine. He didn't go inside. He just sat there in the dark, the radio silent, the events of the day replaying in his mind. He had seen scenarios like this a thousand times in his career—the domestic disputes, the violence, the tragic, messy ends. But it was always from a distance. It was always someone else's family, someone else's tragedy. This was Rick's wife. This was Danny's mother. This was personal. The professional detachment he'd relied on his whole career was gone, leaving him raw and exposed.

After what felt like an eternity, he finally got out of the patrol car, locked it, and walked to his own personal vehicle, a beat-up but reliable old pickup truck. He got in, the familiar scent of his own life—old coffee and the faint smell of sawdust from a long-forgotten project—a strange contrast to the sterile horror of the jail. He started the engine and finally, finally, headed home. The city lights smeared past his window, a river of reds and whites that he didn't see. His mind was a frantic, desperate calculation. How do you tell your wife that the woman who was once like a sister to her is lying in a hospital bed, likely to never wake up? How do you explain that you were standing just feet away while it happened? The questions were a physical weight, pressing down on his chest, making it hard to breathe.

And then there was Danny. The thought of the boy, safe at home, finally finding a flicker of peace, was a new kind of agony. How could he possibly tell him? How could he look into those fragile blue eyes and deliver a piece of news so brutal it would undoubtedly shatter the new, delicate world they were all trying to build around him? The absolute horror of what this would do to Danny, the new layer of guilt and trauma it would place on his already overburdened soul, was paralyzing.

He considered calling Maria, giving her a warning before he walked through the door. But he couldn't. This wasn't news you delivered over the phone. This was a wound that had to be tended to in person, face-to-face. He just kept driving, the silence in the truck a heavy, suffocating thing, each mile bringing him closer to a conversation he had no idea how to begin.

He pulled into the driveway, the crunch of the tires on the gravel sounding unnaturally loud. He killed the engine and just sat there, staring at the warm, welcoming light spilling from his own living room window. It looked like a different world, a peaceful planet he was about to contaminate with the grim reality of his day. He finally forced himself out of the truck. He walked to the front door, his keys feeling heavy and foreign in his hand. He unlocked it and stepped inside.

The first thing he saw was the boys. They were on the couch, a movie playing quietly on the TV. They weren't on opposite ends anymore. Danny was curled up, his head resting in Tony's lap, and Tony's hand was resting gently in Danny's shaggy brown hair. They were a picture of quiet, domestic peace. The sound of the door closing made them both jump. Danny scrambled to sit up, pulling away from Tony as if he'd been caught doing something wrong. He looked at Leroy, his eyes wide with a familiar, conditioned fear, expecting a reprimand, a disapproving look.

The sight of that fear on Danny's face, after everything, was the final straw for Leroy's composure. All the horror, the anger, the exhaustion from the day—it all melted away, replaced by a profound, aching need to make this one small corner of the world safe. He gave Danny a small, tired smile, his voice softer than he'd intended.

"Hey," he said gently. "It's okay, son. You're allowed. This is your home."

He saw the tension in Danny's shoulders ease just a fraction. Leroy walked past them, unbuckling his heavy duty belt and hanging it, along with his hat, on the rack by the door. He continued into the kitchen, where Maria was standing at the counter, her back to him. He came up behind her and wrapped his arms around her waist, burying his face in her hair. He just held her for a long moment, breathing in the familiar, comforting scent of his wife.

"Hey, *mi amor*," she said softly, leaning back into him.

He kissed her, a long, weary press of lips. Then he let her go and walked to the fridge, pulling out a slice of cold pizza from the box he knew would be in there. He needed the simple, grounding act of eating something, of doing something normal, before he could even begin to speak. Maria watched him, her brow furrowed with concern. She saw the deep, bone-weary exhaustion in his eyes, the way his shoulders slumped. This was more than just a long day at work.

"Leroy, what is it?" she asked, her voice low. "What happened? Why did Dina want to see you so badly?" She started to speculate, her own anxiety rising. "Was she trying to fight the CPS case? Did she threaten you? What did she say?"

Leroy took a bite of the cold pizza, chewing slowly, deliberately, buying himself a few more seconds. He looked past her, through the kitchen doorway, to where he could see the boys sitting on the couch, their heads now close together as they spoke in low whispers. He shook his head, finally meeting Maria's worried gaze.

"Not in here," he said, his voice a low, rough murmur. "Let's... let's go out back. This isn't a conversation for the boys to hear."

In the living room, Tony saw his parents' hushed, serious exchange. He saw his dad's grim expression and the way his mom's hand went to her mouth. He saw them both head for the back door that led to the patio. His stomach dropped.

Danny, noticing the sudden tension in Tony's body, looked over at him with a questioning gaze.

"Something's wrong," Tony said, his voice barely a whisper, his eyes still fixed on the kitchen. "Something bad must've happened." He looked at Danny, a new, cold dread creeping into his own heart. "They only go out back to talk when it's something they don't want me to hear."

Leroy slid the glass door to the back patio shut behind them, the sound of a soft, final seal separating them from the fragile peace inside the house. The evening air was cool, and the scent of Maria's late-blooming roses hung sweetly, a stark contrast to the grim topic at hand. They sat at the small patio table, the one where they drank their coffee on Sunday mornings. Maria waited, her hands clasped tightly on the table, her knuckles white. She watched her husband's face, illuminated by the soft glow of the porch light, and saw a level of exhaustion she had never seen before. Leroy stared out into the darkness of their backyard, gathering his thoughts, trying to find the words.

"She wanted me to get her out," he began, his voice low and rough. "Out of general population. She was terrified. She'd been beaten the day before... a warning, she said. The other inmates knew why she was there."

Maria's hand flew to her mouth, a small, horrified gasp escaping her.

"She tried to bargain," Leroy continued, his voice flat, devoid of emotion. "Said she'd sign the papers, give up Danny, tell CPS whatever we wanted. Anything, as long as I got her somewhere safe." He finally turned to look at his wife, his own eyes full of a deep, hollow pain. "I went to talk to the warden, Maria. I told him she was cooperating. I told him she wouldn't make it another night." He paused, the memory of the blaring alarm, the panicked voice on the intercom, replaying in his mind. "And then all hell broke loose. While I was in his office. They got to her again. In the showers."

Maria's resolution, her strength, the wall she had built around her heart to deal with the loss of her friend, began to dissolve with each word.

"Leroy, no..." she whispered, her voice trembling.

"It was bad, Maria," he said, his voice cracking. "They stabbed her. Multiple times. The paramedics said... they said she was circling the drain." He took a shaky breath. "She's at the hospital now. In a coma. They don't think she's going to wake up."

Maria stared at him, her mind refusing to comprehend the horror of what she was hearing. This was Dina. The girl she'd passed notes with in high school. Her maid of honor. The woman who was supposed to be her sister. Reduced to a bloody, broken body on a hospital bed. A wave of nausea and a profound, bottomless grief washed over her. She began to sob, not loud, ragged cries, but the silent, shoulder-shaking sobs of a heart that was truly, finally, broken. Leroy reached across the table and took her hands, his own grip a desperate, grounding force.

The sink was piled high with dishes, the sour stench of spoiled milk and something sharper clinging to the air. Danny's math homework was still spread across the table, pencil smudges pressed deep into the paper, the letters of his name scrawled in that earnest, heavy-handed way he always signed it. And Dina—her best friend since high school, her sister in every way that mattered—was leaning against the counter, jittery. Her eyes were rimmed in red, her pupils blown wide. A tumbler of amber liquid shook in her hand, sloshing over the side.

"Dina…" Maria's voice broke as she stepped forward. "Not with him here. Not like this." Dina laughed, sharp and brittle, a sound that didn't belong to the girl Maria had once shared a prom dress with, who had stood at her side on her wedding day.

"He's fine," Dina spat, waving the glass as if it proved her point. "He's tougher than he looks. He's my kid."

Before Maria could answer, the creak of the stairs split the tension. She spun around and saw him—Danny, no more than ten years old, hair rumpled from sleep, clutching the railing in pajama-clad fists. He blinked at the dim kitchen light, his wide blue eyes catching on the glass in his mother's hand. Confusion tugged at his small face.

Maria's heart lurched.

"Danny," she said softly, forcing warmth into her tone. "Sweetheart, you're supposed to be in bed." She crossed the room quickly, crouching to meet him before his eyes could settle too long on Dina's unsteady sway. She touched his cheek, guiding his gaze to hers. "Come on, mi cielo. Let's get you back upstairs."

He opened his mouth, maybe to ask why his mom was crying, or why the house smelled wrong, but Maria didn't let him. She wrapped an arm around him, shielding his line of sight, and led him up the stairs with a steady, practiced gentleness.

In Dina's narrow hallway, under the flicker of a weak lightbulb, Maria whispered, "Let's pack a bag, okay? Just for tonight. You can come stay with us. Tony will be so excited to see you." Danny hesitated at his bedroom door, small shoulders tense.

"But… what about Mom?" he asked, his voice a thin thread of worry. Maria's chest ached. She kissed his hair, pulling him close.

"She'll be okay. Right now, I just want you safe. Just one night."

She slipped into his room, grabbed the old Spider-Man backpack by his bed, and began stuffing it with the first clothes her hands landed on—socks, a t-shirt, his worn sneakers. Danny stood silently, watching, clutching Peanut. His silence said everything.

Later that night, when Maria crawled into bed beside Leroy, she told him everything in a cracked whisper. "He can stay with us. Just for a little while. Until she pulls herself together."

Leroy lay in the dark, staring at the ceiling. Finally, he turned toward her, his hand finding hers under the blanket. His voice was low, heavy. "Maria… Rick made me promise. He said it with his last breath. 'Take care of my boy.' But he also said not to take him from her unless we had no other choice." He shook his head, jaw tight. "We can't force it. Not yet."

"We can't tell him," Maria choked out through her tears, her first, immediate thought a fiercely protective one. "Leroy, we can't. Not now. Maybe not ever." She looked at him, her eyes pleading. "He's just started to heal. He's just started to feel safe. This… this would destroy him. The guilt… he would think it was his fault. We can't do that to him."

Leroy looked at his weeping wife, his own heart a heavy, leaden weight in his chest. He knew she was right. Telling Danny now would be a cruelty, a burden too heavy for his fragile shoulders.

"Okay," he agreed, his voice rough with an exhaustion that went bone-deep "Okay, *mi amor*. We'll wait. We won't say anything. Not until we have to."

They sat there in the cool night air, holding hands across the table, two partners united in a grim, necessary conspiracy of silence. The news was too gruesome, too exhausting. They needed to compose themselves, to build their walls back up before they could go back inside and face the two boys who were waiting, oblivious, on the other side of the glass.

CHAPTER 24

STILL SCARED

Wednesday morning arrived with the soft, grey light of a day everyone had been dreading. Tony woke first, his back aching slightly from the air mattress he'd insisted on setting up on his floor. After the intensity of Monday night, he had decided Danny needed his own space, a real bed to himself, without the complication of sharing. It felt like the right thing to do, a small, physical act of respect.

He lay there for a moment, listening to the quiet, even breathing coming from the bed. Danny was still asleep. The house was still, but it was a different kind of quiet from the day before. Yesterday had been a peaceful sanctuary; today was the tense, waiting silence before a storm. Today was the day Ms. Jenkins was coming.

Tony slipped out of the sleeping bag, his movements quiet so as not to wake Danny. He pulled on a pair of jeans and a t-shirt and headed downstairs. His parents were already in the kitchen, their movements subdued, a silent, shared anxiety hanging between them. Maria was making coffee, and Leroy was staring into a bowl of cereal he wasn't eating. They both looked up when Tony walked in, offering him small, tired smiles.

A little while later, Danny appeared in the doorway, wearing another one of Tony's oversized t-shirts, his shaggy brown hair a mess from sleep. He looked small and fragile, his blue eyes wide with the unspoken dread of the afternoon to come. No one mentioned it. Instead, Maria poured him a glass of orange juice, and Tony made them both toast, the simple, mundane routine a fragile shield against the looming appointment.

When it was time to go, the tension was palpable. Danny clutched his backpack strap like a lifeline. Tony, seeing the fear on his face, knew he had to take control.

He grabbed his leather jacket and the keys to his mom's minivan. He looked at his parents.

"I'll drive us to school today," he said, his voice quiet but firm. It wasn't a question. It was a statement. *I'm taking care of him.* Leroy's hand twitched as if to stop him—old habit, the father in him ready to object—but then he caught Tony's look. A silent exchange passed between them: I've got this. Leroy gave the smallest nod, conceding ground he'd never given before. His boy wasn't asking. He was stepping up. Maria and Leroy just nodded, a silent, grateful understanding passing between them.

The drive to school was even more silent than it had been on Monday. The unspoken weight of the afternoon's meeting sat between them like a physical presence. Tony gripped the steering wheel, his knuckles white. He could feel the tension radiating from Danny, who sat ramrod straight in the passenger seat, staring out the window, his jaw tight. Tony resisted the urge to reach over, to take his hand, knowing that the gesture, as well-intentioned as it was, might feel like a cage to a boy who was already feeling trapped.

As they pulled into the school parking lot, the familiar morning chaos swirling around them, Tony saw Danny's shoulders hunch even further. He had to do something.

"Hey," he said softly. Danny flinched but didn't turn his head. Tony lifted his right hand from the steering wheel and, keeping his eyes on Danny, gently tapped his thumb over his own heart twice.

Tap. Tap.

He saw Danny's shoulders, just for a second, lose some of their rigid tension. A small, shaky breath escaped him. He didn't turn. He didn't return the gesture. But he eased up, just slightly, a silent acknowledgment that he had received the message. *I'm here. I've got you.* They walked into the school together, a silent, united front. As the first bell rang, they stopped near the main intersection of the hallways.

"I'm... going to the library," Danny said, his voice a low murmur, not quite meeting Tony's eyes. "To read." Tony understood. He needed a quiet, safe space to start the day.

"Okay," he said. "I've got practice." He hesitated for a second, then said, "I'll see you at lunch?"

Danny finally looked at him and gave a small, almost imperceptible nod before turning and disappearing into the river of students. Tony watched him go, then turned and headed for the gym, the weight of the day already settling on his shoulders.

The locker room was a cavern of awkward silence. The usual pre-practice energy — the loud jokes, the complaining about the early hour, the arguments over music — was gone, replaced by a thick, uncomfortable quiet. Marko was at his locker, pointedly ignoring Tony, his movements sharp and angry as he yanked his practice jersey over his head. Jamal, caught in the crossfire, just stared into his own locker, pretending to be looking for something.

Tony changed in silence, the cold shoulder from his best friend a physical ache in his chest. He didn't push. He knew he deserved it. He just pulled on his jersey and headed out to the court, the silence following him like a shadow.

On the court, things were even worse. Tony's body was there, running the drills, but his mind was a million miles away. It was in the library, wondering if Danny was okay, if he was scared. It was jumping ahead to three o'clock, to a meeting with a stranger who held their entire future in her hands. He was a step slow on defense, letting a player blow past him for an easy layup. He threw a no-look pass to where Marko usually was, but Marko had cut a different way, and the ball sailed out of bounds.

"Guzman!" Coach barked, his voice echoing in the half-empty gym. "What the hell was that? My grandmother could have made that shot!" Tony just jogged back on defense, his face a blank mask. There was no flash of anger, no frustrated curse. Just a quiet, weary acceptance. A few plays later, it happened again. A missed defensive assignment. Coach blew his whistle, the sound sharp and angry. "Guzman, get over here!" he yelled. Tony jogged to the sideline. "What is wrong with you today? Your head is so far out of this game it's in another time zone! Sit down. Get your head straight."

"Yes, Coach," Tony said, his voice flat. He took a seat on the bench, grabbed a towel, and draped it over his head, hiding his face from the world.

From the court, Marko saw the whole exchange. He saw the sloppy playing, the coach's anger, and most importantly, Tony's non-reaction. The old Tony would have argued. He would have slammed the ball, kicked the bench, something. This quiet, defeated acceptance was more alarming than any outburst. He looked over at Jamal, who just shook his head, a worried expression on his face. For the first time, Marko's anger began to curdle into a reluctant, grudging concern.

After practice, the locker room was quiet again, but the silence had changed. It was no longer hostile; it was contemplative. Tony sat on the bench, staring at the floor, the coach's words replaying in his head. He hadn't just been a bad player; he'd been a bad teammate. Marko walked over, his own practice gear in hand, and sat down on the bench opposite him. Jamal followed, leaning against the lockers nearby.

"You played like crap today," Marko said. It wasn't an insult. It was a simple, unadorned statement of fact.

"I know," he said quietly, not looking up.

"I've never seen Coach get on you like that," Jamal added, his voice soft.

Tony finally lifted his head, his eyes full of a deep, profound exhaustion.

"I've got a lot on my mind," he said, the understatement of the century. Marko looked at him, at the dark circles under his eyes, at the genuine weight he seemed to be carrying. The anger he'd been holding onto since Tuesday morning finally, completely, dissolved, leaving only a deep, familiar well of concern for his best friend.

"Is he...?" Marko started, the question hesitant. "Is Danny okay?"

Tony was taken aback by the question, by the genuine worry in Marko's voice.

"Yeah," he said, his voice a little rough. "He's just... scared. We have a meeting with a social worker today. After school."

"A social worker?" Jamal asked. "For real?" Tony just nodded.

"It's to make my parents his legal guardians. It's... a whole thing."

Marko scrubbed a hand over his face, letting out a long, slow breath. This was bigger than a simple fight or a breakup. This was real life, heavy and complicated.

"Damn, Tony," Marko said softly. He looked at his friend, really looked at him, and for the first time, he began to understand the depth of the hole Tony was in. "Look, man," he said, his voice full of a familiar, gruff affection. "I'm still pissed at you. And you're still an idiot. But... you're our idiot." Jamal smiled, a small, relieved expression.

"He's right," Jamal said. "We're here, man. Whatever you need."

It wasn't a full reconciliation. It wasn't forgiveness. But it was a start. It was a bridge, fragile and tentative, being extended across the chasm that had opened between them. And for Tony, it was the first good thing that had happened all day.

The news of Tony and Jessica's breakup spread through the school with the speed and intensity of a wildfire. By the time the bell for the second period rang, it was the only thing anyone was talking about. The school's golden couple was done.

Tony felt the constant, prying eyes on him all day, but for the first time, he didn't care. He moved through the crowded hallways, a ghost in his own life: finding a flash of a faded hoodie, a glimpse of shaggy brown hair.

He would catch glimpses of Danny between classes, a fleeting, almost-there presence. He saw him by the lockers, quickly grabbing a book before disappearing back into the stream of students. He saw him by the water fountain, taking a quick drink, his head down. And each time their eyes would meet, for just a fraction of a second across the sea of oblivious faces, Tony would lift his hand to his chest, his thumb resting on the worn fabric of his white t-shirt, and deliver their silent message.

Tap. Tap.

He did it at lunch. He sat with Marko and Jamal at their usual table. Across the chaotic, noisy cafeteria, Danny sat alone, a book open in front of him. Their eyes met over the heads of the crowd.

Tap. Tap.

He saw a faint, shy smile touch Danny's lips before he looked back down at his book.

The bridge between Tony and his friends was still fragile. The conversation was stilted, full of the things they weren't saying. Jamal, in particular, was unusually quiet, pushing his food around his plate, a nervous, unreadable expression on his face. Finally, he pushed his tray away.

"Hey," he said, his voice low, directed at Tony and Marko. "Can we... can we go shoot some hoops? At the court outside. Just for a minute." Tony and Marko exchanged a look. It was the middle of lunch.

"Now?" Marko asked. "Why?"

"I just... I need to talk to you guys about something," Jamal said, not quite meeting their eyes. "It's important."

Tony looked across the cafeteria at Danny, who was still absorbed in his book. He caught Danny's eye one more time and gave him a small, reassuring nod, a silent promise that he wasn't going far. Danny, seeming to understand, just nodded back. A few minutes later, the three of them stood on the familiar, cracked asphalt of the outdoor basketball court. The lunchtime chaos of the school felt a million miles away. Marko and Tony started shooting, their movements easy and practiced. Jamal just stood under the hoop, holding a basketball, turning it over and over in his hands.

"Alright, man, you're freaking me out," Marko finally said, catching a rebound. "What's going on?" Jamal took a deep breath, his eyes on the worn leather of the ball. For a second, it looked like he was going to shut down completely. His shoulders hunched, the words caught in his throat, and he shook his head as if to wave it all away. But then he exhaled, hard, like forcing himself past a breaking point.

"It's about Friday night," Jamal began, his voice quiet. "When I called you, Tony. I... I wasn't just on that bus to 'clear my head'." Tony stopped dribbling, his full attention on Jamal. "I go down to that part of town sometimes," Jamal continued, the words coming out in a quiet, difficult rush. "There's... there's a community center there. An LGBTQ youth center. I don't... I don't go in. I just... I sit at the bus stop across the street. Just to... I don't know. To feel like I'm not the only one."

He finally looked up, his expression a mixture of fear and profound vulnerability. "I saw Danny get on the bus because I was already there. I followed him because... because he looked the way I feel most of the time. Lost." He looked at Tony, a deep, empathetic understanding in his eyes. "When you told us the truth on Tuesday... it made me realize I was a hypocrite, too. Hiding. Being scared." He took a final, shaky breath, the secret he'd been holding finally breaking free. "I'm like you, Tony. I'm gay, too."

The confession landed on the basketball court with the force of a physical blow. Tony stared at Jamal, a wave of shock and a profound, dawning understanding washing over him. Suddenly, Jamal's caution, his quiet support, it all made perfect, painful sense. But it was Marko who reacted first. He just stood there, frozen, the basketball held loosely in his hands. He looked back and forth between Tony and Jamal, his face a mask of pure, unadulterated bewilderment.

"Are you kidding me?" he finally burst out, the words a mix of frustration and disbelief. It wasn't anger. It wasn't disgust. It was the raw, wounded confusion of a man whose entire world had just been turned upside down for the second time in two days. "You too?" He threw the basketball on the ground, the sharp *'thwack'* echoing in the sudden silence. "What is happening? Is everyone in on some secret but me? First Tony, now you?" He looked at them, his expression genuinely hurt. "Why didn't you guys just tell me? We're supposed to be a team. We're supposed to tell each other everything."

The accusation, born not of malice but of a deep, wounded loyalty, hung in the air between them. Jamal looked at Marko's hurt, confused face and took a hesitant step forward.

"I was scared, man," he said, his voice pleading for understanding. "I'm still scared. I didn't know how anyone was going to react." He glanced at Tony, a look of gratitude on his face. "Honestly, what you did on Tuesday... telling us... that's what gave me the courage to say anything at all. It made me feel like... maybe I didn't have to hide it forever." He turned back to Marko. "I didn't want to say anything yesterday," he admitted, his gaze dropping to the ground. "With everything going on with you and Tony, and with Jessica... it was already so tense. It felt... inappropriate. Like I'd be making it all about me." He finally met Marko's eyes again, his own full of a deep, apologetic sincerity. "I'm sorry, man. I never wanted to lie to you."

Marko looked from Jamal's earnest, scared face to Tony's quiet, weary one. The pieces finally clicked into place in his head. His two best friends had been going through their own private hells, and he'd been completely oblivious. His anger, which already felt thin and misplaced, evaporated completely, leaving only a deep, familiar well of affection. He couldn't stay mad. He wanted to crack a joke, he thought something like, *"So what, are we starting our own basketball team? The... Rainbow Rebounders?"* but he bit his tongue. The moment felt too heavy, too fragile for his usual bullshit. He just shook his head, a slow, disbelieving, but ultimately accepting gesture.

"Man," he said, his voice rough. "You guys are a mess." He looked at them both, a small, sad smile on his face. "But you're my mess."

Tony watched the exchange, a profound sense of relief washing over him. He turned to Jamal.

"What you did Friday night," Tony said, his voice low and full of a gratitude that went beyond words. "Making that call. If you hadn't... I don't know what would have happened. You... you started all of this, man. Thank you." Jamal gave a small, watery smile.

"There's... there's another reason I wanted to tell you guys," Jamal said, his voice gaining a small, nervous energy. "Now." Tony and Marko both looked at him, waiting. "You know in Bodowski's class," Jamal started, his gaze dropping to the basketball at his feet, "for the *Mockingbird* project? I got paired with Connor."

Marko's eyebrows shot up.

"Connor? The quiet kid with the glasses? The one who's like, a genius?"

"Yeah," Jamal said, a faint blush creeping up his neck. "That's him." He took a breath, the words coming out in a rush. "I... I really like him. Like, a lot. And I was thinking... I want to ask him out. But I couldn't do it while I was still hiding. It didn't feel right." He finally looked up at them, his expression a mixture of terror and determination. "I want to be able to be honest. Like you, Tony."

The three of them stood there on the empty court, the unspoken secrets finally out, the old foundation of their friendship shattered but the new one, built on a raw and difficult truth, just beginning to set in. From the far side of the school grounds, near the student parking lot, Jessica watched them. She had been heading to her car to get a textbook she'd forgotten when she saw the three of them walk out to the basketball court. She stopped, partially hidden by a large oak tree, and just observed.

She saw them talking, saw Marko's angry, confused gestures, saw him throw the ball down. She couldn't hear the words, but she could read the body language. She saw Jamal's quiet, vulnerable confession. She saw Tony's steady, supportive presence. And then, she saw the shift. She saw Marko's anger dissolve, saw him pull his two best friends into a rough, clumsy, three-way hug.

She saw them reforming, reforging their bond without her. For half a heartbeat, she remembered when Tony used to look at her that way— unguarded, steady, like she was his anchor. But the memory slipped away just as fast, because the truth was undeniable: that version of him had never truly belonged to her.

A fresh wave of pain, sharp and clean, went through her. But underneath it, there was something else. A quiet, sad understanding. She looked at Tony, at the way he stood with his friends, the angry, defensive shell he had worn for the last year completely gone. He looked lighter. He looked more like the boy she had first fallen for. With a final, quiet sigh, she turned away from the scene, from the boys and their newly forged truth, and walked back toward the school, leaving them to their new world.

Between lunch and fifth period, as the three of them were walking through the crowded main hallway, they passed Connor. He was at his locker, talking to a friend. As Connor closed his locker door, his eyes met Jamal's for just a split second across the sea of students. It was a tiny, almost imperceptible moment, but in that glance, Connor gave a small, shy smile before quickly looking away and heading in the opposite direction. Jamal's hand twitched around the strap of his backpack, gripping it too tight, his breath stuttering in his chest. He tried to mask it by moving quicker, eyes down, but Tony caught the way a hidden smile tugged faintly at the corner of his mouth before he smothered it.

Marko, busy complaining about a pop quiz, didn't notice a thing. But Tony saw it all. He saw the look on Connor's face, and more importantly, he saw the way Jamal's breath caught, the way his steps faltered for just a second before he quickly regained his composure.

In class, after they had all sat down, Tony leaned over to Jamal, his voice low and casual.

"Hey, man," he said. "You see that? In the hallway? With Connor?" Jamal immediately got defensive, his eyes darting around to see if anyone was listening.

"See what? I don't know what you're talking about." Tony just smiled, a quiet, knowing expression on his face.

"Dude," he said gently. "I think he likes you."

The simple validation seemed to land on Jamal with a physical weight. He just stared at Tony, a mixture of terror and a new, dawning hope in his eyes. He didn't say anything. He just picked up his pencil and started pushing his book around his desk, a silent, contemplative gesture that told Tony everything he needed to know.

CHAPTER 25

HOME

The final bell of the day was a death knell. The fragile truce Tony had brokered with his friends, the quiet understanding that had passed between him and Danny in the cafeteria—it all evaporated, replaced by the singular, crushing dread of the three o'clock meeting.

The drive home was the quietest it had ever been. It wasn't the tense, angry silence of the week before, or the fragile, hopeful silence of the morning. This was a heavy, suffocating quiet, thick with unspoken fear. Tony gripped the steering wheel, his eyes fixed on the road, his mind a frantic, repeating loop of everything that could go wrong. What if she saw the lingering anger in his eyes and thought he was a risk?

Danny sat in the passenger seat, completely still, his hands clasped so tightly in his lap that his knuckles were white. Danny's knee bounced once, quick and nervous, before he locked it still like he was afraid even that small movement might be held against him. Tony saw it out of the corner of his eye and wanted to say something—anything—but the words stuck in his throat. He'd never felt so useless, sitting right there and still unable to take the weight off the boy beside him. He stared straight ahead, his face a pale, blank mask, but Tony could feel the terror radiating from him in waves. He wanted to say something, to offer some reassurance, but the words felt like lies. He couldn't promise it would be okay, because he didn't know that for sure. So he just drove, the silence a shared burden between them.

Tony pulled into the driveway at 3:15, a strange car—a sensible, four-door sedan—parked at the curb in front of their house. She was already here. His stomach twisted into a knot. They walked into the house to find Maria, Leroy, and a woman Tony didn't recognize sitting in the living room. The television was off. The air was thick with a tense, formal quiet. Ms. Jenkins, a woman in her late forties with kind, tired eyes and a calm, professional demeanor, was in the middle of speaking. Her pressed navy blazer and leather folder made her look like she carried authority in the crook of her arm. To Tony, she felt like a judge and jury wrapped into one—kind eyes or not.

"...and as I mentioned on Saturday, Sergeant, our primary goal is always to minimize disruption for the child," she was saying. She looked up as the boys entered, her expression softening. "Ah, and this must be Daniel and Antonio."

"Boys," Leroy said, his voice a little strained. "This is Ms. Jenkins. From Child Protective Services." Tony just nodded, his throat suddenly dry. Danny seemed to shrink, his eyes immediately dropping to the floor.

"Hello, boys," Ms. Jenkins said, her voice gentle. "Thank you for joining us. Why don't you have a seat?"

Tony and Danny sat down on the couch, a careful, respectable distance between them. The meeting continued, a blur of quiet questions and carefully worded answers. Ms. Jenkins already had the details from her conversation with Leroy, but she went over them again, asking Maria about her history with the Sanders family, their relationship with Rick, their ability and willingness to care for Danny. Her questions were direct but not accusatory.

Then, she turned to Tony. She asked him about his relationship with Danny, both in the past and now. Tony, his heart pounding, answered as honestly as he could, leaving out the most intimate details but making his commitment clear.

"He's my best friend," he said, his voice firm. "I'll do whatever it takes to make sure he's safe." Finally, she turned to Danny. The entire family seemed to lean forward, a silent, protective wall around him.

"Daniel," she said, her voice incredibly soft. "I know this is a lot. I just have a few questions for you. Is it okay if I ask them now?" Danny, who had been staring at his own hands the entire time, looked up. He glanced at Tony, who gave him a small, almost imperceptible nod. He then looked back at Ms. Jenkins and gave a tiny nod of his own. "Do you feel safe here?" she asked.

"Yes," Danny whispered. His voice cracked on the single syllable, and he flushed like he wished he could take it back. Tony caught the way his fingers twisted into the hem of his shirt, like he was trying to anchor himself to something solid.

"Do you want to stay here? With the Guzmans?"

"Yes," he said again, his voice a little stronger this time. Ms. Jenkins smiled, a genuine, warm expression.

"Good. That's what we want, too." She looked at Maria and Leroy. "As we discussed, this is what we call kinship care, and it's always our primary goal. Keeping a child with people he knows and trusts is the best possible outcome."

She made a few notes in her folder, then looked up, her expression turning slightly more formal. "Now, ordinarily, we would have to schedule a hearing to terminate the mother's parental rights, which can be a long and difficult process. However, in this case, that won't be necessary." She looked at Danny, her gaze full of a careful, professional sympathy. "Your mother, Dina, is currently medically incapacitated and will be unable to care for you for the foreseeable future. She had also, before her hospitalization, verbally agreed to surrender her rights. Given the circumstances, the court will be able to grant emergency guardianship to the Guzmans here without a contest."

The phrase—*medically incapacitated*—was a sterile, bureaucratic shield. It was a kindness, a way of delivering a life-altering piece of information without dropping a bomb of traumatic detail on a fragile teenager. Leroy and Maria exchanged a look of profound, silent relief. They had been spared, for now, from having to tell him the violent truth. Ms. Jenkins placed her folder on the coffee table, her expression shifting to one of gentle seriousness.

"Now, while Daniel is physically safe here, which is our primary concern, we also need to think about his emotional well-being," she said, her gaze including everyone in the room. "A child who has been through what he has... it leaves scars we can't see. I'm going to strongly recommend that we get him into counseling as soon as possible." She pulled a pamphlet from her bag and handed it to Maria. "This is a list of state-approved child and adolescent therapists in the area who specialize in trauma and family crisis. The services will be covered. I've highlighted a few I've worked with before who are excellent." She then looked at Danny, her voice incredibly kind. "It's just a safe place for you to talk about things, Daniel. With someone who isn't involved. It can really help." Maria took the pamphlet, her expression grateful.

"Thank you, Ms. Jenkins. We will look into this right away."

Ms. Jenkins smiled, stood up, and gathered her things.

"I'll file my report this afternoon recommending the placement. We'll have a preliminary hearing next week, but it should just be a formality." She looked at Danny one last time, her smile warm and genuine. "Welcome home, Daniel."

The moment the door closed behind her, the entire house seemed to let out a collective, shuddering breath. The storm had passed. They had survived. Maria pulled both boys into a fierce hug, while Leroy stood by, a single, silent tear tracing a path down his weary cheek. The hardest part was over. They were a family.

The family hug was a moment of pure, unadulterated relief. It was a physical acknowledgment that the storm had passed and they had, against all odds, survived it together. When Maria finally let them go, her eyes were shining with happy tears. Leroy was smiling, a genuine, tired smile that reached his eyes for the first time in days. The weight of the world had been lifted from their shoulders.

But for Tony, the relief was something else entirely. It was a wild, soaring, effervescent joy that threatened to burst right out of his chest. It was over. The hardest part was over. Danny was safe. He was *theirs*. He wasn't going anywhere.

He looked at Danny, who was standing beside him, looking dazed and overwhelmed, a single tear tracing a path down his cheek. At that moment, Tony wanted nothing more than to grab him, to pull him close. But he stopped himself.

He saw the fragile, shell-shocked look in Danny's eyes. He knew that a big, dramatic kiss wasn't what Danny needed right now. He was still processing everything—the meeting, the news about his mother, the simple, staggering fact that he was finally, truly, home.

So Tony reined in the overwhelming urge. He took a steadying breath and did the only thing he could. While his parents were turned away, wiping their own happy tears, he looked at Danny. He lifted his hand to his chest and, with his thumb, delivered their silent, secret message.

Tap. Tap.

He saw a small, watery smile touch Danny's lips. It was enough. Danny's shoulders dropped a fraction, like someone had finally eased a too-tight band across his chest. It wasn't just a smile; it was the first breath of relief he'd allowed himself all day.

"Hey," Tony said softly, his voice a little rough with emotion. "You wanna... you wanna go upstairs?" He saw a flicker of uncertainty in Danny's eyes and quickly added, "Just... to hang out. You don't have to talk or anything. You can just... be. And you can find a way to express yourself, in any small way you can, when you're ready."

It was an offering of quiet, private space, away from the intense emotion of the living room. It was a promise of no pressure, no expectations. Just a sanctuary where Danny could process everything in his own time, in his own way.

Danny looked at him, at the open, honest affection on his face, and gave a small, grateful nod.

They went upstairs to Tony's room, the door closing softly behind them, a gentle seal on their private world. Danny immediately curled up on the bed, pulling a pillow into his lap and hugging it to his chest. Tony sat on the air mattress on the floor, leaning against the bed frame, giving him space. They didn't talk. They just existed in the quiet, the shared relief, a tangible presence in the room.Every creak of the house outside the door—the clink of dishes in the sink, the muffled sound of Maria's footsteps—made the little cocoon of Tony's room feel even more private. Tony sat with his knees drawn up, fighting the urge to reach across the mattress. He didn't. But Danny's breathing, steady and close above him, was enough to hold onto.

A little while later, there was a soft knock on the door. It creaked open, and Leroy poked his head in.

"Hey," he said, his voice a low, gentle rumble. "Just... checking in. See how you're doing, son." His eyes were on Danny.

Danny looked up from the pillow he was clutching. He didn't say anything, but he met Leroy's gaze and gave a small, almost imperceptible nod. Tony saw it—the way Danny's shoulders straightened a hair, like Leroy's question had given him permission to admit he was still standing after everything. It was tiny, but to Tony, it looked like the bravest thing he'd ever seen. It was a silent reassurance. *I'm okay.* Leroy's shoulders seemed to relax. He didn't press for anything verbal; he knew the boy had been through more than enough for one day. His gaze shifted to Tony, a new, lighter expression on his face.

"Your mom mentioned you two were in the garage yesterday," he said, a hint of a smile in his voice. "Cleaning up my old bike."

"Yeah. We got a lot of the grime off." Tony's face broke into a genuine, tired grin.

"She said you found a partner who actually knows a thing or two about engines," Leroy added, his eyes twinkling as he looked back at Danny. Danny's cheeks flushed a faint pink, and he looked down at the pillow in his lap, a shy, pleased smile on his face.

"I was thinking," Leroy said, his voice full of a casual warmth. "I've got a bit of paperwork to finish up, but after that... you two want to show me what you did?"

Tony looked at Danny, a silent question in his eyes. Danny gave a small, hesitant nod.

"Yeah, *Papi*," Tony said, his voice bright with a new, uncomplicated enthusiasm.

The evening settled into a new, comfortable rhythm. Tony and Danny helped Maria prepare dinner, the three of them moving around the warm kitchen in an easy, unspoken dance. Danny was quiet, but he followed Maria's instructions, carefully chopping vegetables, his movements precise and focused. For Danny, the simple, domestic act of helping to prepare a meal in a calm, safe kitchen was a revelation. The silence wasn't tense or angry; it was peaceful.

After dinner, once the kitchen was cleaned, the boys led Leroy out to the garage. The single bare bulb overhead cast a warm glow on the newly cleaned Triumph. Leroy circled the bike slowly, a look of genuine, impressed surprise on his face.

"Wow," he said, running a hand over the gleaming chrome fender. "You two weren't kidding. It looks... almost new." He crouched down, examining the engine block that Danny had so carefully wiped down. "You really got in there."

"Danny knew what to do," Tony said, a proud, happy note in his voice. Leroy stood up and looked at his son, a long, thoughtful expression on his face. He saw the new light in Tony's eyes, the quiet confidence, the way he stood just a little closer to Danny. He saw the way he had stepped up, the way he had become a protector, a partner.

"You know," Leroy said, his voice full of a casual gravity, "a man who's going to be working on a machine like this, a man who's taking on this kind of responsibility... he should probably know how to ride it."

Tony's head snapped up, his eyes wide with disbelief.

"You can get your license," Leroy said, a slow, proud smile spreading across his face. "You've earned it. Your support for Danny... for our family... through all of this. You've shown me you're ready." It was more than permission. It was a reward. A vote of confidence. A father's acknowledgment of the man his son was becoming.

Later that night, Tony and Danny went back up to Tony's room. Tony was completely overjoyed with how the day had gone. A lot of unexpected, wonderful things had happened. He was still buzzing from his dad's words, from the simple, shared victory of the day. He lay down on the air mattress, his hands behind his head, staring up at the ceiling with a wide, goofy grin. He heard a soft rustling from the bed above him. He turned his head and saw Danny looking down at him from the edge of the mattress, his expression unreadable in the dim light from the hallway.

"Hey," Tony whispered. "You good?"

Danny didn't answer. Instead, he slowly, deliberately, slid off the bed and onto the floor. He crawled over to the air mattress, his movements hesitant but full of a quiet purpose. Tony's heart started to pound, a frantic, hopeful rhythm in his chest.

Danny lay down on the air mattress beside him, facing him, their faces just inches apart in the semi-darkness. He looked at Tony, his blue eyes searching, and then, without a second's hesitation, he lifted his hand. He placed it gently on Tony's chest, right over his heart, and with his thumb, he returned the gesture.

Tap. Tap.

The signal, so freely given, so unexpectedly returned, was a lightning strike. Tony's breath hitched in his throat. Every rational thought, every promise of patience he had made to himself, evaporated in the face of this one, perfect, reciprocal gesture. Danny wasn't just accepting his affection anymore; he was offering his own. A wave of pure, unadulterated love, so potent it almost hurt, crashed over him. He saw the fragile, hopeful smile on Danny's face, and he knew, with an absolute certainty that settled deep in his soul, that this was it. This was the beginning of everything.

They lay like that for a long time, just looking at each other in the quiet dark, Danny's hand a warm, steady presence on Tony's chest. The air mattress on the floor suddenly felt like an unnecessary and artificial barrier.

"Tony?" Danny's voice was a fragile whisper, full of a hesitation that made Tony's heart ache. They lay in silence so long Tony thought Danny had already drifted off. Then he felt it—Danny's toes brushing clumsy and tentative against his calf under the blanket. A small, accidental touch. Or maybe not accidental at all.

"Yeah?" he breathed back.

"The bed's... it's big enough," Danny said, the words a quiet, vulnerable offering. "You don't... you don't have to sleep on the floor."

The invitation, so simple and so profound, was everything. Tony's throat tightened. He couldn't speak. He just gave a slow, deliberate nod. Together, they moved from the floor to the bed, a silent, coordinated dance. They slipped under the covers, the space between them charged with a new, terrifying, and exhilarating intimacy. They lay on their sides, facing each other, the silence humming with unspoken things. This was it. The culmination of a day that had changed everything. The start of a night that would define their future.

255

CHAPTER 26

NEW NORMAL

As the days passed, the raw, chaotic energy that had consumed the Guzman house had settled into a new, fragile kind of normal. A quiet rhythm had established itself, built on small, tentative steps. Tony no longer slept on the air mattress; after that first night, he had simply stayed in the bed, and Tony had joined him, the two of them navigating the new intimacy with a shy, careful grace. Their days were filled with school, their afternoons were spent in the garage, their hands greasy as they slowly, piece by piece, brought the old Triumph back to life, and their evenings were spent in the quiet company of a family Danny was slowly, cautiously, beginning to accept as his own.

The secret of what had truly happened to Dina remained a heavy, unspoken thing between Maria and Leroy, a necessary shield they held around the boys. The official story was the one Ms. Jenkins had provided: she was "medically incapacitated" and would be for the foreseeable future. It was a vague, sterile truth that Danny seemed to accept without question, too focused on his own healing to probe the dark corners of her fate.

On a Tuesday afternoon, two weeks after the meeting with Ms. Jenkins, Maria sat at the kitchen table, the pamphlet of therapists in her hand. She had made the call. Today was the day. Danny came downstairs, his movements quiet and hesitant. He knew what today was. He stood in the kitchen doorway, clutching the strap of his backpack, his eyes wide with a familiar, hunted look.

"I don't... I don't want to go," he whispered, his voice so quiet it was almost lost in the hum of the refrigerator. Maria's heart ached for him. She stood up and walked over, her expression full of a gentle, unwavering love.

"I know, *mijo*," she said softly. "It's scary. Talking to a stranger about... things." She didn't push. She just stood before him, a calm, steady presence. "But Dr. Sharma... she's just here to help you sort through the noise in your head. It's a safe place. Just for you."

Tony appeared at the top of the stairs, keys to the minivan jingling in his hand. He had a free period every Tuesday afternoon, a fact that had once been for slacking off, but had now become the perfect, unchangeable slot in his schedule for this. He saw the terror on Danny's face, the plea in his eyes as he stood frozen before his mom.

He walked down and stood beside Maria, a silent, united front. He didn't say anything. He just looked at Danny and, with his thumb, gently tapped the space over his own heart twice.

Tap. Tap.

Danny saw the gesture. He took a shaky breath, the silent message a small, steady anchor in the swirling sea of his anxiety. He looked at Maria's kind, patient face, at Tony's unwavering support, and gave a single, tiny nod. He would go.

The drive to the therapist's office was quiet. Tony drove, his hands steady on the wheel, the silence in the car a comfortable, supportive one. The building was an old, converted house in a leafy, quiet part of town, not a cold, clinical office building. The waiting room was warm and inviting, with comfortable armchairs and shelves full of books. A few minutes later, a woman with warm, intelligent eyes and a calm, gentle smile opened the door to the inner office.

"Daniel?" she said, her voice soft. "I'm Dr. Sharma. It's very nice to meet you. Are you ready?"

Danny looked from the doctor's kind face back to Tony, who gave him a small, encouraging smile and a subtle nod. He took a deep, shuddering breath, clutched the straps of his backpack, and took the first, terrifying step on a new, necessary part of his journey. He walked through the door, leaving Tony alone in the quiet waiting room. Tony sat there, the minutes stretching into an eternity. He just listened to the faint, muffled murmur of voices from behind the closed door, his heart aching with a fierce, hopeful prayer that this was working, that Danny was finally finding a place to unload the heavy, invisible burdens he had been carrying for so long.

Dr. Sharma's office was nothing like Danny had imagined. It wasn't a cold, sterile room. It was warm and comfortable, with two soft armchairs, a low wooden table, and a large window that looked out onto a quiet, green garden. It felt less like a doctor's office and more like a cozy living room. Danny chose the chair furthest from the door and sat on the very edge, his backpack clutched in his lap like a shield. Dr. Sharma sat in the other chair, a kind, patient smile on her face. She didn't have a notepad or a pen. She just sat, her hands resting calmly in her lap.

"Thank you for coming in today, Daniel," she said, her voice as gentle as it had been in the waiting room. "I know this can be a difficult first step to take."

Danny just nodded, his eyes fixed on a small, smooth stone that sat on the table between them.

"I've spoken briefly with Ms. Jenkins and the Guzmans," Dr. Sharma continued, "so I have a general idea of what's been going on. But this space," she gestured to the room around them, "is just for you. You don't have to talk about anything you don't want to. We can just sit in the quiet if you'd like. The time is yours."

They sat in silence for a long time, the only sound was the soft ticking of a clock on the wall and the distant chirping of birds from the garden. Danny's heart was a frantic drum against his ribs. He knew he was supposed to talk, to say something, but the words were a tangled, heavy knot in his throat. Dr. Sharma didn't push. She just waited, her presence a calm, accepting anchor in the room. Finally, she spoke again, her voice still incredibly soft.

"That's a very interesting backpack," she said, her gaze on the worn canvas bag in his lap. "It's been on a lot of adventures."

Danny looked down at his backpack, surprised by the question. It wasn't about his mother, or the club, or the fear that was a constant hum beneath his skin. It was just about his backpack. He ran a hand over the faded, patched fabric. He didn't answer.

"Is there anything in there that's particularly important to you?" she asked, her tone one of simple, genuine curiosity.

Danny hesitated. Then, slowly, as if it were the hardest thing he had ever done, he unzipped the main compartment. He reached inside and pulled out Peanut, the small, worn plush elephant. He held it in his lap, his fingers tracing the frayed seams of its ears.

"This is Peanut," he whispered, the words a rough, rusty sound in the quiet room. It was the first thing he had said.

"Hello, Peanut," she said, as if greeting an old friend with a genuine and warm smile. "It's very nice to meet you." She looked at Danny, her eyes full of a deep, gentle understanding. "He looks like a very good friend."

Danny looked down at the small, stuffed elephant in his hands, at the one constant, comforting presence in his life, and gave a single, tiny nod. He took a shaky breath, the words coming out in a hesitant, fragmented whisper.

"My dad... he gave him to me," he said, the memory surfacing, fragile and specific. His voice wavered and for a second he bit down hard on his lip, like trying to dam up a flood before it spilled. His knuckles whitened around Peanut's frayed ear, the effort of holding himself together almost visible in the air. "When I was five. I... I hated getting my hair cut. I cried every time. And one day... after I was done, and I didn't cry... he gave me Peanut." He looked up, his eyes seeming to see a ghost from a happier time. "He said... he said it was for being a strong boy." He clutched the elephant a little tighter, his gaze turning inward. "When things were... bad. Loud. I would hide in my closet. And I'd hold him. He... he kept me safe." Danny's voice cracked, and for a second he bit down hard on his lip, like he was trying to dam up a flood before it could spill. His knuckles whitened around Peanut's frayed ear, the effort of holding himself together almost visible in the air between them. The admission was a monumental offering, a tiny, precious piece of his story finally brought out into the light.

The rest of the session passed in a similar, quiet way. Danny didn't say much else. He answered a few of Dr. Sharma's gentle questions with a nod or a single, whispered word. But he didn't retreat. He didn't shut down. For the first time, he had spoken about his past to a stranger and the world hadn't ended. It was a good start. When the hour was up, Dr. Sharma smiled at him.

"Thank you for sharing Peanut with me, Daniel," she said warmly. "I'd like to see you both again next week, if that's okay."

Danny just nodded, a sense of quiet relief washing over him. He tucked Peanut safely back into his backpack and walked to the door. He pushed it open and stepped back into the waiting room. Tony was still there, sitting in the same armchair, his head bent over a magazine he clearly wasn't reading. He looked up the moment Danny emerged, his expression a mixture of anxiety and profound, hopeful concern. He had waited. He had kept his promise.

Danny walked toward him, a new, fragile confidence in his step. He didn't say a word. He just walked right up to Tony, and as his boyfriend stood to meet him, Danny reached out and, for the first time, unhesitatingly took his hand, lacing his fingers through Tony's. From the doorway of her office, Dr. Sharma watched the quiet interaction. She saw the simple, unhesitating way Danny reached for what he wanted. It was a small thing, just the joining of two hands, but she knew it was a seismic shift. In their session, he had been a passive survivor, recounting the ways he had endured. But this, this was different. This was the first time she had seen him go for something he wanted, a simple, profound act of agency. It was a bigger step than anything he had said in his office. She gave a small, satisfied smile and quietly closed her door, leaving them to their new beginning.

The gesture was so simple, so direct, and so full of a new, unspoken certainty that it took Tony's breath away. He just stared down at their joined hands, a slow, brilliant smile spreading across his face. Danny was okay. And he was holding his hand. It was more than enough. They walked out of the quiet office and into the bright, warm afternoon sun, their hands still linked. The world felt different, lighter. The therapy session, as difficult as it had been for Danny, felt like a pressure valve had been released. As they walked to the minivan, Tony's mind was buzzing with a mixture of relief and awe.

"You were really brave in there, you know," he said, his voice full of genuine admiration. "Going in by yourself. I don't think I could have done that."

Danny looked at their joined hands, then up at Tony. He thought about how badly he had wanted Tony to be in that room with him, to hold his hand while he talked about Peanut. But he also knew, on a deeper level, that this was something he had to do on his own.

"I had to," he whispered, the words a simple, honest truth.

They reached the minivan, and Tony squeezed his hand gently.

"Hey," he said, his voice soft. "The afternoon is ours. We don't have to go home. We can do... whatever you want." Danny looked at him, his expression uncertain. He wasn't used to having choices. Tony saw the hesitation and decided to make it easier. "Okay, how about this," he said, a small, playful smile on his face. "Option A: there's an old-fashioned ice cream parlour a few blocks from here. My treat. Or, Option B: we could go to the mall, and I could buy you some new clothes that actually fit. You can't live in my old band t-shirts forever."

He presented the two options, one a simple, sweet indulgence, the other a practical step toward a new life, a new identity. He waited, letting the choice, for the first time, be completely and entirely Danny's. Danny looked down at the baggy t-shirt he was swimming in. Part of him knew he needed new clothes, things that were his own. But the thought of the mall—the crowds, the bright lights, the overwhelming number of choices in every store—was exhausting. Besides, he didn't mind wearing Tony's clothes. They were soft and smelled like him, a constant, comforting reminder that he was here, that he was safe. It felt like wearing a piece of Tony, a silent, protective shield. He looked back up at Tony, a small, hesitant smile on his face.

"A," he whispered, the single letter a quiet, definitive choice. "Ice cream."

Tony's smile widened.

"Ice cream it is," Tony said, giving Danny's hand a final squeeze before letting go to unlock the car.

The parlour was a perfect slice of nostalgia, a place that seemed untouched by time. It had a checkered black-and-white floor, red vinyl booths, and a long, gleaming counter with dozens of tubs of colorful ice cream on display. The air smelled of sugar cones and vanilla. A bell chimed as they walked in, and they were the only customers. They stood in front of the glass case, a dizzying array of choices before them.

"What's your poison?" Tony asked, his tone light and easy. Danny scanned the flavors, his eyes wide. He wasn't used to this many options. He finally pointed a shy finger at a tub of pale green ice cream. He stared at the case too long, paralyzed by the dizzying number of options. His old life had been about survival, not choices. Choices always belonged to someone else. Picking mint chip felt absurdly huge, like he was daring to want something.

"Mint... chocolate chip?" he said, the words a hesitant question.

"A man of taste," Tony declared with a grin. "I'll have the same."

They got their cones and slid into a booth by the window, the red vinyl cool against their skin. For a moment, they just ate in a comfortable silence, the only sounds were the soft scrape of their spoons and the distant hum of the freezer case. It was the most normal thing they had ever done together—just two boys in a booth, eating ice cream on a Tuesday afternoon.

Tony watched Danny carefully, saw the way he was slowly, cautiously relaxing. The rigid tension in his shoulders was gone, and he was actually enjoying himself, a small, genuine smile playing on his lips as he ate.

"So," Tony said softly, breaking the quiet. "Was it... okay? The session?" Danny looked up, considering the question. He swallowed a spoonful of ice cream, then gave a small, thoughtful nod.

"It was... quiet," he whispered. "She was nice." He paused, then added, "We talked about Peanut."

Tony's heart ached. He didn't press for more. He understood that talking about Peanut was a way of talking about everything else without having to say the words.

"That's good," he said, his voice full of a gentle reassurance. "That's a really good start." Danny looked down at his melting ice cream, then back up at Tony, his blue eyes clear and direct.

"Thank you," he said, the two words carrying the weight of the entire week. "For... waiting for me."

"Always," Tony said, his own voice thick with an emotion he couldn't quite name. He reached across the table and, with his thumb, gently wiped a small smudge of green ice cream from the corner of Danny's mouth. The touch was light, fleeting, but it was electric. Danny's breath hitched, and a soft blush crept up his cheeks.

They sat there, their eyes locked, the half-eaten ice cream forgotten between them. The world outside, with all its complications and fears, seemed to melt away, leaving only the two of them in a quiet, sunlit booth.

As they scraped the last of the ice cream from their bowls, Tony felt a comfortable, easy feeling settle over him. This was good. This was right. He didn't want it to end.

"Hey," he said, his voice casual. "You wanna... you wanna head home? We could... work on the bike for a bit before my dad gets back." Danny's face lit up. It wasn't a wide, beaming smile, but a subtle, genuine brightening of his entire expression. The motorcycle had become their shared project, their neutral ground, a place where they could exist together without the pressure of words. It was a place where they were just two guys, working with their hands, building something.

"Yeah," Danny said, his voice a quiet but eager whisper. "Okay." The simple, enthusiastic agreement was all Tony needed. The afternoon wasn't over. They had a plan. They had something to build, together.

The Triumph sat waiting for them, a half-finished project full of promise. They worked in an easy, comfortable silence, the only sounds the scrape of a wire brush against rusted chrome and the soft rock station playing from a dusty old boombox in the corner.

Danny was crouched down, trying to loosen a rusted bolt on the exhaust pipe. He grunted with effort, his small hands struggling to get a good grip with the wrench.

"Here, let me..." Tony started, moving to help.

"No, I got it," Danny said, his voice a quiet murmur of concentration. He gave the wrench one final, determined twist. The bolt gave way with a sharp, grating screech, and Danny's hand, slick with grease, slipped. The side of his palm scraped hard against the sharp, unfinished edge of a metal bracket.

"Ah, shit," he hissed, dropping the wrench with a clatter and pulling his hand back.

"What? What happened? Let me see." Tony was beside him in an instant.

"It's nothing," Danny said, but he was cradling his hand to his chest, his face pale. A thin line of bright red blood was already welling up from a nasty, inch-long gash on his palm.

"That's not nothing," Tony said, his voice a low, urgent command. All the easy-going calm of the afternoon was gone, replaced by a fierce, protective focus. "Come on. Inside. Now." He led Danny into the house and straight to the kitchen sink, gently turning on the warm water. "Okay, put it under here," he said, his voice softer now.

Danny flinched as the water hit the cut, but he didn't pull away. Tony's presence was a steady, calming force. Tony opened a cabinet and pulled out the first-aid kit. He worked with a surprising gentleness, his large, calloused hands moving with a careful precision. He cleaned the cut with an antiseptic wipe, ignoring Danny's sharp intake of breath, and then carefully dried the skin around it.

"This might sting a little," he warned, before applying a thin layer of antibiotic ointment.

Danny just watched him, his heart a slow, steady drum in his chest. He was used to dealing with his own injuries, to hiding them, to letting them heal on their own. He had never had anyone do this for him before. He had never been the focus of such gentle, unwavering care. Tony finished by wrapping a clean, white bandage snugly around Danny's palm. He held his hand for a moment longer than necessary, his thumb gently stroking the back of Danny's wrist.

"There," he said, his voice a low murmur. "All better." Danny stared at the neat white wrap, stunned. He'd hidden scrapes and bruises for years, waiting for them to scab over on their own. No one had ever stopped the bleeding for him before. The absurdity of it—that a bandage could feel more intimate than a kiss—made his chest ache in a new way.

He finally looked up, and their eyes met. In the quiet of the kitchen, with the afternoon sun slanting through the window, the air was thick with unspoken things. Tony's concern, his gentleness, his simple, profound act of care—it was more intimate than any kiss. Danny looked down at his bandaged hand, then back up at Tony.

"Thanks," he whispered, the single word carrying the weight of a thousand unsaid emotions. It was a thank you not just for the bandage, but for everything. For being there. For being safe.

CHAPTER 27

LOVE LANGUAGE

Two months had passed into the middle of May. A new kind of normal had taken root, fragile at first, but growing stronger with each passing day. The preliminary hearing with CPS had been a quiet formality, just as Ms. Jenkins had predicted, and the Guzmans were now Danny's official legal guardians.

The air mattress on Tony's floor was long gone, folded up and stored in the closet. The space on the bed beside Tony was now simply Danny's, an accepted and unspoken truth. Their days fell into a comfortable routine: school, quiet lunches where a shared glance and a silent tap, tap were often enough, and afternoons spent in the garage. The old Triumph was slowly, piece by piece, coming back to life under their greasy, patient hands, its restoration a mirror of their own. And every Tuesday, without fail, Tony would leave his free period, pick Danny up from the front of the school, and drive him to the quiet, leafy street where Dr. Sharma's office was. He would wait in the comfortable armchair, reading a magazine he never remembered, for exactly one hour, just like he promised.

Little by little, Danny was opening up in those sessions. He had talked more about Peanut, about his dad, about the good memories from before. He had even, in hesitant, fragmented whispers, started to talk about the bad times—the shouting, the loneliness, the constant, gnawing fear of living in that house. But there was one subject he never touched. One name he never said. He talked around the edges of her, of the monster, but he never talked about Dina herself. Dr. Sharma, with her infinite patience, never pushed.

At school, their relationship remained a quiet, private thing. Danny's fear of judgment, of the prying eyes and whispers, was still a palpable thing. He was slowly finding his voice in the safety of the Guzman home and Dr. Sharma's office, but the thought of being a public spectacle was still too much to bear. So they kept their distance in the crowded hallways, their connection a secret language of shared glances and silent signals.

One evening, as they were lying in bed, the comfortable silence was broken by Danny's quiet, hesitant voice.

"Tony?"

"Yeah?" Tony answered, turning to face him in the dark.

"Marko and Jamal," Danny started, the words a little shaky. "Do they... do they know? About us?"

"No," Tony said honestly. "They know how I feel. But they don't know about... 'us'."

Danny was quiet for a long moment. "You can," he finally whispered. "If you want to. You can tell them."

The permission, so freely given, was a monumental gift. It was an act of trust, a sign that Danny was finally starting to believe that their world could expand, just a little, without shattering. Tony was so taken aback he couldn't speak for a moment. He just looked at Danny in the dim light, at the fragile courage in his eyes. He knew what this cost him. He knew that for Danny, inviting anyone else into their small, safe world was a terrifying leap of faith.

"Are you sure?" Tony finally asked, his voice a low, gentle whisper. "You don't have to. We don't have to tell anyone anything until you're ready."

"I know," Danny said, his voice a little stronger now. "But... they're your best friends. They should know. It's not fair to you... to have to keep hiding." He took a shaky breath. "I trust them. Because you do." The simple, profound statement of trust hit Tony harder than any declaration of love could have. He reached out in the dark and gently took Danny's hand, lacing their fingers together. "Okay," he said, his voice thick with an emotion he couldn't name.

"Okay. I'll... I'll talk to them tomorrow." He squeezed Danny's hand, a silent thank you for his bravery, for his trust, for everything. In the quiet of the bedroom, it felt like another wall had just come down, leaving them with a new, more open space to build their future in.

The next day at school felt different. The air was charged with a new, private significance for Tony. He saw Danny by his locker between second and third period, a fleeting glance across the crowded hallway. Danny was just grabbing a book, his head down, trying to remain invisible as always. Their eyes met for a fraction of a second. Tony lifted his hand to his chest, his thumb resting over his heart.

Tap. Tap.

A small, almost imperceptible smile touched Danny's lips before he disappeared back into the river of students. But this time, Tony knew the signal wasn't just his to send anymore. It was a promise of a conversation to come.

At basketball practice, the change in Tony was palpable. The heavy, distracted weight that had plagued him for weeks was gone, replaced by a sharp, joyful focus. He moved with a fluid, confident grace, his passes were crisp and accurate, and every shot he took seemed to swish effortlessly through the net. Marko elbowed Jamal at one point.

"That's the guy we know," Marko whispered and Jamal only nodded, a quiet relief softening his face.He was a leader on the court again, not out of anger or aggression, but out of a pure, uncomplicated love for the game. Marko and Jamal exchanged a look of relieved, impressed surprise. The old Tony, the best version of him, was back. The locker room was steamy and loud, echoing with the familiar sounds of slamming locker doors, hissing showers, and the usual post-practice bullshit. Tony sat on the bench, pulling off his sneakers, but even in the noise, he carried Danny's quiet courage like a steady drumbeat under his ribs.

Marko and Jamal sat down on the bench opposite him, their own conversation dying down. They had been watching him all practice, their expressions a mixture of relief and lingering confusion. The cloud that had been hanging over their friend for months had finally lifted, and they didn't understand why.

"Dude, you were on fire today," Marko said, a genuine, impressed grin on his face. "Felt like old times. Whatever funk you were in, I'm glad it's over."

"Yeah, man," Jamal agreed, his tone softer, more observant. "You seem... different. Better."

Tony finished untying his shoes and finally looked up, meeting their gazes. He saw the genuine concern in their eyes, the unspoken questions. This was it. No more hiding. No more half-truths.

"I need to talk to you guys," he said, his voice low and serious, cutting through the casual atmosphere. "For real this time." Marko and Jamal exchanged a look, their expressions immediately turning serious. Marko stopped bouncing his leg; Jamal leaned forward slightly. They waited. "It's about me and Danny," Tony began, his eyes on his own hands. He took a deep, steadying breath. "We're... we're together now. Like, a couple. Boyfriends."

He looked up, bracing himself, his gaze steady and unwavering. Jamal didn't look surprised; he just offered a small, supportive smile, a silent acknowledgment of the truth he'd already suspected. But Marko just stared, his brow furrowed as he processed the new information, the pieces of the last few chaotic weeks visibly clicking into place in his mind.

"Whoa," Marko said slowly. "Okay. So... the breakup with Jessica... the fight with Kyle... it was all... this?"

"Yeah," Tony said, his voice quiet. "It was all this."

"So... it's official now?" Marko clarified, his tone shifting from shock to something more grounded. "You guys are actually... a thing?"

"Yeah," Tony said, a small, relieved smile touching his lips as he saw no trace of disgust on his friend's face. "We are. And... he told me it was okay to tell you guys. He trusts you." The weight of that trust seemed to land on Marko. His expression softened, the last of his lingering confusion giving way to a simple, uncomplicated happiness for his friend.

"Damn, Tony. That's... that's huge, man." Marko said as he looked at Jamal, then back at Tony, a real grin spreading across his face. "I'm happy for you, dude. For real. It's good to see you... you know. Not miserable." Tony laughed, a real, genuine sound of relief that echoed slightly in the noisy locker room.

"Yeah. Me too. He's in therapy. I drive him."

"So, that's where you disappear to every Tuesday afternoon?" Jamal asked, the question gentle but direct. "You always duck out of your free period without saying anything." Tony's smile faded slightly, his expression turning more serious. The easy part was over. He nodded.

"Yeah. That's... that's for him." The word *therapy* landed with a new weight. Marko's eyes widened slightly.

"Oh. Damn. Is he... is he doing okay with it?"

"He's getting there," Tony said, a fierce, protective note in his voice. "He's talking, little by little. It's... a process." He looked at them, needing them to understand the gravity of it all. "This is all still so new for him. He's still so raw. That's why we're not... you know. Obvious. At school. It's too much for him right now. He needs to feel safe." He looked at his friends, his expression full of a new, vulnerable honesty. "I'm just trying to keep my promises, you know? To be what he needs me to be."

The easy camaraderie in the room was replaced by a new, deeper understanding. The full picture—the abuse, the rescue, the fragile recovery—was becoming clearer. Marko clapped him on the shoulder, his grip firm and supportive.

"We get it, man," he said, his voice full of a quiet respect he rarely showed. "We get it. Your secret is safe with us."

At the same time, across the school, Danny was in the library. The vast room, with its high ceilings and hushed, reverent quiet, felt like a cathedral of whispers. But for the first time, he wasn't hiding in his usual corner. He sat at one of the public computer terminals, his back to the room, his expression one of quiet, intense concentration. He wasn't reading for class. He was searching the library's database, his fingers hesitantly typing in keywords he had never dared to explore before: *Relationships. Communication. Healing from trauma.*

He felt a hot flush of embarrassment, even though no one could see his screen. It felt like admitting he was broken, that he didn't know how to be a person. But the shame was quickly replaced by a stronger, more determined feeling. Tony had been so patient, so kind. He was trying so hard, every single day, to be the person Danny needed. Danny wanted to meet him halfway. He wanted to learn. He wanted to understand how to build something healthy and real from the wreckage of their past, how to be a good boyfriend. He scrolled through the search results, his eyes landing on a title that seemed to call out to him: *"The Five Love Languages."* It sounded simple, not like a dense psychology textbook. It sounded like a place to start. He scribbled the call number on a scrap of paper, a small, secret mission clutched in his heart.

He found the book in the self-help aisle, a section he had never ventured into before, feeling like an intruder in a foreign land. He pulled the slim volume from the shelf, clutched it to his chest like a shield, and retreated to an empty carrel in the back corner, a place where he felt safe and unseen. He opened the book, the smell of paper and ink a small comfort, and his eyes began to scan the first few pages, a new, fragile hope blooming within him. He was so absorbed, so focused on the words that promised a map to a world he desperately wanted to understand, that he didn't notice the quiet footsteps approaching his table. He didn't register the faint scent of vanilla perfume until a shadow fell over his page. He looked up, his heart instantly seizing, a jolt of pure terror flooding his veins.

It was Jessica.

Danny froze, every muscle in his body going rigid. He braced himself for the storm—the anger, the accusations, the confrontation he had been dreading for two months. His first instinct was to slam the book shut, to hide what he was reading, to bolt. But before he could move, he saw the look on her face. It wasn't anger. It was a deep, familiar sadness. And in that moment, a new, different kind of fear took hold: the fear of hurting someone else. He knew it was wrong, what had happened. He had never intended for her to be collateral damage in the war of his and Tony's lives.

Jessica stood there, her own expression a mixture of surprise and a pain that looked bone-deep. Her eyes flickered from Danny's terrified face down to the book on the table. She read the title, and he saw a wave of understanding—and a fresh stab of hurt—wash over her features. She remembered Tony's raw, broken confession in the park: *I'm in love with him.* And now, seeing Danny here, with this book, she could only assume one thing: he was in love with Tony, too. The final, painful piece of the puzzle clicked into place.

She pulled out the chair opposite him and slowly, quietly, sat down. The sound of the chair legs scraping against the linoleum was deafening in the library's silence. Danny just stared, his heart hammering against his ribs, his knuckles white where he gripped the book.

"I'm not angry with you, Danny," she said, her voice a soft, gentle whisper that was completely at odds with the hurricane he had been expecting. "I want you to know that. I was hurt. I'm still hurt." She took a small, shaky breath. "But I'm not angry with you. I could never fault you for this."

Danny didn't know what to say. He just watched her, his eyes wide with a disoriented confusion. This gentle kindness was more destabilizing than rage would have been. Jessica looked at the book, then back at him, her gaze full of a sad, profound empathy.

"He's trying really hard, isn't he?" she asked, her voice quiet. "To be better." The simple, knowing question made Danny's throat tighten. He could only manage a small, almost imperceptible nod. She let the silence stretch just long enough to sting, then added softly... "I know you're scared," she continued, her voice still a gentle whisper. "And you have every right to be. But I need to ask you something, and I need you to be honest with me. It's the only way any of us can move on." She took a breath, her own eyes shimmering with unshed tears that she refused to let fall. "Are you in love with him, too?"

The question, so direct and so full of a pain that wasn't his, made Danny's throat close. He looked at this girl, this kind, beautiful girl who had been nothing but good to Tony, and felt a wave of shame so profound it was almost suffocating. He couldn't lie to her. He wouldn't. He took a shaky breath, the words coming out in a hesitant, fragmented whisper.

"I never... I never wanted to hurt you, Jessica. I... I know it was wrong." He finally met her gaze, his own eyes full of a deep, apologetic sincerity. "I'm so sorry." He couldn't say the words, "*I love him*." They felt too big, too sharp, too much like a betrayal to say to her face. But he had to answer her question. He had to be honest. "He's... he's helping me," Danny whispered, his gaze dropping to the book on the table as if the words were written there. "He makes me feel... safe. For the first time...... in a very long time. And I'm... I'm really grateful for him."

It wasn't a direct confession, but it was everything. It was the absolute truth, spoken in his own quiet, hesitant way. Jessica heard the unspoken volumes in his words. She saw the deep, undeniable affection in his eyes when he spoke of Tony. She didn't need to hear the words "I love him" to know it was true.

She took a deep, shuddering breath, a fresh wave of her own pain washing over her as the final door on her own hope closed. But she pushed it down. She had to be the bigger person. This small, broken boy was not her enemy.

"Okay," she said softly, a single tear finally escaping and tracing a path down her cheek. She wiped it away quickly with the back of her hand. "Okay, Danny. Thank you... for being honest." She still wasn't ready to forgive Tony for using her, for the lies. But looking at Danny, at the fragile hope in his eyes, she knew she couldn't hate him for loving the same boy she did. She gave him a small, sad, and incredibly brave smile. "You two," she said, her voice barely a whisper. "Just... try not to hurt each other anymore. Okay?"

And with that, she stood up and quietly walked away, leaving Danny alone in the carrel, the book still open in front of him, his heart aching with a strange, complicated mix of guilt, gratitude, and a new, fragile hope. Jessica's quiet footsteps faded, leaving Danny alone in the cavernous silence of the library. The echo of her final words, "Just... try not to hurt each other anymore," hung in the air, a sad and gentle plea that settled deep in his heart. He sat for a long time, staring at the empty chair opposite him, a profound ache blooming in his chest for the kind girl whose heart had been broken in the crossfire of his and Tony's long, painful war.

The weight of it all—the guilt, the gratitude, the sheer, terrifying newness of being cared for—threatened to pull him under. But then he looked down at the book in his hands. The simple, clean title felt like a lifeline. *He's trying really hard, isn't he?* Jessica's words came back to him. Tony was trying. He was fighting for them. Danny knew, with a sudden, fierce clarity, that he had to fight, too. He couldn't just be a passenger in his own rescue. He had to learn how to be a partner.

He pushed the painful encounter from his mind and forced his attention back to the page. The introduction was simple, the concept almost shockingly straightforward: different people feel loved in different ways. The book explained that everyone has a primary "love language"—a specific way they best understand and receive affection. If you don't speak your partner's language, your expressions of love, no matter how sincere, can get lost in translation.

He turned the page to the first chapter: **Words of Affirmation.** He thought of Tony, replaying the rough, cracked honesty in his bedroom that night—*I don't know how to be good, but I want to be.* He thought of the quiet, steady *"You good?"* that seemed to anchor him every day since.

The book described people whose primary language was verbal encouragement, compliments, and kind words. They needed to hear *"I love you,"* but also *"I'm proud of you," "You did a great job,"* and *"I'm here for you."* Danny thought of Tony. He remembered the raw, broken confession in his bedroom, the desperate need to explain, to be understood. He thought of the quiet, constant reassurance in Tony's voice since that night, the gentle *"Hey, you good?"* and the fierce, protective *"That is not going to happen."* Tony needed to hear things, but he also seemed to know that Danny needed to hear them, too.

Next was **Quality Time.** This was about giving someone your undivided attention. Not just sitting in the same room, but truly being present, listening, sharing an activity without distraction. The afternoons in the garage immediately came to mind. The easy, comfortable silence as they worked on the Triumph, the shared focus, the simple joy of building something together. It felt like a perfect fit.

He read about **Receiving Gifts.** The book was quick to point out that this wasn't about materialism, but about the tangible thought behind the gift. A gift was a physical symbol that said, "I was thinking of you." Danny remembered the sandwich Tony had placed on his cafeteria table. He had been too scared to eat it then, but now he understood the gesture in a new light. It wasn't a trick. It was a gift. It was Tony trying to speak a language of care, however clumsily.

Then came **Acts of Service.** For these people, actions truly spoke louder than words. They felt loved when their partner did something for them—making breakfast, running an errand, or, in Danny's case, driving him to therapy every single Tuesday and waiting for an hour without complaint. The sheer, unwavering reliability of Tony's actions, of him showing up time and time again, resonated deeply.

Finally, he turned to the last chapter: **Physical Touch.**

He read the description, and a jolt of pure, undeniable recognition shot through him. The book described people who felt most loved and secure through physical connection—holding hands, a hand on the back, a hug, a simple, reassuring touch. He pictured Tony's knuckles brushing his wrist in the waiting room, the press of him on the mattress when Danny whispered *Can you just lie here with me?*—moments that felt more like home than words ever could.

His mind immediately went back to the night of the meeting with Ms. Jenkins. He remembered the terror, the feeling that his world was about to shatter again, and the overwhelming urge he'd had. *Can you just lie here with me?* The memory of Tony's solid, warm presence beside him, of the steady beat of his heart under his palm, was a visceral one. In that moment, he hadn't needed words or gifts. He had just needed to be held. He had needed to feel, physically, that he wasn't alone.

He looked down at his bandaged hand, remembering the surprising gentleness of Tony's fingers as he'd cleaned the cut, the lingering, reassuring weight of his touch. He thought of their first kiss, so soft and tentative, and how it had felt like the first real, safe thing that had happened to him in years.

He closed the book, his heart pounding with a new, startling clarity. He finally understood. Tony had been trying to speak all five languages to him at once, a desperate, shotgun approach to show him he cared in every way possible. But for Danny, the one that broke through the fear, the one that felt like coming home, was touch.

And Tony? What did Tony need? He thought about Tony's confession, his need to be heard, his constant, quiet check-ins. It had to be Words of Affirmation. Tony needed to hear that he was good, that he was forgiven, that he was loved.

Danny sat back in the carrel, the book held tightly to his chest. He felt like he had just been given a secret decoder ring. The path forward no longer felt like a terrifying, dark forest. For the first time, he felt like he had a map. He didn't have to guess anymore. He could learn. He could practice. He could show Tony he loved him in a way Tony would understand. And maybe, just maybe, he could learn to ask for what he needed, too. The fragile hope that had bloomed within him earlier was no longer so fragile. It felt real. It felt possible.

After practice, Tony headed straight for the library, a new, lighter energy in his step. He walked through the tall canyons of bookshelves, his eyes scanning the quiet carrels. He found Danny in his usual spot in the back, but he wasn't reading. He was just staring at a book on the table, his expression lost and distant.

Tony approached quietly, and Danny looked up, his eyes wide and startled. As Tony got closer, he saw Danny, with a sudden, panicked movement, slam the book shut and shove it into his backpack, as if trying to hide evidence of a crime. Tony stopped at the table, a slow, curious grin spreading across his face.

"Whoa, what was that?" he asked, his tone light and teasing. "Hiding something from me?"

"It's... it's nothing," he stammered, his voice a flustered mumble. "Just... a book." Danny's face flushed a deep, mortified red. His hands fidgeted with the zipper of the backpack like he could bury the secret deeper.

"A book?" Tony chuckled, pulling out the chair and sitting down opposite him. "This is the first time I've ever seen you in the library trying to hide a book you were reading. You looked like you were a million miles away."

"I was just... thinking," Danny mumbled, his gaze fixed on a scratch on the table. He was stammering over his words, his usual quiet shyness replaced by a new, more frantic kind of flustered energy.

Tony watched him, his smile softening. He knew Danny. He knew his different shades of quiet. This wasn't the scared quiet, or the sad quiet. This was something else entirely. This was the flustered, embarrassed quiet of someone who had been caught doing something deeply personal. He leaned forward, his voice a low, gentle murmur.

"Hey," he said softly. "It's okay." He lifted his hand and, right there in the quiet library, gently tapped his thumb over his own heart twice.

Tap. Tap.

CHAPTER 28

STOLEN SILENCE

The drive home from school was quieter than usual. Tony could feel a new, nervous energy coming from Danny, who stared out the passenger window, his knee bouncing with a restless rhythm. Tony didn't push it, sensing that whatever was on Danny's mind, he needed to get there on his own terms.

Back in the safety of Tony's room, the silence stretched, thick with unspoken thoughts. Danny dropped his backpack by the door and just stood there, wringing the strap in his hands. Tony watched him, his expression soft with concern.

"Hey," Tony said gently, sitting on the edge of his bed. "You good?" Danny took a deep breath, the kind one takes before jumping off a high dive. He finally looked up, his blue eyes filled with a mixture of fear and fierce determination.

"I, um… I need to tell you something," he began, his voice barely a whisper. He walked over to his own backpack and hesitantly unzipped it. He pulled out the library book—*"The Five Love Languages"*—and held it out, his hand trembling slightly. "I found this. In the library. Today."

Tony looked at the book, then back at Danny's terrified face. He remembered the look of panic when he'd found him in the carrel, the way Danny had tried to hide the cover. A wave of gentle understanding washed over him. He wasn't upset; he was deeply touched.

"Okay," Tony said, his voice calm and even, trying to soothe the fear he saw in Danny's eyes.

"It's just…" Danny struggled for the words, his gaze dropping to the floor. "You… you've been doing so much. For me. You're always so careful, and you're patient, and you… you're trying so hard to understand what I need. To respect my boundaries." He took another shaky breath and finally met Tony's gaze again. "I want to do that, too. For you." He held the book up a little higher, a silent offering. "I want to… to understand what *you* need. How to… be better for you. I don't want it to be just you taking care of me all the time. I want to take care of you, too."

The raw, vulnerable confession hit Tony with the force of a physical blow. He felt a tightness in his chest, an emotion so powerful it almost stole his breath. This wasn't about a book. This was about Danny seeing them as an "us," as a team. This was Danny, who had been taught that his needs didn't matter, actively trying to learn how to care for someone else.

Tony stood up slowly and closed the distance between them. He didn't take the book. Instead, he gently took Danny's face in his hands, his thumbs stroking his cheeks.

"Danny, look at me," he said, his voice thick with emotion. "You don't have to 'be better' for me. You're everything. Just you, right here, right now, is everything." He leaned in, resting his forehead against Danny's. "But this…" he whispered, his eyes closing. "The fact that you would do this… that you're even thinking like this… that's the most incredible gift you could ever give me."

He could feel Danny start to tremble under his touch, the tension finally breaking. Danny let the book fall to the floor with a soft thud and wrapped his arms around Tony's waist, burying his face in his chest and holding on tight. Tony wrapped his own arms around him, pulling him close, just holding him in the quiet of the room.

"I think… I think yours would be Words of Affirmation," Danny mumbled into Tony's sweatshirt. Tony let out a soft, wet laugh, tightening his hold.

"Yeah?"

"And I think… I think mine is this," Danny whispered, his voice small but sure. "Just… this."

Tony didn't need a book to understand what he meant. He just held him closer, knowing that this quiet, shaky confession was a bigger step forward than any therapy session. It was the moment they stopped being a protector and a victim, and truly started being partners.

Tony felt a light, hesitant brush of Danny's hand against his chest, right over his heart. The simple contact was a lightning strike. Tony's heart, which had been beating with a steady, calm affection, immediately kicked into a frantic, wild rhythm. It was beating so fast and so hard, it felt as if it would burst right out of him, a frantic drum against Danny's palm. He held his breath, every nerve ending zeroed in on the boy in front of him.

Danny looked at Tony, his blue eyes wide and luminous in the soft light of the bedroom. He had been trying to find the words for so long, turning them over and over in the quiet of his therapy sessions, whispering them to Peanut in the dark. For weeks, they had been a heavy, precious weight on his tongue, but fear had always held them back. The fear that it was too soon, that it wasn't real, that he didn't deserve to say them.

But now, feeling the frantic, honest beat of Tony's heart beneath his hand, seeing the unwavering love in his eyes, the fear finally dissolved. It was replaced by a quiet, solid certainty. This was real. This was safe. And he was finally strong enough. He took a shaky breath, the sound fragile in the quiet room.

For a heartbeat Tony thought he imagined it—that Danny's hand on his chest, his lips parting like he had something to say. His whole body locked, terrified to hope. What if it wasn't what he thought? What if Danny pulled back again? His chest felt like it might cave in from the pressure of waiting.

"Tony," he whispered, voice catching. His lips trembled around the next word. He bit down hard on his bottom lip, shook his head like he almost couldn't force it past. Then, with a sharp inhale, he let go— "I love you."

The words were spoken so softly, they were almost a sigh, but they landed in the room with the force of a thunderclap. For a second, Tony couldn't breathe. He couldn't think. All he could hear was the echo of that simple, perfect sentence. He felt a hot, stinging sensation behind his eyes as tears of pure, unadulterated joy welled up.

A sound, a choked, half-laugh, half-sob, escaped his lips. "You..." he started, his voice thick and unrecognizable. "You have no idea how long I've waited to hear you say that."

He didn't wait for a response. He closed the small distance between them and captured Danny's lips in a kiss that was nothing like their first. There was no hesitation, no gentle discovery. This was a kiss of pure, unrestrained joy and profound relief, a celebration of a finish line they had finally, miraculously, crossed together. He pulled back, resting his forehead against Danny's, their tears mingling. Danny was smiling, a real, brilliant smile that lit up his entire face.

"I love you," Tony whispered back, the words a fierce, unbreakable vow. "I love you so much."

In the quiet of the bedroom, with the late afternoon sun slanting through the window, they just held each other, two broken pieces that had, against all odds, finally found their way back together and made each other whole. The front door opened softly, and the two boys slipped back into the quiet house. They were both smiling, their hands slightly cold from the river air, their hair a little messy from the evening breeze. The heavy, emotional weight that had clung to them for months seemed to have finally lifted, replaced by a light, easy camaraderie.

They found Maria and Leroy in the kitchen. Maria was wiping down the counters, and Leroy was sitting at the table, scrolling through the news on his phone. They both looked up as the boys entered, their expressions warm and welcoming.

"Hey," Tony said, his voice casual as he leaned against the doorframe. "We were, uh... thinking of going to grab a pizza. If that's cool."

Maria's face broke into a wide, genuine smile. The simple, utterly normal teenage request was music to her ears. It was a world away from the frantic rescues and hushed, tearful confessions. This was just her son, and the boy who was becoming like a son, wanting to go out on a Friday night.

"Of course, *mijo*," she said, her voice full of warmth. "That sounds nice. Do you need some money?"

"Nah, I've got it," Tony said, pulling his wallet from his back pocket. Leroy looked up from his phone, a pleased, relaxed expression on his face.

"Just be back by eleven," he said, the command more of a gentle reminder than a strict order. "And if you bring any back for me, no anchovies. I mean it."

Tony laughed. "Wouldn't dream of it, *Papi*."

"Hang on, I just need to grab something," Danny said quietly. Before Tony could respond, Danny turned and quickly headed back up the stairs. Tony watched him go, a curious, soft smile on his face. A moment later, Danny came back down, shrugging his worn backpack over his shoulders. Tucked under his other arm was a fresh, spiral-bound sketchbook—a gift from Tony the week before, after he'd seen Danny doodling incredible, intricate patterns on a scrap piece of mail.

Danny stood beside Tony, quiet as usual, but he wasn't hiding behind him. He stood tall, offering a small, shy smile to Maria when she looked at him. The haunted, fearful look in his eyes was gone, replaced by a calm, peaceful light. As Tony turned to grab the keys to the minivan from the hook by the door, he felt a subtle movement beside him. He glanced over and saw Danny, with his eyes on the floor, gently tap his own chest twice with his thumb.

Tap. Tap.

The secret message, so freely given, sent a warm jolt straight through Tony's heart. It was Danny's quiet *"thank you"*. It was an *"I'm happy"*. It was an "us." He gave Danny a small, private smile that was just for him.

"Come on," he said, his voice soft. "Let's go."

And as they walked out the door together into the cool summer night, Maria and Leroy exchanged a look of profound, silent relief. Their boys were going to be okay. This was the new normal. And it was beautiful.

"Hey," he said, his voice casual, but with an undercurrent of something more. "I, uh... I want to take you somewhere. A place I go sometimes. When I need to think."

Danny looked up from the part he was cleaning, his curiosity piqued by the rare, almost hesitant tone in Tony's voice.

"Okay," he said simply.

They left the quiet suburb of their neighborhood behind, driving towards the city as the sun began to dip below the horizon. The roar of the minivan felt different as they merged onto the highway, the city lights growing brighter and closer, a sprawling galaxy of steel and glass. Tony didn't say where they were going, and Danny didn't ask.

As the sound of the minivan's engine faded down the street, a comfortable silence settled over the kitchen. Maria watched the taillights disappear before turning back from the window, a soft, thoughtful smile on her face.

"A pizza run," she said, almost to herself. "It's so... normal." Leroy looked up from his phone, his own expression one of quiet contentment.

"He's a good kid, Maria. Tony. He's stepped up." He shook his head in mild disbelief. "The two of them... they spend hours in that garage. I peeked in yesterday. That old Triumph... it's looking almost new. I was tempted to get in there and show them a thing or two, but they looked like they had everything under control. It's their thing."

"They're both good kids," Maria corrected gently, a warmth spreading through her chest. She picked up a dish towel and began to dry the counter, her movements slow and thoughtful. "It's good to see them working on something together. It reminds me..." She trailed off, a wistful, faraway look in her eyes. Leroy watched her, knowing exactly where her mind had gone.

"Of us?" he finished for her, his voice a low, gentle rumble. Maria smiled.

"Of us. Before Tony, before all this..." Maria said as Leroy chuckled, the sound a warm, deep bass. "Remember that time we rode out to the lake with nothing but a tarp and a bag of chips?" Maria laughed, shaking her head.

"Details, details," Leroy grinned, his eyes twinkling.

"We froze, but I wouldn't trade it," Maria sighed. The memory passed between them like a warm blanket—brief, tender, enough.

They stood in silence for a moment, the shared memory a warm, comfortable blanket. The motorcycle wasn't just a machine; it was a part of their story, and seeing the boys bring it back to life felt like watching a new chapter begin.

"You know," Maria said, her voice soft, pulling him back to the present. "Since the boys are graduating soon, we need to celebrate them properly." Leroy nodded, his focus now entirely on her.

"I know. It's coming up fast."

"Originally, I wanted to throw a big party," Maria continued. "A big, loud celebration for Tony. But now... with Danny..."

"No," Leroy agreed immediately. "A party is out. It would be too much for him." He thought for a moment. "What about a dinner? Just the four of us. Somewhere nice. Not too fancy or loud, but... special." Maria's eyes lit up.

"That's perfect."

"I know a place," Leroy said, a slow smile spreading across his face. "An Italian spot I went to for a retirement dinner a while back. It's called *Sotta la Luna*. It's nice, but it's got this... relaxed feeling. Great food. It would be perfect."

"*Sotta la Luna*," Maria repeated, tasting the name. "I like it." The decision was made. A quiet, intimate dinner to celebrate not just a graduation, but the formation of their new, complete family. She leaned her head on Leroy's shoulder, a profound sense of peace settling over her. "A celebratory dinner," she said. "For our boys."

Tony finally pulled the van over on a quiet, industrial-looking street, the kind with more warehouses than houses. From here, they could hear the low, constant hum of traffic from a nearby bridge.

"Come on," Tony said, leading Danny through a gap in a chain-link fence. They navigated a short, dusty path that opened up to a small, secluded patch of rocky shoreline.

The view was breathtaking. The Queensboro Bridge loomed before them, a majestic, intricate web of steel, its lights just beginning to flicker on against the deep twilight sky. The dark, swirling waters of the East River lapped against the shore, and the distant, glittering skyline of

Manhattan was a breathtaking backdrop. The air was cool and smelled of the river and the city.

"This is it," Tony said, his voice quiet. "This is my spot."

He walked to the water's edge and picked up a flat, smooth stone. "When things were... a lot," he began, not looking at Danny, just staring out at the water, "when I had too much in my head... I'd come here. It was the only place that felt quiet, you know? Even with the whole city right there." He pointed with the rock towards the massive bridge. "Right there," he said. "That's where I taught myself how to skip rocks. I'd just... throw them for hours. Trying to make them fly."

With a flick of his wrist, he sent the stone sailing out over the water. It skipped once, twice, three times—perfect, bouncing dimples on the river's dark surface—before finally sinking. He turned to look at Danny, a vulnerable, open expression on his face.

"No one's ever been here with me before," he confessed, his voice barely a whisper. "This was just... my place."

Danny's heart swelled. He looked from Tony's face to the magnificent bridge, then back again. This was more than just a place with a pretty view. This was a piece of Tony's soul, a secret sanctuary he had just been invited into. He understood the immense trust in the gesture. Tony was showing him the part of himself that he had always kept hidden, the quiet, thoughtful boy who sought solace by the water.

Danny walked to the riverbank and found a flat stone of his own. He didn't say anything. He just stood beside Tony, mimicking his stance, and with a clumsy, hopeful flick, sent his own rock skipping across the water. It only managed one short hop before it sank with a soft *plunk*. Tony let out a small, genuine laugh. He found another stone and handed it to Danny.

"Here," he said softly. "Try this one. You have to get low. It's all in the wrist."

And as the sky deepened to a dark, inky blue and the city across the river lit up, they stood side-by-side, skipping rocks in a comfortable, easy silence, two boys sharing a secret world in the shadow of a bridge.

After a few more throws, Danny let his last rock drop to the ground. He stood for a moment, just staring, his artist's eye taking in the breathtaking scene before him: the intricate lines of the bridge, the glittering lights of the skyline reflecting on the dark, moving water, the vastness of the twilight sky.

"I... I want to try and sketch this," he said, his voice quiet but full of a new, certain purpose. He turned to Tony. "If that's okay." Tony's smile widened. He loved seeing this side of Danny—the focused, passionate artist.

"Yeah? Of course it's okay." He looked from the bridge back to their spot on the rocky shore. "But this isn't the best angle. You can't see the whole thing from here." He gestured up the path. "Come on. I know a better spot."

He led Danny up the dusty path, away from the water's edge, and onto a small, grassy lookout area just a little ways up the riverbank. From here, the view was panoramic. The entire magnificent sweep of the Queensboro Bridge was laid out before them, perfectly framed by the glittering towers of Manhattan on one side and the quieter lights of Queens on the other.

"Whoa," Danny breathed, his eyes wide with awe.

"Better?" Tony asked, a proud grin on his face.

Danny didn't answer. He had already dropped his backpack to the ground, pulling out the sketchbook and a charcoal pencil. He sat down on the cool grass, crossing his legs, and opened to a fresh page. Tony sat down beside him, not crowding him, just a quiet, steady presence.

He watched as Danny's focus narrowed, the world seeming to melt away until it was just him, the paper, and the breathtaking view. His hand, which could be so hesitant and trembling, was now confident and sure. The pencil began to move, swift, light strokes that captured the bridge's powerful lines, the shimmer of the city lights, and the vast, quiet beauty of the night. Tony just watched, completely captivated, feeling like he was seeing the world, and the boy beside him, in a whole new light.

An hour passed in comfortable silence, the only sounds the soft scratch of charcoal on paper and the distant hum of the city. The sky, now a deep, cloudless indigo, was dotted with a handful of early stars. A sliver of a crescent moon hung low over the horizon. Tony never moved. He just watched, content to be a quiet guardian of this small, peaceful moment. Finally, Danny stopped. He held the sketchbook out, his arm trembling slightly from the effort, and looked at his work with a critical eye.

"Can I see?" Tony asked softly.

Hesitantly, Danny turned the sketchbook toward him. Tony's breath caught in his throat. It wasn't just a drawing; it was an emotion. Danny had captured not just the bridge, but the *feeling* of the night—the quiet majesty, the vast loneliness, and the electric, hopeful energy of the city lights. In the corner, almost hidden, he'd sketched two small, silhouetted figures on the bluff: them.

"Danny, this is... incredible," Tony said, his voice full of a genuine awe that went beyond a simple compliment. "You're... really talented."

Danny's cheeks flushed a faint pink in the dim light, and he looked down, a shy, pleased smile on his face. He carefully tucked the sketchbook back into his backpack.

The quiet settled around them again, but this time it was different, charged with the intimacy of what they had just shared. Tony knew this was the moment. The fear he'd felt before was gone, replaced by a calm, solid certainty.

"Hey," he said, his voice a little shaky. "I know everything is... still new. And complicated. But I... I want to do this right. All of it." He turned to face Danny, his expression earnest and open. "I was wondering... if you would go out with me," he said, the words coming out in a rush. "Like, on a real date. Not just... hiding in the garage or running from things. A real date."

Danny stared at him, his blue eyes wide in the dim light. A slow, brilliant smile spread across his face, the first completely unguarded, joyful smile Tony had ever seen from him.

"Yeah," Danny whispered, his voice full of a happy, breathless disbelief. "Yeah, Tony. I'd really like that."

CHAPTER 29

OUTING

The living room was cast in the soft, low light of a single lamp. It was nearly one in the morning. On the couch, Maria held a book in her lap, her eyes having scanned the same page for the last hour without registering a word. At the kitchen table, Leroy sat with a stack of paperwork, the faint scratching of his pen the only sound in the tense, waiting silence of the house. Every passing car on the quiet street made Maria's head lift, her heart giving a hopeful, anxious flutter.

Finally, the tell-tale crunch of the minivan's tires on the gravel driveway broke the stillness. A moment later, the front door opened with a soft, nearly silent click.

Tony and Danny slipped inside, trying to be ghosts. Their faces, illuminated by the dim lamp, were still glowing with the quiet, easy happiness of their evening by the river. They were moving in a shared bubble of intimacy, oblivious to the late hour, their shoulders brushing as Tony reached to hang the keys on the hook.

"You two know what time it is?"

Leroy's voice was a low, quiet rumble from the kitchen, but it cut through the air like a razor. Danny flinched as if struck, the light in his eyes instantly extinguished. He froze, his body going rigid, his shoulders hunching as he braced for the storm he had been conditioned to expect. The happy, safe boy from the riverbank vanished, replaced in an instant by a terrified child waiting for the screaming to start.

Tony saw the transformation, and a hot, sickening wave of guilt and protective anger washed over him. He immediately stepped slightly in front of Danny, a subconscious shield.

"I know, *Papi*. I'm sorry," he said, his voice firm and clear, taking all the blame. "It's my fault. We were just talking, and I completely lost track of time. It won't happen again." Maria, seeing the raw terror on Danny's face, set her book aside and stood up.

"It's okay, *mijo*," she said, her voice a soft, soothing balm directed at Danny.

"You're not in trouble." She walked over to them, her expression gentle. "We just worry. When it gets this late and we don't hear from you, we worry that something has happened. That's all."

Leroy came to stand beside her, his expression serious but not angry. "Next time, a simple text message to let us know you'll be late," he said, establishing the rule calmly and fairly.

"That's all we ask. We trust you. But we need to know you're safe." The simple, healthy parental boundary was so foreign to Danny he didn't know how to react. He just stared, his heart still hammering.

"Now get upstairs, both of you," Leroy said, his voice softening. "It's late. Go on, get to bed." The boys nodded and quickly headed up the stairs, leaving the two parents alone in the quiet living room. Maria let out a long, shaky breath, her hand over her heart.

"Did you see his face, Leroy?" she whispered, her voice aching with empathy. "He was terrified. He thought you were going to..."

"I know," Leroy said, his own voice rough with a pained understanding. He wrapped an arm around his wife's shoulders, pulling her close. "It's going to take a long time, *mija*. A long, long time."

The sounds of the next summer morning—the distant rumble of the subway, the shouts of kids playing on the sidewalk, the hiss of a neighbor's sprinkler—filtered through the open windows. After a relaxed breakfast of pancakes that Maria insisted on making, she clapped her hands together, a determined, happy glint in her eye.

"Okay," she announced to the boys. "With graduation next week and your birthdays right after, we are going out. Both of you need proper clothes for the dinner at *Sotta la Luna*, and I will not take no for an answer." Danny, who had been relaxed just a moment before, immediately tensed. He looked down at his plate, his shoulders hunching slightly.

"Out.... where?" he asked, his voice barely a whisper. "Like... to the mall?" The thought of the mall on a Saturday—the endless sea of people, the noise, the vast, overwhelming spaces—made his stomach clench with a familiar, cold dread. Tony saw the look on his face instantly. He saw the way Danny's hands clenched under the table, the subtle shift in his posture from relaxed to braced. Before Maria could even answer, Tony jumped in.

"Actually," he said, his tone casual but deliberate, "there's this smaller shop I've been wanting to check out. It's in Astoria, a place called 'The Foundry.' They have really cool stuff, more our style than some big department store." He looked at Danny, his expression gentle. "It's a lot smaller. Quieter. I think... I think it might be better." Maria looked from Tony's considerate face to Danny's relieved one, and her heart swelled with pride.

"That," she said, her voice full of warmth, "sounds like a perfect idea, *mijo*."

An hour later, Tony pulled the minivan into a parking spot on a tree-lined street in Astoria. The area buzzed with the relaxed energy of a summer Saturday—people wandered in and out of quirky shops and cafes, their laughter mixing with the distant rumble of the N train, a steady, familiar hum.

The Foundry was exactly as Tony had described: a quiet, intimate space with exposed brick walls, warm lighting, and racks of carefully curated clothing. As the four of them stepped inside, Maria felt the familiar maternal instinct to take charge—to start rifling through shirts, choosing things for the boys to try on. But she stopped herself.

She watched Tony point Danny toward a rack of soft, vintage-style t-shirts in the corner, his voice low and steady. She saw the way Danny looked around the shop—not shrinking, not folding inward as he would have just a few months ago—but genuinely curious. He ran a hand over the sleeve of a denim jacket, his artist's fingers seeming to take in the texture, the quality of the fabric. He was exploring. There was no trace of the frightened, haunted boy they'd first brought home. Something deep inside Maria, a knot of worry she hadn't even realized she was still carrying, finally unclenched. She leaned toward Leroy and spoke softly, her voice full of a quiet wonder.

"You know... I think they've got this." She nodded in their direction. "They don't need us hovering."

Leroy followed her gaze. He watched the quiet, easy rhythm between the boys—the way Danny paused before lifting a shirt, waiting for Tony's nod—it was a rhythm that didn't need words.

"You're right," he said, his own voice heavy with a quiet pride. Maria reached out and squeezed his arm.

"There's a coffee shop on the corner, and I saw a dress in a boutique window that might be perfect for the dinner." Her eyes sparkled with a rare, uncomplicated desire to just be a woman shopping with her husband. "Why don't we give them an hour? Let them be teenagers while we play grownups." Leroy chuckled, a warm, genuine sound. He was already pulling out his wallet. He approached the boys, who were now debating the merits of a dark grey hoodie. He handed Tony a few folded bills.

"Your mom and I are going to look around a bit," he said. "Get what you need for dinner—and if something else catches your eye, go for it. We'll be back in an hour." Tony blinked, surprised by the sudden freedom. Then his face softened into something more meaningful—an expression of gratitude that ran deep.

"Okay, *Papi*. Thanks."

The bell above the door chimed softly behind them as Maria and Leroy stepped out into the bright afternoon. They settled at a small patio table outside the café, the warm sun on their faces. After ordering their drinks, a quiet comfort settled between them—the kind born of years, of weathered joys and shared scars.

"I can't get over how much things have changed," Maria said at last, her gaze distant as she watched the people drift past. "In just a few months... our house feels different. Calmer. Like it finally took a breath and can relax."

"It's Tony," Leroy said, his voice heavy with pride. "He's... different. Not just protective—he's *present*. He knew the mall would be too much for Danny. He planned for that. He's patient now. He *sees* him. I think this whole thing—hell, all of it—it forced him to grow up." Maria let out a breath that was half-sigh, half-smile.

"And Danny... he seems lighter. Just watching him look through clothes like any other kid... it felt like a tiny miracle." She traced a slow circle in the condensation on her glass. "Every time he smiles? A real smile? I feel like we won something." Leroy reached across the small metal table and took her hand, his large, calloused fingers enveloping hers.

"It is a win, *mija*. Every quiet, normal moment? That's a win."

They sat in the warm hush of the city, laughing now and then, talking about what they might wear for the dinner. For the first time in a long, long while, it felt like a real Saturday. Just as Maria was giggling over an absurdly large sunhat she'd seen in a shop window, Leroy's work phone buzzed on the table, a harsh, intrusive sound.

He glanced at the screen—and the air around him changed.

His smile vanished. His posture straightened, his shoulders subtly squaring. The easy warmth slipped away, replaced by the measured, impenetrable silence of a man who knew what came next. The husband was gone; the cop was back.

Maria's laughter died in her throat as she saw the shift.

"What is it?" Maria asked as Leroy placed the phone facedown on the table and looked at her, his eyes now holding the grim weight of his profession.

"That was the precinct," he said, his voice low and devoid of its earlier warmth. "The file I've been waiting on just came in. I have to go pick it up."

Maria's chest tightened. She already knew.

"Dina's?"

Leroy nodded slowly, the weight of the name hanging in the air between them.

"The full case file. Photos. Notes. The works." The words hung in the warm Saturday air, a sudden, cold weight that displaced all the easy happiness of the afternoon. "The completed case file. For Dina." Maria stared at her husband, her mind racing. The images her imagination conjured were a chaotic, terrifying blur. She felt a wave of nausea.

"Now?" she whispered, her voice tight. "You have to go right now?"

"It's better to just get it over with," Leroy said, his voice grim. He was already pulling out his phone, but he wasn't looking at his contacts. He was opening a ride-share app. "I'll get a cab of some kind. There's no reason for you and the boys to have to sit at the precinct. You stay. Finish your shopping. I'll meet you back at the house later."

It was a clear, protective gesture. He was drawing a line, separating the grim necessities of his job from the fragile, normal life they were trying to build. Maria just nodded, unable to speak, a profound sense of gratitude for his quiet strength warring with the cold dread in her stomach. Leroy stood, leaned over, and gave her a quick, firm kiss on the forehead.

"I'll be fine," he said, a promise he wasn't sure he could keep. "I'll see you at home."

She watched him walk to the curb, a solitary, determined figure heading off to confront the ghosts of their past. After his car disappeared around the corner, Maria sat alone at the small table, the cheerful sounds of the Astoria street a jarring counterpoint to the turmoil inside her. She took a deep, shuddering breath, forcing herself to push the image of Dina from her mind. She had to be strong. For them.

She paid for the coffees, left a generous tip, and walked back across the street, pausing for a moment outside the window of The Foundry. She took another steadying breath, smoothed the expression on her face into one of calm, maternal warmth, and pushed the door open, the small bell chiming her return.

She found the boys by the dressing rooms. A small pile of clothes was draped over a nearby chair. Tony was leaning against the wall, his arms crossed, a look of amused patience on his face. And Danny was standing in front of the full-length mirror, looking at his own reflection with an expression of quiet, startled surprise. He was wearing the deep blue button-down shirt, tucked into a pair of dark, perfectly fitting jeans. He looked... different. Taller. More solid. The scared, haunted boy who had arrived on their doorstep months ago was gone, replaced by a handsome young man who was just beginning to see himself for the first time.

Tony saw his mom enter and pushed off the wall.

"Hey," he said. "Where's *Papi?*"

"Oh, he just got a message from work, *mijo*," Maria said, her voice a perfect imitation of casual annoyance. "Something urgent came up that needed his attention. You know how it is." She waved a dismissive hand. "He said he'll meet us back at the house later."

The lie was smooth, effortless, a shield she expertly placed between the boys and the grim reality. She immediately turned her attention to Danny, her face breaking into a genuine, warm smile that masked the cold knot in her stomach.

"What do you think?" Tony asked, his voice soft.

"It's... okay," Danny mumbled, though his eyes told a different story. He smoothed a hand down the front of the shirt, a small, shy smile touching his lips.

"It's more than okay," Maria said, her own voice full of a genuine warmth that masked the cold knot in her stomach. "You look wonderful, Danny. Truly." Danny's cheeks flushed a faint pink. Tony held up a dark grey hoodie from the pile on the chair.

"He picked this out, too," Tony said to his mom. "And I found a new pair of jeans that don't have holes in the knees." Maria looked at the small collection they had assembled—the thoughtful, stylish choices, the simple act of two boys picking out clothes together—and her heart ached with a fierce, protective love. This. This was what mattered. This quiet, normal moment. It was a victory.

"They're perfect," she said, her smile unwavering. "Let's get them all." She looked from the clothes to Danny, a new idea sparking in her eyes. "You know," she said, her tone gentle, "I was thinking we could do something special for dinner tonight. Have you ever had sushi, *mijo?*" Danny looked a little startled by the question and shyly shook his head.

"Well, then it's settled," Maria declared, her smile turning bright and warm. "There's a wonderful little place not far from here. My treat. It's time you had your first taste."

She walked to the counter to pay, leaving the two boys to get changed, her mind a chaotic battleground of love for the family she was building and a deep, sorrowful dread for the news her husband was on his way to collect.

Maria's suggestion hung in the air, a bright and unexpected offering. Danny looked a little startled, his eyes wide. He'd never even seen sushi up close before, let alone eaten it. The idea was foreign, intimidating. But then he saw the gentle, hopeful look on Maria's face and the quiet, encouraging smile Tony gave him. He trusted them.

"Okay," he whispered, the single word a small leap of faith. Maria's smile turned brilliant.

"Wonderful! There's a place just a few blocks from here. We can walk."

The walk itself was a new experience. Danny, usually so hyper-aware of the people around him, found himself insulated between Maria and Tony. They flanked him, not in a smothering way, but like a quiet, protective honor guard, their presence a buffer against the bustling Saturday afternoon crowds of Astoria.

The restaurant, called "Kumo," was a small, serene oasis tucked between a noisy bakery and a laundromat. Inside, it was calm and minimalist, with smooth wooden tables, soft lighting, and the quiet hiss and clink of the sushi chefs working behind a long, clean counter. There was no loud music, no shouting—just a low, peaceful hum of conversation. Danny felt the knot in his stomach loosen just a little.

They were shown to a small booth in the back. Maria and Tony slid in on one side, and Danny took the other, giving him a view of the whole room. When the menus came, Danny's anxiety returned in a rush. He opened the glossy pages to a dizzying array of words he didn't recognize—*nigiri, sashimi, maki, unagi, tobiko*. It was another language, another set of rules he didn't know. He stared at the menu, completely lost, the fear of doing something wrong, of looking stupid, creeping back in. Tony, sensing his panic, leaned across the table.

"Hey," he said softly, his voice a low murmur just for him. "Don't worry about it. It's a lot." He pointed to a picture of a colorful roll. "This one's a California Roll. It's just crab, avocado, and cucumber. It's what everyone tries first." He then pointed to another. "And this is a shrimp tempura roll. It's fried shrimp, so it's cooked. It's my favorite."

He was giving him a map, a safe place to start. Maria, watching the quiet exchange, smiled to herself. She ordered a large platter for them to share, making sure to include the two rolls Tony had pointed out. When the food arrived, it was a work of art. A lacquered tray, bright with colors Danny had never seen on food, was set between them. He stared like it was art, not dinner. Then came the next challenge: the chopsticks. He watched as Tony and Maria expertly picked theirs up. He fumbled with his own, the two thin sticks feeling clumsy and alien in his hand.

"Here," Tony said, his voice gentle. He reached over, his hand covering Danny's, and adjusted his grip. "Like this. You hold the bottom one still, and just move the top one. Like a claw." He guided Danny's hand, helping him pick up a piece of a California roll. It wobbled precariously but held.

Danny brought the piece to his mouth. The flavor was a complete surprise—clean, fresh, and subtle. The creamy avocado, the slightly sweet crab, the cool cucumber, all wrapped in perfectly seasoned rice. It was nothing like the heavy, greasy food he was used to. It was… light. He tried another piece, this time on his own. He successfully picked it up, and a small, almost imperceptible smile of pride touched his lips. He ate it, and the smile widened just a fraction. He liked it.

Maria watched him, her heart aching with a quiet joy. It wasn't just about sushi. It was about seeing him try something new and not be afraid. It was about watching him discover a small, simple pleasure in a world that had, for so long, only offered him pain. Tony caught her eye across the table and gave a small, almost imperceptible nod. He saw it too. This quiet, normal moment, in this quiet, normal restaurant, was another victory.

As they finished their meal and walked back out into the bright afternoon, Danny felt a new, fragile sense of confidence settle in his chest. He had navigated a new restaurant, tried new food, and learned a new skill. It was a small thing, but it felt monumental. As they walked, he let his hand brush against Tony's, a small, tentative touch. Tony immediately took it, lacing their fingers together, a silent, solid reassurance.

Maria walked beside them, the shopping bags rustling with their new clothes. The afternoon had been a success, a perfect picture of their new family. But as they turned the corner toward their street, her mind inevitably drifted back to Leroy. The happy, light feeling from the restaurant began to recede, replaced by the cold, heavy dread of the news he was on his way to collect.

While Maria and the boys were navigating the delicate art of chopsticks and discovering the clean, fresh taste of sushi, Leroy was at home, locked in his small office. The room was his sanctuary, usually a place of quiet order, with his police commendations framed on the wall and his books on law and history arranged neatly on the shelves. But tonight, the order felt like a mockery.

The large, thick manila envelope sat on his desk, an ugly, ominous presence. He had stared at it for a long time after getting home from the precinct, his stomach a tight, acid-filled knot. He knew he shouldn't. He knew it would only bring the horror of that day at the jail flooding back. But he had to. He was the lead officer on the case. He had to review the evidence.

With a heavy, weary sigh, he pulled the tab and slid the contents onto his desk. The official reports were one thing—cold, procedural language detailing the incident. But then came the crime scene photos.

He spread them out, his professional gaze scanning the images of the shower, the tile, the evidence markers. But then his eyes landed on one, and he stopped. It was a close-up of Dina's face, taken in the harsh, clinical light of the hospital. Her features were swollen and distorted, her skin a grotesque canvas of deep purples and angry reds. Her eyes were closed. He sat with that photo for just too long, the image burning itself onto the back of his eyelids. He saw not just a victim, but the ghost of a friend—the vibrant, laughing girl from his wedding photos, now a broken, unrecognizable shell.

He pushed the photos away, his breath catching in his throat. A wave of profound, soul-deep exhaustion washed over him. This was the secret he now carried. This was the brutal truth he and Maria had sworn to shield Danny from. He thought of the boy at the sushi restaurant, his face lit with the small, proud victory of mastering a pair of chopsticks, and the weight of his promise felt immense, almost crushing. He would carry this darkness so that Danny could have the light. He would live with these images so that Danny wouldn't have to.

Suddenly, he heard the familiar crunch of the minivan's tires on the gravel driveway. The sound jolted him back to the present. He heard the car doors slam, followed by the light, happy sound of Maria's laughter and the lower murmur of the boys' voices as they approached the front door. A surge of pure, protective panic shot through him.

His hands moved with a frantic, desperate speed. He quickly, almost violently, shoved the photos and the reports back into the manila envelope. He didn't just place it to the side; he yanked open the bottom drawer of his heavy oak desk—the one filled with old, forgotten files and personal effects—and thrust the envelope deep into the back, burying it beneath a stack of tax records from a decade ago. He slammed the drawer shut, the sound a loud, definitive *thud* in the quiet office.

He stood there for a second, his heart hammering, his breathing ragged. He ran a hand over his face, forcing the mask back on. By the time the key turned in the front door lock, he was just *Papi* again—waiting in the hallway with a tired smile.

He stood there for a second, his heart hammering, his breathing ragged. He ran a hand over his face, forcing the grim, professional mask back into place, erasing the horror from his expression. By the time he heard the key turn in the front door lock, he was just a father in his home office, waiting to greet his family after their outing. He walked out into the hallway, a tired but gentle smile on his face.

"Hey," he said, his voice a little rougher than he intended. "Smells like you guys found the perfect place for food."

"We did!" Maria said, her face bright as she walked in, the boys trailing behind her. "It was wonderful. Danny tried everything." She set a few shopping bags down on the floor. "And the shopping trip was a huge success." Tony dropped his own bag and started pulling out the contents.

"*Papi*, check it out," he said, holding up a dark green button-down shirt. "I can actually wear this to the graduation dinner without looking like I'm going to a punk show." Maria's smile was brilliant. She reached into another bag and pulled out the deep blue shirt they had picked for Danny.

"And look at this," she said, her voice full of a soft pride as she held it up for Leroy to see. "For Danny. He looks so handsome in it." Danny, who had been standing quietly by the door, looked down at his feet, a shy, pleased blush creeping up his neck.

Leroy looked at the clothes, at the happy, normal chaos of his family returning home. He looked at Tony's proud grin and at the faint, genuine smile on Danny's face. These simple, tangible things—new shirts for a celebration, the easy chatter, the smell of takeout sushi—felt like a shield against the brutal, ugly contents of the envelope now buried in his desk drawer.

"They're great," he said, his voice full of a warmth that was entirely real, even as it covered a deep, cold secret. "You'll both be the best-dressed guys there."

He watched as Maria shooed the boys upstairs to put their new things away, her laughter filling the small house. He stood there in the entryway, but the warmth of the moment couldn't reach him. Maria turned back from the staircase, her own smile brilliant, but it faltered the moment she saw his face. The mask was slipping. She could see the haunted look in his eyes, the deep, bone-weary exhaustion he couldn't quite hide.

"Leroy?" she said, her voice dropping, all the lightness gone. "What is it? What's wrong?"

"It's nothing, *mija*," he lied, turning away to hang his keys. "Just a long day."

"Don't," she said, walking over to him, her voice firm but gentle. "Don't lie to me. I can see it on your face. It was the file, wasn't it?" Leroy let out a long, shuddering breath and finally nodded, the weight of the secret too heavy to carry alone.

"It was bad, Maria. It's police business. You don't want to see it."

"She was my friend, Leroy," Maria insisted, her own voice trembling slightly. "For a long time, she was my best friend. I have to know. I need to see."

He looked at her, at the fierce, determined set of her jaw, and knew he couldn't protect her from this. He led her into his office and closed the door. With a heavy, reluctant hand, he opened the desk drawer and pulled out the envelope. He didn't show her all of them. He just took out the one photo he couldn't get out of his own mind and laid it face down on the desk.

"Are you sure?" he asked one last time.

She just gave a single, sharp nod. He slowly turned the picture over. Maria's reaction was silent but violent. Her breath caught like she'd been punched. One hand clamped to her mouth, her face bleaching white as she stared at the image.

"Oh, God," she whispered, stumbling back a step until she hit the wall. "Leroy... that's not... that's not her."

He was beside her in an instant, wrapping his arms around her as a single, silent sob wracked her body. He held his wife, surrounded by the light and warmth of the life they had built, and felt the immense, crushing weight of the darkness they now had to carry together.

CHAPTER 30

THIS IS IT

The early morning light of late June streamed through the window, carrying with it the fresh, clean scent of a new summer day. For the first time in what felt like a lifetime, the day didn't begin with the harsh blare of an alarm clock, but with the soft, gentle quiet of a house holding its breath in anticipation.

Tony woke first. He lay still for a moment, listening to the even, peaceful rhythm of Danny's breathing beside him. He turned his head on the pillow and just watched him, a profound, aching tenderness swelling in his chest. Danny looked younger in his sleep, the lines of worry and fear that had been etched on his face for so long completely smoothed away. Today was graduation day. They had made it. The thought felt monumental, almost impossible.

He thought back to that first day he'd seen Danny at school, huddled and broken. It felt like a different century, like he was remembering a different person. He had been so cruel, so consumed by his own fear. And now... now he was waking up next to him, his arm instinctively draped over Danny's side, and the thought of a future without him was simply unimaginable. As if sensing his gaze, Danny's eyes fluttered open. They were still clouded with sleep, but when they focused on Tony, a slow, soft smile spread across his face.

"Hey," Danny whispered, his voice a rough, sleepy murmur.

"Hey, graduate," Tony whispered back, leaning in to press a gentle kiss to his forehead. "You ready for this?" Danny's smile faltered slightly, a flicker of the old anxiety returning to his eyes. He gave a small, uncertain shrug. The idea of the ceremony—the crowds, the stage, all the eyes on him—was still a terrifying prospect. Tony saw it immediately. He tightened his arm around him, a silent, steady reassurance.

"We'll do it together," he said, his voice a low, firm promise. "Side-by-side. The whole time. I'm not going anywhere." Danny looked at him, at the unwavering sincerity in his eyes, and the fear began to recede, replaced by a fragile, hopeful courage. He gave a small, deliberate nod.

"Okay," he whispered. "Together."

Downstairs, the house was already humming with a quiet, happy energy. Maria was at the stove, making a special breakfast of pancakes and fresh strawberries, while Leroy sat at the table, a proud, contented smile on his face as he read the morning paper. The air was filled with the warm, comforting smells of coffee and melting butter, a perfect domestic scene that felt a world away from the chaos that had consumed them just a few short months ago.

An hour later, the four of them were sitting around the kitchen table, the remnants of a celebratory breakfast pushed aside, the air humming with a happy, nervous energy. The sound of the doorbell cut through the chatter. Maria's face broke into a wide smile.

"They're here!"

She opened the front door to find Miguel and Leo standing on the porch, both dressed smartly and holding a small, wrapped gift. The greeting was a warm flurry of hugs and congratulations as they stepped inside, filling the house with an even brighter energy.

"I couldn't have my boys graduating without our whole family there," Maria said, beaming as she led them into the kitchen. "Miguel was sweet enough to close up Freddy's for the day." Miguel waved a dismissive hand, though he was smiling.

"Please," Miguel laughed. "As if we'd miss this. Leo has been planning his outfit for a week." Leo just grinned and gave Tony a friendly clap on the shoulder. Miguel then turned his attention to the two graduates, looking them up and down with a theatrical, appraising eye. "Okay, the happy, well-fed glow is a good start," he declared. "But the hair is a disaster, and you are not wearing wrinkled t-shirts to get your diplomas." He winked, his expression full of a warm, brotherly affection. "Come on, you two," he said, gesturing with his head toward the stairs. "Upstairs. Your personal stylist has arrived. I'm making sure you both look perfect for your big day." Tony let out a laugh, shaking his head.

"Dude, I can dress myself."

"That's debatable," Miguel retorted without missing a beat. "Now move it. We have work to do."

He shooed them toward the staircase. Tony went willingly, laughing, and after a moment's hesitation, Danny followed, a small, shy smile on his face. The three of them disappeared upstairs, their footsteps echoing softly, leaving the adults smiling in the quiet kitchen.

Tony's room was in its usual state of organized chaos—clothes draped over a chair, a guitar leaning against the wall, and stacks of books on the floor. Miguel walked into the center of the room and put his hands on his hips, surveying the scene with the critical eye of a director.

"Okay, this room is a disaster, but we have a mission and we will not be deterred," he announced dramatically. He pointed to the shopping bags from the day before. "Let's see the wardrobe options."

Tony rolled his eyes, but he was smiling. He pulled out the dark green button-down he'd picked, while Danny shyly produced the deep blue one.

"Excellent choices," Miguel said with a genuinely impressed nod. "Your mother has taste. Okay, you two, get changed. We have to see what we're working with." Tony just sighed and started unbuttoning his t-shirt.

"I still maintain that I know how to dress myself, man."

"That's adorable," Miguel said without looking up from the comb he was now pulling out of his jacket pocket. "Now, hurry up. Hair is next, and that's where the real magic is going to happen."

Danny changed quickly and quietly, his movements still hesitant. He watched the easy, familiar banter between Tony and Miguel, a small, curious smile on his face. He had never had friends like this, a friendship so comfortable it felt like family. Once they were both in their new shirts and jeans, Miguel went to work. He sat Tony down on the edge of the bed.

"Hold still," he commanded. "I'm trying to make you look less like a rock star who just rolled out of a tour bus." He expertly worked a little product through Tony's long hair, pulling it back from his face and tying it at the nape of his neck in a way that was sleek and stylish—a clear upgrade from Tony's usual messy ponytail. Then, Miguel turned to Danny, a bright, professional smile on his face. "Your turn."

As Miguel took a step toward him, comb in hand, Tony subtly moved between them, a casual but deliberate motion.

"Hey, man," Tony said to Miguel, his voice low and quiet so only he could hear. "Just... go easy, okay? He's still not big on people... you know. Touching him." Miguel's expression immediately softened. He stopped, his gaze flickering to Danny with a new, more profound understanding and a hint of apology in his eyes. He hadn't even thought about it.

"Right," he murmured, his own voice dropping. "Of course. My bad."

Tony looked over at Danny, a silent, questioning look on his face. *Are you okay with this? You don't have to do anything you don't want to.* Danny saw the exchange. He saw Tony's quiet, fierce protection and Miguel's immediate, respectful understanding. He saw that his boundaries, for the first time in his life, were something to be acknowledged and honored. He took a small, steadying breath and gave Tony a quiet nod. He was fine with this. He trusted them.

"Okay," Miguel said, his voice gentle now. He pulled the desk chair out for Danny. "Have a seat. And just tell me if you want me to stop at any point. No questions asked."

Danny sat hesitantly in the chair. Miguel's touch, when it came, was incredibly light and professional, his movements slow and deliberate as he worked a small amount of pomade through Danny's hair, giving it shape and texture, sweeping it off his forehead in a way that framed his face. For Danny, the simple, respectful touch was a revelation. He slowly relaxed into it, closing his eyes, trusting.

When Miguel was done, he stepped back.

"Okay," he said, his voice full of satisfaction. "Turn around. Look in the mirror."

Tony stood beside Danny, and they both looked at their reflections in the long mirror on the back of Tony's closet door. They looked… different. Older. They looked like two handsome, confident young men on the verge of a new chapter in their lives. Danny stared at his own reflection, a look of quiet wonder on his face. He slowly lifted a hand and touched his hair, as if to make sure the person in the mirror was real.

Tony looked at their reflection together—the dark-haired, confident boy and the quiet, blue-eyed one—and he felt a surge of pride and overwhelming love.

"There," Miguel said, his voice soft but full of pride. "Perfect." He clapped them both on the shoulder. "Now you're ready to graduate."

Downstairs, the rich aroma of fresh coffee filled the kitchen. Maria poured three mugs and brought them to the table where Leroy and Leo were sitting. She remained standing, leaning against the counter, a soft, happy smile on her face as she listened to the faint, muffled sounds of movement from upstairs. Leroy took a slow sip from his mug, a look of quiet amusement in his eyes.

"It's gotten awfully quiet up there," he said, his voice a low rumble. "You think he's actually letting Miguel tell him what to do without a fight?" Leo let out a short, knowing laugh, shaking his head.

"Oh, you have no idea," Leo began. "Once Miguel gets into what he calls 'curation mode,' there's no stopping him. He tried to reorganize my entire dorm room last semester because my bookshelf wasn't 'telling a clear narrative'." Maria chuckled, the sound warm and full.

"I can't even imagine. Tony has been dressing himself in the same uniform of a t-shirt and jeans since he was thirteen. The idea of him taking fashion advice from anyone is a miracle."

"Tony doesn't stand a chance," Leroy added with a grin.

"Not a single one," Leo agreed, his expression softening. "But he means well. He just... likes things to be perfect for the people he cares about."

The light, easy laughter faded into a comfortable silence. Maria looked from her husband to the kind young man sitting at her table, her heart feeling full to the point of bursting.

"It's good for him, though," she said, her voice a little thick with emotion. "For both of them. To have someone like Miguel looking out for them." She took a deep, happy breath. "I'm just so glad you're all here. Our whole family." Just then, they heard the sound of footsteps on the stairs, and the three of them turned, their faces full of anticipation, ready to see the results of Miguel's work.

The boys were greeted by the sight of Maria, Leroy, and Leo, who all looked up at the same time. The casual conversation in the kitchen died instantly. Maria's hand flew to her mouth, a soft gasp escaping her lips. Her eyes immediately welled up, and she tried to hold back a wave of emotional sobbing, her heart overwhelmed by the sight of the two young men on the staircase. Leroy, masking his own surge of emotion with a gruff joke, looked Tony up and down.

"Well, look at that," he said, a slow, proud grin spreading across his face. "You finally cleaned up. Don't look like a roadie for a punk band for once."

Tony just laughed, shaking his head as he reached the bottom step. But then, all three adults' focus shifted to the boy standing just behind him.

It was Danny. Danny, who was this scared, scarred boy who had walked into their lives broken and ready to give up. Danny, who rarely made eye contact and whose smiles were small, hesitant, and heartbreakingly fragile. But now, standing there in his new clothes, his hair perfectly styled, bathed in the warm, supportive attention of this family, something inside him broke free. He actually gave his widest smile ever, a real, unguarded, brilliant smile that reached his eyes and revealed his teeth.

Tony, who had turned to look at him, stopped dead in his tracks. He was so used to Danny's shy, closed-lip smiles that he was surprised to notice, for the very first time, that Danny had a cute, slightly crooked snaggle tooth on one side. The small, endearing imperfection, revealed in a moment of pure, uninhibited joy, was the most beautiful thing Tony had ever seen.

The cap felt too big, slipping down over his eyes, but when the crowd roared for him, he stood taller than he ever had before. The ceremony itself was long and formal, but for Tony, the only moment that mattered was seeing Danny walk across the stage. When the principal called his name—"Daniel Sanders"—a cheer erupted from the Guzman section that was loud enough to draw stares.

Danny, for his part, had been terrified, but as he walked across the stage, diploma in hand, he chanced a look out at the crowd. He saw Maria openly weeping with joy, Leroy giving him a proud, steady nod, and Tony on his feet, clapping so hard his hands were red. And in that moment, a wave of pure, unadulterated happiness washed over him, and he broke into the same wide, snaggle-toothed smile from the morning. Tony, seeing him so genuinely happy and proud, celebrating an accomplishment he had earned against all odds, wanted so desperately to run right across the stage and give him the biggest hug ever.

Later that evening, the four of them were seated in a comfortable, quiet booth at *Sotta la Luna*. The restaurant was beautiful, with low, warm lighting, dark wood, and the soft clinking of glasses and silverware providing a gentle, intimate soundtrack. The air smelled of garlic, rosemary, and melting cheese.

"I still can't believe you two are officially high school graduates," Maria said, her eyes shining as she looked at the boys. "It feels like just yesterday I was dropping you off for your first day of kindergarten, Tony."

"And now you're an old man," Leroy added, a proud grin on his face as he raised his water glass. "To the graduates. We are so incredibly proud of both of you. To the future, whatever it may hold."

"To the future," they all echoed, their glasses clinking softly above the table.

Danny, who had been quiet but relaxed since they arrived, took a sip of water. The overwhelming anxiety he'd felt the first time he'd been in a restaurant like this was gone, replaced by a calm, happy sense of belonging.

"So," Maria said, her tone gentle as she turned to Danny. "Now that the hard part is over... have you given any more thought to what you might want to do next? No pressure at all, *mijo*. Just... dreaming a little." Danny looked down at his plate for a second, then met her gaze, a new, fragile confidence in his eyes.

"I... I think I'd like to take a class," he said, his voice quiet but clear. "At the community college. Just... one. An art class. To start." The simple declaration felt monumental. It was the first time he had, on his own, voiced a desire for his own future. For the first time, the idea of a future didn't scare him. It pulled. Tony reached for his hand under the table, lacing their fingers together, and gave it a firm, proud squeeze. Before Maria could express her overjoyed reaction, Tony's phone buzzed on the table. He glanced at the screen, a grin spreading across his face.

"Hey," he said to his parents. "Marko, Jamal, and the others are just getting out of a movie. Would it be cool if I invited them to meet us here for dessert? To celebrate."

"Of course, *mijo*," Maria said, her heart feeling full to bursting. "The more the merrier."

A few minutes later, the quiet, intimate atmosphere of the restaurant was gently interrupted by the arrival of the first guests. Jamal walked in, a nervous but brilliant smile on his face, and walking beside him, their hands loosely but unmistakably intertwined, was Connor. Tony's jaw dropped slightly in surprise, which quickly morphed into a wide, genuine grin. Maria's eyes lit up, and she immediately began signaling for the waiter to add more chairs.

"Well, look at you two," Tony said as Jamal and Connor approached the table, a pleased, teasing note in his voice. He looked at their joined hands. "When did this happen?" Jamal's cheeks flushed a deep red, but he didn't let go of Connor's hand.

"Uh, a little while after you pointed out in class that he might like me," Jamal said, giving Tony a grateful look. "Turns out, you were right." Just as they were pulling up chairs, Marko arrived, looking a little breathless.

"Sorry, man, I couldn't find parking," he said. He gave a friendly nod to everyone, his gaze lingering for a moment on the new couple with a look of happy approval. "Don't get too comfortable yet," he announced to the table. "There's one more person joining us. She's just parking her car now." Before Tony could even ask who, the answer walked through the door.

It was Jessica.

The easy, celebratory atmosphere at the table didn't just fade; it evaporated. A sudden, thick silence descended, so absolute it felt like the air had been sucked out of the room.

Tony froze, his smile vanishing, his expression shock and a sharp ache he wasn't ready for. He saw Danny, who was seated beside him, physically recoil, his shoulders hunching as he curled in on himself, his eyes immediately dropping to the floor as if the entire situation was his fault. Jessica stopped just inside the doorway, her own face a mask of nervous resolve as she took in the scene. Marko, looking deeply apologetic, gestured for her to join them, the tension so thick it was a physical thing.

The silence stretched, thick and suffocating. No one moved. Danny looked as if he was trying to physically will himself to disappear, his gaze locked on the empty plate in front of him. Tony was a statue of pale, shocked guilt. It was Maria who broke the spell. Her eyes, full of a deep, maternal understanding, took in the entire, painful tableau: she saw Tony's shock, Danny's immediate, self-inflicted guilt, and the nervous apprehension on Jessica's face. She knew this was a conversation for kids, not for parents.

She placed her napkin on the table and caught Leroy's eye, giving him a look that was both a plea and a command. He understood instantly.

As Leroy discreetly flagged down a passing waiter, Maria stood up. She didn't address the table at large. Instead, she walked around to where Jessica was sitting, her movements calm and deliberate. She placed a warm, steady hand on Jessica's shoulder. Jessica flinched slightly at the contact, looking up at her with wide, uncertain eyes.

"Jessica, honey," Maria said, her voice a low, sincere murmur that was just for her. "It is so good to see you. You are always, always welcome at our table." The simple, unconditional warmth of the gesture seemed to break something in Jessica. Her shoulders slumped with relief, and her eyes immediately welled with grateful tears.

"Thank you, Maria," she whispered, her voice choked with emotion.

By this point, Leroy had finished his quiet conversation with the waiter. He stood up.

"Your mother and I are going to move to that smaller table over there," he announced calmly to the group, gesturing to a recently vacated two-top across the room. "Give you all some space to catch up." He gave Tony a look—not of anger, but one that clearly said, *Handle this. And be a man about it.*

Maria gave Jessica's shoulder one last, reassuring squeeze before she and Leroy gracefully excused themselves, leaving the six teenagers alone in the heavy, charged silence, the emotional spotlight now focused squarely on them. Just as Tony was about to sit back down, Marko caught his eye and gave a slight, almost imperceptible shake of his head.

"Hey, man," Marko said, his voice a low murmur. "Can I talk to you for a sec? By the bar." Tony's stomach tightened, but he nodded.

"Yeah."

He followed his best friend, weaving through the tables to a relatively quiet spot near the service station. Marko shoved his hands in his pockets, unable to look Tony in the eye.

"Look," Marko began, his voice rough with a discomfort Tony had never heard from him before. "I know this is a mess. Her being here. I didn't plan it." He finally looked up, his expression a mask of conflicted guilt. "I couldn't leave her hanging after the park. One check-in turned into a hundred conversations." Tony just listened, his own heart a heavy stone in his chest. "I'm starting to really fall for her, Tony," Marko confessed, the words a difficult, painful rush. "And I need to ask you something." He took a deep breath. "Would you be okay with it? If... if I asked her out? If we started dating?"

The question hung in the air between them, heavy and absolute. Tony felt a sharp, irrational sting of jealousy, a ghostly echo of a life he had already chosen to leave behind. But it was immediately extinguished by the crushing weight of his own actions. He had lied to her. He had used her. He had broken her heart. What right did he have to an opinion? His blessing wasn't a gift he was entitled to give; it was a permission he had no place to grant. He looked at his best friend, at the genuine, agonizing conflict on his face, and knew there was only one right answer.

"You don't have to ask me that, man," Tony said, his voice quiet but steady. "I lost the right to have a say in who she dates a long time ago." He forced a small, sad smile. "She deserves to be happy. And you're a good guy, Marko." He met his friend's gaze, his own expression full of a painful, final closure. "Yeah. You should ask her out." He clapped a hand on Marko's shoulder, a gesture that was both a release and a resignation. "Just... be good to her. Okay? Be better than I was."

"Of course," Marko promised, his voice thick with a profound, grateful relief.

They stood there for a moment, two brothers navigating the wreckage Tony had created. Then, together, they walked back to the table, the decision made, ready to sit down and pretend to eat dessert.

CHAPTER 31

FIRST OF MANY

The drive home from *Sotta la Luna* was thick with a quiet, contemplative energy. The drama of the evening had settled, leaving behind a strange sense of resolution. In the back of the minivan, the friends had all gone their separate ways, leaving just the four members of the Guzman family to process the night.

"That was..." Maria started, searching for the right word as she looked out the passenger window. "...a lot."

"You can say that again," Tony said from the driver's seat, his voice a low murmur. He glanced in the rearview mirror, his eyes finding Danny, who was staring out at the passing streetlights. He then looked at his parents. "Marko pulled me aside at the restaurant," he said, deciding to get it all out in the open. "He told me he's falling for Jess." Leroy and Maria turned to look at him, their expressions surprised. "He asked me if I'd be okay with him asking her out," Tony continued, his knuckles white on the steering wheel. "He asked for my blessing."

"What did you tell him?" Leroy asked, his voice laced with a careful curiosity.

"I told him he didn't need it," Tony said, shaking his head. "I told him I lost the right to have an opinion a long time ago. That she deserves someone like him, someone who's going to be honest with her." He let out a long breath. "I just told him to be good to her." Maria reached over and placed a hand on her son's shoulder, squeezing it tightly.

"I am so proud of the man you are becoming, Antonio," she whispered, her voice thick with emotion.

When they got home, the emotional exhaustion of the day finally caught up with them. Maria and Leroy, carrying the unseen weight of the file locked in the office, declared they were heading straight to bed.

"Don't you two stay up too late," Maria said, giving both boys a tired but loving kiss on the cheek before she and Leroy disappeared upstairs.

Tony and Danny were left alone in the quiet living room, bathed in the soft glow of a single lamp. Tony's heart sang with a joy so pure and so profound it felt like it might lift him off the ground. He looked at Danny, who was standing by the couch, looking small and a little lost in the sudden quiet. They had navigated so much—pain, fear, forgiveness, and now, the messy, complicated world of their friends. They had survived it all, together.

"Hey," Tony said softly, walking over to him. Danny looked up, his blue eyes questioning.

"Can I... can I put on some music?" Tony asked, his voice gentle. He pulled his phone from his pocket, already scrolling through a playlist. "Something... quiet."

Danny gave a small, almost imperceptible nod. Tony found what he was looking for, and a moment later, a soft, instrumental melody—a simple, soothing piano piece—began to play from the phone's speaker, filling the quiet room with a gentle, hopeful sound. Tony set the phone on the mantle and turned back to Danny. "I know this is probably weird," he began, his voice a little shaky with the force of his own happiness. "But... I feel like we need to mark this moment. Right here. The end of this insane week. The beginning of... everything else." He took a deep breath, his heart pounding. "Would you... would you feel comfortable... dancing with me?"

Danny stared at him, his eyes wide. The thought was both terrifying and impossibly wonderful. A dance. A quiet, private celebration of how far they had both come, with their own soft music playing just for them. He looked at Tony's open, hopeful face, at the boy who had saved his life and was now, so gently, showing him how to live it. He gave another small nod.

"Okay," he whispered.

Tony's face broke into a brilliant smile. He gently took Danny's hand and placed his other on the small of his back, pulling him in slowly. Danny rested his free hand tentatively on Tony's shoulder. And in the silent, dimly lit living room, with the soft notes of the piano filling the space around them, they began to sway, a quiet, clumsy, and utterly perfect first dance. Danny stepped too close and caught Tony's foot with his own. He froze, mortified, but Tony just laughed softly and tightened his arm around him.

"Perfect," Tony whispered, and Danny's cheeks flushed hot, but his smile didn't fade. If anything, it grew.

The Saturday morning after graduation was a lazy, golden affair. Tony and Danny slept in late. When they finally made their way downstairs just before noon, they found Maria in the kitchen humming to herself as she made a fresh pot of coffee, and Leroy sitting at the table, a look of quiet, happy anticipation on his face.

"Well, look what the cat dragged in," Leroy said, his voice a warm, teasing rumble. "I was starting to think you two were going to sleep until your birthdays next weekend." Tony just grinned, running a hand through his messy hair as he stumbled toward the coffee pot.

"Long week, *Papi.*"

"I know," Leroy said, his smile softening. "Which is why, after you've had your coffee, I have something to show you. In the garage."

A flicker of curiosity passed between Tony and Danny. Once the boys had taken their time to wake up and enjoy the morning peace, Leroy led them out into the cool, gasoline-scented air of the garage. The Triumph sat in the center of the space, gleaming, a near-finished masterpiece of their shared effort. But it wasn't the bike Leroy gestured to. Sitting on the workbench, side-by-side, were two brand new, full-faced helmets. They were identical, their glossy black surfaces reflecting the light from the open garage door. Tony stopped, his breath catching in his throat. He just stared at them.

"Figured a driver needs a helmet," Leroy said, his voice full of a quiet pride. He then looked over at Danny, a gentle, welcoming smile on his face. "And so does his passenger. For whenever he's ready for a ride." Danny looked down, a shy, pleased blush creeping up his neck. He understood the gesture perfectly. It was an invitation, a promise of shared adventures, a symbol of his permanent place in their world. Tony finally found his voice.

"*Papi*… these are… wow. Thank you."

"That's not all," Leroy said, a twinkle in his eye. He reached into his pocket. "I know you've been studying that manual ever since I gave you the okay. And I know you were planning on booking your road test after your birthday." He unfolded a small piece of paper and handed it to Tony. "I figured, why wait? Your test is booked. This coming Monday. 8 a.m. sharp." Tony stared at the confirmation slip, his jaw dropping.

"This Monday? For real?" The news hit him like a jolt of pure, unadulterated joy. It was happening. It was real. He looked from the paper to his dad, then over to Danny, a brilliant, ecstatic grin spreading across his face.

"You're ready," Leroy said simply, clapping a firm, proud hand on his son's shoulder.

Tony looked at the two helmets sitting on the bench, then at the beautiful, quiet boy smiling shyly at him, and for the first time, the future didn't feel like a terrifying, unwritten map. It felt like an open road. Tony could hardly keep it together. The confirmation slip in his hand felt like a winning lottery ticket.

"Monday," he kept repeating, a dazed, happy grin plastered on his face. "This Monday. I can't believe it."

The rest of the morning was a blur of excited, frantic energy. The surprise from Leroy had lit a fire under them, turning the vague, long-term project of the Triumph into an immediate, urgent mission. The long days they had already spent cleaning every part, the weekend trips to a specialty auto shop in Flushing to order brand new parts to replace ones that had eroded over years of neglect—it was all culminating in this final, thrilling push.

"We have to go now," Tony announced, already pulling his wallet out. "If the test is Monday, we need to get the last few things today."

"What's left?" Leroy asked, leaning against the garage doorframe, watching the boys with a fond, amused expression.

"New spark plugs, for sure," Danny said quietly, speaking up with a new, technical confidence. "And the new gas tank we ordered came in yesterday. The old one's too rusted out. And the seat. And I'm ready to start painting," Tony added, his eyes gleaming. "I'm doing it in a classic, glossy black. It's going to look so sick."

An hour later, they were walking out of "Cycle Tech," the small motorcycle parts shop in Flushing, their arms loaded with boxes. The new gas tank was pristine, the replacement seat was made of smooth, uncracked black leather, and a small box of spark plugs rattled in the bag Danny was holding.

Back in the garage, the air was thick with the smell of degreaser and the promise of new beginnings. They laid their new parts out on a clean rag on the floor like a surgeon preparing for an operation.

"Okay," Tony said to Danny, clapping his hands together, a general leading his troops. "You work on getting the old tank and the spark plugs out. I'm going to start prepping the frame for the first coat of paint."

He pulled on a pair of worn work gloves and picked up a sheet of fine-grit sandpaper, his movements full of a new, joyful purpose. Danny, with a quiet, focused intensity, selected a wrench from the toolbox and crouched down by the engine. They worked in a comfortable, syncopated rhythm, the sound of Tony's sanding a soft, steady *shush* against the metallic clink and scrape of Danny's tools, the radio on the workbench playing a backdrop of classic rock to their shared, happy labor.

The air in the garage was thick with the scent of metal, grease, and the faint, sharp tang of paint thinner. A dusty old boombox on the workbench was playing a classic rock station, the familiar guitar riffs a perfect soundtrack to their afternoon. The wide garage door was open, letting in the warm, golden light of the late Saturday.

Tony was completely in his element, his earlier excitement now channeled into a state of pure, focused energy. He worked meticulously, sanding down the last rough patches on the motorcycle's frame, his movements economical and sure. He was preparing his canvas, and he wanted it to be perfect. Danny worked in a quiet, syncopated rhythm beside him. He carefully drained the last of the old fuel, the liquid a sick, brownish color, before expertly unbolting the rusted, dented gas tank. He set it aside like a discarded shell, then turned his attention to the engine, his smaller, more nimble fingers reaching deep into the bike's guts to carefully remove the old, fouled spark plugs.

He was excited, too, but his excitement was a quieter, warmer thing. He found himself pausing his work just to watch Tony. He had never seen him like this—so completely unburdened, so full of a simple, uncomplicated joy. This Tony was bright and loud and full of a restless, happy energy. He would hum along to the radio, his focus absolute, a small, contented smile on his lips. Danny's heart ached with a feeling so tender and so profound it almost hurt. This was the Tony he had missed so desperately. This was the boy he was falling in love with all over again.

They had worked so hard for this, put in countless hours side-by-side in this garage, their shared project a silent language that had allowed them to heal. This moment, this easy, happy day, felt like the first real reward. After another hour of focused work, the final pieces were in place. The new, pristine gas tank was bolted on, gleaming under the garage lights. The new spark plugs were set, and the smooth, uncracked leather seat was secured. Tony stood back, wiping a slick of sweat and grease from his forehead with the back of his hand.

"Okay," he said, his voice a low, nervous hum. "I think... I think that's it." Danny stood beside him, his own heart starting to hammer against his ribs. This was the moment of truth. All their work, all their hours, all came down to this. Tony connected the battery cables, his movements slow and deliberate. He took a deep breath and looked at Danny. "You ready?"

Danny couldn't speak. He just gave a single, tight nod. Tony swung his leg over the bike, the new leather of the seat creaking under his weight. He put the key in the ignition and turned it. The bike gave a low, pathetic cough, a single, wheezing sputter, and then fell silent. A wave of crushing disappointment washed over Tony.

"No, no, come on," he muttered, his shoulders slumping. He was about to try again when Danny, who was peering intently at the engine, pointed.

"Wait," Danny said. "That lead... I think it's loose." Tony looked and saw it—a small electrical lead near the new spark plug was sitting just slightly off its contact. He reached down and pressed it firmly into place with a satisfying *click*. He looked at Danny, a new, fragile hope in his eyes. "Okay," he said, his voice a shaky whisper. "One more time."

He turned the key again.

This time, the engine caught with a loud, hacking cough, then another. It sputtered, fighting for life, and then, with a final, triumphant roar, it exploded into a steady, powerful rumble. The sound filled the garage, a deep, throaty, and utterly beautiful noise. It was alive! Tony let out a whoop of pure, unadulterated joy that echoed off the walls. He looked over at Danny, who was standing there, covered in grease, with a brilliant, wide, snaggle-toothed grin on his face, his eyes shining with happy tears. His hands were blackened with grease, streaks smudged across his forearms, and Tony could feel the vibration of the engine buzzing up through the soles of his boots. The air was thick with exhaust, hot metal, and triumph—it was the smell of something reborn.

They had done it. Together. They had taken something broken and, piece by piece, they had brought it back to life.

While Tony and Danny were celebrating their victory in the garage, Maria and Leroy were in the kitchen, the quiet of their Saturday afternoon suddenly shattered by an impossible sound. It started as a cough, then a sputter, and then it erupted into a deep, throaty, and utterly unmistakable roar—the sound of a Triumph motorcycle engine that hadn't been heard in nearly twenty years.

Maria dropped the dish towel she was holding. Leroy looked up from his newspaper, his face a mask of pure, unadulterated shock. They exchanged a wide-eyed look of disbelief.

"No way," Leroy breathed out.

Without another word, the two of them headed for the back door. Leroy pulled open the door to the garage, and they were met with a scene of joyous, greasy chaos. The air was thick with the smell of exhaust fumes, and the Triumph was rumbling in the center of the floor, alive and humming with power. Standing on either side of it were the two boys, covered in grease, their faces split with identical, triumphant grins.

"I'll be damned," Leroy said, his voice full of a genuine, impressed awe. He walked slowly into the garage, circling the bike as if it were a ghost. "You actually did it. You boys actually did it."

"It was Danny!" Tony shouted over the noise of the engine, his voice buzzing with excitement. "There was a loose lead on one of the new plugs! He spotted it! He's the genius!"

Danny just shook his head, a happy, embarrassed blush creeping up his neck.

Maria stood in the doorway, her hand over her heart. She wasn't just looking at a motorcycle; she was looking at two boys who had taken something broken and forgotten and, through their shared patience and hard work, had brought it roaring back to life. She saw Tony, no longer an angry, conflicted kid, but a proud and capable young man. And she saw Danny, not as a victim, but as a quiet, competent partner, his face lit with a rare, brilliant smile of pure accomplishment.

"I haven't heard that sound since before Tony was born," she said, her voice thick with unshed, happy tears.

Leroy walked over to his son and clapped a firm, proud hand on his shoulder. He then looked at Danny, his own eyes shining with a respect and affection that went beyond words. The promise he had made to his dying best friend all those years ago—to keep his boy safe—felt more complete in this one, loud, grease-stained moment than it ever had before.

The four of them stood there in the garage, united by the beautiful, deafening roar of the engine, a new, complete family celebrating their first, hard-won victory together.

Before Tony knew it, it was Monday morning. The previous night he had barely slept a wink from the excitement of knowing his road test was coming up. Leroy gave a firm nod.

"Alright. Let's go."

It was decided that Leroy would follow in his pickup truck, just in case, while Maria and Danny would ride with him. Tony would ride the Triumph to the test site himself. It wasn't just a practical decision; it was a vote of confidence. Tony swung his leg over the bike, the leather seat cool and solid beneath him. He turned the key, and the engine roared to life with a satisfying, deep rumble. He took a deep, shaky breath, the smell of gasoline and hot metal filling his lungs. He was terrified and more excited than he had ever been in his life. He could feel his palms sweating inside his leather gloves as he gripped the handlebars.

He gave a final, tight nod to his dad, clicked the bike into first gear, and with a slight, nervous lurch, pulled out of the driveway and onto the quiet residential street. For the first couple of blocks, his control was stiff and overly cautious. The bike felt heavy and unwieldy, every small bump in the pavement a potential disaster. He could feel his dad's pickup truck a steady, watchful presence in his rearview mirror, which only added to the pressure.

But as they turned onto a wider avenue, something shifted. The muscle memory from the countless hours in the garage, the patient lessons with his dad in an empty parking lot, began to take over. His shoulders relaxed. His grip on the handlebars softened. He leaned into a turn, and the bike responded perfectly, a seamless extension of his own body. The fear didn't vanish, but it was overshadowed by a new, exhilarating feeling—the pure, unadulterated freedom of the open road. The wind rushed past his helmet, the city unfolded around him, and for the first time, the Triumph didn't feel like a project or a test. It felt like second nature. It felt like flying.

In the truck behind him, Leroy watched the transformation in his rearview mirror. He saw the initial, jerky start, and felt a familiar pang of fatherly concern. But then he saw his son settle into the ride, saw the stiff, nervous posture relax into one of easy, confident command. A slow, proud smile spread across his face. He was ready.

They arrived at the DMV testing ground in a quiet corner of Kissena Park to a scene of quiet, nervous tension. A handful of other hopeful riders were waiting their turn, their faces a mixture of bravado and sheer terror. Tony parked the Triumph and walked over to where his family was waiting by Leroy's truck.

"You got this," Leroy said, his voice a low, steadying presence. He gave Tony's shoulder a firm squeeze. Maria just hugged him, a fierce, silent gesture that said everything. Danny stood a little ways back, his hands shoved deep in his pockets, but his eyes never left Tony's face.

When the examiner, a stern-faced woman with a clipboard and an impenetrable expression, called his name, Tony's heart hammered against his ribs. He swung his leg over the bike, the engine rumbling to life beneath him. The first part of the test was a simple, slow ride around the perimeter of the lot. But Tony's nerves were shot. His hands, slick with sweat inside his gloves, felt clumsy on the handlebars. He let the clutch out too fast on the initial pull-away, causing the bike to lurch forward with a jerky, unprofessional motion. The examiner, watching from the center of the lot, made a sharp, deliberate mark on her clipboard.

Tony's stomach plummeted. *"I blew it. I already blew it."*

From the sidelines, Maria gasped, her hand flying to her mouth. Leroy's jaw tightened, but he remained silent. Danny just clenched his fists tighter in his pockets, his knuckles white. Tony took the first corner too wide, his movements stiff and uncertain. The Triumph, which had felt like second nature just an hour before, now felt like a wild, unpredictable beast. He was failing. The panic began to close in, his vision narrowing.

He was about to make the turn for the second leg of the course when he glanced over at his family. He saw his mother's worried face, his father's stoic one. And then he saw Danny. He wasn't looking at the bike or the cones; he was looking right at Tony, his expression one of absolute, unwavering faith. A voice, calm and familiar, cut through the noise in his head. *"Control, not speed. You are in command of the machine."* His dad's words.

Tony took a deep, steadying breath, the cool morning air filling his lungs. He blocked out the examiner, the other riders, the fear. He focused on the hum of the engine, the solid weight of the machine between his legs, and the quiet belief in Danny's eyes. He eased into the next part of the course: the slow, controlled weave through a line of bright orange cones. His movements were different now—fluid, precise, almost elegant. The bike moved with him, a perfect, synchronized dance.

It was the same rhythm he'd found in the living room two nights before—Danny's quiet faith steadying his steps, guiding him through clumsy fear into something graceful. The cones blurred past like music he could finally keep time to.He navigated the tight figure-eight, his turns clean and confident. He brought the bike to a smooth, abrupt halt, the front tire stopping perfectly inside the small, painted box.

Finally, he rode the bike back to the starting point and killed the engine. The sudden silence was deafening. He watched, his heart pounding, as the examiner walked toward him, her face still an unreadable mask. She made a few final notes on her clipboard. It felt like an eternity. She looked up at him.

"You're a little jerky on the takeoff," she said, her voice flat. "But your control maneuvers are excellent." She tore the sheet from the pad and handed it to him. Stamped at the bottom in bold, block letters was the word: **PASS**.

A wide, brilliant, disbelieving grin split Tony's face. He let out a whoop of pure, unadulterated joy that echoed across the quiet lot. The tension on the sidelines broke instantly. Maria rushed forward, pulling her son into a fierce, relieved hug. Leroy clapped him hard on the shoulder, his face breaking into a rare, wide smile.

"Knew you had it in you," he said, his voice thick with pride.

But amidst the happy chaos, Tony's eyes searched for and found Danny's. Danny hadn't moved. He just stood there, a real, unguarded, snaggle-toothed smile of pure happiness stretched across his face. It was a smile entirely *for Tony*. Tony's heart felt like it was going to burst. He lifted his hand to his chest and, right there in the middle of the crowded DMV lot, delivered their silent message.

Tap. Tap.

Danny's smile somehow widened.

Later, as Tony proudly rode the newly-legal Triumph back into the garage, the engine rumbling with a satisfying purr, he saw Danny waiting for him. He parked the bike and took off his new helmet, his hair a mess, his face flushed with victory. He placed it on the workbench, right next to the second, identical helmet that sat waiting. He looked at Danny, then at the empty passenger seat on the bike, and then back at Danny, a hopeful, gentle question in his eyes. He didn't have to say a word. Danny's gaze lingered on the empty leather seat, his pulse quickening. It wasn't just a ride—it was an invitation, a promise of belonging. When his eyes lifted back to Tony's, the answer was already there, quiet and certain.

CHAPTER 32

TWO AGAINST THE WORLD

Tony looked at Danny, his heart pounding in his chest. Then, his gaze moved pointedly to the empty black leather passenger seat behind him, and finally, to the pristine, untouched helmet that was Danny's. He didn't have to say a word. The invitation hung in the air, a silent, hopeful question. Danny's own gaze followed Tony's. He looked at the helmet—*his* helmet, a solid promise of shared adventures. A flicker of the old, familiar fear tightened in his stomach.

But then he looked at Tony. He saw the open, hopeful, and patient look on his face. He saw the boy who had pulled him back from the edge of a bridge, the boy who held him when he shook with fear, the boy who had taught himself the language of patience just for him. Trust in Tony was a stronger force than any fear. Slowly, deliberately, Danny reached out and picked up his helmet. It felt heavy and solid in his hands. He gave Tony a small, shy, but determined nod.

"Okay," he whispered, the single word a quiet declaration of courage. A brilliant, relieved smile broke across Tony's face. He took the helmet from Danny and gently placed it on his head, his fingers carefully adjusting the straps under his chin, the touch a tender, protective gesture.

"Ready?" Tony asked, his voice a low murmur. Danny took a deep breath and nodded again.

"Ready."

Tony got on the bike first, his movements sure and confident. He waited as Danny hesitantly swung his own leg over the back, settling onto the seat behind him.

"Hold on tight," Tony said.

Danny's arms tentatively wrapped around Tony's waist. He pressed his cheek against the worn, familiar leather of Tony's jacket, and as Tony started the engine, the powerful vibration rumbling through both of them, his grip tightened. And together, they pulled out of the garage and into the bright Monday morning, leaving the quiet suburban street behind as they headed for the open road.

The ride was a revelation. For Danny, who had only ever experienced the city through the smudged window of a rattling bus or on foot with his head down, this was like seeing the world for the first time. They moved through the heart of Queens, the familiar rumble of the elevated 7 train passing overhead as they rode under the tracks. The world was a vibrant, chaotic mural of different cultures—the fragrant smells of a hundred different cuisines, the sound of languages he didn't recognize, the colorful storefronts and bustling sidewalks.

Tony was a confident and careful driver, navigating the traffic with an easy grace. He was hyper-aware of the precious cargo he was carrying, his every move calculated to be smooth and reassuring. And as they left the dense, urban streets behind and turned onto the roads leading south, the landscape began to change. The buildings grew smaller, the sky opened up, and a new scent hit the air—a sharp, clean, salty tang that Danny had only ever dreamed of.

The fear that had been a cold knot in his stomach at the start of the ride had long since melted away, replaced by a feeling of pure, unadulterated exhilaration. He wasn't running *from* anything; he was riding *toward* something. The wind whipped past them, a cleansing force that seemed to scour away the last remnants of the past, leaving only the rumble of the engine and the solid warmth of Tony's body pressed against his. They finally crossed the bridge into the Rockaways, the vast, glittering expanse of the Atlantic Ocean suddenly stretching out before them. Tony found a spot to park along the quiet, off-season boardwalk, and killed the engine. The sudden silence was immediately filled by a new, more powerful sound: the rhythmic crash and sigh of ocean waves.

Tony helped Danny off the bike, and they took off their helmets, their hair a wild, windswept mess. They walked, wordless, from the concrete boardwalk down onto the soft, cool sand. They were the only two people on this stretch of beach. It felt like their own private world.

They found a spot far from the boardwalk and just sat, their shoulders brushing, and watched the endless, hypnotic roll of the waves. The sun was warm on their faces, the sea breeze cool and clean. After a long, comfortable silence, Tony finally spoke.

"What do you think?" he asked, his voice a quiet murmur, almost lost in the sound of the ocean. Danny didn't answer right away. He just stared out at the horizon, at the impossibly vast line where the deep blue of the water met the pale blue of the sky.

"It's… big," he finally whispered, and Tony knew he wasn't just talking about the ocean.

Tony smiled and reached over, his fingers finding Danny's in the sand. Danny's hand closed around his, their grip firm and sure. He leaned his head against Tony's shoulder, a simple, profound gesture of peace and belonging. They sat like that for a long time, their hands intertwined, two boys at the edge of a continent, their whole future as wide and open as the ocean stretching out before them.

After a long while, Tony stirred. He let go of Danny's hand and stood up, a playful, challenging glint in his eyes. Danny watched, confused, as Tony began to unlace his heavy combat boots, pulling them off and setting them neatly on the sand. He followed with his socks, then shrugged out of his iconic black leather jacket, folding it carefully and placing it on top of his boots.

The setting sun cast him in a golden, almost ethereal light. He was just a boy in a t-shirt and jeans, stripped of all his usual armor. He gave Danny a big, wide grin.

"Last one in's a rotten egg," he declared, and before Danny could even process the words, Tony was jogging toward the water. He hit the edge of the surf and let out a loud, sharp gasp as the cold Atlantic water swirled around his ankles. "Whoa! Okay, that is freezing!" he yelled, laughing, but he didn't stop. He waded in deeper, up to his knees, the cold water dark and churning around him.

He turned back to Danny, who was still sitting on the warm, dry sand, watching him with wide, disbelieving eyes.

"Well?" Tony shouted over the roar of the waves, his smile a brilliant slash of white against the twilight. "You coming, or are you just gonna sit there?"

Danny's first instinct, the one honed by years of fear and self-preservation, was to say no. To stay right where he was, safe and warm. But then he looked at Tony—truly looked at him. He saw him standing in the freezing ocean, shivering, lit by pure, uninhibited joy.

He was tired of being the boy on the shore. With a sudden, decisive movement, Danny scrambled to his feet. He kicked off his own worn-out sneakers, pulled off his socks, and, without giving himself a second to think, he ran. He sprinted down the sand and plunged into the surf, the shock of the icy water so intense it stole his breath and made him cry out.

Tony's laughter echoed as Danny splashed toward him, a huge, genuine smile finally breaking across his own face. The cold was brutal, but the feeling of shared, reckless joy was a fire in his chest, warmer than any summer sun. The initial, brutal shock of the cold water gave way to a giddy, breathless laughter that echoed over the sound of the waves. They splashed at each other, two boys lost in a moment of pure, uncomplicated fun, the city a distant, glittering memory behind them. After a few minutes, a deep, bone-chilling shiver wracked Danny's body.

"Okay," he said through chattering teeth, his smile never leaving his face. "Can we... can we get out now? I can't feel my toes."

"Yeah, say less," Tony agreed without a second's hesitation. He was shivering too, his lips tinged with blue, but his eyes were bright with happiness.

They scrambled out of the surf, their wet jeans heavy and clinging to their legs, and collapsed onto the cool, dry sand. They didn't bother to get dressed right away. They just sat, shoulders brushing, and watched as the last sliver of the sun disappeared below the horizon, leaving the sky a deep, bruised purple. As the light faded, dozens of seagulls began to congregate on the water's surface, their dark shapes bobbing gently on the rolling waves, their calls a lonely, plaintive sound.

Danny watched them, a feeling he couldn't quite name settling over him. It was peace, but it was a kind he'd never known before. It wasn't the fleeting, anxious quiet he'd find hiding in his closet or the sterile silence of an empty library. This was a deep, steady calm, a peace that wasn't defined by the absence of fear, but by the solid, warm presence of the boy sitting next to him. He felt an involuntary smile spread across his face, a real, wide, snaggle-toothed grin, and he didn't even try to hide it. Tony turned his head, watching the pure, uninhibited joy on Danny's face. His own heart felt so full it was almost painful.

"So," he said, his voice a low, gentle murmur that was almost lost in the sound of the waves. "For a spur-of-the-moment thing..." He hesitated, a flicker of hopeful vulnerability in his eyes. "Are you enjoying our first date?"

Danny finally tore his gaze away from the ocean and looked at Tony. He looked at the boy who had just run into the freezing Atlantic with him for no reason at all, the boy who was now shivering beside him, his hair a mess, a stupid, happy grin on his face.

"Yeah," Danny whispered, his own smile unwavering. "It's... perfect."

The simple, heartfelt word—"perfect"—hung in the cool, salty air between them. Tony just looked at him, his heart so full he felt like he couldn't speak. He saw the last of the fear and hesitation melt from Danny's eyes, replaced by a quiet, shining confidence he had never seen before. Then, Danny moved.

He leaned in, his movements sure and deliberate. He braced his hands on Tony's shoulders to support himself and pressed his lips to Tony's. The kiss was cold from the sea and tasted of salt, but it was the warmest thing Tony had ever felt. It was a kiss of pure, unadulterated affection, a quiet *"thank you"* and a bold *"I'm here"* all at once. Danny held the kiss for a long, perfect moment, pouring all the newfound peace and unspoken joy of the day into the gentle pressure of his lips.

He held it for as long as his shivering arms could hold his weight. Suddenly, his tired muscles gave out, and he collapsed backward with a soft *oomph* into the cool sand.For a second, there was just stunned silence. Then, a loud, barking laugh erupted from Tony. It wasn't a mean laugh; it was a sound of pure, surprised delight, a joyous, unrestrained belly laugh that echoed across the empty beach. He fell back onto the sand beside Danny, laughing with tears streaking from his eyes.

"Oh, jeez," Tony gasped, wiping a tear from his eye. "I'm sorry. I'm sorry. I shouldn't laugh at that. Are you okay?"

Danny looked at Tony's face, at the genuine, helpless joy radiating from him, and a slow grin spread across his own face. He wasn't being made fun of. He was being laughed *with*. He just felt... silly. Free. A laugh bubbled up from his chest, a sound he hadn't heard in years. Soon, they were both lying on their backs on the sand, side-by-side, their shoulders shaking with shared, uninhibited laughter under the vast, starry sky.

The shared, easy laughter slowly faded, leaving them in a comfortable, happy silence under the vast, starry sky. A cool breeze drifted off the water, and Tony, acutely aware of their still-damp clothes, finally shivered. He sat up, pushing his windswept hair out of his eyes.

"Okay," he said, his voice soft. "We should probably get going before we actually freeze." He looked at Danny, a gentle, warm smile on his face. "There's a little all-night cafe a few blocks from here. We could... we could stop, grab a hot chocolate to warm up before we head all the way back." Danny sat up too, nodding in agreement.

"Yeah," he whispered. "I'd like that."

They stood, brushing the sand from their clothes. Before turning to walk back toward the boardwalk, they both paused, taking in their surroundings in greater detail. The beach was bathed in the soft, pale light of the crescent moon. The waves washed onto the shore with a gentle, rhythmic *shush*, and in the distance, the lights of the beach houses along the shore twinkled like a second, grounded constellation. The air was clean and salty, and the world felt quiet, peaceful, and immense. Tony looked at the quiet houses, then over at Danny, who was staring out at the dark water with a look of profound, quiet awe on his face.

"It's... different out here," Tony said, his voice a low murmur. "Calm."

Danny finally turned his gaze from the ocean to Tony, and he gave a small, almost imperceptible nod. He understood exactly what Tony meant. This place, with its quiet streets and the endless, soothing sound of the ocean, felt a world away from the frantic energy of the city, and even further from the suffocating confines of their pasts. It felt open. It felt possible.

They shared an agreed look, a silent, profound understanding passing between them. They could see it. They could see themselves in an area like this at some point in their lives, in a small house by the water, a place built on the quiet peace they were just now discovering. It almost felt like a home away from home, a future they hadn't even known they were looking for.

Without a word, Tony reached for Danny's hand, and together, they walked off the beach and back to the motorcycle parked on the side streets. A gentle smile touched Tony's lips. He helped Danny with his helmet, his fingers lingering for a moment as he made sure the strap to this helmet was snug and secure. The gesture was full of a quiet, protective care that made Danny's heart ache in the best possible way.

Tony helped Danny onto the back of the motorcycle and got his helmet adjusted properly. He swung his own leg over, the familiar weight of the machine solid and reassuring beneath him. Danny's arms wrapped around his waist, his grip sure and confident now, no longer hesitant.

The ride back into the city was just as illuminating as the ride out toward the beach. They flew through the cool night air, a single, dark shape against the sprawling galaxy of city lights. The roar of the Triumph's engine was a constant, powerful presence, a deep rumble that vibrated through Danny's entire body.

And the sound of the engine was akin to Danny in a way he never knew. All his life, loud noises had meant danger. The shattering of a bottle, the slam of a door, the raw, grating sound of Dina's voice rising in a drug-fueled rage—these were the sounds of his trauma. They were chaotic, unpredictable, and always, always a prelude to pain. He had learned to crave silence, to equate it with safety.

But this was different. This noise wasn't chaotic; it was constant. It wasn't angry; it was powerful. It was the sound of the machine that was carrying them forward, away from the past. Pressed against Tony's back, feeling the steady, controlled vibration of the engine, Danny realized that this was what safety could sound like, too. It could be loud and fierce and strong. It was the sound of Tony's promise, a protective roar against the quiet, insidious whispers of his old life. It was the sound of them, together, moving forward. And for the first time, he didn't want the noise to stop.

They walked into the house, their cheeks flushed from the cold night air, a shared, happy silence hanging between them. The living room was bathed in the soft, flickering light of the television. They found Maria and Leroy curled up together on the couch, a cozy tangle of limbs under the soft afghan, completely engrossed in one of their favorite *novelas*. Maria looked over as they entered, her expression warm and unsurprised.

"Hey, you two," she said softly, her eyes flicking to the clock on the wall, which showed it was just past ten. "Have fun?"

She and Leroy didn't ask what the boys had gotten up to. They had heard the Triumph leave and figured that with Tony's newfound license, they would want to go exploring. And explore they did. It was an act of trust, giving them the space to have their own lives, their own firsts.

"Yeah," Tony said, a wide, unguarded grin spreading across his face. He looked over at Danny, his eyes full of an affection that was impossible to miss. "It was the best date I've ever been on."

Danny's cheeks immediately flushed a deep red, but he didn't look away. A small, brilliant, snaggle-toothed smile bloomed on his face. Maria's heart swelled. She caught Leroy's eye over the back of the couch, and he gave her a slow, contented smile. This was it. This was the new normal they had prayed for.

"Okay, lovebirds," she said, a playful, teasing note in her voice. "You two look wiped out. Go on, get ready for bed…. It's a school night. You two may be graduates, but there's still another few more days of class."

"Okay, Mom," Tony said, still smiling. He reached for Danny's hand, lacing their fingers together without a second thought, and led him toward the stairs, leaving his parents to the soft, dramatic whispers of their show.

CHAPTER 33

DECLARATION

The Tuesday morning after their first date felt different. The air in the house was still and quiet as Tony and Danny got ready for school, but it was a comfortable silence, filled with the warm, unspoken memory of the day before. The scent of the salty ocean air seemed to still cling to them, a lingering trace of the freedom they'd tasted together.

Tony was pulling on his black leather jacket, the familiar weight a comforting shield, when he looked over at Danny, who was quietly packing his sketchbook into his backpack. An idea, bright and exhilarating, sparked in his mind.

"Hey," he said, his voice a little hesitant, but his eyes were shining with a hopeful energy. "What if... what if we took the bike to school today?"

Danny froze, his hand still inside his backpack. He looked up at Tony, his own eyes wide with a sudden, familiar panic. The school. The crowds. The whispers. It was one thing to hold hands on a deserted beach in the dark; it was another to willingly ride into the heart of the lion's den on a gleaming black motorcycle, a moving spotlight that would draw every eye in the student parking lot. They weren't "out" out. He wasn't ready for that kind of attention. Tony saw the terror on his face instantly and kicked himself for being so impulsive. He immediately backpedaled, his voice soft and reassuring.

"Hey, no, it's okay. Forget I said it. It was a stupid idea. We can take the van. It's no big deal." He started to turn away to grab the minivan keys from the hook by the door, but Danny's quiet voice stopped him.

"No. Wait."

Tony turned back. Danny was still standing by the bed, his expression a chaotic battle of fear and a new, fragile resolve. He thought of the feeling of flying down the highway, of the solid strength of Tony's back against his cheek, of the freedom of the open ocean. He thought of the boy who had so patiently waited for him, who had shown him what it felt like to be safe, who had never once pushed him.

"Maybe it doesn't always have to be this way," a quiet, defiant voice whispered in his mind. *"Maybe I don't always have to be the boy who hides."* He looked at Tony, at the boy he loved so deeply, and for the first time, the desire to be seen *with* him was stronger than the fear of being seen *by* everyone else. He took a deep, shaky breath, a single, deliberate nod signaling his decision.

"I... I want to," he said, his voice quiet but steady. "Let's take the bike." A slow, brilliant, disbelieving smile spread across Tony's face.

"Yeah?" he breathed out.

"Yeah," Danny confirmed, a small, terrified, but incredibly brave smile touching his own lips.

"Okay," Tony said, his heart feeling like it was going to beat right out of his chest. "Okay. Let's ride."

The journey to school was a tense, silent countdown. As Tony guided the Triumph into the student parking lot, he could already feel the eyes turning toward them. The deep, throaty rumble of the vintage bike was an anomaly in a sea of sensible sedans and beat-up hatchbacks. He found a spot, killed the engine, and for a moment, neither of them moved, the sound of the engine replaced by the frantic thumping of their own hearts.

"Dude! No way!" a familiar voice boomed. Tony and Danny turned to see Marko and Jamal jogging toward them, their faces split with identical, impressed grins.

"You actually got this thing on the road!" Marko said, circling the Triumph with a look of genuine awe. "It looks sick, man. The black paint is perfect."

"For real," Jamal agreed, his eyes wide. "It looks amazing." He then looked from the bike to the two of them, a knowing, happy smile on his face. "It's really cool you guys rode in together."

Just then, another figure approached, his steps a little hesitant as he navigated the parking lot. It was Connor, a stack of textbooks clutched to his chest. He saw Jamal and his face broke into a small, shy smile.

"Hey," he said, his gaze immediately falling on the gleaming motorcycle. "Whoa. Is this yours?"

"Tony and Danny fixed it up," Jamal said, slinging an arm proudly around Connor's shoulders.

"It's incredible," Connor said, his eyes wide with genuine admiration. He looked from the bike to Tony, then to Danny, offering them both a warm, kind smile. "You guys did an amazing job. And riding it to school? That's seriously cool."

The easy, uncomplicated acceptance from all three of them was a shield against the curious stares from the rest of the parking lot. Danny looked over at Tony, who was beaming with pride, and felt a new, fragile sense of courage take root. The first bell shrieked, and their friends said their goodbyes, melting into the river of students. Tony and Danny were left alone in the relative quiet. Tony took off his helmet and ran a hand through his hair, his heart a nervous, thumping drum.

"Hey," he started, his voice a low, considerate murmur. "When we go in there... people are gonna ask questions." He looked at Danny, giving him all the power. "What do you want me to say? We can just say it's because we live together. No one has to know anything else."

He was offering him an out. A shield. Danny looked at Tony, at the incredible, painstaking care he was taking with his feelings. He was tired of hiding. He was tired of being a secret.

"You can tell them the truth," Danny said, his voice quiet but full of a new, unwavering strength. "You can tell them we're together. That we're boyfriends."

The word *"boyfriends"* spoken aloud by Danny for the first time, landed in the quiet parking lot with the force of a beautiful, perfect thunderclap. A slow, brilliant, and utterly adoring smile spread across Tony's face. He reached out and, with his thumb, gently tapped the space over his own heart twice.

Tap. Tap.

He then helped Danny with his helmet.

"Ready?" Tony asked. Danny took a deep breath and gave a firm nod.

"Ready."

Tony started to turn toward the school entrance, but a small, hesitant touch on his hand stopped him. He looked down. Danny had reached out, his own fingers trembling slightly, and had tentatively laced them with Tony's.

Tony's breath hitched. He looked at their joined hands, then back up at Danny's face. Danny's eyes were fixed on the school doors, his jaw tight with resolve, but he didn't pull away. He was scared, but he was choosing to be brave. He was choosing *them*.

A wave of love so fierce it almost buckled Tony's knees washed over him. He gave Danny's hand a firm, reassuring squeeze, a silent promise that he would not let him go. And together, hand in hand, they walked toward the school doors, ready to face whatever came next.

The moment they walked through the school doors hand-in-hand, a tangible shockwave rippled through the crowded main hallway. It wasn't loud or dramatic. It was a sudden, noticeable drop in the usual morning chaos—a dozen conversations faltering at once, a hundred heads turning in near-unison. The normal, roaring river of students seemed to part around them, creating a small, silent bubble of intense scrutiny. The gossip ignited instantly, spreading from person to person like a lit fuse. It was a cascade of whispers, of wide-eyed glances, of phones being discreetly pulled out to text friends who were not in the immediate vicinity.

"Is that Tony Guzman? Who is he holding hands with? Wait, isn't that the new kid? The quiet one? No way. Tony and another guy?"

Tony Guzman—the effortlessly cool, leather-jacket-clad boy who moved through the school with the easy confidence of a king in his own court, the boy who had just broken up with the beautiful and popular Jessica—was walking through the hallway holding hands with the shy, almost invisible Danny Sanders. The whispers spread like wildfire, shock turning into instant legend.

Tony felt the stares like a physical weight, but he kept his head held high, his gaze fixed straight ahead. His grip on Danny's hand was a warm, solid anchor in the storm. He could feel a fine tremor in Danny's fingers and knew the sheer, terrifying effort it was taking for him not to bolt.

For Danny, it was a waking nightmare. Every whisper was a judgment, every stare a hot poker against his skin. The urge to pull his hand back, to drop his head and disappear into the anonymity he had clung to for so long, was so strong it was a physical ache. But through it all, there was the steady, grounding pressure of Tony's hand in his. He focused on that feeling, on the simple, solid connection that was his only anchor.

The walk to Danny's locker felt like a mile-long gauntlet under a thousand spotlights. When they finally reached it, the small metal alcove felt like a private sanctuary. Danny let go of Tony's hand, his own trembling slightly as he fumbled with his combination lock. Tony leaned against the locker next to his, creating a small, private space for them, his body a subtle shield against the rest of the hallway.

"You okay?" Tony asked, his voice a low murmur that was just for them.

Danny didn't look at him. He just stared into the cluttered space of his locker. After a long moment, he gave a single, shaky nod.

"Yeah," he whispered. He then slowly turned his head and looked at Tony, his blue eyes still wide with fear, but with something else there, too—a deep, profound, and shining gratitude. "Thanks... for not letting go."

"Never," Tony promised, his voice a fierce, quiet vow.

The second bell shrieked, a final warning before class. Tony escorted Danny to their first class together, AP English. Tony stared at Danny, lifting his hand to his chest.

Tap. Tap.

A small, watery, but genuine smile touched Danny's lips. He had survived the first five minutes. The school was in an absolute buzz, but for the first time, he felt like he wasn't facing it alone.

Mr. Bodowski, oblivious, launched into a lecture on symbolism in *To Kill a Mockingbird*. But no one was listening. The room was buzzing with a silent, intense energy, all of it directed toward the back of the room. Tony could feel the stares. He saw a girl two rows ahead turn and whisper to her friend, her eyes wide. He just stared straight ahead, a defiant, protective wall around the two of them.

The hallways between classes were worse. The whispers were louder, the stares more blatant. Tony kept a hand on the small of Danny's back as they navigated the human currents, a small, grounding gesture of solidarity. He saw Marko and Jamal by the lockers and gave them a tight, stressed nod. They nodded back, their expressions a mixture of support and a clear understanding that this was a storm the two of them had to weather on their own.

By the time the lunch bell rang, Tony's stomach was a tight knot of anxiety. This would be the real test. He saw Danny hovering uncertainly by the cafeteria entrance. Tony walked over, and without a word, he gently placed a hand on the small of Danny's back and guided him toward the lunch line. They got their food and scanned the roaring, chaotic room. Tony's eyes immediately found their usual table, where Marko, Jamal, and Connor were already sitting, saving them two spots. As they approached, Marko looked up, saw them coming, and a slow, wicked grin spread across his face.

"Okay, I get it now," he said, his voice a loud, theatrical whisper. "Tony got a motorcycle, and now he's got a boyfriend to ride on the back. It's like a whole biker gang aesthetic. I respect it." Jamal just rolled his eyes, but he was smiling.

"Shut up, man."

The joke, as clumsy as it was, was a gift. It was Marko's way of saying, *"I see this, and I'm still your idiot best friend, and we're still going to be idiots together."* The tension in Tony's shoulders eased. They sat down, Tony taking the seat next to Danny, creating a solid, united front.

The bubble of their table couldn't protect them from the rest of the cafeteria. The stares were constant. Then, a figure stopped at the edge of their table.

It was Jessica.

She stood there, her books clutched to her chest like a shield, her expression a mask of nervous resolve. The easy chatter at the table died instantly. Tony's heart dropped into his stomach. Her focus was entirely on Danny.

"Hi, Danny," Jessica said, her voice quiet but clear. "I, um... I just wanted to say congratulations. On graduating. After everything... it's a really big deal. And I'm... I'm happy for you."

The simple, impossibly graceful words hung in the air. Danny just stared at her, his throat too tight to form words. He could only manage a small, almost imperceptible nod of thanks. Jessica finally turned her gaze to Tony. There was no anger in her eyes, just a deep, final sadness.

"You too, Tony," she said softly. "Congratulations."

And with that, she gave a small, sad smile, turned, and walked away, leaving a profound, altered silence in her wake. It hit him all at once— she had just shown more grace in thirty seconds than he had managed in their entire relationship. He looked at Danny, who was still staring after Jessica, his eyes shining with unshed, grateful tears. In that moment, in the middle of the roaring, gossiping cafeteria, Danny reached out under the table and, for the first time, tentatively took Tony's hand. A wave of shame and deep, aching respect washed over Tony. He saw the hurt, but also the strength in her. And he knew, in that moment, that just letting her walk away wasn't enough. He had to do more than just accept his punishment; he had to actively try and fix the friendships he had broken.

"Jess, wait," he called out.

His voice wasn't loud, but it was clear, and it cut through the buzz of the surrounding tables. Jessica stopped, her back still to him. She hesitated for a second, then slowly turned around, her expression a mixture of surprise and weary apprehension. Tony stood up. He looked at the empty seat beside Marko, then back at her, his expression open and sincere.

"Please," he said, his voice quiet but full of a genuine, pleading warmth. "Sit. With us. I know it's weird. But... please."

Jessica looked at him, then at Marko, who gave her a small, encouraging nod. She seemed to have a silent battle with herself for a moment, then, with a deep, steadying breath, she walked back to the table and slid into the empty spot, creating a new, impossibly complicated seating arrangement. An awkward, heavy silence descended. Tony looked from Jessica's guarded face to Marko's hopeful one, and then over to Danny, who looked like he wanted to be anywhere else in the universe. Tony knew this was on him. He took a breath and looked directly at Marko, then shifted his gaze to Jessica.

"I know... what's going on between you two," he said, the words difficult but necessary. "Or, what could be. And I just... I need you to hear this from me." He finally looked Jessica square in the eye, his own expression full of a painful, honest sincerity. "He's a good guy, Jess. He's my best friend. And he'll treat you right. He'll be honest with you in a way I never was." He then looked at Marko. "And you... you'd be lucky to have her. She's the best person I know." He leaned back, the confession leaving him feeling raw and exposed, but also... lighter. "You guys have my blessing," he said, forcing a small, sad smile. "For whatever that's worth. You both deserve to be happy."

The table was silent. Jessica stared at him, a storm of conflicting emotions in her eyes. Marko looked stunned, and then a look of profound, grateful relief washed over his face. It was Danny who moved first. In the middle of the roaring, gossiping cafeteria, with everyone at the table watching, he reached out under the table and, for the first time, tentatively took Tony's hand. Tony's fingers immediately closed around his, a silent, solid anchor in the most difficult moment of his life.

When the 12:45 bell rang, Tony was waiting by Danny's locker, leaning against the cool metal, a silent, solid presence that dared anyone to look too long. Danny approached, his movements still a little hesitant, but the hunted, terrified look in his eyes was gone, replaced by a quiet, weary resolve.

"Ready?" Tony asked softly.

Danny just gave a small nod. They walked out of the school and to the motorcycle, a new kind of silence between them. It wasn't awkward; it was the shared, tired quiet of two soldiers who had made it through a long and difficult battle together.

Instead of heading home, Tony turned in the other direction, toward the leafy, quiet part of town they had come to know well. It was Tuesday. The drive to Dr. Sharma's office was different this time. Before, it had always been a tense, quiet journey, with Danny coiled into a knot of anxiety in the passenger seat of the minivan. Today, on the back of the Triumph, it felt like a continuation of their ride from the day before. Danny's arms were wrapped securely around Tony's waist, his cheek pressed against the familiar, worn leather of his jacket. The rumble of the engine was a comforting, protective sound. It was the sound of them, together, moving forward.

Tony parked the bike and they walked into the warm, inviting waiting room. As always, Tony settled into the comfortable armchair, picking up a magazine he had no intention of reading. A few minutes later, Dr. Sharma opened her office door, a kind, gentle smile on her face.

"Daniel," she said warmly. "It's good to see you."

Danny looked from her calm expression to Tony, who gave him a small, encouraging nod. Danny took a deep, shuddering breath, and for the first time, he walked through her door not with a sense of dread, but with a quiet, determined purpose.

He sat in his usual chair, but he didn't clutch his backpack to his chest like a shield. He set it on the floor beside him. Dr. Sharma settled into her own chair, her presence a calm, accepting anchor.

"So," she said, her voice gentle. "How was your week?"

Danny was quiet for a long moment, gathering his thoughts. He thought about the chaos of the last few days—the graduation dinner, the motorcycle test, the terrifying, exhilarating act of walking into school holding Tony's hand. But underneath all of that, there was a new, shining memory, a perfect, quiet moment that had changed everything. He took a breath, the words coming out in a hesitant, but clear whisper.

"We... we went on a date," he said. Dr. Sharma's smile widened slightly, but she didn't push. She just waited, letting him tell the story in his own time.

"On the motorcycle," Danny continued, a small, shy smile touching his own lips. "He has his license now. We... we drove to the beach. To Rockaway." He looked up, his blue eyes shining with the memory. "It was... big. The ocean. We were the only ones there."

He recounted the day, his voice growing a little stronger with each detail. He told her about the freezing, exhilarating shock of the ocean water, about Tony's unrestrained, joyous laughter, about their shared, silly collapse into the sand. He even told her about the kiss, his cheeks flushing a faint pink as he described the feeling of it—cold and salty and perfect.

"He called it our first date," Danny finished, his voice a soft, wondering murmur. "And... it was. It was the first time... the first time I've ever just... been happy. Without being scared. I think... I think I'm starting to believe him now. That I'm allowed to be happy."

CHAPTER 34

LET THEM EAT CAKE

The last week of June descended upon the city, cloaking the borough in the thick, soupy humidity of a New York summer. Heat waves shimmered in visible, dancing ribbons above the asphalt, and the very air felt heavy, a tangible presence buzzing with the drone of cicadas and distant traffic. Inside the house, however, a different kind of atmosphere had settled. The fever-pitched storm that had followed Tony and Danny's public coming out had finally broken, leaving behind a new and settled quiet. After the initial blast of gossip and shocked whispers from the student body, burdened by the looming dread of final exams, had simply absorbed the new reality. Tony and Danny were a couple. The novelty eroded, the stares lessened, the whispers faded into the general din of the hallways. They were no longer a spectacle, but a single, undisputed unit, their hands finding each other with an easy, unconscious gravity.

The week itself became a quiet festival of milestones. On Wednesday, Danny turned eighteen. The day began not with a party, but with a personal offering: a mountain of Maria's golden-brown pancakes, served with a small candle flickering in the center. It ended with a small, beautifully wrapped box from Tony. Danny had carefully peeled back the paper to reveal a professional set of charcoal pencils in a sleek tin case and a thick, textured artist's sketchpad, its pages heavy and full of promise. He hadn't said a word, just stared at the gift, his blue eyes shining with unshed tears. The unspoken message hung between them, more powerful than any birthday song: *"I see you. I see this part of you that you guard so closely. And I love it."*

Friday was Tony's turn, a much louder affair. Marko and Jamal had burst through the door, serenading him with a version of *"Happy Birthday"* so violently off-key it was a masterpiece of intentional chaos, Connor trailing behind them with a sheepish grin and a six-pack of soda. They'd dumped a pile of video games on the living room floor and waged digital war until well past midnight, the sounds of explosions and triumphant shouting filling the house.

Now it was Saturday. The culmination. Their official joint celebration, a backyard barbecue that felt less like a party and more like the coronation of a life they were finally allowed to build in the open.

Tony woke incrementally, surfacing from his dreams into a world defined by two sensations: the rich, earthy smell of fresh coffee from downstairs, and the warm, solid weight of Danny curled against his side. He kept his eyes closed for a moment, letting the peace of it soak into him. He could feel the slow, even rise and fall of Danny's breathing against his ribs, a steady, living rhythm that had become the new metronome of his life. He carefully turned his head on the pillow, the cotton cool against his cheek, and just watched him.

In the soft morning light filtering through the curtains, Danny looked younger, almost boyish. The anxious lines that had for so long been etched around his eyes and mouth were gone, smoothed away by sleep, leaving his pale skin almost translucent. The old, faded scar on his upper lip was a faint, silvery crescent in the dim light. Tony's eyes traced it, a silent catalog of their history. A few short months ago, this—this quiet, this effortless domesticity—would have been an impossible, dangerous fantasy. Now, it was the bedrock of his entire world.

He leaned in, gently pressing a kiss to Danny's messy brown hair, breathing in the faint, clean scent of his shampoo.

"Hey," he whispered, his voice a low, sleepy rumble. "Happy birthday weekend, baby."

Danny stirred with a soft murmur of contentment, his eyelids fluttering. His eyes, still clouded with sleep, took a second to focus. When they landed on Tony, a slow, unguarded smile spread across his face. It was the smile reserved just for him, the one that made Tony's heart feel like it was physically expanding in his chest.

"You too," Danny murmured, his voice thick and raspy. He instinctively shifted closer, burrowing his face into Tony's shoulder, chasing the last vestiges of warmth and sleep.

They lay like that for a few minutes, suspended in the rare, perfect stillness of a Saturday morning with no demands. The muffled sounds of Maria and Leroy moving around downstairs—the clink of a plate, a low laugh—were a comforting, distant hum, the soundtrack to a life Tony hadn't even known he was missing until he had it.

"Come on," Tony said finally, the words laced with a reluctant resolve as he began to untangle himself from the sheets. "Let's get some coffee before my mom drafts a chore list."

Danny groaned, but he followed. They made their way downstairs, a silent pair in their sleep clothes—Tony in a pair of worn gray sweatpants, Danny swallowed by one of Tony's old t-shirts that hung down to his knees. The kitchen was empty but filled with the welcoming aroma of a freshly brewed pot. Through the open screen door, they could see Maria and Leroy in the backyard, engaged in a low, serious debate over the placement of the massive, gleaming new barbecue grill Leroy had insisted on buying for the occasion.

Tony moved with familiar ease, pouring two mugs of coffee. He added a generous pour of milk and two spoonfuls of sugar to one, sliding it across the counter to Danny without a word. They leaned against the cool granite, side-by-side, taking slow, quiet sips in the warm, sunlit kitchen.

"It's a big day," Tony said, his voice a low murmur, watching his parents through the window.

Danny gave a small, almost imperceptible nod, his eyes also fixed on the scene outside. He saw Leroy gesticulate wildly at the grill, and Maria throw her head back and laugh, a joyous, uninhibited sound that carried on the breeze. A small, genuine smile touched Danny's own lips, a mirror of her happiness.

"Yeah," he whispered, the single word full of a quiet awe. "It is."

They stood there for another moment, two eighteen-year-old boys in a quiet house, their shoulders brushing. It was a simple, perfect peace, a stark and beautiful contrast to the tense, fearful silence that had once defined so much of their time together.

The moment shattered as Maria slid the back door open, entering the kitchen like a whirlwind of happy, maternal energy. A dish towel was thrown over her shoulder like a general's sash.

"There are my birthday boys!" she announced, her face beaming. "Okay, drink up. The time for lazing about is over. I have a list of duties." She pointed a playful, accusatory finger at Tony. "Your father is losing a battle of wits with a propane tank and an instruction manual written in Martian. He needs a translator. Go help him before he starts cursing in three different languages." Tony laughed, a real, easy laugh.

"On it. Just give us a second here, Mom." Maria's gaze then softened as she turned to Danny.

"And you, *mijo*," she said, her voice warm as she opened a drawer and handed him a clean spoon. "I have a very important and very serious job for you. You are my official taste-tester for the potato salad. Your unbiased opinion is crucial to the success of this entire operation." She winked, and Danny felt a warm, happy blush creep up his neck. The quiet morning was officially over.

They headed back upstairs. The easy domesticity of their new life had become a comfortable, unthinking rhythm. Tony disappeared into the en-suite bathroom for a quick shower. Danny, with a quiet confidence that would have been unthinkable just months ago, went directly to Tony's dresser, pulling out a pair of soft, worn-out sweatpants and a faded Ramones t-shirt for himself. He was sitting on the edge of the bed, already dressed, when Tony emerged, a towel slung low around his waist, water dripping from his long black hair. They traded places in silence, practiced dance, and a little while later, both showered and dressed in their work clothes, they descended the stairs again, ready to face their assignments.

Tony found his dad in the backyard, standing over a baffling array of shiny metal parts and screws, a single, cryptic page of diagrams held in one hand.

"This is junk, Antonio," Leroy grumbled, gesturing at the metal heap. "This piece cannot possibly fit in that piece. It defies physics."

"Okay, *Papi*," Tony said, taking the manual and trying to stifle a grin. "Let's see what the Martians have to say."

Meanwhile, in the kitchen, Danny stood beside Maria at the counter. He held the spoon she'd given him, a small, thoughtful frown on his face as he contemplated the creamy potato salad. He took a small taste, his expression serious. "It's really good," he said, his voice quiet but sure.

"But... maybe a little more.... paprika? For color, and.... a little... smokiness?"

Maria's heart swelled. She looked at this boy, this quiet, gentle boy who had weathered so much, now standing in her kitchen, so carefully and seriously giving his opinion on her recipe.

"Paprika," she declared, reaching for the spice jar as if it were a royal decree. "An excellent suggestion, my official taste-tester."

The day unfolded in that comfortable, easy rhythm. By early afternoon, the barbecue was miraculously assembled, a testament to Tony's diplomatic translations and Leroy's grudging patience. The platters of food were prepared and covered, and the boys had retreated upstairs to get ready for the party. In Tony's room, the air hummed with a low, happy energy. Tony pulled out the new dark green button-down shirt his mom had bought him, while Danny laid out a similar one in a deep, rich blue.

They changed in a comfortable silence, the shared space of the bedroom now as natural to them as breathing. Tony, buttoning his shirt, caught a glimpse of their reflection in the mirror. He saw Danny smooth down the front of his own shirt, and for a fleeting second, a small, shy, and genuinely happy smile broke across Danny's face as he looked at himself. Seeing it, Tony felt a surge of protective love so fierce it almost buckled his knees. It hit him harder than any gift, because Danny wasn't just surviving anymore—he was beginning to like the boy in the mirror. It humbled him, filling him with an aching respect for just how far Danny had come.

Just as they were about to head back down, the doorbell rang, its chime signaling the official start. Their core group spilled into the house: Marko, Jamal, and Connor, their arms loaded with bags of chips and bottles of soda, their voices loud and full of life.

"Alright, where's the food? I was told there would be burgers, and I am prepared to riot," Marko announced, making a beeline for the kitchen with the subtlety of a freight train.

Jamal just rolled his eyes, a fond smile playing on his lips. His hand found Connor's as they bypassed the chaos and walked straight out into the backyard.

Leroy, now a proud king in his "Kiss the Cook" apron, was placing the first seasoned patties on the grill. The sharp sizzle and plume of fragrant smoke filled the air just as the back gate creaked open.

It was Jessica.

She stood there for a moment, holding a small, tastefully wrapped gift, her expression uncertain. A brief, charged quiet fell over the group, the laughter and chatter momentarily suspended. Then Maria, ever the gracious diplomat, broke the silence with a brilliant, welcoming smile that erased all the tension.

"Jessica, honey! I'm so glad you could make it. Come, come give me a hug."

Jessica's shoulders visibly relaxed as she stepped forward and returned the hug. She wished Tony a happy birthday, the exchange a perfect model of mature, quiet friendship. Then, she turned to Danny. He stiffened slightly, an old reflex.

"This is for you," she said, her voice soft as she handed him the small gift. "Happy birthday, Danny." She met his eyes, her own clear and sincere. "I'm really happy for you. For both of you."

"Thanks, Jess," Danny managed, a small, surprised smile gracing his lips. "That... that means a lot."

Later in the afternoon, Miguel and Leo arrived, completing the circle of their found family. The backyard was alive, a symphony of laughter, the sizzle of the barbecue, and the rhythmic thump of a reggaeton beat from a portable speaker. For the first time in what felt like his entire life, Danny wasn't hovering on the sidelines, an anxious satellite. He was in the middle of it all, laughing freely—a loud, unburdened sound—at one of Marko's painfully stupid jokes about a nun walking into a bar.

Across the yard, Tony was leaning against the house, a bottle of soda in his hand, just watching. His heart was so full it felt like it might actually burst. He watched Danny take a sip of his drink, his blue eyes sparkling with mirth, and he felt a profound sense of rightness settle over him. This was it. This was everything. He caught Danny's eye across the lawn. With his thumb, Tony gently tapped his own chest twice, over his heart.

Tap. Tap.

Danny's smile widened. He didn't even hesitate. He subtly lifted his own hand and returned the gesture.

As the sun began to set, casting long, golden shadows across the lawn, Maria emerged from the house bearing a large chocolate cake, its surface blazing with a forest of candles. After a loud, joyous, and truly terrible rendition of *"Happy Birthday"*, Tony and Danny leaned in together, sharing a look before blowing out the candles in a single, combined breath.

The gifts were a testament to how well they were known and loved. Maria and Leroy gave them a single, large framed photo from graduation day—the four of them, Maria, Leroy, Tony, and a genuinely smiling Danny—and announced they'd opened savings accounts for both of them, "for college, for an apartment, for whatever comes next."

Then, it was Danny's turn. He shyly handed Tony a flat, rectangular gift wrapped in simple brown paper. When Tony unwrapped it, his breath caught in his throat. It was the charcoal sketch. The one he had made on the bench overlooking the Queensboro Bridge, from Tony's personal space. But it was no longer just a drawing on a page. It was matted and beautifully, professionally framed, the dark wood highlighting the delicate lines of the charcoal. It was a memory made permanent. A promise solidified. A gesture so full of love and meaning it left Tony completely speechless. He couldn't form words. He just pulled Danny into a fierce, desperate hug, burying his face in his hair, holding on as if Danny were an anchor in a storm.

"It's perfect," he whispered into Danny's ear. "It's the most perfect thing I've ever seen."

Later, long after the last friends had gone and his parents had retreated inside, they sat together on the back steps. The remnants of the party—a few stray napkins, the cooling grill—were a happy, quiet mess behind them. The night was warm and alive with the chirping of crickets, the sky a deep, star-dusted indigo.

"Best birthday ever," Tony said, his voice a low murmur in the dark.

"Yeah," Danny whispered, leaning his head on Tony's shoulder. He felt solid, real. "It was."

Tony turned his head, his lips finding Danny's in a kiss that was soft and sure and utterly unhurried. It was a kiss that tasted of chocolate cake and contentment, a kiss full of the quiet promise of a thousand more days just like this one. It wasn't just a promise of the next sunrise, but of a lifetime of them, side-by-side, finally and completely home.

The last of the party's energy finally seeped out of the house, leaving a profound and welcoming silence in its wake. The low hum of the refrigerator and the distant sigh of city traffic were the only sounds as Tony and Danny padded up the creaking stairs. Tony felt heavy, pleasantly overstuffed with burgers, cake, and the sheer joy of the day. He moved with a lazy contentment, his arm slung over Danny's shoulders.

Danny, by contrast, felt almost weightless, buzzing with a kind of high-octane happiness that was entirely foreign to him. The whole day felt like a dream he was terrified of waking up from. It was more laughter, more acceptance, more uncomplicated fun than he had ever felt he was allowed to have in one lifetime, let alone one afternoon.

They entered Tony's room, their shared sanctuary, and closed the door, shutting out the rest of the world. The moonlight cast a pale blue rectangle on the floor. On the dresser, the collection of birthday gifts sat like monuments to the day. Front and center was the framed sketch of the Queensboro Bridge, its dark wood catching the faint light.

"Oof," Tony grunted, collapsing onto the edge of the bed and pulling off his shoes. "I think I ate three-and-a-half burgers. Your official taste-testing duties should've extended to quality control on my stomach." Danny didn't answer right away. He walked over to the dresser and gently ran a finger along the edge of the frame. He felt a tremor in his hand, the last aftershock of the day's overwhelming emotion.

"Hey," Tony's voice was softer now, all teasing gone. "You good?" Danny turned, his blue eyes looking huge in the dim light.

"That was..." He shook his head, struggling for the right word. "...a lot."

"'Good' a lot? Or 'bad' a lot?" Tony asked, already knowing the answer but giving him the space to say it.

"Good," Danny breathed out, the word full of wonder. "It was too good, Tony. Your mom calling me *mijo*... Jessica being so... nice. Marko actually making me laugh instead of just making me want to disappear." He let out a shaky, quiet laugh. "It just doesn't feel real. I don't feel like I'm allowed to have a day like this." Tony's heart ached with a familiar, protective love. He stood up and crossed the room in two strides, gently taking Danny's hands in his. They were still cool.

"Hey. Look at me," he said, his voice a low, firm anchor. "You are allowed to have this. You're allowed to have all of it. This isn't a dream, and it's not a one-time thing. This is your life now, okay? Our life."

Danny's gaze flickered down to their joined hands, then back up to Tony's face. He gave a small, jerky nod, a wave of emotion making his throat tight.

"C'mere," Tony murmured, pulling him into a hug. Danny melted against him, burying his face in the hollow of Tony's neck, breathing in his familiar scent. He wrapped his arms around Tony's waist and just held on, letting the sheer force of Tony's presence ground him. This was real. Tony was real.

After a long moment, they broke apart. An easy, practiced intimacy took over as they began to shed the day. They changed out of their party clothes, moving around each other in the small space. Tony stripped off his button-down and jeans, leaving him in just his boxers. Danny pulled on one of Tony's soft, worn-out t-shirts that smelled like him, the worn cotton a comforting weight against his skin. Finally, clean and comfortable, they climbed into bed, pulling the comforter over them despite the warm night. They lay on their sides, facing each other, the space between them charged with a quiet, sacred energy.

"Seeing you laugh today," Tony said, his voice a sleepy rumble as he brushed a stray piece of brown hair off Danny's forehead. "That was the best gift I got." A real, soft smile touched Danny's lips.

"Better than the framed masterpiece?" Danny whispered, his own attempt at a joke. Tony's expression turned serious.

"That," he said, his thumb gently stroking Danny's cheek, "is in a whole other category. That's... everything." Danny's eyes fluttered shut as he leaned into the touch. The nervous buzz inside him finally settled, replaced by a deep, bone-weary peace. He was full, not of food, but of a quiet, life-altering joy. Here, in the dark, with Tony's hand on his face and his steady breathing mingling with his own, it all finally felt real. He was allowed to have this.

They lay in the comfortable silence for a long time, simply breathing in the quiet of the room. The initial wave of exhaustion had passed over Tony, replaced by a restless energy. His stomach was still full, and his mind was still replaying the day's highlights on a happy, endless loop. He felt a sudden need for air, for movement.

"I can't sleep," he whispered into the darkness, his voice barely disturbing the quiet. "Too much cake. Too much... everything." He rolled onto his back, staring at the ceiling. "Wanna go for a walk?"

Danny, who had been drifting in a pleasant haze, opened his eyes. The idea settled over him not as a disruption, but as a perfect, logical conclusion to the day. The party was for everyone else, a loud and beautiful declaration. The quiet moments in this room were for them. A walk, through the sleeping streets of their neighborhood, felt like it belonged in that same private category.

"Yeah," he said, his voice soft. "Okay."

Getting dressed for the second time that night felt like a secret mission. They moved with a hushed efficiency, pulling on jeans and sneakers, their socked feet silent on the wood floor. Tony grabbed a plain white t-shirt, and Danny, out of habit, pulled on an old, familiar hoodie. They crept out of the bedroom, leaving the door open just a crack. The floorboards in the hallway gave a familiar groan, and they both froze for a second, listening, before continuing their tiptoed descent. The front door lock made a soft, oily *snick* as Tony turned it, and then they were outside, enveloped by the warm, humid embrace of the summer night.

The street was bathed in the hazy orange glow of the streetlights. The air was thick and still, smelling of asphalt, cut grass, and the faint, sweet scent of honeysuckle from a neighbor's fence. It was a different kind of quiet from the one in the house. This was a living silence, punctuated by the rhythmic chirping of crickets and the distant, lonely wail of a siren.

They started walking with no destination in mind, their sneakers scuffing softly on the pavement. For a block, they didn't speak, simply letting the peace of the night settle over them. Then, as they rounded the corner onto the main avenue, Tony's hand found Danny's, their fingers lacing together in a gesture that was as natural as breathing.

"It's weird," Danny said, his voice low. "The streets are always so loud during the day. At night, it feels like it's just ours."

"It is," Tony agreed, giving his hand a gentle squeeze. "Tonight, it all is."

They walked on, their easy, familiar silence returning. It wasn't an empty quiet, but one filled with everything that had been said and felt throughout the day. It was the echo of Maria's laugh, the sizzle of the grill, the off-key birthday song, the weight of the framed sketch in Tony's hands. There was nothing left that needed to be said, so they just walked, their shoulders brushing, their linked hands a steady, warm anchor between them.

The walk served its purpose, gently burning off the last of the day's frantic energy. The pleasant lethargy returned to Tony's limbs, and the buzzing in Danny's chest subsided into a calm, steady hum of happiness. After circling the block a few times, they found themselves back in front of the house. The windows were all dark, save for the pale moonlight reflecting off the glass. Tony stopped on the sidewalk, turning to face Danny under the halo of a streetlight. He looked at the boy in front of him—at the soft, shaggy hair, the old hoodie, the faint, happy tiredness in his blue eyes—and felt a wave of profound peace. All the fighting, all the fear, all the hiding—it had all led them here, to this quiet street, to this perfect, ordinary moment.

"Happy birthday, Danny," he said softly, the words meant only for him. A slow smile spread across Danny's face, reaching his eyes.

"Happy birthday, Tony."

CHAPTER 35

BETRAYAL AND RETREAT

Tony was the one Danny truly opened up to, pouring out years of silent torment in whispered late-night confessions. With Maria and Leroy, his openness was limited to small gestures—a shared laugh over dinner, a lingering presence in the kitchen, a quiet nod of agreement. He'd been going to therapy for months after Leroy and Maria had taken him in, and it had helped, slowly chipping away at the walls he'd built. Tony was always there, too, a fierce protector who'd stand up to anyone who dared pick on Danny at school, a constant reminder that he wasn't alone anymore.

There were laughter-filled evenings, stolen kisses in the hallway, and the quiet comfort of simply existing next to someone who saw him, truly saw him, and still chose to stay. Danny was even sketching more using his new charcoal set he got from Tony. His sketches loosening, a tentative smile appearing more often. Therapy helped, but Tony's belief was the truest tether — pulling Danny back into the world.

One Friday afternoon in early July, Tony was in his dad's small home office, looking for a stapler for his college essay, which was due the next week. He rummaged through the top drawer of the old metal filing cabinet, his fingers brushing past paper clips, old pens, and stray rubber bands. Nothing.

"*Papi*, where's the stapler?" he called out.

"Should be in the bottom drawer, *mijo*!" Leroy's voice called back from the living room.

Tony pulled open the heavy bottom drawer. It was filled with old case files, neatly labeled. But one file, a simple, unlabeled manila folder, was sitting right on top, out of place. Curiosity, a simple, innocent impulse, got the better of him. He lifted the flap. The first thing he saw was a close-up, clinical photograph of a woman's face. It was so swollen and bruised, so horrifically broken, that it took him a second to even recognize her. Dina. His stomach lurched. He felt a cold, sick dread wash over him as he flipped to the next photo. The next shot: Dina on a gurney, jumpsuit soaked, paramedics pressing frantically against stab wounds.

Tony dropped the file as if it had burned him, the photos scattering across the floor. His mind flashed back to that night, weeks ago, when his parents had gone outside to talk, their faces grim and secretive. He remembered the vague, sterile phrase Ms. Jenkins had used: *medically incapacitated.* This was what they had been hiding. This brutal, bloody, horrific truth. A white-hot rage, born of shock and a fierce, protective love for Danny, surged through him. He scooped the photos back into the folder, his hands shaking, and stalked out of the office and into the kitchen, where Leroy was just getting a glass of water.

"What the hell is this?" Tony's voice was a low, menacing growl. He threw the folder onto the kitchen table, the photos spilling out again across the polished wood. Leroy froze, the glass of water halfway to his lips. He saw the photos, then the look of pure, unadulterated fury on his son's face.

"Tony," he started, his voice a low warning. "You shouldn't have seen those."

"Shouldn't have seen them?" Tony's voice rose, incredulous. "This is what happened to her? This is what you've been hiding from us? From *him?*"

"It was to protect him," Leroy said, his own voice hardening. "What good would it do for him to see this?"

"He has a right to know!" Tony shot back. "You can't just lie to him, not after everything!"

The argument was so intense, so focused, that neither of them heard the soft footsteps on the stairs. Neither of them saw Danny appear in the kitchen doorway, his expression open and curious, drawn by the sound of their raised voices. He saw the photos before they saw him. His gaze fell upon the scattered images on the table—the blood, the bruises, the waxy, pale, and broken face of his mother. In an instant, the sanctuary of the last months collapsed. Raw terror swallowed him whole.

He didn't scream. He didn't cry. He didn't make a sound. The color drained from his face, leaving it a stark, ghostly white. The fragile light in his blue eyes extinguished, replaced by a vacant, hollow look of pure, unadulterated horror. He took a single, stumbling step backward, his hand flying to his mouth as if to stifle a sob that wouldn't come.

"Danny," Tony breathed, turning, his own anger evaporating, replaced by a dread so cold it froze the blood in his veins. But it was too late. Danny just stared at the photos for a second longer, his mind processing the unspeakable, and then he turned and fled. They heard his frantic, stumbling footsteps as he ran back up the stairs, followed by the violent, definitive slam of Tony's bedroom door.

Tony and Leroy stood frozen in the kitchen, the horrific photos a damning indictment between them. The silence in the house was absolute, a profound, terrifying emptiness where a fragile, healing peace had been just moments before. The progress they had so carefully, so lovingly nurtured over the last few months had just been completely, and perhaps irrevocably, undone.

His hands started to tremble. The room seemed to tilt. Suddenly, he wasn't in the kitchen; he was back in their cramped house, hearing Dina's saccharine voice turn sharp, seeing her hand raised, the book he was reading snatched away, the casual, cutting cruelty. The memory wasn't just visual; it was visceral. He could feel the familiar cold knot of shame and terror in his stomach, the desperate need to make himself invisible.

He dropped the book with a dull thud and muttered something about feeling unwell before retreating to his room, the familiar scent clinging to his skin like a curse. Tony found him later, curled tight on his bed, facing the wall.

"Hey, you okay?" he'd asked gently, sitting on the edge of the mattress.

Danny just grunted, burying his face deeper. He felt the familiar darkness creeping in, suffocating the fragile light Tony had painstakingly built around him. He *knew* it wasn't fair to Tony. Tony deserved someone whole, someone unburdened by ghosts and the constant threat of a fractured mind.

He began to pull away. Small things at first. Missing meals he'd previously enjoyed. Retreating to his room more often. His sketches became frantic, dark, filled with distorted shapes and harsh lines, then he stopped sketching altogether. The light in his eyes dulled. He'd nod at Tony's concern, but his silence only deepened the weight; every gesture of care twisted into proof that he was unworthy of it.

Tony tried. He cooked Danny's favorite foods, brought him books, played his guitar softly outside Danny's door, but Danny's walls had gone up again, thicker and higher than before. Tony's frustration grew, laced with raw fear. He saw the light dimming in Danny's eyes, saw the physical manifestation of withdrawal. He pleaded, he cajoled, he offered space, he offered closeness.

"Danny, please, talk to me," Tony desperately pleaded "What's going on? You're not alone." But Danny was trapped in a silent scream. The thought festered.

"If I'm this broken, I can only hurt him. It's better if I just... disappear." Danny's thought rang in betrayal. The weight of his own existence became unbearable, a suffocating blanket he couldn't throw off. He

didn't want Tony to witness it, to have to live with the aftermath of his inevitable collapse.

He just needed it to stop. The pain, the shame, the certainty of being unfixable. The Queensboro Bridge, looming in his mind, began to appear not as an end, but as a release.

The gnawing pull in Danny's mind had grown from a whisper to a roar. It wasn't about pain anymore, not exactly. It was about *cessation*. About silence. The lavender and mothball scent still clung to his clothes, his skin, even his thoughts, an invisible shroud reminding him of everything he was, everything he had endured, everything he felt unworthy of. He saw Tony's worried glances, Maria's gentle questions, Leroy's quiet presence, and the crushing weight of their goodness only amplified his self-loathing. He was a burden. A broken thing. They deserved better than his constant shadow.

He waited until the house was quiet, the soft hum of the refrigerator the loudest sound. The city outside was a blurred tapestry of distant lights. He didn't write a note. What was there to say?

"I'm sorry I'm broken. I'm sorry I couldn't be fixed. I'm sorry for being a burden." The words felt inadequate, futile. He simply slipped out of bed, dressed in the dark, and moved with a quiet, practiced stealth honed from years of trying to be invisible. The front door clicked shut with an almost imperceptible sigh. Danny jumped on the 10-speed bike sitting in the front lawn, blindly pedalling in any direction that got him further away from Tony, swallowed by the vast indifference of the night.

2 a.m. Tony woke up with a start. Not from a sound, but from an abrupt, chilling emptiness in the bed beside him. Danny was always there, a warm presence he'd grown accustomed to, even when Danny was quiet and withdrawn. This was different. This was a void. He sat up, heart hammering, fumbling for his phone. No text. No call. He flicked on the lamp, casting long shadows across the room. Danny's side of the bed was cold, the blankets undisturbed. Too undisturbed. This wasn't a trip to the bathroom. This was... deliberate.

A cold dread coiled in Tony's stomach, tighter than any fear he'd known. He checked the bathroom, the kitchen, and the living room. Empty. His frantic calls to Danny's phone went straight to voicemail, each ring amplifying the sickening certainty blooming in his gut. Then, it clicked. A horrifying, ice-cold certainty that slammed into him with the force of a physical blow.

Tony returned to his desk — Danny's charcoal sketch of the Queensboro Bridge. He hadn't noticed before, but there was a small, lonely figure perched on the railing. Now the detail burned into him like prophecy.

He remembered the escalating intensity of Danny's recent withdrawal. This wasn't just a bad mood; this was a complete retreat, a shutting down that felt terminal. The way Danny had looked at him, not with anger, but with a profound, resigned sadness, as if he was already saying goodbye. The light in Danny's eyes had been getting steadily darker.

A gut-wrenching certainty seized Tony. He didn't waste another second. He grabbed his keys, threw on a hoodie, and burst out of the house, not even bothering to wake Maria. There was no time. His only thought was the bridge. He had to get there. Now.

The roar of Tony's motorcycle tore through the stillness of the timeless night, a desperate counterpoint to the thunder in his chest. He didn't even remember throwing on his helmet, just the cold bite of the handlebars and the furious surge of the engine beneath him. Every speed limit became an invisible suggestion, every yellow light a challenge to be overcome. The city's familiar streets blurred into an indistinguishable tunnel, the streetlights stretching into frantic streaks. He wove through the sparse traffic like a ghost, his mind a singular, terrifying focus: the bridge.

Maria's eyes flew open in the darkness, her heart instantly hammering against her ribs with a sick, frantic rhythm. The sound wasn't coming from the garage; it was already outside, tearing down their quiet residential street, fading into the distance with a gut-wrenching finality.

No, no, no.

She threw back the covers, her bare feet hitting the cold wood floor. A primal fear, cold and sharp, propelled her from the room.

"Tony?" she called out, her voice a choked whisper in the profound silence the engine had left behind. She half-ran, half-stumbled down the hallway to his room. The door was ajar. She pushed it open, her hand trembling as she fumbled for the light switch. The room sprang into view, stark and empty. The bed was a tangled mess of sheets, the imprint of where two heads had been still visible on the pillows. The window was open, a light breeze stirring the curtains, carrying the last ghost of the engine's sound. The framed sketch of the bridge, their symbol of hope from the party, sat on the dresser, looking like a relic from another lifetime.

"Danny?" she tried, her voice cracking. Panic seized her throat. She spun around and hurried to the guest room at the end of the hall, praying she'd find him there, that he'd been scared by the sound, too. She didn't even need to turn on the light. The perfect, undisturbed comforter on the bed told her everything. He had never been in there. They were both gone.

The realization struck like a fist to her chest, squeezing all the air out at once. Hours ago, the house had been full of light; now, it felt hollow. Her mind, frantic and illogical, supplied a hundred terrible scenarios, each one more vivid and horrifying than the last. An accident. A fight. Someone coming after them.

Her breath came in ragged gasps. She scrambled back to her bedroom, her shaking hands searching the top of her nightstand for her phone. The screen was blindingly bright in the darkness. Her fingers trembled, nearly dropping the phone, before she pressed the only name that mattered.

Leroy.

She pressed the call button, listening to the electronic ring with a rising sense of hysteria. It felt like an eternity. Come on, come on, pick up. Finally, the ringing stopped.

"Maria? What's wrong? Why are you awake so late?" Leroy's voice was thick with sleep, but instantly alert. He knew her well enough to know a call at this hour meant only one thing.

"They're gone," she sobbed, the words tumbling out in a breathless rush. "Leroy, they're gone. Tony—he took the bike. They're both gone."

"What? Slow down, Maria. What are you talking about?"

"I heard the motorcycle," Maria cried, her words a frantic torrent as she paced the length of her dark bedroom. "It woke me up. I came to check and their room is empty. They're gone, Leroy. I don't know where they've gone."

On the other end of the line, there was a rustle of movement, the sound of a man sitting bolt upright. Leroy's voice came back, no longer sleepy but sharp and strained with an authority that cut through her panic.

"Okay, Maria. Maria, listen to me. Take a deep breath. I need you to breathe. I'm on my way, but I need you to be my eyes and ears until I get there. Can you do that for me?" She tried to inhale, but her breath hitched on a sob.

"I... yes, okay."

"Good. Now, did they leave a note? Look on the dresser, on the pillows. Anywhere."

Spurred by the instruction, Maria moved back into Tony's room, her phone clamped between her shoulder and her ear. Her eyes scanned every surface, her heart sinking with each empty space. She shook the pillows, ran a hand over the cold sheets.

"No. Nothing. There's nothing here, Leroy."

"Okay, okay," Leroy's voice was a steady, grounding force against her rising hysteria. *"Go check again. Did they take their wallets? Their phones? We need to know if they have their phones, Maria."* She went to the dresser where their things had been left after the walk. Tony's wallet wasn't there. Danny's was gone, too.

"Their wallets are gone," she reported, her voice trembling. The fact felt ominous, a sign of intent. This wasn't a joyride.

"Was the door locked?" Leroy pressed. *"Did anything look broken or out of place? Tell me exactly what you see."*

"No, everything's normal," she whispered, looking around the horribly normal, empty room. "It's just... they're not here."

"Okay. Here is what we are going to do," Leroy stated, his tone leaving no room for argument. *"First, I want you to call Tony's phone. If he doesn't answer, hang up and immediately call Danny's. Tell me if it rings or goes to voicemail."*

Maria fumbled as she ran to the wall phone in the kitchen, her thumb slick with sweat as she navigated the screen of her cell. She found Tony's contact and dialed his number. The phone on her end went silent as she listened to the ringing on his. One ring. Two. Three. Each one was a fresh spike of dread in her heart. After the fourth, it clicked over. *"Hey, it's Tony. Leave a message."*

"It went to voicemail," she choked out, fighting back a fresh wave of tears.

"Call Danny's. Now."

She did, her hand shaking so badly she almost dropped the phone. The result was the same. Then, Danny's quiet, hesitant voice on the recording. She hung up before he could finish.

"His too. Straight to voicemail." A heavy silence hung on the line for a second. She could hear Leroy take a long, controlled breath.

"Okay, I'm talking to my supervisor right now," Leroy's voice was firm, resolute. *"I'm leaving. I will be home in twenty minutes, you understand? Twenty minutes. We will handle this together. I love you. I'm on my way."*

The line clicked dead. Maria stood alone in the hallway, the silence of the house pressing in on her from all sides. The frantic, screaming panic had subsided, replaced by a cold, focused dread. She had her orders. A timeline. Twenty minutes. Taking a shuddering breath, she pulled up Marko's number, her thumb hovering over the call button.

A late swerve to avoid a delivery truck sent the bike skidding on its side, the tires screaming in protest as he fought for control. For a terrifying second, the world tilted, a cascade of sparks spitting from the asphalt as he wrestled the machine upright. His heart lodged in his throat, a sharp, metallic taste filling his mouth, but there was no time for fear, no time for anything but the desperate, unyielding need to get to Danny. The close call barely registered; it was just another obstacle in the race against the dark.

Finally, the bridge silhouette loomed into view, its massive steel cables and towering frame a stark, imposing presence against the bruised pre-dawn sky. Tony cut the engine, the sudden silence deafening after the bike's frantic roar. He threw the kickstand down with a violent thud and scrambled off, his legs shaky but propelled by raw adrenaline.

He sprinted onto the pedestrian walkway, his eyes scanning wildly, heart threatening to punch through his chest. The wind whipped at him, cold and merciless, carrying the faint scent of the black river below. And then he saw him.

Danny.

He was there, on the wrong side of the rail, a slender, dark silhouette etched against the faint glow of the city lights reflecting on the churning black water far below. He wasn't moving, just standing there, gazing down into the void.

Tony's world stopped. His breath caught in his throat, a silent scream lodged behind his teeth. The cold terror that had been building in him since waking to an empty bed finally erupted, a sickening wave that threatened to buckle his knees. His heart, already pounding from the frantic ride, suddenly felt like it was going to stop altogether. Danny was right there. On the rail.

"Danny!" Tony's voice ripped from his lungs, a raw, desperate sound that was immediately torn by the wind. He took a hesitant step forward, arms outstretched, as if he could physically bridge the impossible gap between them. "Fuck, Danny, please! Don't move!" Danny's head barely tilted, a slow, almost imperceptible turn. His eyes, in the dim light, seemed vacant, fixed on something beyond Tony, beyond everything. "Danny, look at me!" Tony pleaded, his voice breaking now, a choked sob escaping his throat. Tears blurred his vision, hot and stinging against the cold wind. "Please, just... just come back. Get off the rail." He extended a trembling hand, palm open, offering everything he had.

"It'll be better this way, Tony," Danny's voice was a whisper, carried on the wind, devoid of its usual warmth. "For everyone. I can't take it anymore. I have nothing left in me." His words chilled Tony — as if Danny was already half-swallowed by the dark below.

"No!" Tony cried, desperation making his voice crack. "No, that's not true! Don't you dare say that! Danny, please, think about it! You're my whole world, I'm nothing without you! Without you, there would be nothing, no more sunrise for me if you're not in it! No more anything!" He was barely coherent, his words tumbling out, fueled by pure, unadulterated terror. "Think about our family, Danny. Think about those wonderful sketches you do. Think about... us."

He took another agonizing step forward, moving slowly, cautiously, as if approaching a skittish deer. "Danny, I love you. God, it hurts how much I love you — but it's the hurt that means I'm alive, because you're here. It means you're here. It means *we're* here." His chest heaved with the force of his cries. "Please, just give me your hand. Just come back to me. We can fix this. Anything. Just... don't go."

Danny's eyes finally met Tony's, but there was a deep-seated agony in them, a profound brokenness that seemed to ripple through his very core.

"You don't understand, Tony," he choked out, his voice cracking, thick with despair. "I'm broken. I'm just... I'm a burden. Dina made me this. It's in me. I'll never be anything but this ruin, and you deserve someone untouched." His gaze flickered back to the churning darkness below, the pull seemingly physical, unyielding.

"I don't care, Danny!" Tony's voice rose, a fierce, unwavering declaration against the roar of the wind and Danny's despair. "I love *this mess*! I love every single part of you, without fail! You're not a burden! You're my heart! Don't you dare leave me!" His words tore from him like a vow, as if sheer force could tether Danny to the railing.

Something in Tony's absolute conviction, in the raw, aching love pouring from him, seemed to pierce through Danny's shroud of despair. His eyes twitched away from the water, just for a heartbeat — catching Tony's face like it was the last star left in the sky.

Then Danny's foot, numb and trembling, slipped on the slick steel — and the void opened its mouth. He slipped, body lurching forward into the open air.

"DANNY!"

CHAPTER 36

I'VE GOT YOU

Tony lunged, a scream tearing from him. Time seemed to stretch, agonizingly slow. His arm shot out, propelled by an instinct born of terror and love, a desperate reach across the chasm. His fingers, miraculously, snared Danny's wrist, just as the boy's body plunged into the open air. The jarring impact sent a searing pain up Tony's arm, nearly yanking him over too. He braced himself against the railing, feet scrambling for purchase on the solid ground, every muscle screaming as he held on, gritting his teeth.

With a superhuman grunt born of pure adrenaline and love, Tony used every ounce of his strength, pulling with a desperate, jerking motion. Inches. Centimeters. Slowly, agonizingly, he began to haul Danny's dead weight back up. Danny's body scraped against the cold metal of the railing. Danny felt the sudden heat of Tony's grip, fierce and unrelenting, as if sheer will alone was dragging him back to the world. And then, with one final, impossible heave, Danny's torso cleared the rail. Tony scrambled backward, pulling Danny with him, until they both collapsed in a heap on the cold, hard concrete of the walkway, far from the terrifying edge.

For a long moment, there was only the sound of their laboured breathing and the cold rain. Tony let out a ragged breath, his body trembling with the aftershock of adrenaline. He gently moved, pulling Danny more fully into his arms, until Danny was sitting on his lap, wrapped tight against him. They sat there in the rain, two separate islands of warmth in a cold, chaotic world, clinging to each other for dear life. Tony buried his face in Danny's chest, and Danny's grip on his shoulders was unwavering. After some time had passed, Tony helped Danny up, and they began the ride home.The ride back to Tony's place was a blur of silence and cold rain. Danny remained on the back of the motorcycle, his grip on Tony's waist unwavering, his head resting against Tony's back. He wasn't just holding on; he was anchoring himself to the impossible strength that had just pulled him back from the void.

Home. Tony hit the killswitch on his bike and began his dismount. Danny stayed seated for a beat, clutching Tony's trembling hand, his eyes fixed on him as if he couldn't believe the man was still real. He saw the shivering, the goosebumps on Tony's arms, the exhaustion etched around his eyes. It wasn't just rain; it was the physical manifestation of Tony's frantic race against death, of the impossible strength that had just pulled Danny back from the void. In that moment, seeing Tony so raw, so utterly spent, the truth solidified in Danny's mind like a cold, hard stone: he had never truly appreciated how amazing Tony was. He had never truly grasped the almost boundless lengths Tony would go for him, the sheer depth of his love. It was a stark, brutal realization, a turning point that cut through the lingering despair.

Slowly, reverently, Danny brought Tony's still-trembling hand to his lips and kissed his knuckles, a silent vow passing between them.

"I'm so sorry," he whispered, his voice hoarse, broken. "Tony, I'm so, so sorry. I'm sorry." The apologies tumbled out, a continuous stream of raw regret. Tony's breath hitched. He squeezed Danny's hand, a faint, tired smile touching his lips.

"You're a dork, you know that?" he murmured, the endearment thick with relief and affection. "A complete and utter dork."

He helped Danny to dismount the bike. Still soaked, shivering, and clinging to each other, they tried to make their way silently through into the house

The night had been the longest of their lives. Every creak of the house, every passing car, had sent a fresh jolt of adrenaline through Maria's exhausted body. She sat huddled on the sofa, a cold, half-empty mug of coffee on the table in front of her, a crumpled tissue clutched in her hand. Leroy paced the worn path between the window and the fireplace, a thunderous, contained fury in every step. The first, pale, sickly grey light of dawn was beginning to seep through the blinds, illuminating the dust motes in the air and offering no comfort at all. They had called Marko, who knew nothing. They had called the hospitals. Nothing. All they had was the silence and their mounting terror.

Then, they heard it.

The soft, metallic sound of a key sliding into the front door lock.

Both of them froze, their heads snapping towards the sound. The door handle turned with agonizing slowness, and the door swung inward.

Tony and Danny stepped inside, looking like ghosts. They were pale, disheveled, and cloaked in an exhaustion so profound it seemed to be the only thing holding them up. Danny's eyes were fixed on the floor, and he stayed a half-step behind Tony, using him as a shield from the world. Tony's face was a grim, tight mask, his jaw set. For a heartbeat, there was only stunned silence. Then the dam of Maria's control broke.

"Oh, thank God," she cried, surging to her feet. She rushed towards them, her hands fluttering, wanting to touch them, to check for injuries, to simply confirm they were real. "Where have you been? Are you hurt? We've been out of our minds with worry!"

Leroy cut her off, his voice a low, dangerous rumble that filled the room. He took a step forward, blocking their path to the stairs, his entire body radiating a furious, paternal rage.

"Don't you dare ask if they're hurt," he said, his eyes locked on his son. "You get in this living room. Right now. You're going to tell us what the hell happened."

Tony didn't flinch. He met his father's glare, but his arm tightened protectively around Danny's shoulders.

"Dad, not now."

"Not now?" Leroy's voice rose, cracking with the strain of a whole night spent wrestling with his worst fears. "We have been calling hospitals, Tony! Your mother has been crying for three hours straight! 'Not now' is not an option!"

"I promise, I'll explain everything soon," Tony said, his own voice strained but firm. He looked from his father's furious face to his mother's distraught one, his expression pleading. "I promise. But for now, he and I need privacy. We need to talk."

He made a move to guide Danny toward the stairs, but Leroy shifted, blocking them again. "This is my house. You will not walk away from me." Maria's hand closed tight around Leroy's wrist, not to restrain him but to remind him — their son was standing between them and something fragile.

"Dad, please!" Tony stopped, his voice dropping, losing its defensive edge and becoming something raw and heavy. "Just... look at him!"

For the first time, Leroy's gaze shifted past his son and properly landed on Danny. He saw the boy's tremor, the way he was shrinking into himself, the vacant, haunted look in his eyes. It wasn't the look of a teenager who'd been out for a joyride. It was the look of someone who had just survived something terrible. The fury in Leroy's face didn't vanish, but it faltered, complicated now by a dawning, sickening understanding. Maria saw it too. She put a hand on her husband's arm.

"Leroy," she whispered. "Let them go."

Leroy held his ground for another tense second, a silent, furious battle raging within him. Finally, with a sharp, defeated exhalation, he stepped aside.

"Thank you," Tony murmured. He didn't wait for another word, immediately guiding Danny past them and up the stairs. A moment later, they heard the soft, definitive click of his bedroom door shutting.

Leroy and Maria were left standing in the living room, the space suddenly feeling vast and empty. The immediate, frantic panic for their sons' safety was over. It was replaced by a new, colder, and far more specific dread. They were home. They were safe. But they were not okay. And the question was no longer *where* they were, but what in God's name had happened to them in the dark.

Once in Tony's bedroom, the cold rain still dripping from their clothes onto the floor, they moved with a quiet, shared understanding. There was no need for words. They helped each other. Tony unzipped Danny's hoodie, pulling the sodden fabric away. Danny's fingers fumbled with the buttons of Tony's shirt. Wet jeans sloshed to the floor. In moments, they were both standing there, stripped of the cold, wet barriers, finally free of the weight of the night.

They crawled into bed, pulling the warm blankets high around them. They lay facing each other for want of the profound, simple need for connection. Skin against skin. The incredible warmth of another body pressed close, chasing away the cold, the fear, the isolation. Just the steady rhythm of their breathing, the feeling of each other's skin and body heat, a silent testament to life, love, and the sunrise they had almost missed.

The pale, hazy light of a new day bled through Tony's bedroom window, painting the room in a soft, grey wash. Tony and Danny lay tangled in a mess of blankets, their naked bodies still damp from the rain, their wet clothes a forgotten heap on the floor. They were facing each other, close enough that Tony could feel Danny's soft breaths ghosting across his lips, close enough that the lingering chill from the night before seemed to melt away in the shared warmth. Tony let out a long, slow sigh of pure exhaustion, but beneath the weariness, a profound sense of peace settled over him. Danny was here, he was safe, and that was all that mattered.

Danny shifted slightly, his gaze fixed on Tony's face, a faint, almost imperceptible tremor running through his slim frame.

"Tony?" he murmured, his voice a quiet rasp.

Tony hummed in response, his eyes already closing, heavy with the promise of sleep.

"Mmm?"

"I… I can feel something poking me," Danny whispered, his eyes widening slightly, a hint of something unreadable in their blue depths.

Tony's eyes shot open. All the peaceful drowsiness vanished instantly, replaced by a searing wave of mortification that left him speechless. He knew exactly what Danny was talking about. Every muscle in his body stiffened with a mortifying blend of surprise and overwhelming embarrassment. He felt heat rush to his face, a blush that seemed to spread to every inch of his skin.

"Oh god," he whispered, his voice cracking. He began to pull away, untangling himself from the blankets with a frantic urgency. "I'm so sorry. I'll just… I'll go find some underwear. Or my jeans. Something." He swung his long legs out of the bed, his back to Danny, desperate to cover himself, to hide the undeniable evidence of his body's betrayal. As Tony stood, the pale light from the window caught the subtle, faded lines of old scars – a jagged one near his left shoulder blade, a faint, almost invisible white streak on his ribs.

Tony reached for a clean pair from an open drawer, his hand trembling slightly, but before his fingers could even brush against the fabric, Danny moved. Quiet as a shadow, he slid out of the bed, the blankets pooling at his feet like a discarded cloud. Tony felt a soft touch on his arm, and then Danny was standing before him, small and slender, his own pale body illuminated by the weak morning light.

Danny's gaze wasn't on Tony's face. It was on his body, a slow, deliberate journey of observation. There was no hint of teasing, no trace of lust, just a quiet, almost reverent curiosity. His eyes traveled over the hard, coiled muscles of Tony's chest, down the defined lines of his abdomen, over the smooth curve of his hips, and then, inevitably, to the prominent erection that was the source of Tony's shame.

"Don't," Danny said, his voice soft but resolute, a quiet plea that vibrated with an unexpected strength. Tony froze, his arm still outstretched toward his clothes, his breath caught in his throat.

"Danny, I..." Tony began

Danny took a single step closer, his eyes still fixed on Tony's body. His gaze was an act of quiet exploration, a silent acknowledgment of the strength that had just saved him, the vulnerability that had just been exposed. His mind wasn't on sex; it was on the overwhelming reality of Tony himself—the man, the body, the love. He reached out a trembling hand, his fingers feather-light as they traced the hard line of Tony's bicep, then moved down to the faint, jagged line of a scar on Tony's side, a memory from a bike accident years ago.

"I've never seen you like this," Danny continued, the words tumbling out of him in a rush, his voice gaining a newfound, though still fragile, confidence. "So... undone. And it's... I don't know. You're beautiful. It's not a thing to hide." His gaze returned to Tony's nakedness, but again, there was no smirk, no lust in Danny's eyes. It was a look of quiet, genuine awe, a profound acceptance that seemed to strip away Tony's last layers of defense. "This is you," Danny whispered, his voice imbued with a quiet conviction. "All of you. The strength that pulled me back. The body that was so tired and cold on the bridge. The... the wanting. It's all just... you. And I want to see it." His hand lingered at Tony's side, feeling the heat still radiating from him, grounding himself in the proof that Tony had survived the same nightmarish storm.

Tony just stared at him, the embarrassment slowly giving way to a profound, gut-wrenching shock. The cold room, the damp air, the sunrise, all of it faded. All he could feel was the soft pressure of Danny's hand, and all he could hear was the quiet conviction in Danny's voice. This was about an adoration so complete, so total, it knocked the air from his lungs. It was about Danny looking at the most vulnerable part of him, and instead of shame, seeing something to be cherished.

Slowly, Tony lowered his arm and let it fall to his side. He didn't reach for his clothes anymore. He just stood there, fully exposed, letting Danny see him.

Danny's hand continued its gentle exploration, tracing the lean line of Tony's hip, the curve of his thigh. His touch was light, almost like a whisper against Tony's skin, a silent language of reverence. With a soft tug on Tony's hand, Danny pulled him back towards the bed. Tony stumbled slightly, caught off guard, but allowed himself to be guided. They fell back into the warmth of the blankets, their bodies intertwining once more.

Danny shifted, pressing closer, and then his lips were on Tony's. It was a loving kiss, not frantic or demanding, but deep and searching, a silent conversation that spoke of relief, of gratitude, of a burgeoning, undeniable connection. Tony's arms wrapped around Danny, pulling him tighter, as if to absorb every inch of him.

Even as their lips moved together, Danny's hand continued its silent journey. His fingers brushed over Tony's shoulder, down his spine, across the taut curve of his back side. As his fingertip skimmed the sensitive skin of Tony's butt, Tony let out a sudden, involuntary gasp, a sharp intake of breath. His hand shot out, lightly grabbing Danny's wrist, stopping the movement.

Danny froze, his eyes widening, a flicker of fear crossing his face. His body tensed, and his voice was a mere whisper, laced with immediate anxiety.

"Did I... did I do something wrong?" Danny timidly asked.

Tony's heart ached at the sudden worry in Danny's eyes. He squeezed Danny's wrist gently, reassuringly.

"No, no, god no," Tony murmured, his voice thick with tenderness. A soft, embarrassed laugh escaped him. "It's just... I'm really ticklish there. Always have been." He leaned in, pressing a soft kiss to Danny's forehead. "You didn't do anything wrong, Danny. Not ever."

A small, weary chuckle escaped Danny, the sound almost lost against Tony's chest.

"Ticklish?" Danny repeated, a fragile smile touching his lips. He tried to move his finger back to the spot, a playful glint in his blue eyes, but Tony quickly intercepted his hand again, a low, weak laugh rumbling in his own chest. They both dissolved into soft, shared laughter, the sound quiet and intimate in the still morning.

This feeling of simplicity didn't last; the images flooded him, chaotic and sharp. The biting wind on the top of the bridge, a physical thing that tried to push him away from the city lights. The terrifyingly solid feel of the metal railing under his hands. The dizzying, siren call of the black water so far below. He remembered the feeling of letting go, the split second of weightless surrender before a grip of iron seized his arm.

Tony.

The memory wasn't of the calm, confident Tony he knew. It was a vision of someone else entirely. Tony's face, contorted in raw terror, screaming his name until his voice was shredded. The desperate, animal strength as he heaved him back over the railing, both of them collapsing onto the walkway in a tangle of limbs. He remembered Tony pinning him to the ground, not with anger, but with the sheer weight of his body, his face buried in Danny's neck, sobbing with a helpless, racking violence Danny had never imagined possible. Tony, his anchor, his rock, had been utterly and completely exposed, stripped bare by the terror of almost losing him.

Then, the memory of the front door. The look on Maria's face—the beautiful, soul-deep relief giving way to a mother's profound hurt. The sight of Leroy, his father figure, his quiet protector, looking at him with a rage born from six straight hours of picturing his sons dead in a ditch.

It was too much. The horror of what he had almost done, the crushing guilt of the pain he had inflicted on this family that had only ever shown him kindness—it all converged into a single, overwhelming wave. A tremor started in his hands, then spread through his entire body. A choked sound escaped his throat, a raw knot of pain. Tony's arm tightened around him instantly.

"I got you," Tony whispered, his voice thick and rough against Danny's ear. "It's okay. I'm right here."

But it wasn't okay. The dam broke. A sob tore through Danny, a wrenching, full-body convulsion. Every tear he'd locked away on the bridge came crashing free, wracking his body in ragged waves. He curled into a tighter ball, and the grief poured out of him in ragged, agonizing waves. He wept for the boy who had felt so lost he'd climbed that railing, for the parents downstairs whose hearts he had broken, and most of all, for the boy holding him, the boy he had almost destroyed.

Tony didn't say anything else. He just held on, his grip an unbreakable promise. He was an anchor in the storm, silent, immovable, there. Eventually, the violent sobs subsided into exhausted, shuddering breaths. Danny felt hollowed out, scraped clean. He shifted slightly, turning his head just enough to look at Tony.

"You were crying out there," Danny whispered, the words barely audible. It was the most shocking part of the whole night.

Tony's eyes were red-rimmed, his face etched with a weariness that seemed to have aged him ten years. He simply nodded, a raw honesty in the gesture.

"I thought I lost you," Tony murmured, his lips brushing against Danny's temple. "I'm never letting you go."

Danny closed his eyes, a single tear tracing a path into the pillow. He didn't have the strength to reply. He just held onto the arm draped across his chest, clinging to the one solid, true thing in a world that had almost fallen away completely. They were home. They were together. And for now, in the quiet wreckage of the dawn, that was enough.

CHAPTER 37

RELAPSE

Tony continued to lay there, holding Danny in a steady, silent embrace, a human anchor in the swirling tide of guilt. The quiet stretched on, filled with the unspoken truths of the night. Finally, Danny knew what he had to do. He couldn't let them live with the questions. He couldn't let Tony carry this burden for him. He had to own his own story. He shifted slightly, pulling back just enough to look at Tony.

"Hey," Danny whispered, his voice a rough, morning rasp. Tony's eyes fluttered open, immediately finding his.

"Hey," he murmured back, his voice thick with sleep and concern.

"We... we need to go downstairs," Danny said, the words tasting like stones in his mouth. "We need to talk to them. They deserve... we owe them an explanation."

Tony looked at him, at the fragile, terrified resolve in his blue eyes. He knew, without a doubt, that this would be the hardest conversation of Danny's life. And he also knew he had to let him lead it. He just nodded, a silent, unwavering promise of support.

Getting dressed was a slow, deliberate act. They moved around each other in the quiet room, a silent, shared dread hanging in the air. A little while later, they stood at the top of the stairs, two boys bracing themselves for a confession that would change everything.

They found Maria and Leroy in the kitchen, sitting at the small table, two half-empty mugs of coffee between them. They looked up the moment the boys appeared, their faces etched with a weary, waiting anxiety.

"Boys," Maria said, her voice a little too bright. Tony and Danny walked into the room and sat down at the table, the silence thick and heavy. Leroy finally broke it, his voice a low, steady rumble, his eyes fixed on his son.

"Tony," he began. "You need to tell us what happened last night. Why you tore out of here like the devil was on your heels." Tony opened his mouth, ready to spin the story, to take the blame, to shield the boy beside him. But before he could speak, a small, quiet voice cut him off.

"It wasn't his fault." All three of them turned to look at Danny. He was staring down at his own hands, which were clasped so tightly on the table his knuckles were white. "He... he was coming to get me," Danny continued, his voice a trembling whisper. He finally looked up, his gaze meeting Leroy's, his own eyes swimming with unshed tears. "I... I relapsed. After I saw the photos of my mom... the emotional weight was just... it was too much for me to bear." He took a shaky breath, the confession tumbling out in a rush of pain. "I went to the bridge. I was... I was going to jump. Tony saved me. He pulled me back."

The words landed in the quiet kitchen with the force of a physical blow. Maria let out a choked, horrified sob, her hand flying to her mouth. Leroy just stared, his face a mask of stunned, ashen shock, the full weight of his own inaction crashing down on him. In an instant, Maria was out of her chair and kneeling beside Danny, wrapping her arms around his shaking shoulders, pulling him into a fierce, protective hug.

"Oh, *mijo*," she wept into his hair. "You are not a burden. Do you hear me? You are loved."

Danny finally broke, a raw, ragged sob tearing from his chest as he collapsed against her, the full weight of his pain and guilt pouring out in the safety of her embrace. Tony sat frozen, watching, his own heart shattering and healing all at once. He looked at his father, and for the first time, he saw not a cop, not an authority figure, but a man completely undone by his own regret.

"This is on me," Leroy said, his voice a rough, broken whisper. "I should have gotten him out of that house sooner. I promised his father..." He trailed off, unable to finish. Tony reached across the table and, for the first time in years, placed his hand on his father's arm.

"We have him now," Tony said, his voice quiet but firm. "That's what matters. We have him now."

They sat there for a long time, a broken and healing family, the raw truth finally out in the open, the quiet of the morning filled with the sounds of Maria's soft reassurances and Danny's long-overdue tears.

The raw, ragged sobs that had wracked Danny's body slowly subsided, leaving him hollowed out and trembling in the circle of Maria's arms. She continued to hold him, stroking his hair, her own tears staining the collar of his t-shirt. Tony and Leroy remained at the table, silent witnesses, the air thick with the weight of the confession. The storm had passed, leaving a fragile, wounded quiet in its wake.

Danny finally pulled back, wiping his wet face with the back of his hand. He looked small and exhausted, but for the first time, his eyes were clear of the frantic, haunted look they usually held. He took a shaky breath and turned his gaze from Maria to Leroy, who sat watching him with an expression of profound, aching guilt.

Against his better judgment, against every instinct that screamed at him to retreat back into silence, Danny asked the question that had been festering in his mind since that horrible afternoon.

"Leroy?" he began, his voice a raw, fragile whisper. "The photos... why did Dina look..... the way she did in those photos?"

The question landed in the quiet kitchen like a stone. Tony's head snapped up, his own expression a mixture of dread and surprise. Maria froze, her hand still on Danny's back, and her eyes immediately flew to her husband's. A silent, panicked conversation passed between them in a single glance. *"What do we say? We can't tell him the truth. Not now. It's too much."*

Leroy saw her look and the plea in her eyes. But then he looked back at Danny, at the fragile courage it took for him to even ask that question, at the boy who was finally, desperately, seeking the truth about his own life. To lie to him now, to shield him with a story that wasn't real, felt like a betrayal. He had earned the right to the whole, ugly story. Leroy took a deep, steadying breath. He leaned forward, his voice low, even, and stripped of all judgment. It was the voice of a cop delivering a difficult report, a tone meant to create a safe, factual distance from the horror.

"Danny," he began, his gaze steady and direct. "What you saw in those pictures… it happened after I arrested her all those months ago. It happened in jail." Danny flinched, a look of profound confusion on his face. He didn't understand. Leroy continued, his voice flat and steady. "When an inmate is brought in, their charges are part of their record. The other women in there… they found out why Dina was arrested. They learned about the child endangerment charge." He paused, letting the weight of the implication settle before he said the final, terrible words. "The inmates have their own way of dealing with that, son," Leroy said, his voice laced with a grim finality. "What you saw in those pictures… they did that to her. It was their form of… justice. They did that to her because of what she did to you."

The truth landed with a deafening, shattering silence. Danny stared at Leroy, his mind struggling to process the information. The violence he had seen in those photos wasn't because of drug dealers or money. It was because of him. The realization was a dizzying, sickening blow. A storm of impossible emotions crashed over him—horror at the brutality, a terrifying, shaming flicker of validation, and an overwhelming, crushing wave of guilt. He had caused this. His pain had created more pain. He physically recoiled, pulling away from Maria's embrace as if her touch had suddenly burned him. He wrapped his arms around himself, a choked, guttural sound escaping his throat as he started to rock back and forth in his chair.

"No, no, no," he whispered, his eyes wide with a new kind of horror. "It's my fault. It's my fault."

"No!" Tony's voice was sharp, cutting through Danny's spiraling panic. He was out of his chair in an instant, kneeling in front of Danny, forcing him to look up. "Danny, look at me. That is not on you. Do you hear me? Her choices, what happened in that jail—that has nothing to do with you. That is the consequence of the life *she* chose to live." Leroy stood and came around the table, his own face a mask of pained resolve.

"Tony's right, son," he said, his voice a firm, grounding anchor. "The world she was in has its own brutal rules. You are not responsible for that. You are the victim here. Not the cause." Maria, her own face streaked with fresh tears, reached for him again, this time just placing a gentle hand on his arm.

"We are so sorry you had to hear that, *mijo*," Maria whispered. "But you are not to blame. You are safe now. And that is the only thing that matters."

Danny just shook his head, unable to speak, and buried his face in his hands, a silent, shuddering sob wracking his body. The truth was out, but it was a heavier, more complicated, and more terrible truth than he could have ever imagined.

Tony's and Leroy's reassurances were a desperate shield against a truth that was too heavy for an eighteen-year-old's shoulders, but the words couldn't penetrate the storm of guilt raging inside Danny. He continued to sob, his body curled into a tight, protective ball in the kitchen chair, the sound a raw, ragged testament to a pain too deep for words.

Maria, her own heart shattering with every one of his cries, knew they couldn't stay there, frozen in the harsh light of the kitchen where the wound had been ripped open. She looked at Leroy, her expression a clear, maternal command. *"Help me."*

"Come on, *mijo*," she whispered, her voice a soothing balm as she gently rubbed Danny's shaking back. "Let's go to the living room. It's more comfortable. Come on, we're all right here with you."

Tony was already moving. He knelt in front of Danny again, his presence a solid, unwavering anchor.

"Danny, hey, look at me," Tony said softly. "Let's get you to the couch, okay? I've got you. Do you want me to get you Peanut?" Danny looked at Tony, and without needing to say a word, he knew the answer. "Alright I'll go get him for you."

Slowly, as if moving through deep water, Danny allowed himself to be guided. He let Tony gently pull him to his feet, his legs unsteady beneath him. Leaning heavily on Tony, he let himself be led the few short steps into the living room. Leroy followed behind them with a glass of water and a box of tissues, his movements quiet and deliberate, the strong, silent guardian of his broken family.

They settled Danny on the soft couch. He immediately curled up against the cushions, turning his face away from them, his sobs quieting to a series of long, shuddering breaths. Maria grabbed the familiar, soft afghan from the back of the chair and gently draped it over him, a gesture of warmth and protection.

No one tried to force him to talk. No one offered any more platitudes. They simply gathered around him, a silent, unbreachable fortress. Maria sat on the edge of the coffee table, her hand resting lightly on his covered leg. Tony sat on the floor, his back against the couch, his shoulder pressed firmly against Danny's side so he would know, without a doubt, that he wasn't alone. Leroy took up a position in the armchair opposite them, a silent, watchful sentinel.

They sat like that for what felt like an eternity, the only sound in the room was the soft ticking of the clock on the mantle and Danny's ragged, uneven breathing. They didn't need words. Their presence, their unified, unwavering vigil, was the only language that mattered. It was a silent, powerful vow: *"We are here. We are not leaving. You will not go through this alone."*

Finally, after a long, long time, there was a small movement from under the blanket. A hand emerged, pale and trembling, and reached out, not toward Maria, but toward Tony. Danny's fingers found the back of Tony's neck, a light, desperate touch that was both a plea and an anchor.

Tony's own hand came up to cover Danny's, holding it there, his heart aching with a love so fierce it felt like it might just be enough to hold the shattered pieces of this boy together until he could learn how to heal.

By the time afternoon light dimmed, the only sounds were the soft ticking of the clock on the mantle and Danny's quiet, ragged breaths. He remained huddled on the couch, Tony a solid, warm presence on the floor beside him, their hands still linked. The violent storm of his sobs had passed, leaving behind a profound, unnerving stillness. Danny's gaze was hollow, shock settling into his bones like a second skin. It was Maria who finally moved, her maternal instincts overriding the paralysis of the moment. She knew they couldn't just sit in the wreckage; they had to start rebuilding, one small, gentle brick at a time. She stood up, her movements slow and deliberate.

"I'm going to make some tea," she announced softly to the room at large, her voice a fragile anchor in the quiet.

Leroy looked up, his expression grateful for the sense of purpose. He stood as well, his own role in this sad play becoming clear. While Maria went to the kitchen, the comforting clatter of a kettle and mugs a small sign of life returning. Leroy walked over to the couch. He didn't speak. He simply picked up the afghan that had slipped to the floor and gently, carefully, draped it back over Danny's shaking shoulders, tucking it in around him. It was a simple, paternal gesture of care, a silent promise of warmth and protection.

Tony never moved from his spot on the floor. He just tightened his grip on Danny's hand, a constant, physical reminder. *"I'm here. I'm not letting go."* He could feel a fine tremor running through Danny's fingers, a testament to the war still raging inside him. A few minutes later, Maria returned with two steaming mugs. She handed one to Tony and then knelt in front of Danny, just as Tony had done earlier.

"Here, *mijo*," she said, her voice a soft, steady murmur. "It's chamomile. It will help. Just a small sip."

Danny didn't seem to register her words at first. He just stared blankly at the wall behind her. Maria gently took his free hand and wrapped his cold fingers around the warm ceramic of the mug. The warmth seemed to penetrate the fog. He blinked, his focus slowly returning to the room, to her kind, tear-streaked face. He took the mug, his movements stiff and robotic, and brought it to his lips, taking a small, shaky sip.

They sat in silence as he drank, the sweet, calming scent of the tea filling the air. He was still trembling, but the violent shudders had ceased. The family watched him, their shared gaze a protective, loving shield. Finally, Leroy spoke, his voice low and full of a quiet, steady authority that was meant to be a comfort, a plan.

"First thing in the morning," Leroy began, looking at Maria but speaking for Danny's benefit, "we'll call Dr. Sharma. We'll get you an emergency appointment. You don't have to carry this alone, son. We'll get you the help you need to work through it."

The words—*work through it*—seemed to hang in the air, a monumental task that felt impossible. Danny looked from Leroy's resolute face to Tony's, a flicker of the old, familiar despair in his eyes. He didn't have the strength to work through anything. He just wanted it all to stop. Tony saw the look and knew he had to do something. He squeezed Danny's hand.

"One minute at a time," Tony whispered, the words a low, fierce promise meant only for him. "That's all you have to do. We'll just get through this minute. And then the next one. I've got you."

Danny looked at him, truly looked at him, and in the depths of his exhaustion and despair, he saw the unwavering truth in Tony's eyes. He wasn't alone. He took another sip of tea, the warmth spreading through his chest, a fragile truce against the cold. He leaned his head against Tony's shoulder, a silent surrender, and for the first time since hearing the news, he closed his eyes, finally allowing the sheer, bone-deep exhaustion to begin pulling him under. The long, difficult process had already begun.

The dreary, heavy feeling from the difficult conversation could not be shaken. It clung to the air in the house, a silent, unwelcome guest that settled over the rest of the afternoon and into the evening. The day crawled by, each tick of the clock on the mantle a stark reminder of the fragile new reality they were all navigating. Maria, ever the matriarch, insisted on the simple, grounding ritual of dinner. She made a pot of chicken soup, its warm, savory aroma filling the kitchen—a stark contrast to the cold knot of grief that had settled in everyone's stomach. At the dinner table, Danny's spoon never left the wood beside his bowl. The soup cooled untouched, steam curling up like a cruel reminder of warmth he couldn't reach.

Tony grew increasingly worried about Danny. He watched him from across the table, his own food forgotten. Every moment of Danny's silence, every shallow breath he took, was a fresh spike of anxiety for Tony. His hand twitched toward Danny's bowl more than once, aching to coax him into just one bite, but the words wouldn't come.

Later, as a movie they weren't watching played on the television, Danny finally succumbed to the sheer, bone-deep exhaustion of the day. He had curled up on one end of the couch, falling into a fitful, shallow sleep, with Peanut clutched tightly to his chest. Tony sat on the floor, his back against the couch, a silent, watchful guardian, his own anxiety a thrumming, restless energy in the quiet room. He got up to get a glass of water, his movements stiff. Maria followed him into the kitchen, finding him staring out the dark window over the sink.

"He's not eating, Mom," Tony whispered, his voice tight with a fear he was trying desperately to control. "He won't even talk. He's just... gone. What if he doesn't come back from this? What if what I did... what if it broke him for good?"

Maria came and stood beside him, her presence a calm, quiet anchor in his storm. She took his hand instead, the simple, steady touch saying what words couldn't.

"He will be fine, *mijo*. I promise," she said, her voice a low, steady murmur. "It will just take time. This is a very deep wound. You cannot expect it to heal overnight." She looked at her son, at the genuine anguish on his face, and her heart ached for him, too. "But this time is different for him. This time, he is not alone. That he has the support system of home to help him through this difficult time. He has us. He has you. That's the difference. Our job now is to be his quiet, safe place to heal. We just have to be patient."

Tony let out a long, shuddering breath, his mother's words a fragile shield against his own overwhelming fear. He nodded, not trusting his own voice. He walked back into the living room and sank to the floor beside the couch, resuming his vigil over the sleeping, broken boy he loved so fiercely, ready to be patient for as long as it took.

CHAPTER 38

ONE MINUTE AT A TIME

Monday morning arrived with the soft, grey light of a day everyone had been dreading. The weekend had been nothing if not still and silent. The violent, emotional storm had passed, leaving a profound quiet in its wake. Tony had tended to Danny with a gentle, unwavering focus, his presence a constant, comforting shadow. Maria, ever the matriarch, kept the rhythm of the house going with warm meals and fresh coffee, her quiet strength a shield against the lingering sorrow. And Leroy had been a silent guardian, his watchful presence a promise of safety that needed no words.

The morning played out with this new, somber grace. Maria was already in the kitchen when the boys came downstairs, the rich aroma of coffee a small, grounding comfort. Danny was pale and there were dark circles under his eyes, but he walked with a quiet resolve. He sat at the table and tried to eat the toast Maria placed in front of him. His stomach was still uneasy, a tight knot of anxiety and grief, but he knew he had to try. He had to show them he was trying. If not for himself, then for the family that was fighting so hard for him.

When it was time to go, Tony stood, ready to grab the keys to the minivan, but Leroy was already getting up from the table.

"I'll take you boys today," he said, his voice a calm, steady rumble. He picked up his own keys from the counter. The decision was quiet but monumental. It was a father stepping in, a silent declaration that this burden was his to help carry, too.

The drive to Dr. Sharma's office was a quiet one, but it was a comfortable, supportive silence. Danny sat in the back, watching the familiar streets of Queens pass by, the solid presence of Leroy in the driver's seat and Tony in the passenger seat creating a protective barrier around him.

In the warm, inviting waiting room, Danny was called back almost immediately. He gave Tony a quick, nervous glance, and Tony responded with a small, reassuring nod. As the door to Dr. Sharma's office closed, Leroy sat down in the armchair next to his son. He looked at Tony, at the deep, weary concern etched on his face.

"You did good, son," Leroy said, his voice a low, rough murmur. "That night. You saved him." Tony just stared at the worn carpet, a wave of emotion making his throat tight.

"I'm just so worried about him, *Papi*."

"I know," Leroy said, placing a firm, heavy hand on his son's shoulder. "We all are. But he's strong. And he's not alone anymore. That's what matters. But look *mijo*, I'm going to leave you two boys here for now. This is your thing and I don't want to intrude." Leroy lightly shook Tony's shoulder and smiled wearily before leaving.

Inside the session, Danny sat in his usual chair, his hands clasped tightly in his lap. Dr. Sharma settled opposite him, her expression one of calm, gentle patience.

"Good morning, Daniel," she said softly. "How was your weekend?" The simple, open-ended question was a key, and the lock on Danny's carefully constructed composure immediately gave way. He took a deep, shuddering breath.

"They told me," he whispered, the words a raw, painful rush. "About my mom. About what happened to her... in jail." He finally looked up, his blue eyes swimming with a fresh, agonizing wave of guilt. "It was because of me. She... they hurt her because of what she did to me." His voice cracked on the last word, and a single, hot tear traced a path down his pale cheek. "It's my fault."

Dr. Sharma listened, her expression never changing from one of deep, unwavering empathy. She waited until his words had settled in the quiet room before she spoke, her voice incredibly gentle but firm.

"Danny," she began, "thank you for telling me that. I know how heavy that must feel." She leaned forward slightly. "This feeling you have, that everything is your fault... that's a very heavy weight to carry. Is that a feeling you've had for a long time?"

Danny flinched at the question. He looked down, his gaze finding the worn backpack on the floor beside him. He thought of Peanut, tucked safely inside. He thought of all the times he'd hidden in his closet, clutching the elephant, the world outside a terrifying storm of noise.

"When things were... bad," he whispered, his voice barely audible. "Loud."

"What made things loud, Danny?" Dr. Sharma asked softly. He took a shaky breath, the name he had so carefully avoided in this room finally breaking free.

"Dina," he said, the name a strange, bitter taste on his tongue. "She... she was the one who was loud." He finally looked up, his eyes meeting hers, and the dam he had held back for so long finally broke. Danny lightly brushed the faded scar on his upper lip. The ridge gave him the courage for what he was about to say next.

"She would... hit me," he confessed, the words a torrent of long-suppressed pain. "When she needed money, for... for her stuff. And I didn't have any. She would get so angry." His hand instinctively went to the old, faded scar on his upper lip. "She said I was... useless. A burden. That she wished I'd... never been born." He was openly weeping now, the tears he had held back for years finally falling. "And I believed her.

I thought it was my fault — that if I were better, if I weren't so useless, she wouldn't have to be like that."

Dr. Sharma's expression remained calm and full of a profound, gentle sadness. She let him cry, giving his pain the space it had been denied for so long. When his sobs began to quiet, she spoke, her voice a clear, unwavering anchor of truth in the storm of his guilt.

"Danny," she said, her voice firm but kind. "Listen to me very carefully. What she did to you was wrong. It was abuse. And it was never, ever your fault. You were a child. Her child. A parent's job is to protect you, not to harm you. Nothing you could have ever done or said would have made you responsible for her choices, for her violence." She leaned forward, her gaze direct and full of a strength he could feel from across the room. "You are not useless. You are a survivor of something terrible. And the fact that you are sitting here, bravely telling your story… that is the strongest thing in the world." She let the words sink in, a powerful counter-narrative to the toxic self-blame he had carried his entire life. "The guilt you feel about what happened in the jail is a testament to your own kindness," she continued softly. "But it is a weight that does not belong to you. Your only job now is to let us help you set it down." She gave him a small, warm smile. "And we will. One minute at a time."

Dr. Sharma's words hung in the quiet, safe space of the office, a powerful and unequivocal validation that Danny had never heard before. He took a shaky breath, wiping his eyes with the sleeve of his oversized t-shirt.

"You said she was the one who was 'loud'," Dr. Sharma said gently, her voice a calm anchor. "Was she always like that?" Danny shook his head, his gaze dropping to the floor.

"No," he whispered. "Not before. Before… before my dad died." He clutched the stuffed elephant, Peanut, a little tighter, the worn fabric a familiar comfort. "It all changed after the funeral." Dr. Sharma remained silent, giving him the space to continue. "I was ten," Danny began, his voice small, the memory vivid and sharp. "I remember my suit felt too big and stiff, and the whole church smelled like lilies". He looked up, his eyes seeing a ghost from a different lifetime. "My mom… Dina… she just looked so fragile. She was crying the whole time, leaning on Leroy. She looked broken". He took a shaky breath. "I think… I think she broke that day. And she never got put back together."

He recounted the blur of the day, the quiet, hushed whispers of the adults, the heavy silence that seemed to suffocate everything.

"I didn't really get it," he confessed. "I just knew my dad wasn't coming home, and everyone was so sad, and I just… I felt so alone". "At the reception," he continued, his voice dropping even lower, "my mom was just sitting in a corner, with this… hollow look in her eyes. Everyone was talking to the adults. No one was looking at me." He paused, the memory of that profound, childhood loneliness still aching. "And then… he was there."

"He?" Dr. Sharma prompted gently.

"Tony," Danny whispered, the name itself a mixture of pain and solace. "He was ten, too, and he looked just as lost and confused as I felt. He came over to me. I couldn't even talk. And he… he just put his arm… around my shoulder. It was this clumsy, awkward hug." A small, watery, and incredibly sad smile touched his lips. "It was the first time all day I didn't feel completely invisible," he said, his voice cracking. "My whole world was gone. My dad was gone, and my mom… she was already disappearing. But Tony was there. He was my anchor. When I had nothing left, he was the only thing that felt real. He was… he was everything." Dr. Sharma listened, her expression full of a deep, gentle empathy.

"It sounds like, even when you were both just children, Tony was a very important source of comfort and safety for you." Danny nodded, clutching Peanut a little tighter.

"He was," he whispered.

"Tell me what happened to that friendship," Dr. Sharma prompted, her voice still incredibly soft. "How did your relationship transform over the years after the funeral?" Danny took a shaky breath, the memories a bittersweet flood.

"For a long time... it was comfortable," he began. "We were inseparable, just like we had been since we were little kids. He was... he was the cool one. He was good at basketball, and I'd just sit and watch him, and that was enough." He remembered one afternoon, sprawled on the grass next to the court, when Tony had turned to him with a rare seriousness. "He told me I was the only person he could really talk to about anything" . He paused, the memory still sharp and painful. "That's... that's when I told him," he whispered, his gaze dropping to the floor. "I told him I was gay".

Dr. Sharma waited, the silence in the room a safe space for the difficult memory.

"He just... froze," Danny said, his voice cracking. "He told me it was wrong, that he couldn't be friends with someone 'like that'. And that was it. He just... he cut me out. He stopped talking to me. When I saw him again at the new school, he acted like he didn't even know me. He was just... cruel. He called me a 'lost puppy' in front of his ex-girlfriend. He made it clear he didn't want anything to do with me."

He took another shuddering breath, the pain of that year of rejection still raw.

"And then," he continued, his voice shifting, "shortly after, everything changed again. I was in a really bad place, and I ended up at this club downtown... and he came for me. He rescued me."

He recounted the events of the last few months, his voice a quiet, wandering murmur. He told her about Tony's raw, tearful confession, how he had blamed his cruelty on the "poison" his aunt had fed him. He spoke of their shared, quiet hours in the garage, slowly bringing the old Triumph motorcycle back to life, a project that allowed them to heal without having to talk .

"He came up with a signal," Danny whispered, a small, shy smile touching his lips. He lifted his hand and showed her, tapping his own chest twice with his thumb. "He said it means he's thinking of me, that he's being my shield. So we can talk... without anyone else knowing" .

He finally looked up, his blue eyes shining with a fragile, new hope.

"And just last week... he took me on our first real date. To the beach". He told her about their reckless plunge into the freezing ocean and the quiet peace of watching the sunset. "He asked if he could kiss me. I said yes. And it was the best."

The memories, both painful and beautiful, hung in the quiet room.

"He's... trying so hard," Danny finished, his voice full of a quiet awe. "To be what I need. He makes me feel... safe." He looked down at his hands, at the faint, lingering feeling of Tony's fingers intertwined with his. "He's my anchor again."

Dr. Sharma listened, her expression full of a deep, gentle warmth as Danny's story tumbled out—the anchor Tony had been after the funeral, the painful rejection, and finally, the slow, tentative journey back to each other.

"He is my anchor again," Danny finished, the words a quiet, profound truth in the still room.

"That's a beautiful way to put it, Danny," Dr. Sharma said, her voice a calm, validating presence. "It sounds like you have both been through an incredible journey, and that his presence in your life is a source of immense safety for you now." She paused, her gaze kind but direct. "You've just done something incredibly brave by sharing your side of this story. And Tony... he's sitting right out there in the waiting room."

Danny's head snapped up, his eyes wide with a flicker of panic at the thought.

Dr. Sharma immediately softened her tone.

"I know this is sudden, and you absolutely do not have to if you're not ready. But sometimes, when the feelings are this close to the surface, it's the most powerful time to share them. How would you feel about inviting him in *now*? To give him a chance to share his perspective, and for him to hear from you how important he is?"

The thought was terrifying. This room was his one safe space to be completely, utterly vulnerable. But then he thought of Tony, waiting patiently for an hour just because he'd promised he would. He thought of Tony's own raw, tearful confession, and his desperate need to be honest. This was a chance to meet that honesty with his own. He took a deep, shaky breath, the decision a quiet, solid thing in his chest.

"Okay," he whispered, giving a single, deliberate nod. "I… I think that would be okay." Dr. Sharma gave him a warm, proud smile.

"Thank you for trusting me, Danny. I'll be right back." She left the room, leaving Danny alone with his hammering heart. A moment later, the door opened again. Tony stepped in, his expression a mask of pure anxiety. He saw Danny, looking pale and emotionally raw, and immediately rushed to his side.

"Hey, are you okay? What's wrong?" he asked, his voice a low, urgent whisper.

Dr. Sharma followed him in, closing the door softly.

"Everything is okay, Tony. Danny was just sharing some very important parts of his story, and he was brave enough to allow you to be a part of the conversation."

She gestured to the empty armchair next to Danny. Tony hesitated, then sat, a silent, supportive presence. Dr. Sharma turned to him, her voice calm and inviting. "Tony, thank you for joining us. As Danny's anchor, your perspective is incredibly important. I was hoping you could share your side of the story, your journey with him, from start to finish." She then leaned forward slightly, her gaze kind but intent. "And more importantly, I'd like for you to tell us... how do you see Danny now, as he is today?"

Tony looked from Dr. Sharma's calm, expectant face to Danny, who was watching him with wide, uncertain eyes. He took a deep, shaky breath, the air in the quiet office suddenly feeling heavy. This was it. No more hiding.

"From the start..." he began, his voice a low, rough murmur. He looked at Danny, a sad, nostalgic smile touching his lips. "We were kids, maybe five. It was... easy. We were inseparable". He remembered Leroy's story about the day they'd met, a memory that felt like someone else's life . "He was just... my person. The only person I could talk to about anything". His smile faded, his gaze dropping to his own hands, which were clenched tightly in his lap. "And then one day, he trusted me. He told me he was gay". Tony's throat tightened, the shame of the memory still raw. "And I... I freaked out. I was a coward." He finally looked up, his expression a mask of self-loathing. "I told him it was wrong. That I couldn't be friends with someone... like that".

He took a shaky breath, forcing himself to continue, to own the ugliest parts of his story.

"For almost a year after that, I was a monster to him. I was cruel". He shook his head, the memory of his own words making him sick. "I called him a 'lost puppy' in front of my ex-girlfriend, talked about his mom... just to hurt him, to push him away" . He looked at Dr. Sharma, his eyes pleading for understanding. "My Tía Isabella... she filled my head with all this poison about it being a sickness, a sin. And I used her words as a shield because I was terrified of how I really felt" . He glanced at Danny. "I was cruel."

"And then he came to our school," Tony said, his voice dropping. "And everything started to fall apart. Seeing him... I couldn't keep lying to myself." He recounted the turning point, the moment he saw the fresh, angry cut on Danny's cheek . "Something just... snapped. All that anger I'd aimed at him for a year... it just shifted. It wasn't about him anymore. It was for him." He briefly described the frantic rescue from the club and the raw, painful confession in his bedroom that followed . "I finally told him the truth. All of it."

Dr. Sharma listened, her expression full of a deep, gentle understanding.

"Thank you for sharing that, Tony. That took a lot of honesty." She paused, her gaze kind but intent. "And now? How do you see Danny now, as he is today?"

Tony turned in his chair to look directly at Danny. The analytical part of the session was over; this was just the truth.

"I see the strongest person I've ever met," he said, his voice thick with an emotion so powerful it almost stole his breath. "I see a survivor. I see someone who has been through hell and still gets up every morning, who still tries to eat breakfast when his stomach is in knots, who still has the courage to sit in this room and talk about the worst parts of his life."

He reached out, resting a steady hand on Danny's knee — grounding, certain.

"When I look at him," he said, his voice dropping to a raw whisper, "I see the boy I fell in love with when we were kids. And I see the man I want to spend the rest of my life protecting and learning from." His hand tightened, a vow in touch as much as in words. "I see my anchor. I see... my everything."

Tony's words, a raw and honest confession, settled in the quiet room, leaving a profound, vibrating silence in their wake. He kept his hand on Danny's knee, a grounding, physical connection to the boy he had just laid his entire soul bare for.

Danny just sat there, his head spinning. He had braced himself for an apology, for a difficult explanation of Tony's past cruelty. He had been prepared to hear about Tía Isabella, about fear, about hypocrisy. He was ready to navigate the wreckage of their shared, painful history.

But he had never, in his wildest dreams, expected *this*. This raw, poetic declaration of love and admiration. The words echoed in his mind, overwriting years of internalized worthlessness. Tony hadn't just said he was sorry; he had called him strong. He had called him a survivor. He had called him... everything.

He looked from Tony's earnest, tear-streaked face to Dr. Sharma's calm, gentle one, as if trying to confirm that what he had just heard was real. A single, choked sound escaped his lips.

"Strong?" he whispered, the word a fragile, disbelieving question. Dr. Sharma's voice was incredibly soft.

"Is that not how you see yourself, Danny?"

Danny just shook his head, a fresh wave of tears blurring his vision. He had never been strong. He had been a hider, a runner, a quiet ghost who knew how to make himself invisible. Strength was Tony, loud and confident and fearless. Strength was Leroy, a solid, unbreachable wall. Strength was not a word that belonged to him.

"Tony," Dr. Sharma said, turning her gentle gaze to him. "Tell him what you see."

Tony leaned forward, his focus entirely on the boy in front of him, his voice a low, fierce, and unwavering testament. "I see someone who survived a monster every single day. I see someone who got up and went to school even when his home was a nightmare made real. I see someone who had every reason to give up, to become hard and mean, but instead, he stayed kind. I see someone who walked into a school full of people who stared and whispered, and he did it with his head held high. I see someone who was brave enough to tell me he missed his best friend, even after I had been a complete asshole to him for as long as I was."

He looked Danny right in the eye, his own gaze full of a profound, absolute conviction.

"I see strength in every piece of him — the kind that humbles me, the kind I'll never stop being in awe of."

CHAPTER 39

A SIGH OF RELIEF

Tony's words, a fierce and unwavering testament, settled in the quiet office, leaving a profound, vibrating silence in their wake. He kept his hand on Danny's knee, a grounding, physical connection to the boy he had just redefined, not as a victim, but as a hero.

Danny just sat there, the tears that had been welling in his eyes finally spilling over, tracking silent paths down his cheeks. But these weren't the ragged, terrified tears of before. They were quiet tears of shock, of disbelief, and of a fragile, dawning hope so overwhelming it felt like a physical ache in his chest. He had spent a lifetime feeling invisible, useless, and broken. And in the space of a single afternoon, the two most important men in his life had looked at him and called him strong.

Dr. Sharma let the powerful moment hang in the air, allowing the truth of Tony's words to settle deep into the foundation of Danny's fractured self-worth. She looked at the two boys—one so raw with a love he was just learning how to properly express, the other so stunned by an admiration he never believed he deserved—and a warm, genuine smile touched her lips. She finally broke the silence, her voice a soft, steady anchor.

"Thank you both for your honesty today," she said, her gaze moving between them. "What happened in this room… this was a huge success. For both of you."

She looked at Danny. "You were brave enough to share your deepest pain." Then she looked at Tony. "And you were brave enough to meet that pain with your absolute truth." She leaned back in her chair, her expression full of a gentle, professional pride. "This is just one step, a very big one. But this is how the healing happens. There will be more successes along the way. More moments like this." She looked directly at Danny, her final words a powerful affirmation of the new reality he found himself in. "Danny, you are not alone in this anymore. Your way forward is paved by people who want to see you regain yourself, to become whole and stay that way."

The session was over. The hour had flown by in a torrent of emotion, leaving them all feeling drained but fundamentally changed. Tony and Danny stood, a silent, shared understanding passing between them. As they walked to the door, Danny hesitated for a second, then reached out and, with a new, quiet confidence, took Tony's hand in his.

They walked out of the quiet office and into the bright, warm afternoon sun, their hands still linked. The world felt different, lighter. The therapy session, as emotionally draining as it had been, felt like a pressure valve had been released. As they walked outside, Tony looked at Danny, at the quiet resolve on his face, and his heart swelled with a profound, aching admiration.

"You were really brave in there, you know," he said, his voice full of a genuine awe that mirrored a similar conversation they'd had weeks ago. "That was… a lot. And you faced it. I'm so proud of you." Danny looked at their joined hands, a faint, shy blush creeping up his cheeks. Tony squeezed his hand gently, a new tradition already forming in his mind. "I was thinking," he said, his tone light and easy, "that kind of bravery deserves a reward. Are you in the mood for ice cream?"

Danny looked up, a small, genuine smile spreading across his face. This time, there was no hesitation, no fear in his eyes. He just gave a simple, happy nod.

"Yeah," he whispered. "I'd like that." Tony pulled out his phone and scrolled through his contacts. He tapped on Leroy's name and typed:

Hey Papi,

Danny and I are going to grab some ice cream. We just want a little time alone. Thanks for driving us today. You're the best.

He slipped the phone back into his pocket, and they set off down the tree-lined street toward the ice cream parlour. The afternoon breeze carried a faint hint of summer, brushing against their skin like a quiet promise of better days.

As they walked, they passed cozy boutique shops and a small open park. Tony gave Danny's hand a light squeeze when they spotted a tabby cat sprawled lazily in a patch of sunlight on the grassy knoll. Danny smiled at the sight, the first real one since their session.

Within minutes, the familiar sign of the ice cream parlour came into view. Danny's mind wandered to the glass case and all its options, already beginning to weigh his choices. Tony bumped his shoulder lightly.

"You want Mint Chocolate Chip again?" Danny nodded without a word, a quiet yes written in the small smile that tugged at the corner of his mouth. Tony grinned and pulled open the door. "Then that's what we're both getting."

The parlour was just as they remembered it—a perfect slice of nostalgia with its checkered floor, red vinyl booths, and the sweet smell of sugar cones . They slid into their usual booth by the window, the afternoon sun warm on their faces. It was quiet, just like their first time here, a peaceful sanctuary that felt like it belonged only to them. They ate in a comfortable silence for a moment, the simple, normal act of sharing a treat a welcome balm after the emotional intensity of the session.

"So," Tony said softly, breaking the quiet. "How are you... feeling?"

Danny looked down at his melting ice cream, considering the question. He thought about the storm he had just unleashed in Dr. Sharma's office, the painful words he had finally spoken aloud.

"Tired," he admitted, his voice a quiet murmur. He looked up, his blue eyes clear and direct. "But... lighter. It was hard. But it felt... good. To finally say it."

"I'm glad," Tony said, his own voice thick with an emotion he couldn't quite name. He reached across the table and, with his thumb, gently wiped a small smudge of green ice cream from the corner of Danny's mouth, a callback to their first time here. The touch was light, familiar, and electric. Danny's breath hitched, but this time, he didn't just blush. He reached out and placed his own hand over Tony's, holding it there on the table.

"Thank you," he whispered, the two words carrying the weight of the entire day. "For... waiting for me. Again."

"Always," Tony said, his heart so full he felt like he couldn't speak. He turned his hand over, lacing his fingers with Danny's. They sat there, their hands intertwined, a silent testament to the promises kept and the long, hopeful road ahead.

They sat in the quiet, sunlit booth, the half-eaten ice cream forgotten between them. Their fingers stayed laced on the tabletop, a silent testament to the promises kept and the long, hopeful road ahead. He thought about the immense courage Danny had shown in the session, the raw honesty that had left Tony himself feeling shaken and full of awe.

"You know," Tony began, his voice soft, his thumb gently stroking the back of Danny's hand. "Dr. Sharma talked about finding a safe place for your thoughts. A way to work through... everything." Danny looked up from their joined hands, a flicker of the old, familiar caution in his eyes. "I was thinking," Tony continued, choosing his words with care, "Your art... that's your safe place, isn't it? The drawing you did of the bridge… it was incredible, Danny. You have a real gift." He saw a faint, pleased blush creep up Danny's neck. "I was thinking maybe… maybe you need better tools. Your own stuff. Not just the charcoal I got you, but whatever you want." Danny's eyes widened, and he started to shake his head, a protest already forming on his lips.

"Tony, you don't have to…"

"I want to," Tony said, his voice firm but gentle, cutting off the protest before it could fully form. "There's a small art supply store a few blocks from here. We could just… go look? No pressure to buy anything. I just want to see the stuff you like." The offer was so unexpected, so deeply considerate, it left Danny speechless. This wasn't about a crisis. This wasn't about protection. This was about Tony seeing a part of him that had nothing to do with his trauma—his passion, his talent—and wanting to nurture it. After a long moment, a small, shy, but incredibly grateful smile touched his lips. He gave a single, solid nod.

The art supply store was a quiet, sun-drenched cathedral of creativity. The air smelled of clean paper, oil paints, and sharpened pencils. Canvases of all sizes were stacked against one wall, and towering shelves were filled with a rainbow of paints, pastels, and inks. For Danny, who had only ever worked with a few scavenged pencils, it was a wonderland.

At first, he was too overwhelmed to move. He just stood near the entrance, his eyes wide, taking it all in. Tony didn't rush him. He just gently led him down an aisle stacked high with sketchbooks of every shape and size.

"This one looks like the one you have," Tony said, picking up a thick, textured pad. "The paper feels nice." He was showing interest, validating Danny's world, giving him a place to start.

Slowly, cautiously, Danny began to explore. He ran his fingers over a set of soft pastels, his touch light and reverent. He uncapped a marker, testing its sharp, clean line on a scrap piece of paper. He was no longer a frightened boy; he was an artist in his element.

Finally, he stopped in front of a beautiful wooden box of professional-grade colored pencils, their sharpened points a vibrant, perfect spectrum. He just stared at them, a look of profound, quiet longing on his face.

"You should get those," Tony said softly from behind him.

"They're… they're too expensive," Danny whispered, already turning away.

"I don't care, I only want you to have the best," Tony said, taking the box from the shelf. He added the high-quality sketchbook he had been holding and a set of fine-tipped ink pens for good measure. He walked to the counter, leaving Danny standing in the aisle, a chaotic, wonderful mix of guilt and gratitude swirling in his chest.

They walked out of the store and back into the bright afternoon, Danny clutching the bag of new supplies to his chest as if it were a precious treasure. Tony pulled out his phone, a new, easy feeling settling between them.

"Okay," Tony said, his thumb tapping the screen of a ride-share app. "I'll call us a cab to get home. My dad felt we needed the space today."

While they waited on the quiet, sunlit sidewalk, the silence between them was comfortable, full of the easy peace of the afternoon. When the cab arrived, they slid into the back seat, the quiet intimacy of their day creating a small, private bubble against the backdrop of the city. The drive home was a peaceful one, a silent journey back to the safety of the house where they could enjoy the rest of their day. Danny felt a new sense of ownership, of possibility, that was entirely new. Tony just watched him, a soft, proud smile on his face.

They walked into the house to the comforting, savory smell of grilled cheese sandwiches and tomato soup. They found Leroy and Maria in the kitchen, just as they expected. Maria was at the stove, flipping a perfectly golden sandwich, while Leroy sat at the table, reading the paper.

"There are my boys," Maria said, her voice full of warmth as she looked up. "Perfect timing. Lunch is almost ready."

Leroy lowered his newspaper, his eyes immediately landing on the large, unfamiliar bag in Danny's hands.

"Looks like you had a successful trip," he said, a curious smile on his face. "What's in the bag?" Danny immediately looked down, a familiar shyness washing over him.

"Just some things," he murmured. Tony stepped forward, his own voice full of a pride he didn't bother to hide.

"We went to the art store," he explained, reaching over to help Danny pull out the new supplies and place them on the table. He showed them the professional sketchbook, the pristine box of colored pencils, and the fine-tipped ink pens. "I told him he needed some real tools if he's going to be a serious artist."

"Oh, *mijo*, these are wonderful!" Maria said, wiping her hands on her apron and coming over to admire the collection. She picked up the wooden box, feeling its smooth weight. "This is a real investment in your talent, Danny. It's a beautiful thing." Leroy just nodded, a look of deep, quiet approval on his face.

"That's good, son. Real good."

The lunch that followed was the most normal, relaxed meal Danny could remember. They talked about the different kinds of pencils, and Leroy told a funny, self-deprecating story about the one time he tried to paint their house and ended up with more paint on himself than on the walls. For the first time, Danny found himself joining in the easy laughter, a real, unforced sound that made Maria's heart swell.

After lunch, the boys went up to Tony's room. The quiet, comfortable energy from the kitchen followed them upstairs. Tony flopped onto the bed, scrolling through his phone, but Danny just stood by the desk, looking at his new art supplies, which were now neatly arranged on the surface. He ran a hand over the cover of the new sketchbook, a mixture of excitement and a deep, paralyzing intimidation on his face. He was an artist with new tools, but he was still a boy who was scared to make a mark, scared it wouldn't be good enough.

Tony looked up from his phone, sensing the shift in Danny's mood. He saw him just standing there, frozen, and he knew exactly what he was thinking. He sat up, his voice gentle.

"You know," he began, "with all that new stuff, you could start putting a real portfolio together. For the art school applications we were looking at."

Danny flinched at the idea, the old self-doubt immediately rushing back in.

"I don't know, Tony..." he whispered, shaking his head. "I don't think my work is... good enough."

"Not good enough?" Tony stood up and walked over to him, his voice full of a firm, unwavering belief that left no room for argument. "Danny, are you kidding me? The sketch you gave me at our joint birthday celebration... the one of the bridge? I hung it on the wall right next to our bed. I look at it every single day. It's the most perfect thing I have.... aside from you though." He placed a hand on Danny's shoulder, forcing him to meet his gaze. "You are more than good enough. You just have to start." He gave him a small, encouraging smile. "And you don't have to do it alone. We can figure it out. Together."

Danny looked at Tony, at the absolute, unconditional faith in his eyes. He then looked over at the pristine, empty sketchbook on the desk. It was no longer a terrifying, blank page. It was a promise. It was a beginning. A slow, determined nod was his only reply.

In that moment, a comfortable, productive silence settled over Tony's room. Tony sat on the edge of his bed, his laptop open, scrolling intently through a website for local mechanics apprenticeships. Danny sat on the floor, surrounded by his new art supplies. He opened the pristine, textured sketchbook, the blank page both a promise and a challenge.

He needed a subject for his portfolio, something that was his. Something real. He thought long and hard, his mind a quiet slideshow of images—the majestic arc of the Queensboro Bridge, the hushed, peaceful sanctuary of the beach at sunset, the worn, comforting face of his stuffed elephant, Peanut. But none of them felt quite right. None of them captured the feeling that was currently taking root in his chest—a fragile, powerful thing that felt like hope.

His gaze drifted up from the blank page and landed on Tony. He was leaning against the headboard, his expression one of quiet, intense concentration as he read about engine diagnostics and certifications. The late afternoon sun streamed through the window, illuminating the dust motes dancing in the air around him and catching the silver of his nose ring.

In that quiet, unguarded moment, Danny didn't just see his friend, his rescuer, his boyfriend. He saw a young man seriously and passionately planning his future. He saw the boy who had faced down his own demons, who had broken his own heart to tell the truth, who had become a shield for someone else's pain. Then it hit him. He was going to draw the most inspiring thing he could think of: Tony.

With a quiet, solid certainty, Danny opened his new sketchbook. He chose a graphite pencil from the professional set Tony had given him, the tool feeling balanced and full of potential in his hand. He looked at Tony, who was still absorbed in his laptop, and began to draw.

His hand moved with a new, confident energy. He wasn't sketching a memory or an imaginary world; he was capturing a real, living moment. He drew the way Tony's hair fell across his forehead as he concentrated, the intense, focused line of his jaw, the gentle curve of his shoulders as he hunched over the screen. He poured all of his focus, all of his newfound hope, into the lines taking shape on the page.

Tony, feeling a pair of eyes on him, finally looked up from his laptop. He saw Danny on the floor, completely engrossed in his work, his brow furrowed in concentration. The intensity was so different from the fearful, withdrawn quiet Tony was used to. This was the focus of an artist lost in their craft. A warm, curious smile spread across Tony's face.

"Whatcha working on over there?" he asked, his voice a low, gentle murmur. "You look pretty serious." Danny looked up, startled, and instinctively shielded the sketchbook with his arm, a shy, protective gesture.

"You can't see yet," he said, a faint blush creeping up his neck.

"Come on, just a peek?" Tony teased, leaning forward from the bed to try and get a better look. Danny shook his head, but this time, a small, mischievous smile played on his lips. It was a new expression for him, and it made Tony's heart skip a beat.

"Not yet," he insisted, his voice quiet but firm. "It's a surprise. I'll only show you once it's finished."

Tony stopped, taken aback by the gentle but clear boundary. He saw the look on Danny's face—the playful determination, the quiet confidence—and he felt a surge of pure, uncomplicated happiness. This wasn't the scared, silent boy he always had to protect. This was a partner, with his own secrets and his own surprises.

"Okay, okay," Tony said, leaning back with a laugh, holding his hands up in mock surrender. "A surprise. I can handle that." He picked his laptop back up, a wide, pleased grin on his face. "Just... don't make me wait too long?"

Danny just smiled back, a silent promise, before turning his full attention back to the page, to the drawing of the boy he loved. The quiet of the late afternoon settled around them, a comfortable, shared peace. Tony went back to his laptop, but he wasn't really reading anymore. He kept glancing over at Danny, who was a study in absolute concentration. He was hunched over the sketchbook on the floor, his body shielding the page, the only sounds the soft, rhythmic scratch of pencil on paper and his own quiet, focused breaths.

An hour melted away like that. The sun dipped lower, and the light in the room turned a warm, deep gold. Finally, the scratching sound stopped. Tony looked over and saw Danny leaning back on his hands, staring down at the finished page with an expression that was a complex mixture of exhaustion, pride, and a deep, terrifying vulnerability. He took a long, shaky breath.

"Okay," Danny whispered, his voice barely a sound in the quiet room. "It's... it's done." Tony's heart gave a hard thump. He closed his laptop and set it aside, giving Danny his full, undivided attention.

"Can I... can I see it?" he asked, his own voice a low, nervous murmur. For a long moment, Danny didn't move. He just looked at the drawing, his creation, this fragile, honest piece of his soul that he was about to share. Then, with a final, steadying breath, he picked up the sketchbook, stood, and walked over to the bed where Tony sat. His hands were trembling as he held it out. Tony took the sketchbook, his fingers brushing against Danny's. He looked down at the page. And the world stopped.

It was him. But it was a version of him he had never seen before. Danny hadn't just drawn a portrait; he had drawn an emotion. He had captured him in that moment from earlier, sitting on the bed, his hair a mess, looking at his laptop. But he had stripped away all the anger, all the defensive shields Tony had worn for years. The drawing was all clean, strong lines, but the expression in the eyes was one of gentle, quiet contemplation. He looked... peaceful. He looked kind. He looked like the man he so desperately wanted to become. Danny hadn't just captured his likeness; he had captured his hope.

Tony's breath hitched in his throat. He just stared at the drawing, a wave of emotion so powerful it almost buckled him. He slowly lifted his gaze from the page to the boy standing before him, his own eyes shining with unshed, disbelieving tears.

"Is this…" he started, his voice a choked, raw whisper. "Is this really how you see me?" Danny looked at him, at the raw, vulnerable awe on his face, and for the first time, he didn't look away. A small, sure smile touched his lips.

"Yeah," he said softly. "It is."

The simple, profound confirmation was everything. Tony carefully set the sketchbook on the bed beside him and stood up. He closed the small distance between them and wrapped his arms around Danny, pulling him into a hug that was full of a desperate, grateful, and overwhelming love. He buried his face in Danny's clean hair, a single, silent tear escaping and landing on his shoulder. This was it. This was what it felt like to be truly seen.

CHAPTER 40

THEN IT'S HOME

The late July air hung thick and heavy over the city, the kind of heat that promised a thunderstorm later but for now just baked the asphalt. At home, it was cool and quiet. The mail had just arrived, sitting in a small, unassuming pile on the kitchen table. In that pile were two envelopes that felt like they could alter the course of their entire lives.

Tony, unable to stand the suspense, tore his envelope open first. As he scanned the letter from the mechanics union, a slow, brilliant grin spread across his face, but he kept his celebration muted. He looked across the table at Danny, who was just staring at the thick manila envelope from the New York School of the Arts as if it might bite him.

Danny traced the edge of the seal with a trembling finger. For years, a future was something that happened to other people. The idea that one might be waiting for him inside a paper envelope seemed impossible.

Tony got up from his chair and walked around the table to stand behind Danny, placing his hands gently on his shoulders. He leaned down, his voice soft and low, just for him.

"Hey... whatever it says, we're good. Okay? Just breathe. Let's see it together."

With Tony's hands grounding him, Danny took a shaky breath and carefully tore open the tab. He pulled out a sheaf of papers, his eyes finding the bolded word first: CONGRATULATIONS. He sank back into the chair as if his bones had turned to liquid, reading the words without them making sense.

"...your portfolio demonstrated exceptional technical skill and a profound emotional depth... the portrait series of 'Tony' and the singular piece 'Queensboro Bridge' were of particular note to the committee..."

Under the table, his other hand clutched Peanut, the familiar anchor steadying him even in this impossible new moment. He looked up, turning his head to see Tony, his blue eyes wide with disbelief.

"I got in," he whispered, the words catching in his throat.

Tony's grin finally broke free, full of pure, unadulterated joy *for him*. He squeezed Danny's shoulders.

"Of course, you did," he said, his voice thick with pride. "There was never a doubt in my mind. Your art... it's everything, Danny." He then held up his own letter with a triumphant shake. "And it looks like you'll have a ride. I got the apprenticeship." Danny's gaze fell to Tony's acceptance letter, and a genuine smile, bright and overwhelming, finally reached his eyes. He pointed to a line in the letter's body.

"You... you credited me on the Triumph?"

Tony leaned down and kissed the top of his head.

"Of course," he said simply. "We restored her together. Equal partners." He pulled out the chair beside Danny and sat down, taking his hand and lacing their fingers together on the table. "So. Looks like we're both officially going somewhere." The weight wasn't gone, but it had changed. It was no longer the weight of dread, but the heavy, solid, and wonderfully real weight of a shared future.

The front door clicked open, followed by the heavy sound of a purse landing on the entryway table. Maria's tired sigh floated through the hall, worn but familiar, the sound of someone finally off their feet after a long shift. Leroy's boots followed a beat later, solid against the wood, his police uniform creaking faintly as he shed the weight of the day.

"Tony? Danny? We're home," Maria called, her voice carrying warm through the hall.

She reached the kitchen doorway and stopped dead. There they were—her son and the boy who had become her son—sitting close, hands laced together on the table. Two official-looking letters lay beside them like proof of some impossible dream. Both their faces were taut, lit with disbelief and something fragile and electric. Maria's hand flew to her mouth.

"Tell me," she whispered.

Tony was already on his feet, unable to keep still. He practically bounced in place, his words tumbling out. "He got in! Danny got into the Arts program!" He pointed at Danny like he was showing off a prize, pride radiating from every line of his face. "And I got the apprenticeship. Both of us. We both got in!"

Maria bypassed Tony without hesitation, her eyes wet, and wrapped Danny up in her arms. She pulled him against her chest, one hand cradling the back of his head as if he were still the boy she had first welcomed into her home.

"Oh, *mijo*. My talented, brilliant boy. I knew it. In my heart, I knew it." She rocked him gently, her voice trembling with love. Then she drew back just enough to hold his face between her hands, thumbs brushing across his cheeks. "All that work. All that courage."

Danny swallowed hard, stunned by the weight of her pride. He tried to answer but his throat locked up. All he could do was nod.

Leroy had been silent in the doorway, arms folded, watching with a rare softness in his eyes. He stepped forward now, scanning the two letters. He laid one steady hand on Tony's shoulder, giving it a firm squeeze, then looked at Danny with a quiet gravity that made his chest ache.

"An artist and a mechanic," Leroy said, his voice gruff but thick with emotion. "Look at you two. You've built a future." He paused, gaze steady on Danny. "Your father would be so proud of you, Danny. So damn proud."

The word father detonated inside him. For a heartbeat, the kitchen tilted. The sound of Maria's laugh dimmed, the table blurred, and Danny was somewhere else: cold wind against his skin, iron beneath his fingers, his father's smile at Coney Island curling like burnt paper. He tasted metal on his tongue. His stomach lurched.

His mask almost slipped. Almost.

Then—warmth. Tony's hand sliding across under the table, lacing their fingers together. A slow rhythm pressed against Danny's knuckles, grounding him. *Here. Now. With me.*

Danny blinked, forcing the world to steady. Maria was still beaming, Leroy watching proudly, the house unchanged. He gave Tony a quick, grateful glance. Tony's answering smile was soft, knowing.

Maria clapped her hands together, breaking the silence. "Right. This requires a celebration. No one is eating leftover chicken tonight." She looked at them with sudden determination, already turning toward the counter. "I'm making pozole. We are celebrating our boys!"

The decision filled the room with a new energy. The sound of Maria moving about the kitchen—pots clattering, pantry doors opening— replaced the stillness of a few moments before. Soon the first savory notes of garlic and simmering broth began to wind their way through the air, promising comfort.

Tony pulled Danny close again, his excitement bubbling over. "Told you, babe," he whispered, a grin tugging at his lips. "They're over the moon."

Danny tried to smile, and almost managed it. The weight in his stomach remained, heavy and unsettled, but the smell of home-cooked food and Tony's hand tight around his own kept him tethered in place.

Maria moved through the kitchen like she'd been preparing for this moment all her life. The sound of a pot pulled from the cupboard, the quick chop of onions, the hiss of oil on the stove—it was a rhythm, a celebration in motion. Leroy took his seat at the table, loosening the collar of his uniform shirt, his eyes still flicking toward the letters on the table every so often, a small smile ghosting across his face. Tony had finally sat down again, though his body vibrated like a live wire. He kept Danny's hand locked in his, his thumb drawing that steady rhythm against Danny's knuckles.

"Pozole," Maria announced as if declaring a holiday. "No arguments. I want you both eating until you can't move."

The smell came quickly—the deep, savory perfume of simmering broth filling the air, garlic and chilies blooming in the oil before she stirred them in. It was a smell that had come to mean family, safety, home. Danny felt it wrap around him like a blanket, and yet at the same time his stomach twisted with nerves.

Tony, never one to sit still, hopped up to help, darting around Maria to grab bowls, spoons, limes, anything she'd let him touch. She swatted at him with the back of her spoon, but her face glowed with affection.

When they finally sat to eat, the table was alive with warmth: the steam rising off the bowls, the squeeze of fresh lime juice, the crunch of radishes and shredded cabbage. Tony dove in with his usual gusto, exaggerating a groan of delight after the first bite.

"Best in the boroughs," he declared with a grin, and Leroy chuckled into his own spoon. Tony nudged Danny's knee under the table, leaning close to whisper, "Stay with me, babe."

Danny picked up his, trying to mimic their ease. He took a bite—rich, hearty, delicious—and felt the taste turn to ash in his mouth. The stone in his stomach sat heavy, immovable. He forced himself to keep chewing, then swallowed, smiling faintly as though he agreed with Tony's enthusiasm.

But his jaw ached with the effort of holding the mask.

Maria leaned forward, watching him with her soft eyes. "And you, Danny—you must make sure you have all your supplies before the first day. We'll go to that big art store in Manhattan. We'll get you the best brushes, the best paper, everything you need."

Danny blinked, throat tight. Supplies. Brushes. Paper. Things that meant he was really going. Things he wasn't sure he deserved. He nodded quickly, afraid his voice would betray him.

Tony, oblivious to the tension under the surface, launched into a story about the Triumph's restoration—how they'd nearly lost a piece down a storm drain, how Danny's sharp eye had saved the whole project. He embellished the details until Leroy barked a laugh and Maria swatted him, though she was laughing too.

Danny sat beside him, quiet but present, the laughter brushing against him like sunlight through glass. For a fleeting second, he let himself feel it—the pride, the love, the safety.

As the meal wound down, Maria set her spoon aside and looked between the two boys, her eyes thoughtful. "You know," she began, her tone gentle, "with your program starting, Danny, and Tony with his apprenticeship… your schedules will be different. You'll be coming and going at all hours."

Tony and Danny both looked at her, uncertain. She smiled, warm and knowing.

"It's a big step. A wonderful step. It might be time to think about the next one. For you two to find your own place. A home to start this new part of your lives in. Just for you."

The suggestion hung in the air. Not heavy, not demanding—just a blessing.

Tony's eyes lit up instantly, that spark of adventure firing to life. "Our own place?" he breathed, almost reverent.

Danny's breath caught. The flicker of anxiety stirred—change had always meant danger—but alongside it came something else. Warmth. The thought of a space that was theirs, not borrowed, not hidden. A home. He looked at Tony, whose eyes gleamed with excitement, and something inside him loosened.

Leroy nodded, his voice steady. "She's right. It's the right time. And don't worry," he added, his gaze settling on Danny, "we'll help you look. Make sure you find somewhere good. Somewhere safe."

Safe. The word hit like a balm. Danny swallowed against the lump in his throat, nodding once.

The conversation drifted then, laughter picking up again as Tony joked about which neighborhood would tolerate his singing in the shower. The air had lightened, filled with warmth, but Danny still felt that stone in his stomach. The joy was real, but so was the weight pressing beneath it.

Later, when the dishes were cleared and Maria and Leroy had gone to bed, the house quieted into a softer rhythm. The boys were upstairs in their room. Tony sprawled across his bed, phone held above his face, scrolling through apartment listings with all the restless energy of a boy on the cusp of something new.

"Okay, okay—listen to this one," he said, grinning at the screen. "Two windows. That's their big selling point. 'Two windows!' Like they expect us to live in a cave everywhere else."

Danny sat across the room, rummaging in a drawer for a t-shirt, but really just giving himself space. He smirked faintly at Tony's joke, though it barely touched his eyes.

Tony scrolled again. "Oh, here we go: 'Charming railroad style.' Which means… no doors. Just one long hallway you sleep and eat in. Perfect if you want to trip over me every morning."

Danny nodded, but the heaviness in his chest lingered as they slid under the covers. Tony curled instinctively around him, warm and grounding. Danny stayed stiff for a long moment before finally letting himself sink back into the embrace, eyes wide open in the dark.

The mask held. Barely.

The light that slipped through Tony's curtains was sharp and golden, the kind that promised another sweltering day. Birds chattered in the trees outside, their song at odds with the heavy quiet in the room. Tony stirred first, stretching until his joints popped, the hum of excitement from the night before still buzzing in his veins. He rolled over, grinning, ready to nudge Danny awake. But Danny was already curled tight on his side, arms drawn into his chest, face pale against the pillow. His breathing was shallow, uneven.

"Hey, sleepyhead," Tony murmured, brushing his knuckles lightly along Danny's arm. "C'mon, big day. We've got apartments to find."

Danny winced at the touch, a small grimace tugging at his mouth. He shifted but didn't uncurl. "Stomach hurts," he whispered.

Tony's grin dropped instantly. He sat up, hand warm and steady against Danny's forehead. "You're clammy," he said quietly, voice tight with concern.

At the mention, Danny's stomach twisted. He forced a small shake of his head. "No. Just… sick. It's fine."

Tony studied him for a long moment, lips pressed together. He hated the way Danny's skin felt under his palm—too cool, too damp. "I'll get Mom," he said, already swinging his legs over the bed. He all but sprinted down the hall, socks sliding on the floorboards. "Mom—Danny's sick," he blurted, already tugging at her arm. Maria nearly spilled her coffee in surprise.

"Dios mío, Antonio, slow down!" she muttered, but she was already setting her mug aside, letting him pull her up the stairs. "Oh, *mijo*," she cooed when she saw Danny. She sat on the edge of the bed, pressing the back of her hand to his forehead. "You're pale. Don't move. I'll make you tea—ginger and honey. It will help settle your stomach."

Danny managed a nod, guilt gnawing at him even as the warmth of her care wrapped around him. He hated feeling like this—hated looking weak in front of them, hated the worry etched on Tony's face.

"I don't want to mess up today," he murmured, voice almost too soft to hear.

Tony crouched beside the bed, his hand finding Danny's and giving it a firm squeeze.

"Hey. You're not messing anything up. We've got time. Apartments aren't going anywhere. We'll go when you're ready," Tony said, trying to reassure Danny everything was fine.

Maria returned with tea, the sharp scent of ginger filling the room. "Sip slowly, cariño. You'll feel better." Leroy lingered in the doorway, still buttoning his shirt. His voice was low but softer than usual: "Take it slow, son. Safe decisions come easier when you're steady." Danny nodded, throat tight.

For the next hour, the house moved gently around him. Maria brewed more tea, Tony hovered close, Leroy finished his coffee and headed for the station with a reassuring clap on Tony's shoulder.

By late morning, the ache in Danny's stomach had dulled, no longer sharp but a lingering heaviness. He sat at the kitchen table, Peanut tucked discreetly against his side, while Tony set up his laptop with the energy of a man launching a mission.

"Alright," Tony said, rubbing his hands together. "Let's do this. I've got a few rental sites and some random one that looks like it was coded in 1998 but promises 'hidden gems.'" He grinned at Danny. "And you've got… what, the classifieds?"

Danny held up the folded newspaper, a red pen in hand. "The classifieds," he confirmed quietly. He had already circled two.

Maria chuckled over the frying pan. "Don't tease him, Antonio. The paper is where you find the real deals. Internet landlords just want to steal your money."

"See?" Danny murmured, half a smile tugging at his lips.

Tony rolled his eyes dramatically but turned back to the laptop, fingers flying over the keys. "Okay, okay—listen to this one. 'Astoria, top floor, partial skyline view.' Translation: you lean out the window at a forty-five degree angle and maybe see the tip of the Empire State Building."

Maria snorted. "Check the water pressure. And the corners. Mice love corners."

"Noted," Tony said with mock gravity, typing it into his spreadsheet.

Danny circled another listing in red ink, the sound of the pen scratching quiet against the page. "This one's Sunnyside. Says it's a corner unit. Lots of light. And it's near that little park we like."

Tony leaned over, peering at the tiny print. "Yeah, but the Astoria one has a balcony, babe. Balcony means plants. Balcony means barbecues. Balcony means—"

"Is the entrance well-lit?" Danny interrupted, voice soft but steady.

Tony blinked, caught. He clicked through the listing photos, his grin faltering just a touch. "Uh… kinda. Hard to tell."

From the doorway, Leroy's voice rumbled, freshly back in after dropping paperwork at the precinct. "Astoria's good, but that street can be loud." He tapped the paper where Danny had circled Sunnyside. "This neighborhood's solid. Good patrol presence. Safe."

Tony looked between Danny's careful circles and Leroy's approving nod. His grin softened into something quieter, more thoughtful.

Danny glanced at him, waiting for the protest, the balcony argument. But Tony just reached across the table, brushed his knuckles against Danny's wrist, and said, "Okay. Sunnyside stays at the top of the list."

Danny lowered his eyes to the paper, his chest warm. For the first time that morning, the ache in his stomach loosened its grip.

By noon, their list was finalized—half chaotic Tony-spreadsheet, half Danny's neat red circles. Maria kissed them both on the cheeks before heading to work, reminding them to check faucets, open windows, and look for traps one last time. Leroy had gone back to the station, leaving behind a final nugget of advice: *trust your gut more than the photos.*

That advice sat with Danny as he and Tony pulled on shoes and stepped outside. The Triumph gleamed at the curb, its polished chrome catching the heavy summer light. Tony swung a leg over first, offering Danny a hand with a grin that never quite dimmed, even in the heat.

"Ready to ride, babe?"

Danny hesitated only a moment before sliding on behind him, arms wrapping instinctively around Tony's middle. The familiar roar of the engine came alive under them, steady as a heartbeat. As they pulled into traffic, the city surged around them in waves of motion—horns blaring, kids shouting, the scent of street vendors mixing with hot asphalt.

Danny held on, the vibration of the bike blurring the edge of his unease. He thought they'd be heading for Astoria first—the balcony, the so-called skyline view Tony couldn't stop talking about. He leaned into Tony's shoulder, ready to follow his lead.

But Tony didn't take the turn for the bridge. Instead, he guided the Triumph deeper into Queens, his movements confident, certain. Danny frowned against his shoulder, realizing only as they slowed that they were pulling onto a quiet, tree-lined street in Sunnyside.

Tony cut the engine, and silence settled—broken only by the sound of children playing somewhere down the block. Danny looked up, recognition sparking. The brick building on the corner stood sturdy and handsome, its wide windows catching the afternoon light. Across the street, the little café with green awnings. A block away, the park they'd walked through on lazy afternoons.

Danny's eyes widened. "This is… the one I circled," he said slowly. His voice was tinged with confusion. "I thought we were going to Astoria first."

Tony swung off the bike, tugging off his helmet with a crooked smile. He pushed a hand back through his hair and leaned casually against the Triumph, watching Danny. "Yeah… I got carried away with the balcony thing. Cool factor, you know? But on the ride over, I kept thinking about what you said. About light. About the entrance. About feeling safe."

Danny blinked, caught off guard by the seriousness under Tony's tone.

Tony nodded toward the building. "A balcony's just concrete. A skyline view doesn't mean anything if you don't feel good in the space. This is about us, Danny. About finding a home. Not a bachelor pad. Not something flashy. A home."

The words landed heavier than Danny expected. His chest ached with sudden warmth, and he looked at Tony like he was seeing him fresh. Tony, who laughed too loud, who leapt before thinking—who had also listened, who had noticed the quiet things, the things Danny never thought anyone saw.

"Oh," Danny breathed, almost dizzy. "Okay."

Tony's smile gentled. He stepped close, covering Danny's hand with his own. "So? Should we see if it's as good inside?"

Danny's throat tightened, but he nodded. "Yeah."

They crossed to the entrance together. The heavy oak and glass door gave way to a lobby filled with soft light. Original tile in black and white gleamed underfoot, brass sconces warm against cream-colored walls. The air was cool, not stale. Safe.

Danny let out a breath he hadn't realized he was holding.

At the tenant directory, Tony pressed the buzzer for 4B. A woman's voice crackled through the intercom: sharp, no-nonsense. "Yeah? Who is it?"

"Hi, uh, we saw the ad for the apartment. 4B," Tony said, polite, steady.

"You got an appointment?"

"No, ma'am. We were just in the neighborhood. Hoping for a quick look."

There was a long pause. Danny braced himself for rejection, for the clipped tone that would send them back outside. Then—*BUZZ*. The inner door clicked open.

"Fourth floor," the voice commanded.

They climbed the stairs, the building solid beneath each step. By the time they reached the landing, both were a little breathless, but there she was: Mrs. Rossi, short and sturdy, with silver-streaked hair pulled back in a bun and a floral apron tied around her waist. Her dark eyes were quick and perceptive.

"Boys," she greeted. Her gaze flicked down to their hands—still joined instinctively from the climb—then back up.

But Mrs. Rossi only smiled, warm and knowing. She waved a hand as though brushing his fear aside. "None of that here, ragazzo. Love is welcome in this building." Danny almost staggered with a relief so fierce it was almost painful. Tony squeezed his hand once, firm and proud.

She turned and unlocked the door. "Come. It's a good one." The door swung inward, and sunlight poured across polished hardwood floors. The ceilings were high, the walls freshly painted, the molding graceful with age. The air smelled faintly of old wood and fresh paint, warm and grounding.

Danny stepped inside slowly, his eyes wide. The light caught in the dust motes, making them glow like tiny sparks. He checked first: the corners of the room, the heavy lock on the window, the sightlines down to the street. The hallway outside had been well-lit, the stairwell solid beneath their feet. All of it noted, stored, measured. He walked to the windows, pausing first to glance at the corners, the lock on the frame, the street below. Old habits—check the exits, check the light, check if it felt safe. Safe enough.

The block was quiet, the café across the street steady with life, the park in sight. Safe enough. Only then did he let his gaze soften, imagining his easel by the glass, Tony's boots by the door, mornings with coffee, evenings with quiet laughter.

For once, the future didn't terrify him. For once, it felt like his. He didn't have to speak. Tony came up behind him, arms circling his waist, chin resting against his hair. Together they stood in the sunlight, their shadows long across the floor.

"So?" Tony whispered.

Danny closed his eyes, breathing it in. The warmth, the promise, the safety. "I think I like it," he said, voice careful but steady.

Tony's arms tightened around him. "Then it's home." And for the first time, Danny believed it. A new sunrise waited, and this time, it was theirs.

Danny let himself believe it. For once, the word didn't scare him. The ghosts hadn't vanished—he doubted they ever would—but for the first time, they didn't feel stronger than the ground beneath his feet. Healing, he realized, wasn't a finish line. It was a choice. One he could keep making, again and again. And with Tony's arms wrapped tight around him, Danny knew he wouldn't have to make it alone.

www.ingramcontent.com/pod-product-compliance
Lightning Source LLC
Chambersburg PA
CBHW031519150726
47990CB00001B/15